Virtuous Deception 2:

Playing for Keeps

Virtuous Deception 2:

Playing for Keeps

Leiann B. Wrytes

www.urbanbooks.net

Urban Books, LLC
300 Farmingdale Road, NY-Route 109
Farmingdale, NY 11735

Virtuous Deception 2: Playing for Keeps

ISBN 13: 978-1-64556-129-3
ISBN 10: 1-64556-129-1

First Mass Market Printing November 2020
First Trade Paperback Printing August 2019
Printed in the United States of America

10 9 8 7 6 5 4 3 2 1

This is a work of fiction. Any references or similarities to actual events, real people, living or dead, or to real locales are intended to give the novel a sense of reality. Any similarity in other names, characters, places, and incidents is entirely coincidental.

Distributed by Kensington Publishing Corp.
Submit Orders to:
Customer Service
400 Hahn Road
Westminster, MD 21157-4627
Phone: 1-800-733-3000
Fax: 1-800-659-2436

Virtuous Deception 2:

Playing for Keeps

by

Leiann B. Wrytes

PROLOGUE

Her body shivered as she wavered on the edge of hopelessness. Peter shared a light joke, something about a monkey and two dogs, but it barely registered. His infectious laugh never failed to elicit one from her, pulling one from her subconscious, pushing it through her pain one letter at a time. She adored how his voice danced when something amused him. Sophie, joining in his blissful moment, laughed along with him.

The laugh she mustered was much harder than the joke merited, as she tried to mask the inundated ache swirling through her, facing the inevitable conclusion that this battle was one she would ultimately lose. The moment she dreaded, the one looming around the corner, would force her to utter the words that would likely kill her romance. Slowly but surely, the pain threatened to swallow her whole.

Her exceptional intelligence quotient was no match for her father's, the formidable Richard Freemont. Blinking back tears, she smiled at Peter, absorbing all that their moment had to offer, cementing every little detail into her memory; coveting the way a few rebellious strands of his sienna-brown hair rested on his forehead, the brilliance of the full moon captured in his pea-green eyes, passing on to them a glow comparable to the awesome stars loitering about in the sky above them. Without question, Peter was the love of her young life.

Countless nights, he had lent his shoulder to catch her tears, allowed her to empty her heart into his open ear, proving to her that it was possible for a person to love unselfishly. This would not be an easy thing for her to do—letting him go—but the choice was not hers. Richard had decided for her.

Peter held her small, delicate hand in his, trembling as he spoke. He recounted their fairytale, gushing over the treasure trove of love they had stumbled upon inside one another. The stained wooden park bench swing swayed slightly as she shifted her body, struggling to give him her undivided attention. The sun had set hours ago, filling the sky with wondrous shades of violet, ruby, and orange before relenting to the calm of the dark-blue summer night.

Her parents had insisted their infatuation would flame out as their teenage hormones gave way to more mature dispositions. Their youthful zeal had survived three years of high school and the esteemed walk across the stage. Graduation, only a month old, was still a fresh memory.

Having accelerated her class schedule to graduate from her private school a full two years ahead of schedule, Sophie understood, intellectually, that the ability to make a lifelong emotional commitment at sixteen was unlikely. The odds of their bond stretching beyond their twilight years were not favorable, but her rationale had no answer for the way he made her feel. The safety she sought from him, and his willingness to provide it, was present in his stare, a warmth that never failed to disarm her. He gave her everything he had each moment they were together.

As he gently grazed the softness of her cheek with his hand, his eyes penetrated the windows to her soul. Relishing the magnetic pull his gaze had on her, she returned his stare, trying her best to reciprocate the abundance of love she felt sweltering inside.

"Luce, you know how I feel about you. These last three years have been the best of my life. They say home is where the heart is, and I think my home is right here with you." Caressing her hand as he spoke, Peter continued, his country twang resting in the spaces between the words. "You are my best friend. I didn't truly know what a friend was before you, before us."

Sophie froze, unsure of what to do with the surge of energy he was sending her. His desire washed over her like a tidal wave, overwhelming her thoughts. Overcome with emotion, her sentence derailed, issuing a set of tears in its place.

"Peter, I—"

"Luce, don't cry." Peter lovingly wiped the tears from her eyes as they fell. "I have something I want to give you."

Reaching into his pocket to retrieve the small diamond it housed, he chuckled lightly. Holding it in his fingers for her inspection, he beamed with pride. "I saved up all year to get it for you."

Quickly clasping her hands over her mouth, Sophie gasped audibly. She could not hide her surprise. On the verge of hyperventilating, Sophie suddenly found it hard to breathe. Tears cascaded down her cheeks as she tiptoed the thin line between joy and pain.

"This is a promise ring. Here, let me put it on for you." Peter slid the one-carat diamond onto Sophie's finger. "I was going to give it to you earlier this week, but—"

Peter didn't need to finish the sentence. His touch still warmed her frame. Sophie gazed at her newest piece of jewelry, holding it up, inspecting it through blurry eyes. Peter did not have the money to make a purchase of this kind. It was completely unexpected.

"Do you like it?" Peter asked anxiously, unable to conceal his excitement. "It's spent the last two weeks in my pocket. Every time I meant to give it to you, it just didn't feel right, but tonight was so special with the moon so pretty up there."

"Peter . . . it's beautiful." Hatred began boiling beneath her surface, spurred by what she was being forced to do. It was not fair.

"Sophie Lucille Freemont, this ring is a symbol of the promise I made to you. And the promise you made to me."

The dam broke. The last of her defenses had been shattered. "Oh my God, Peter—"

Sophie cried uncontrollably, nervously twisting the ring on her finger. Staring into his eyes, she felt their souls connect, driving the stake deeper into her heart. She wanted to speak, to reciprocate the love he was pouring into her, but no words would come; only more tears.

Still without an answer, Peter tried to persuade her, mistaking her tears for reluctance. Rubbing her shoulder, a gesture aimed to assure her, he inched closer to her on the bench.

"I know I don't have much now, but I'm going to medical school. I'm going to be a doctor, Luce. I'll be able to take care of you. You don't have to worry."

His voice was calm, but she could see panic creeping into his eyes. Sophie shook her head, trying to force the words from her lips. Her vision blurred as her sobs took over, choking her words.

"Peter, I love you so much. I really do." She cried even harder, watching his face transition from happiness to confusion. "I really wish that I—"

"Luce, what's wrong? Why are you crying like this?" His thick eyebrows arched with worry, the question holding his world hostage, awaiting her answer.

"Oh God, Peter." Sophie could barely speak through her despair. "You have been an amazing friend. I don't deserve you."

"Luce, don't say that. Sure you do. We both do."

"Peter, I can't accept this," Sophie managed to whisper through her tears, taking the ring off and offering it to Peter.

Peter shrank back, treating the offering of love she tried to return like it had been stricken with a virus. He refused to take the ring, unable to accept what she had just told him.

"What are you saying, Luce? I'm not going anywhere. I'll always be here for you, no matter what."

"I am so sorry, Peter." Sophie felt weak. Her heart physically ached in her chest. This was too much for her young mind to bear. She knew it would be painful, but not like this. She strained her resolve, trying to focus on what needed to be done as her entire world came to a grinding halt.

"But I love you. I want us to explore this world together. We made a promise. You can't—"

More tears ran from the wells of her blues, each word like a shard of glass, tearing the soft tissues of her mouth on its way out. The last thing she wanted to do was hurt Peter; he meant everything to her.

"I love you, too. I just . . . I can't . . . Peter."

As he stared in no particular direction, tears began to drip from his eyes as the realization slowly seeped in. He could barely look at her. Rustling his hands through his hair, then brusquely down the sides of his face, Peter turned his gaze to Sophie.

"You don't want me? Is that it? I'm not good enough for your family?"

Sophie felt she might die at the sight of him. She had never seen him so broken. She placed a comforting hand on his face. Peter jerked away from her, leaping up from the bench, causing it to swing wildly.

"Peter, no . . . please. We are family."

"Your daddy told me, but I told him you were different. I told him . . . he didn't know you." Peter's face revealed the destructive blow the night's events had dealt him. As he stood there, it looked like the universe had lost its power. The light from his eyes, once brilliant and iridescent, was now snuffed out.

She stood from the bench, reaching out to him, but Peter backed away from her. He rushed from the backyard, racing toward her house before disappearing around the corner, taking the best of her with him as he ran.

Movement from her back porch caught her attention, causing her to look in that direction. Though she was roughly one hundred fifty yards away, she could easily make out the shadowy figure's outline perched on the deck. After being spotted, the form vanished into the house. Collapsing back down onto the bench, she wept until her eyes burned and were swollen shut. She felt like someone had taken away her ability to dream, to hope.

She spent the remainder of the night there, on the bench, too hurt to go inside. Losing Peter, her champion, was painful enough, but to realize that the person responsible had borne witness to her horror was too much to process. Sophie had done what was required of her, and it had torn her soul from her. Her spirit was in agony.

She lay there until Nanette helped her into the house, right before dawn, where she had a nice hot bubble bath waiting for her. Promptly after the bath, Nanette returned to Sophie with instructions.

"Chile, we have to get you ready. Richard wants you dressed real nice."

Currently seated on a stool facing the full-length mirror in her powder room, Sophie felt less than enthusiastic about her impending plans. Nanette rarely assisted Sophie in this way, but the hurt in Sophie's sunken eyes compelled her.

Sophie felt the need for answers. "Why, Nan? What is it now? Another political function?"

Nanette grunted, arched her brow, throwing Sophie a knowing look. "You know it isn't, now, don't you?"

Sophie shook her head, acknowledging Nan's statement.

"Peter left a long time ago, chile."

"Nan, I don't want to discuss it, please."

Nanette, who had been standing behind Sophie, moved to her side. She gently turned Sophie's face toward her own, peering intently into her eyes. She rushed her words in what could only be described as a harsh whisper.

"I don't know everything, but I know a broken heart when I see it. If ya need me, talk to me, understand?"

"Yes, ma'am." Offering Nan a weak smile, Sophie tried to absorb a bit of comfort from the softness she always found resting in her irises. Nan's eyes carried a kind of sadness Sophie could not interpret, but Nan refused to discuss it with her. Sophie knew that whatever caused that ache had not defeated Nan. Nan was a warrior, the best woman she knew, and the only person in the world she knew truly *loved her*, besides Peter.

"Thank you, Nan."

"No need for that. Just be a loving person, Lucille. That's all, and God will work it all out." Patting Sophie lightly on her cheek, Nan leaned in to leave a feather's kiss on her forehead, forcing the corners of Sophie's mouth to stretch out into a genuine smile.

"What time will Leonard be here, Nan?"

Returning to her position behind Sophie, Nanette fluffed her hair, not certain what to make of the matted mess. "Soon is all I can tell ya, chile."

"I really hate him, Nan."

"Leonard? Did he do something, Lucille?"

"What? Goodness no, Nan. He's been awkward and very uncomfortable these last two months, but nothing inappropriate. I was referring to our fair patriarch."

"Richard is a hard man. I would neva call the way he does things love, chile, but he's yo' daddy."

"Why won't he let me be happy? I'll never have anything here. Never."

"Give it time, Lucille. Prayer is a powerful thing."

"He says prayer is for those who are too lazy to do for themselves."

"Do you believe him?"

"That matters very little in this house. The empty ramblings of the girl child. He only cares for himself—and mother *sometimes*."

"Sophie Lucille Freemont!"

"You know it's the truth. He strangles the life out of every good thing I acquire, Nan."

Nanette had no words to refute that, her silence submitting her regrettable agreement. "Maybe so, but at least the Leonard boy don't seem so bad. Better than the others."

"He is a nice boy, Nan, but he is not Peter."

"I know, chile, but yo' daddy needs it this way."

"I hate him."

"Lucille, you hush speakin' that way 'bout yo' daddy. He's takin good care of you now."

"Financially."

"You went to the best schools. You're a smart girl."

"That's because I had you, Nan. You don't have to defend him. We both know that I'm nothing more than a pawn. Eventually, he'll sacrifice me . . . just like he did Angela."

Nanette sank her thin fingers into Sophie's shoulders, a hand on either side, using the mirror to lock Sophie into a gaze she could not break. "I will never, ever let him do that, Lucille. You hear me? Pray and watch what happens."

Nan had always managed to comfort her with her wisdom, but her words were ineffective in this instance. Richard had gone too far, and only a violation equally repulsive would turn the tide in Sophie's favor.

"Perhaps, Nan, but I cannot wait for *time* to speak on my behalf." Sophie intended to free herself from her father. As the devil with the blue eyes returned her stare, she knew exactly what to do. Sophie would make her move tonight, an act of rebellion. "He cannot get away this. I won't let him."

"Don't go against that man, chile. That was your sister's mistake."

"I know, Nan, but I am not her. I am not afraid of him anymore; not afraid of losing any of *this*. I want *love*, Nan, and he took it from me. He needs to be stopped."

CHAPTER 1

Michelle stood with eyes blazing like embers, narrowing into slits, as her lungs scraped the atmosphere for the oxygen she was suddenly without. The hurried cadence of her heartbeat bellowed in her ears, effectively muting all other sounds. The sight of Charlie, her father's very pregnant mistress, shaking her mother's hand left her speechless.

Their first meeting flashed across her mind, blinding her to the present happenings. There were no visible signs of pregnancy then, at least none that she could recall. Following a lead, Michelle had found herself sitting across from Charlie to gather information regarding a case, when the sound of her father's boisterous voice rattled the hotel room.

Lewis, ignorant of Michelle's presence inside the suite, unwittingly confirmed his association with Charlie. Both she and Charlie had been disturbed by her father's menacing ramblings from the other side of the door. She remembered Charlie rubbing her stomach, and this belly was certainly absent. Michelle would not have believed there was any type of relationship between them had she not heard it for herself. Much to her dismay, she soon learned he had many partners, as it were; one of whom was Lisa, Michelle's twin sister's adopted mother. His untimely death left him unable to obviate, forcing Michelle to inescapably accept most of what she heard as gospel.

Now this woman made herself available for the reading of his last will and testament. She stood a few feet from Michelle, speaking with her mother, Sophie, like they were old friends. Michelle seethed. Here this woman was, staking a claim in the inheritance that her father left for his children, politely holding her round belly, professing that his DNA mingled with hers to form that bastard child.

Her very presence in Sophie's home was nothing short of contemptuous. Not only had she shown complete and utter disrespect for Sophie by bedding her husband, but she sauntered into her home, adding insult to injury. Michelle left her fiancé, Armand, seated on the couch, allowing her mounting displeasure to force her legs into action, quickly moving her toward the source of her rising anger.

Her torso tightened as a recollection of the accusation pitted itself in her lower abdomen. Her father's last words to Charlie replayed in her mind, insinuating the truth of Charlie's claims. *No one disappears with anything that belongs to me.* As far as Michelle was concerned, the truth was irrelevant. Charlie had no right to be there.

"Get your ass out!" Michelle's words cracked the air like the tip of a whip. Her mother may have been willing to play nice, but she was not. She could see Brianna, her twin sister, watching from the corner of her eye, appearing a bit amused by it all.

Sophie damn near broke her neck turning to see Michelle at her side. "Michelle Kaye!"

Though Michelle had not spoken to her mother much over the last month, she was not about to let this trick disrespect her mother in her presence. She ignored her mother's beleaguered stare, keeping her eyes trained on Charlie, who had yet to move. Michelle's body grew rigid, her fists hanging like hammers at her sides.

"Didn't you hear what I said? Leave my mother's home. *Now!*"

"I have a right to be here! This is your brother, and he—"

POP!

Before Charlie could complete her sentence, Michelle rammed her fist into her open mouth. Charlie's thin lips swelled as blood filled her mouth. She stumbled back in shock, careful not to fall.

Sophie watched the scene unfold in horror, stepping in front of Michelle out of reflex. She draped her arm around Michelle's body in a crescent moon. Entrapped by the moment, Sophie wedged herself between Michelle and Charlie, trying to clasp her hands together behind her back. She kept Michelle behind her as she continued to hurl profanities at Charlie.

"*Bitch*, why would you disrespect my mother like this? Get out!"

Michelle's eyes were like lasers, sending the sensation of legions of spiders scurrying up her arms. Charlie's fear-fraught eyes revealed that she realized the mistake she had made with her decision to come. Michelle watched as she frantically scanned the room for a friend, finding none. She had no intention of fighting Charlie, especially in her condition, but she would not allow her to stay.

Charlie regained her balance and walked toward Sophie. Permitting her open hand to connect with Charlie's face again, Michelle, who stood a few inches over her mother, stretched her arm over her shoulder fairly easily.

SLAP!

"Damn whore! Let me go!" Michelle tried to wiggle free of her mother's grasp. Her body, long since surrendering itself to the maddening rage, jerked impulsively. "Let me go!"

Sophie held onto Michelle as best she could. She didn't want her daughter getting into any trouble over this slut. A winded Sophie stared wildly at the whore.

"Why won't you leave? Are you trying to cause trouble?"

Hearing the distress in her mother's voice, Brianna sprang to her feet to assist Sophie in corralling Michelle. She closed the distance between them in seconds, stepping in front of Sophie but facing Michelle. She attempted to deescalate the situation by communicating with her twin. Brianna lifted her hands like goal posts into the air, motioning for Michelle to relax. She maintained eye contact as Michelle momentarily stopped trying to get free.

"Chel, it will be okay. Calm down. We—"

At that precise moment, a sharp pang in Brianna's back propelled her forward onto Sophie, causing the three to stumble away from Charlie. The impact was from the one and only punch Charlie would have the opportunity to throw. Brianna winced at the slight pang in her lower back, then turned and immediately swung in retaliation.

This time, it was Brianna's fist that connected with Charlie's nose, causing a fresh river of red to flow, but Brianna did not stop. She kept swinging until Armand grabbed her and dragged her, kicking and screaming, into the kitchen.

Fortunately for Charlie, Michelle had begun pulling her toward the door, away from Brianna's jabs and out of harm's way. The sharp prick from Michelle's nails digging into her shoulders was mild compared to the bruises she would have had if one more of Brianna's punches had gotten her.

Charlie did not have time to offer a word of thanks, though; Michelle opened the front door and dragged her sore, swollen body outside.

"Don't ever bring your ass back to my mother's home."

Charlie gasped audibly as she looked up at Michelle and saw that same evil in her brown eyes that she had once seen in her father's. Michelle went back into the house and slammed the door, locking it behind her.

Sophie was still standing in the same spot Michelle had left her when she came back into the living room. The lawyer who had read the will seemed to be frozen in place by the hoopla, too. Armand and Brianna were missing in action. Michelle started to go and find them when Sophie called out to her.

"Michelle . . . can we talk a minute?"

Michelle still did not want to talk to Sophie. She was her mother, and she loved her, but she had not figured out how to forgive her, though a day rarely passed without Sophie asking for it. Charlie needed to be checked. Although Michelle was upset with her mom, she was not about to let anyone disrespect her like that.

"Please, *Number One*."

Michelle decided to oblige her and took a seat on the couch. Sophie sat down beside her and motioned for the lawyer to give them a minute. The gesture freed him from his trance, and he quietly left the room, signaling that he had to make a phone call.

"Michelle Kaye, what was that about?"

Michelle looked at her mom, incredulous over the question. Surely she was not referring to her kicking out her husband's mistress after she had boldly waddled her ass into her home like she had an invite.

"Mom, you know what that was about."

"Michelle, you assaulted a pregnant woman."

"I hit a bitch. The fact that she was pregnant was not lost on me."

"Michelle!" Sophie lowered her voice and spoke sternly, like the change would usher in some understanding Michelle had yet to realize, in an effort to drive home some important point. "That is not the issue. Do you realize what you've done?"

Michelle shot Sophie a questioning glance.

Sophie shook her head in frustration. "She has grounds to press charges against you. Do you get that?" She paused to allow her words to register. "She could have you locked up over this."

Michelle stared blankly. It was not that she didn't understand; she simply didn't care. *Let her try. I have a few tricks of my own.*

CHAPTER 2

"Brianna, you need to calm down. What were you thinking, hitting that woman?" Armand sat on a stool at the kitchen island, watching Brianna pace back and forth across the black-and-white tiled floor.

Brianna rolled her eyes and blew out an exasperated breath. "What are you talking about? Your fiancée started it, not me!"

Armand shook his head. Brianna's head was as hard as limestone. "I know that, but you attacked that woman."

"After she hit me! It was self-defense."

"Brianna—"

Brianna stopped pacing and looked at Armand. "Why are you even in here talking to me? Shouldn't you be having this conversation with your future wife?"

Armand's body stiffened a bit. He rubbed his hands over his face to calm himself. "Look, I am just trying to look out for you."

"Well, don't. I don't need you." Brianna spoke the words, but she knew she was lying. She wanted Armand to care. Needed him to care. Since the kidnapping, being with him was the only thing that gave her peace. But each time he left her . . . she was reminded that he did not belong to her. He never would.

"You are living too reckless, Brianna. Taking unnecessary risks."

Brianna knew he was referring to Javan, the monster who had kidnapped her a month before. Armand had rescued her from that nightmare—some real cowboy, guns-blazing type stuff. He had stormed in to where she was being kept, grabbed her, and scooped her off to safety, but when he returned to the house to finish the job, Javan was nowhere to be found.

He had made her his personal responsibility. He even moved her into the new house that he and Michelle had recently purchased. He spent time with her every single night, if only for a few minutes. He tended to her even more than Michelle did.

Brianna could not lie; she was terrified. Everything scared her. She had to fight to function. This was not her fault. The numbness she resided in was the result of her being afraid of absolutely everything. She found it was the most effective means by which she could attain some semblance of a life. Brianna knew it was not the healthiest way to live, but it was the only way she could for now.

"Javan is not coming back, Armand. You kicked his ass, remember?"

Armand's thick eyebrows furrowed, and she knew her sarcastic indifference had not gone unnoticed. Sarcasm fared better than the truth.

"Brianna, I never found him. He's still a problem until I do. It is better to have a definite no than a probable yes, especially in this situation."

"Yes, yes . . . I know. But I'm not worried. As long as you are around to protect me, I have nothing to worry about, right?"

Armand stared at Brianna sincerely. He ran his hands through his curly hair and took a deep breath. "That's right. I'll be around to take care of you."

There was a real love smoldering for her within him, and it was plainly visible to her. As long as she needed him, he would be there, pure and simple. Michelle was his world, his life partner, but Brianna knew her stock increased a little each day.

CHAPTER 3

Shit. The look on Michelle's face foreshadowed the storm headed in his direction.

Ignoring Brianna, Michelle walked past her, stopping just inches away from him. "Where were you, Armand?"

Squinting his eyes and biting his bottom lip, Armand cut his eyes at Michelle. He glanced at her for a mere moment before picking a spot beyond the island, the breakfast nook, and through the French doors, to a spot in the backyard to focus on.

"Clearly, I was in here, Michelle."

"That is obvious . . . *isn't it*?" Michelle cocked her head to the side and lowered her face to his, intentionally interrupting his line of sight. "Why are you in *here*?"

Armand threw a subtle look in Brianna's direction, catching the smile plastered across her face. There was nothing amusing about this situation to him. Using the island's counter to force himself upright, Armand staggered back until he felt the hard edge of the large steel country-style sink cutting into the small of his back. Folding his arms across his chest, Armand tried to rest against it comfortably.

"Michelle, can we not do this right now?"

Michelle did not move an inch. She stood so still he wasn't sure she had even taken a breath. She didn't bother to look in her sister's direction, but it was painfully obvious who she referred to with her next request.

"Give us a minute, please."

Good luck, Brianna mouthed to Armand before vacating the kitchen.

Satisfied that they had the space to themselves, Michelle picked up their conversation.

"Why are you in here, Armand?"

Armand sighed deeply, already seeing where this banter was going. He didn't want to answer, but his silence would only prolong his torment.

"I grabbed Brianna and brought her in here, Michelle, but you knew that."

"So, you chose to help her again?"

"Michelle . . ."

"You chose her over me . . . again?"

"Don't do this shit right now. I am begging you. She was fighting a pregnant woman, Michelle. Do you know how much trouble she could get into if that woman presses charges?"

"Yes! Probably about as much as I could get into since I hit the bitch first. Or were your eyes too fixated on my sister to notice?"

Armand dropped his arms to his sides and walked toward Michelle, his eyes wide with disbelief. His voice ballooned into a loud whisper as he struggled to keep his voice at a respectable volume in her mother's home.

"You are bugging the fuck out! What is wrong with you?"

"You didn't come to my rescue. Didn't rush in to protect me."

"Stop with the theatrics. This is fucking stupid."

"Stupid?"

"Stop talking like I left you in a dark alley or something. I left you, temporarily, with your mom. Brianna didn't have anyone. *She doesn't have anyone*! I am just trying to look out for her."

"She's a grown damn woman. You are supposed to have my back, Armand! Mine!"

Armand felt his patience thinning. Michelle was being completely unreasonable. "You should be glad that your man cares about your family, your sister."

"Don't do that, Armand. That isn't what this is about. Of course I'm glad you care, but not at my expense! You proposed to me, Armand, but you act like you've got the wrong twin."

Armand threw his hands into the air in frustration. "I cannot believe you went there. That is straight bullshit, and you know it, Michelle. You are the only woman I have ever loved, besides my mom. You're jealous over nothing."

As she folded her arms across her chest, Michelle's face conveyed her disbelief. "I know what I see, Armand."

"What you think you see, you mean? I know the woman I fell in love with over two years ago, and she is not this jealous *little girl* standing in front of me now."

"She is not the only one that needs you, Armand."

"So, I'm not here for you? Is that what you're saying?"

"No, you are not, evidenced by your behavior today."

"You are making me fucking crazy. Seriously."

"The feeling is mutual."

Shaking his head in bewilderment, Armand decided to end this battle. "Whatever, Michelle. I'm going to check on your mother, *if* that's okay with you?"

Accepting her silence as consent, Armand left the kitchen to find Sophie. Michelle was losing her mind, but her words still cut him. He didn't want her thinking of him that way. He loved her, no matter what. He loved her, and that should not be something she was still questioning.

CHAPTER 4

The sea of blood surrounding his wife sent Frank crashing to his knees, crying out to no one in particular. Lisa's body lay still, covered in her life's liquid after collapsing on the floor just below the bar. There was so much crimson that Frank could not tell where the self-inflicted injury had occurred. He crawled to his wife's side, visually checking for any signs of life. Though his eyes failed to locate any, his heart refused to concede to her departure. Reaching for the cordless phone on the bar's surface, the catalyst for this tragic event, with shaky hands, he called for help.

"Please state ya emergency."

"Please, someone help me." His words, echoing his distress, were barely audible as tears continued to fall from his eyes. "My wife. She needs help. And I can't . . . I can't help her."

"Sir, what's ya name?"

"Frank."

"Thank ya, Frank. Help is on the way. I need ya to answer a few questions."

"My wife. Please."

"We are sending help to ya wife. What is ya wife's name, sir?"

"Lisa." Frank continued sobbing, his voice barely above a whisper.

"Are ya calling from Le Petit Hotel, sir?"

Frank nodded, thinking he'd answered the question.

"Sir? Is that correct?"

The repetition of the question jolted him out of his haze. "Yes."

"Thank ya, Frank. Can ya tell me what happened to Lisa?"

Frank began heaving heavily. His body shook with grief.

"Frank, Frank . . . stay wit' me, sir. I need ya to stay calm. Help is coming. I need ya to tell me what happened."

"That bitch! She did it!" A yell stretching from the deep recesses of his soul suddenly came roaring out as he realized Charlie was to blame. His deep, baritone voice raggedly poured through the walls of Lisa's suite and down the hallway of the chic hotel.

The operator strained to hear his words through his incessant cries. "Sir, I am sorry. Could ya repeat that?"

"She killed my wife!" Frank continued to cry into the phone.

"Who, sir? Who killed ya wife?"

Frank, teetering on the edge of sanity, could scarcely speak. "Charlie."

"Charlie killed ya wife, sir? Am I hearing that correctly? Is this Charlie in the room, sir?"

The emergency operator dispatched the ambulance and the police.

"Can you describe Charlie, sir? Did ya see her harm ya wife?"

"No, but . . . but she did it. It's her fault."

While the operator transcribed the details of the circumstances as he relayed them to her, she alerted the authorities about a probable suspect in the area, possibly armed and dangerous.

"Frank, help should be dere any minute."

The operator contacted the front desk to confirm that they were aware of the developing situation and passed along Lisa's room information to the officers en route.

"Frank, are ya still there?"

Frank was lying beside Lisa with his head resting atop her stomach. Her hazel eyes were hidden from his view. He closed his and reviewed their last conversation, just thirty minutes old.

They had laughed and played like old times. He'd had real hope for their future together. The prospect of them repairing their marriage looked promising. He had traveled from the States all the way to Saint-Martin to get her back, only to lose her like this. One phone call had destroyed his entire world. Why had she done this to herself, to him? Didn't she know how much he loved her?

Lisa, please don't leave. I'm sorry, baby. I'm so sorry. Don't leave me.

"Frank, are ya there, sir? Please respond."

"I'm here."

"Good. Can ya open the door, please? The paramedics are dere."

Frank reluctantly left Lisa's side to open the door. The paramedics rushed in, and one of them, upon noticing the blood he was covered in, attempted to assist him.

"It's not mine."

He looked at his beautiful wife and fell apart all over again. His eyes were so puffy he could barely see. The paramedics put her on a gurney and prepared to take her to LCF.

"Sir, are you Frank? My name is Fabrice. Frank, can you walk?"

Frank didn't respond. He simply put his arm around the medic and looked at him with bloodshot eyes, still oozing with pain. Nothing else was said. He and the medic headed out the door just ahead of the gurney.

A detective flashed his badge, stopping them in the hallway. Frank tried to figure out why he was there, but it soon became evident once the proper introductions were made.

"Excuse me. I'm Detective Baptiste. That there is my partner, Detective Saenz." He pointed to an older gentleman standing just down the hall, speaking with the paramedics moving Lisa. "Are you Frank?"

Frank nodded but did not speak.

"I need for you to answer some questions for me now. Tell me what happened here?" Topping out at five feet eight inches, the young detective was roughly five or six inches shorter than Frank, but he made up for his height with a few extra pounds of muscle that his dirty gray suit failed to hide.

"She killed her."

The detective looked at the medic holding Frank up. The medic shook his head. Lisa had not been pronounced dead as far as he knew. He could not confirm one way or the other. He had spent his time with Frank.

"Say that again? Who you say did this?" Baptiste flipped through the pages of his pocket pad, scribbling a note for reference later. "Are you talkin' about a Charlie, no?"

The young detective looked at Frank's eyes to gauge his response to the name the dispatcher had given him. He processed the gleam in his eyes and the slight quivering of his lips as confirmation that Frank was familiar with the proposed assailant.

"Where is this Charlie person?" Baptiste pressed Frank for Charlie's whereabouts. Time was a precious commodity, but he was doubtful that Frank's claims were true. "Tell me da truth now. Describe dis Charlie person. Come on now."

Detective Saenz had concluded his part, allowing the others to proceed with the transport. The paramedic did not want to interfere, but with his own sordid history with the police on his mind, felt he had no choice. "Detective Baptiste, we really need to be going now. His wife's condition is critical. The others cannot go without me, *and him*."

"Don't think I don't know what'cha doin'. You are interfering in my investigation!"

Shaking his head, the paramedic explained further. "I think any husband would want to be with his wife at a time like dis one."

Baptiste eyed the paramedic but conceded to his request. Locking eyes with Frank, he made himself perfectly clear. "Fine, take him, but don't ya try to leave the island, sir. I have eyes at Princess Juliana Airport."

This story did not make sense to Detective Baptiste. There were too many details missing. The proposed assailant was conveniently missing, and with no physical description, this "Charlie" was practically invisible. Perhaps this person had hurt Ms. Mason, but Detective Baptiste had no choice but to start with what he had: Mr. Mason.

He called to the station. "Officer Claude, run a background check on a Mr. Frank Mason, registered at Le Petit Hotel. Use his passport information and anything else you can find on him. I need to know everything on dis guy as soon as possible."

CHAPTER 5

The tarred four-lane road felt like a narrow back alley as Frank's world continued closing in on him. He sat near Lisa's head, holding on to her hand, wishing, hoping, praying for her to be okay. Conditions in the ambulance resembled a sauna, and he couldn't seem to fill his lungs with enough air, regardless of how many breaths he took. Sweat leaked from every pore in his body. The possibility of losing her overwhelmed him. If he didn't relax, he would end up in a bed right beside hers.

Finding it difficult to sit comfortably on the small, tattered, plastic-covered cushion in the back of the ambulance, Frank struggled to will his body still. He forced his eyes away from his wife, concentrating on the small, square window pane carved in the back door of the ambulance. He used that focal point as a temporary means of escape for as long as he felt he could.

Rolling hills of plush green grass stretched as far as the eye could see, interrupted only by stints of the sea flanking the French side of the island. Flashes of Lisa, lying on the floor, covered in blood, assaulted his mind as the ambulance shuffled him about, roaring westward, to the nearest hospital, Hôpital Louis-Constant Fleming.

The chatter of the emergency workers did not register. No sirens rang in his ears, only the soft crush of the water upon the beach and his name on her lips tickled his hearing.

Nature's impressionist stroke animated their life's canvas in his mind. Reminiscent of an early Hitchcock film, their years together replayed in silence, bringing him closer to the edge of a world he could not imagine without her. Mustering his mental strength, Frank focused on the tauntingly blue Caribbean waters, a therapeutic technique aimed to combat his anxiety. But even as he submitted his thoughts to the fading waters, a little voice within him echoed a bitter sentiment. Nothing short of a miraculous healing could succor his heart at this moment.

As the medical vehicle hugged the curves of the winding road, loosening his perspective of the sea, Frank turned his gaze again to Lisa. He desperately needed her to smile, to laugh, to come back to him.

This could not happen. Frank could not let her die in paradise. It didn't seem fair that the place where she felt most alive should be the place that would take her life. Surely karma would not be so cruel. He believed that, much like the winding road shifted the shape and size of the massive sea, this moment only appeared to weaken Lisa, but it had no more power over her than the road had over the waters. She would come out of this stronger and more beautiful than before.

Without warning, a mordant pain sprouted from his temple, wrapping itself around the crown of his head. Instinctively cupping each side of his head, Frank scrunched his body inward, blinking rapidly as the intensity of the throbbing continued to increase. Frank's vision deteriorated, the pain acutely impairing his ability to see. His body felt aflame as he closed his eyes, praying the hell would pass. His square jaw line grimaced in agony, yet no sound escaped him, not even a small grunt.

Frank sat mute, writhing in pain for what seemed an eternity. He lost twenty seconds but opened his eyes to the white sands of the beach, the grand shadow of Le Petit Hotel looming over him. He could feel Lisa standing behind him, her finger playfully poking the palm of his open hand as it hung at his side. *Lisa.*

"Excuse me, sir."

Something was pulling him away from his thoughts. He shook his head, trying to hold onto the fading image. He spun around, and with her hand clasped in his, traced her profile with his free hand. *I love you.* His pain was a distant memory, like it had never happened it all. Lisa was smiling, joking, very much alive. Nothing else mattered. He could hear children laughing in the distance, feel the sun on his face. He felt a peace come over him, his heart finding a calm place to hide as fantasy became reality.

"Move, sir. Move quickly now," a voice instructed from somewhere outside of his vision, pilfering the scene, confusing his thoughts as he blinked, toggling pictures of reality and dreamlike slides on a projector. He stared at a pixelated Lisa as Frank felt his body swaying. He looked down to find an unfamiliar hand gripping his arm, shaking it with enough force to pop it out of place. Searching Lisa's eyes for an answer, his heart began to splinter as she faded. *No, no no. Where are you going? Don't leave!*

"Move now, sir. Move!"

His eyes grew wide as Lisa, the beauty of the day, and the beach disappeared completely, replaced with the interior of what he thought was a small room. Frank gaped wildly at his surroundings, trying to reclaim the last few minutes, fighting the disorientation as best he could. Nothing looked familiar to him. There was only a kaleidoscope of colors and shapes. He couldn't make anything out. A chill swept over him as he scrambled his thoughts to make sense of things.

"What is going on?" he mused out loud.

He looked down again at his arm. The *man* was still shaking it. Frank did not see the medical equipment scattered about, packed into the back of the ambulance. He did not notice the uniform the emergency technician wore to identify himself.

"Let go, sir! Ya have to let her hand go now!" the man requested more urgently than before.

Lisa's hand remained tucked firmly within Frank's grip. The two large glass doors of the hospital's emergency entrance were open and awaiting them. The tech had been trying to open Frank's hand so that they could take Lisa inside, but Frank had not budged. Despite the technician's pleas, he remained unresponsive.

"Sir, ya have to let her go! Please!"

Let her go. Frank repeated the order in his head, its true meaning skewed into something frightening, life-threatening. Falling victim to the panic slowly taking control of his mind, he loosed a booming declaration. "No! I ca . . . n't!" His words were fragmented like the images in front of him.

The technician dropped his arm with the outburst. Puffing air like a small locomotive, Frank slid to his right, casting a contemptuous glare at the tech in the process.

"No!" he barked, reaffirming his decision. Reaching across Lisa's body, Frank tried pushing the technician toward the open back door of the bus, but an emotionally-depleted Frank couldn't muster the strength. With his back to the internal wall of the ambulance, the thin piece of metal separating the back area from the cab, he settled near the crest of Lisa's head.

He stared at the tech sitting across from him, angling to reconstruct the moments he felt were missing, precious seconds that would explain things, including the IV bag he noticed hanging casually over Lisa near the technician.

"What's going on? Tell me!"

The technician did not answer his question. He did not say anything at all. Frank's patience wore thin in the silence.

"Why won't you answer me? Who are you? What the fuck is happening?" His knees rattled together as an inescapable sadness anchored itself in the base of his stomach. The dam sheltering his hazel eyes broke as fresh streams of tears inched from its reservoir. Wiping his face with his palm, he tried to shake himself free of the hurt smothering him. "Something's not right. Tell me, how did we get here?"

Frustration, gassed by his mounting confusion, collided with his anxiety, rendering him emotionally defenseless. His questions, multiplying by the minute, circled around his head. Still holding tightly to Lisa's hand, he realized that in all the commotion, she had not moved or made a sound.

Crouching beside Lisa on the gurney, Frank lowered his face until it was level with hers. "Lisa, baby. . . . Lisa?" Patting her hand, he continued to try to wake her. "Lisa, baby, wake up. Lisa . . ." His eyes burned as tears ran without ceasing. Closing them, he whispered to her. *"I'm not leaving, baby. I'm right here. Okay? I'm sorry. I'm here. Please get up."*

"Fra–Frank." Adrenaline punched through his words, forcing a stammer Frank easily ignored. The gentleman had been riding as a passenger in the front of the ambulance, and after convincing the surgeon of his ability to defuse the situation, he stood at the back of the bus, stumbling through his technical training. "Frank . . . look to me. I mean . . . look at me now."

Frank still had not taken notice of him. Aside from the technician across from him and Lisa, no one existed.

"No one is taking her," Frank mumbled under his breath, not bothering to lift his head in the direction of the voice. He could not follow his memory into his present. There were too many blank spots.

Frank sat up straight, flattening his back against the wall of the ambulance. Seeing her on the beach was the last thing he could remember. His anxiety revved as he tussled with the unknown in search of clarity. The complicated, fickle situation fueled a relentless urge to protect her as his misgivings escalated the tension with each second that passed without an answer.

Quickly scanning the area for something to defend himself with, Frank grabbed a needle, wielding it like a weapon toward the technician who had previously held his arm.

"No one is taking her!" Frank lowered his eyes at the technician, feeling a telekinetic energy surge through him, pushing the scrawny, sunburned man sprawling from the back of the ambulance. He immediately turned his attention back to Lisa, frantically darting his eyes between her and the door. Then, cutting through the confusion, he heard a familiar voice.

"Frank, look at me. Frank."

Frank's blank glance toward the source of the voice trying to get his attention was evident. It was the technician who had escorted Frank to the ambulance, the same one who had intervened for him with the detective. Frank slowly turned his eyes toward the familiar voice.

"That's it. That's good. Frank, do you remember me?"

Frank shook his head and did not move from Lisa.

"Think. Come on. You remember now. I know ya do."

Frank maintained eye contact with the man, who seemed to know him, and lowered his defenses a bit.

The technician continued to jog his memory. "Fabrice, remember? From the hotel."

Fabrice? Frank didn't remember anyone named Fabrice.

"You know who I am, don't ya, Frank?"

Frank still couldn't remember him, but pieces of his memory started coming back to him. He could recall following Lisa into her suite after she had found him on the beach.

"Frank, look at Lisa."

Frank looked down at his wife. She still had not moved.

Fabrice continued talking, plugging the holes in Frank's story. "Lisa, your wife, is hurting really bad. You called emergency services from the hotel, and we came to get ya two."

Frank visibly tensed up, causing Fabrice to explain himself further. He motioned toward the hospital with an exaggerated sweep of his arms. "Behind me is the hospital. Doctors are waiting to help ya wife."

Frank looked out the back of the ambulance, behind Fabrice, and noticed the large hospital for the first time.

Fabrice kept his tone even and calm to keep from agitating Frank. "We are trying to save her. Let us help ya, Frank."

Frank looked again at his wife laying on the gurney, but this time he noticed her white bikini bottoms soaked in blood. "Oh, gawd . . . oh, gawd…" Seeing his own hands stained red exasperated his ever-increasing alarm. "Lisa . . ." His memory resurfaced in tiny flashes of light; not enough for him to get a clear picture of what had transgressed, but enough to know that it was something terrible.

Sensing Frank was on the verge of panicking again, Fabrice reclaimed his attention. "Frank look at me. She is stable, but we need to hurry."

In the midst of the unfolding horror, Frank tried to maintain his composure. There was so much blood—all over him, and all over her. Did he do this? Surely, he didn't hurt her? Why couldn't he remember?

"Do you understand? We are here to help. Too much time has passed already." Fabrice motioned for his partner to assist. "Ian is going to climb back into the bus, and we are going to take her into the hospital."

Releasing her hand, Frank conceded to his request. The technicians, Ian and Fabrice, along with Frank, gingerly lowered Lisa to the ground and quickly rolled her into the hospital. Within seconds, security swarmed Frank, tackling him to the ground while the emergency room unit whisked Lisa away to the operating room.

Frank struggled to get free as his torso slid on the frigid surface of the tiled floor. "Lisa! No, wait! Don't take her! I promised her I wouldn't leave!" Frank thought he might die. His head was spinning so violently that he could hardly stand upright. He needed to be with Lisa. She needed him.

"Frank, calm down. Frank."

He peered up at Fabrice hovering over him. Fabrice held his hand up to alert the officers. "You can let him go. I will see to him."

The security officers released Frank, but he didn't have the energy to move much. With some effort, he made it to his feet and managed to take one step before his system started shutting down. His legs buckled. Fabrice caught him, wrapping him in a bear hug as he collapsed to the ground. Frank's body went limp in his arms, exhausted from the emotional ride.

"I promised her. I can't leave her. I can't—" Erupting in a volcano of sobs, Frank stretched out on the floor in the middle of the walkway. Fabrice, sat beside him, resting a comforting hand on his back, creating a safe space for Frank to grieve.

CHAPTER 6

Sophie thought about the events of Monday night as she sat on a stool, sipping on a glass of freshly-squeezed lemonade. Things had gone from sugar to shit in the blink of an eye. It did not go at all as she had intended. It should have been a nice, respectable evening for their family, but it quickly turned into a scene from a *Love & Hip Hop* reunion show, complete with the hostile surprise guest.

Given all the sticking-and-moving her husband had done, a child was merely a mathematical inevitability. Though Sophie was not expecting *Charlie*, that child came as no surprise. In fact, twenty-eight thousand dollars less in her bank account warned her of the probability. It was money well spent, in her opinion. Michelle's behavior, on the other hand, was not something Sophie had been prepared to manage. She was not acting like herself at all. Sophie cringed knowing that her decisions—some directly, others indirectly—were the root cause.

She fought back the tears, seeking release as she gazed out of the large bay windows behind the kitchen sink. Michelle had left her phone calls unanswered. A new day loomed around the corner, marking the passing of day three since the incident, and Sophie wanted some assurances that Michelle was okay. She could only imagine how painful it must have been to be confronted with her father's philandering in such a public manner.

Brianna's frequent calls, though welcomed and needed, did not replace the ones from Michelle she sorely missed. Her soul ached for the undertones of her voice. Taking hold of her drink, she placed her feet on the tiled floor, got down from the bar stool, and proceeded down the hall into the den. The spaces of the newly bare walls haunted her as she passed through. Gone were the frames that once held the memories of her lengthy marriage to Lewis. They were packed in a box, awaiting the furnace. A similar fate was intended for the man himself. Arrangements had been made, and it was only a matter of time before she could be completely free of Lewis once and for all.

Thinking about him made her flesh crawl. Even in death, Lewis prevented her from doing as she pleased. Stepping onto the dark hardwood floor of the den, Sophie smiled as its icy surface tickled the soles of her feet. She took her time walking to her coveted lazy-Suzan in the corner of the room, angled near the window, allowing the cool to travel up to her mind, forcing her to relax. She slouched into the seat, gently placed her drink on the small table beside her, and reclined in her chair. She focused on the chirping of the grasshoppers, rioting just beyond the window sill. The quiet sounds of a peaceful country night provided the deep spiritual massage Sophie so desperately needed.

She sat, basking in the silence, until her landline began to sing, interrupting her quiet. Thinking that perhaps it was Michelle calling, she excitedly grabbed the cordless off the small stand within arm's reach, nearly knocking her drink to the ground.

"Hello?"

"Sophie Lucille Freemont."

Slightly distracted by the ruckus she'd created, Sophie did not hear the caller immediately. "I'm sorry. Hello? Who is this?"

"Luce, it's me." The pleasant tenor, sprinkled with a few years of sleepless nights, serenaded Sophie through the receiver. She no longer needed to ask to whom the voice belonged. The lump in her throat and the clattering of her knees cemented her knowing. "I have missed you."

"Peter Ray Baxter!" Sophie's voice filled with glee. "I can hardly believe it's you. How did you find me? How did you get this number?"

Dr. Baxter cleared his throat, hesitant to share the details with her. "It was no simple task, but simply hearing your voice made it all worth it. It still warms my heart after all these years."

Momentarily removing the cordless phone from her ear and placing it close to her chest, she took a deep breath. Her nerves were on high alert. The mere sound of his voice sent her heart into a frenzy. Clearly, the love she once reserved for him still abided within her; it was still there to give.

"Peter, this is such a surprise. I don't know what to say."

"Say that I may come over, Ms. Freemont."

"Please. I mean, of course. I would love to have you come visit. Just . . ."

"Right now."

Sophie laughed uncomfortably. "Now?"

"Yes, now! I need to see you, Luce."

Postponing their meeting seemed to be the most viable option for Sophie. Her mind wandered in search of an answer to delay their reunion, longing to say anything but the resounding yes pounding against her lips in rhythm with the quick tempo of her heart.

"This is really sudden. I . . ."

"Luce, don't push me away again."

"I am not pushing you away." Her defenses rose, and the phrase came out much harsher than she had intended. Peter's presence would be a welcomed change, but she was not certain of what their rusted union meant for her current situation. How would he fit into everything?

"Don't try and lie to me. That was something you never did very well. I need you to give me your address. Whatever *that* is . . . your hesitance . . . we can discuss it in person. Don't I deserve that much?"

"Peter, that was over twenty years ago." The statement rolled clumsily off her tongue like bits of rock down a jagged hill. "I have moved on."

"No, you haven't. You just moved. There is a difference, and I think you know that."

Sighing heavily, Sophie resigned to give in to his request. The hurt in his voice anchored her decision, making it impossible to dismiss him. In the wake of her seemingly endless list of questionable choices, Sophie did not want to add to it, but perhaps this would work out for both of them.

"Fifty-six seventy-seven Wimbledon Lane."

"I am on my way."

Sophie held the phone in her hand until it beeped excessively, alerting her that the line was clear. Peter Baxter was on his way to her home. She wondered how time had changed things, if he would accept the explanation she had to give him, and if she would have the answers to his questions.

Ding Dong.

Puzzled, Sophie got up to answer the door. She had figured she would have at least thirty minutes to prepare for his arrival, but barely five minutes had passed. Oh, well. She was ready to see him.

"Who is it?" Sophie questioned as she neared the door, but there was no response. She thought it strange but opened the door anyway— an act that she instantly regretted.

"Charlie."

"Ms. Lewis. Or should I say Sophie Freemont?"

Turning her body to the side, Sophie motioned for Charlie to enter with her arm. "I don't have a lot of time. What can I do for you?"

Charlie shuffled down the hall and into the den where their last meeting had taken place. Bracing herself with one hand on the back of the couch, she made the slow drop to the cushion.

"I want what is owed to my son."

"Don't get comfortable. As I stated before, I don't have time for you."

"Ah, see, what you said was that you don't have a lot of time." Charlie fluffed the throw pillow, tucking it under her arm as a rest. "I don't need a lot of time."

The Louis Vuitton knock-off bag gracing her arm, large plastic hoop earrings, and the facial MAC overkill helped Sophie to deduce Charlie's angle within seconds. It was one of the few skills she'd acquired during her time with Lewis. The wardrobe was a drastic change from the designer threads she had worn in the days prior.

"Charlene, I am trying to be civil and adult about this, but you are making that exceedingly difficult."

Charlie laughed, her round belly jiggling a bit from the movement. "Civil? Is that what you call siccing the Bella Twins on me?"

"Why are you here? This is twice now that you have come to my home uninvited."

"I thought you were trying to back out of our deal. Made my own play."

"Planning is not your strong point. Leave that to me. I did not know that you, Charlie, were the Charlene that our mutual friend and I had discussed."

"Well, now you know."

Sophie smirked at the remark. "How do you know Michael?"

"Who?"

"Mike. How do you know Mike?"

"Why?"

Sophie wanted to piece this puzzle together. She could not figure out how Charlie had come to be at her house that day. The only person she had told about the reading, aside from the girls, was Michael, but she hadn't realized that Charlie and Charlene were the same person.

"Curious."

"He saw Lewis roughing me up once, and . . ." Charlie rubbed her neck, remembering how Lewis had nearly strangled her to death. "He consoled me after."

Sophie reflected on her own bout with Lewis. "He was a volatile bastard."

"How do *you* know him?" Charlie smirked, raising her brow. "Is it a *biblical* connection?"

Sophie knew Michael from her days at the Freemont Estate. He had been conceived during one of her campaign ploys for her father. Mr. Sterling's contribution was the largest it had ever been that year, none of which was any of Charlie's business.

"It isn't important."

Seeing that she was not going to get an answer, Charlie returned to her original question. "Why did you let your pit bulls attack me?"

"That situation, as is your pregnancy, is your fault. You slid in where you did not belong." Sophie had chosen to remain by the entrance, not fully entering the room, planting her feet near the door to emphasize the temporal nature of this visit.

"Very funny, but it was your husband, Lewis, who should not have *come* . . . inside me, that is." Rubbing her belly, she smiled. "This baby is my get-out-of-jail free card, my lottery ticket, insurance policy. Whatever you want to call him."

"Leave my house, Charlene, before I call the police."

"I need money, Freemont. Even if you don't have it, I know Daddy does."

"So you *can* read? Where did you get that information, huh? Google? Did you Google me, Charlene? Aww . . ."

The smile left Charlie's face. Her body stiffened like a pair of jeans with too much starch, hard as cardboard.

Sophie began her own recount, letting Charlie know she did not come unprepared. "Charlene Grae, daughter of Benjamin and Linda Grae, twelve sixty-seven Boggin Lane, Terre Haute, Indiana."

Charlie opened her mouth to speak, but Sophie raised her hand, silencing her for a moment longer. "They still live there with your youngest sister, Debra Nolani Grae, class of 2017."

"Fuck you, you uppity white bitch."

"That is completely unnecessary. It isn't pleasant, is it? For someone to insert themselves into your life? To assume to know anything about your family? To threaten that family in any way."

"I wish you would."

"I promise that is the last thing in the world you want. I have the power to make wishes come true. *That* little tidbit is free, because I am positive it did not show up in the search results. Take it and go."

Charlie pulled herself up from the couch and walked toward Sophie. "This is not over."

Sophie shook her head dismissively. "I am not concerned with your shenanigans, your empty threats. This is my city. You are here because I am allowing you to stay, understand?"

"What about our deal? I need that money." Charlie's voice squeaked with desperation. She had nothing with Lewis gone.

"I paid what I agreed to. Don't expect a penny more from me."

"But I don't have anything else. That was not enough." Charlie crossed the threshold of the front door, walking out into the mild sauna of the night. She turned around to face Sophie, who was now directly behind the door, preparing to close it. "If you don't give me more, I will proceed with my claim for his share in the will."

"Charlene, I have been a lot of things, but stupid is not one of them. You will receive nothing more from the Lewis family, not even his damn name. If you think I am going to let you take anything away from my girls, think again. It will not happen."

"I'm getting what's mine!" Charlie barked.

Sophie laughed. "Take a look around you, *Charlene*. If you try this shit again, I'll fill this big, beautiful yard with all of your dirty little secrets. Consider this *warning* an expression of Southern hospitality." Slamming the door in her face, Sophie went to go freshen up for Peter's arrival, leaving Charlie outside once again.

CHAPTER 7

The house was well over an hour away from his home in Allen, and he couldn't get there fast enough. Time seemed to stand still as he sped down the highway. He imagined time had not done much to alter the beautiful blue-eyed young girl who stole his heart when he was seventeen.

His vintage, metallic 1968 Camaro rode like a dream. He thought about their last night together. The knife he didn't see coming had created a wound so deep it had yet to heal. The blame did not belong with his dear Sophie. No, the fault was his to shoulder.

Peter, the product of a single-parent home, attended a very exclusive private school, where he had befriended his love. Attending the school via a scholarship, as opposed to his father's checkbook, served to develop feelings of inadequacy. As a shy, awkward, scrawny kid with a part-time job that regularly prevented him from life outside of academia, Peter didn't exactly garner any votes for class president. He often found himself at the painful end of too many jokes, causing him to be aloof and distance himself from his classmates.

Sophie was different. Her warm and inviting spirit allowed him to be himself. He thrived in large part because of their friendship. Finding favor with her relieved the sting of the stigmatism resulting from his lifestyle. No one really bothered him after she accepted him. His love for her was genuine, steady, and unconditional.

He worried about the backlash she suffered as a result of their relationship. Not everyone approved. Peter thought that perhaps if he could blend in more, fade into the high society crowd, that he could protect her from those unfavorable opinions. Conceivably, it was that thinking that led him to ask her father, the formidable Richard Freemont, for permission to marry his daughter. It seemed like the proper thing to do at the time, and he thought it would show the sincerity of his intent regarding Sophie, but the future mayor had scorned and rejected him. Peter's lack of financial freedoms that the Freemonts enjoyed made him unworthy in her father's eyes, but life had matured him. She was much too young, and he must have been out of his mind asking her father for permission. That was either really brave or really stupid. Something told him the latter was true.

To this day, he couldn't help but lean toward the theory that his gentlemanly gesture cost him Sophie. No words had been exchanged between them after that night, until now. However, his love for Sophie had not waned. If anything, it had grown stronger. With each failed relationship, he longed for her.

The universe had answered his prayer the night he happened upon Brianna.

Peter rolled into the circular driveway in front of Sophie's home. His hands rattled the steering wheel. He took a deep breath, filling his lungs, settling his nerves. His heart was racing a mile a minute. He opened the glove box and grabbed his travel-size gel. After working up a good lather, using his hands, he restyled his hair in the rearview mirror. Satisfied, he got out of the car, closing the door to give himself a final inspection. He felt like that fifteen-year-old kid asking her to study for the first time, but he didn't want to look like it. He curdled his nerves and walked to the door.

There he stood, willing himself to ring the doorbell. What was the issue? A second chance with Sophie was exactly what he wanted. Now that the moment had finally arrived, the thought of being rejected terrified him. He didn't know if he could survive it. He took a deep breath and pressed the small, pearl-shaped button. There was no backing down now.

To Peter, an eternity passed by before Sophie appeared at the door. For one celestial moment, no one said a word, silenced by the enormity of it, a meeting twenty-four years in the making. His heart pounded against the bones protecting it. As she stood there in the foyer, her beauty suppressed his need for air, rearranging his priorities, arousing more than his curiosity and producing an urge more compelling than the impending inquisition moseying about in his head.

"Luce." Peter, unprepared for the lechery overriding his thoughts, felt powerless as his movements sprang to life without him. With a hand cupping each side of her face, moisture lightly coating his lips, which spread as they connected with hers. Clumsily, he entered into her home, half falling, half floating, feeling more and more out of control as his mental ramblings were consumed with those of a salacious nature. It all was happening so quickly that Peter hardly had time to process it.

Once inside, he peered into her beautiful blues, seeking permission through the lustful haze before erasing the space between their lips again. He tasted traces of the mint still coating the insides of her mouth. Their tongues danced to the beat of an old love song. Refusing to break their kiss, he swung the door closed with a swift kick, the loud thud intensifying the electricity flowing effortlessly through them.

She rustled her hands through his thick, freshly styled mane with an angry lust, her hunger swelling into an uncontrollable typhoon. Leaving her lips to explore, he rested his nose in the nape of her neck, perforating his lungs with lavender, honey, and strawberry as he stole the oxygen surrounding him. His lips moved furiously along her collar bone, creating a trail of the sweetest kisses Sophie had ever felt. Wasting no time, his hands rid her body of the few articles of clothing she wore.

"Peter . . ." Sophie whimpered, helpless as her body went limp under his touch.

"Luce . . . don't." Placing his index finger gently across her lips, he withdrew from her, stepping back to admire her natural canvas.

Like a mannequin in a storefront window unable to move, a nude Sophie draped lazily against her front door. The hard oak creaked, echoing the hunger Peter longed to sate, providing an audible record. Her chest heaved, her body swaying with desire.

Peter teased as he brushed her lips with his, fueling the fire. The heat radiated from her body, spurring his advances as her murmurs filled his ears with her demands. Ignoring the groans of his throbbing manhood, Peter opted to take things slowly, gingerly massaging her supple breasts with one hand while exploring the wet terrain of her underworld with the other. Passion oozed from his lips to hers as he carefully laid her down on the bare floor, beneath the archway marking the hall's entrance.

Sophie scrunched her body as her skin made contact with the floor's cold surface. Her momentary discomfort was soon forgotten as Peter disappeared into *her*, quickly developing a taste for her sweet nectar. A series of moans escaped her lips. Her legs trembled, crossing behind his neck, restricting his movement.

Lost in the inferno between her legs, neither he nor Sophie noticed the pair of eyes watching through the oval glass pane of the door, leering at their private moment, fist raised, tempted to interrupt their session with a knock on the door.

CHAPTER 8

Sweat beads formed small waterfalls across his brow. He took a deep breath and invited the rank aroma of cheap perfume and other musty odors to fill his lungs. The air was thick and sticky with remnants of his alcohol-driven sexual escapade carried out just hours before. The scene was so familiar he didn't even need to open his eyes to recount it in detail. Empty liquor bottles and faceless women had become a part of his living décor. Same shit, different day. The silk sheets clumsily draped over his chiseled six-foot frame clung to him so tightly he could barely move. The red-head lying across his ankles didn't help matters. He kicked his leg abruptly and watched the young girl's naked body tumble awkwardly to the floor.

"Ouch!" Rachel screamed as her head collided with something sharp on the carpet. She reached a shaky hand underneath her head and found the small piece of metal responsible for the blood oozing from the fresh cut in her temple. She picked it up and inspected it. It took her a second to focus her eyes and corral her mind before she realized the spiral object she held was a corkscrew. "Damn it."

"Wake up."

She sat up with her back against the bed for support, intentionally avoiding eye contact with Micah, who had managed to turn over onto his back but was still lying in bed. Her vision was blurred as she struggled to manage the battle of the bands contest going on in her head.

"My head hurts."

"Stop all that damn screaming."

Rachel rolled her emerald-green eyes and grunted her frustration. She was in no mood to deal with his craziness. "You kicked me, Micah."

"And? Do I care?"

She didn't want to argue with him. Besides, there was no winning, no negotiating with him. He was tripping, and her challenging him would only make things worse. Micah was controlling as hell. She had learned that if she just kept her head down and her mouth closed, she could get what she needed and move on. So, she remained silent.

Micah had little, if any, concern for her pain. He wanted quiet, time to gather himself in preparation for the day. "Rachel, come here."

Rachel gingerly rose to her feet, instantly regretting the preceding hours spent emptying the bottles of wine. She climbed onto the bed and slowly, seductively inched her way to across Micah's body until her face meshed with his. "Yes?"

While grabbing a fist full of her cherry-red hair, Micah sucked her lips so hard it left them itching and tingling. She took an audible breath as he released her, guiding her face to his lower region. While her mind was spinning from the sudden movement, he grabbed his girth with his free hand and shoved it into Rachel's mouth.

Rachel cringed as tears fell from her eyes, mixing with the blood still dripping from her temple. She fought the urge to throw up the steak and lobster from their night before, relaxed her throat, and took his inches until she felt his scrotum against her chin. If the pounding in her head were not bad enough, the salty taste of his manhood surely made the act even more unbearable. Rachel could not move under Micah's grip. Her bulletproof love ballad joined the madness in her head.

He groaned as his manhood made contact with the soft, wet tissue inside her throat, imagining that her lips held power enough to deliver him from the swelling ache of his heart. He wished the warm, moist feeling would be enough to distract him from the irreconcilable sadness this new day was ushering in.

Micah lifted his head and looked down at Rachel. Tears were streaming down her face. He struggled to maintain his erection as his heart splintered and crashed into hers. Broken and demoralized, Rachel was a soul-churning reflection of himself. It was not purely her hurt that shook him; it was more so the acceptance of the situation. Despair and hopelessness were very clearly drawn into the outline of her small face, and it rocked him to the core. Rachel was once a vibrant, strong, determined woman, but for the first time, he noticed that woman was no more. Micah was responsible for her heartache. What had he done to her? What was he doing?

Throwing her off of him, Micah rolled onto the side of the hotel bed and sat up. Lacking the courage to face her, he grabbed the sheet, covered himself, and walked into the massive bathroom, skulking with a sullen look etched on his face.

Rachel lay on the bed, curled up like a small child with her arms holding her legs in the fetal position, crying silently. Reality tore through the silence, announcing the call for change.

"I am sorry. You need to leave."

Though Micah spoke gently through the closed door, his words rang loudly in Rachel's ears. She slowly gathered herself and prepared to leave. Into her overnight bag, she threw the few outfits she had brought with her: her red-bottoms—a gift from Micah—Summer's Eve Lotion, and her perfume. A plain white V-neck T-shirt and a pair of gray warmup pants were the only things she kept out for wear.

Even with the pounding in her head and Micah's horrible treatment of her, Rachel was not eager to leave. Some part of her wanted him, loved him. She scanned the room to look for anything she may have missed, and her eyes settled on the bathroom. She sighed heavily, wishing she could fit Micah into her bag and take him with her.

On her way out of the room, she stopped briefly by the door. "I love you, Micah."

Micah opened the door once he was certain Rachel had gone. He was completely disgusted with himself. Rachel was a good girl, and she deserved better. He had known for some time how she felt about him, but the feelings were not mutual. She could never have his heart, and she would have been better off had she never met him. He grabbed a few things for the shower, but he knew not even the scalding hot water would cleanse him of the guilt eating away at his soul.

CHAPTER 9

Brianna loathed the idea of having to endure another forty-five minutes with "Dr. WonderBra," but the lenient judge her uncle had lobbied for must have had a stick up his ass that day in court when he made her sessions mandatory for the next year. The silver lining was the train ride downtown. Brianna would have never ridden the train before. It both amused and saddened her to see how much her world had changed in such a short period of time. One measly little second had completely changed everything. Her beautiful, powder-white BMW convertible sat untouched in her garage since her trip to Cancun. Either Armand or Michelle took her where she needed to go, or she used public transportation. Fortunately, DART, a decent city bus system, made getting around Dallas fairly simple.

Brianna had never glanced at anything remotely public before the events of last month, not even the library. Besides, with the convenience of having access to any and everything from her home, she viewed public facilities and resources as beneath her. Those things were for poor people, people in search of what she had, not an educated, sophisticated woman such as herself. She never took the time to attempt to connect herself to the plight of those she assumed were less fortunate, but in the wake of all she'd lost, she found herself trying to do exactly that. She was running from who she was, from the life she had lived—that privileged, proper woman she used to be.

The artificial train light danced around, carving its own picture with its passengers. Brianna felt at home there, comforted by what she perceived to be a solemn atmosphere of people searching for what she was trying to elude. That comfort, however, was temporal as her mind betrayed her. Every glance, gesture, or acknowledgment from a fellow passenger turned into a symbol of their disgust and rejection. The self-inflicted judgment wrapped itself around her psyche, further damaging her fragile self-image, relaying to her that somehow, she did not belong there, either. That even without her expensive heels and designer threads, she was an imposter. Her external presentation did little to reshape the internal impression; the ache of not belonging anywhere imbedded in her. She wanted desperately to *fit* in, to be wanted, loved, and appreciated for the woman she was. The problem was, not even Brianna was sure what that meant. She was looking for herself.

The train screeched as the tracks whined under its weight. She closed her eyes and let her head rest gently on the window to the right of her.

Now Arriving at the West End Station. Doors will open to the right. Please remember to take all your personal belongings. Thank you for riding DART.

The announcement signaled the end of her ride. She made her way down the short metal steps off the train and headed toward the Bank of America building on the next block. Cars and people alike zipped around her as the city roared to life.

She arrived at her appointment at 10 a.m. on the dot. Dr. Shepherd's assistant greeted her warmly, her bright fiery red hair seeming a little lackluster this morning, but Brianna didn't give it much thought.

"Ms. Mason, good morning. Dr. Shepherd is a little behind schedule. Please take a seat, and I'll let you know when she's ready."

Brianna returned the smile but did not speak, taking a seat on one of the two vanilla love seats in the waiting area. The false limitation created by the lack of open space made Brianna uncomfortable. She nervously ran her fingers through her hair, trying to keep her marbles in the jar. Something about Dr. Shepherd rubbed her the wrong way. She hadn't dealt with her inappropriately, but Brianna had a hard time trusting her. The assistant had a tendency to pry, asking Brianna random questions, fishing for details about her life, and Brianna did not feel like playing dodge ball with her.

Beep. Beep. Beep. The intercom buzzed.

"Yes, Dr. Shepherd?"

"Rachel, please send in Ms. Mason. I am ready for her."

Rachel swallowed hard, trying to pause the concert in her head long enough to follow her boss's request. "Yes, Dr. Shepherd."

Rachel did not need to say anything. Brianna stood and walked into the good doctor's office. She grinned and winked at her as she passed by her desk and entered the office. She closed the door behind her.

Dr. Shepherd stood to greet Brianna, walking around her desk to close the space between them. "Brianna, how are you? Please, sit wherever you'd like. I'm going to take my regular seat in the chair over by the window." With that, Dr. Shepherd, with her pen and pad in hand, took her seat.

Brianna again chose not to speak. She stood for a moment, with her back against the closed door, and observed the good doctor. Noticing the silk V-neck blouse that barely covered the 38 DDs propped up on display, and the skirt so short that Brianna could see that the good doctor hadn't bothered to cover her garden, Brianna smirked. Chuckling to herself, Brianna took her attire as a good sign, figuring the good doctor must have plans immediately after work. Dr. Shepherd was generally more pleasant when she had something to look forward to.

"Brianna, are you going to sit?"

Brianna took a seat on the couch across from Dr. Shepherd, closed her eyes, and prepared for the minor interrogation.

"I'd like to begin with what happened at your mom's. Do you mind if we start there?"

"Yes, I do, actually. I don't want to talk about that." Brianna did not want to dredge up anything that had happened at her mother's that day.

Dr. Shepherd removed her glasses and toyed with the plastic handle in her mouth. She did not want to push Brianna too hard. She was on the verge of shutting down, as it were, but she needed to talk.

"I must insist."

Brianna rolled her eyes. This woman drove her crazy. "Fine. What do you want to know?"

"How do you feel about it?"

Brianna did not know how to frame her sentiment. She felt a plethora of things, but she also felt nothing. Her guilt was accompanied, and in some ways overpowered, by her indifference. She loved her family, but she was desperate to get back to her core. That desperation afforded her the ability to compromise her moral center with little regret. She was not devoid of emotion, but she had not yet learned how to operate from such a sensitive state. Everything felt bigger than life and grossly affected her. Having lived such a pampered life prior, she was not equipped to handle that degree of emotional activity, and her indifference was an act of self-preservation. The reaction was not something she did consciously, and although it was a defense mechanism of sorts, it was simultaneously causing her irreparable harm.

"Brianna, I understand how difficult and uncomfortable this may be. This is a safe environment. Anything you say here stays between us."

Brianna did not believe that for a minute. She scoffed and rolled her eyes again, indicating to Dr. Shepherd how she felt about her statement.

"I am bound by law." Dr. Shepherd was losing her patience with the *little girl.* "Your words will stay between these walls. Let me help you."

Brianna considered the good doctor's words. She was bound by law, and Brianna knew she needed help. She could not stop or make any changes on her own. She had tried many times and failed. She may as well give Dr. Shepherd a real try. She had nothing to lose.

"Confused. I felt confused."

"That's good. Can you pinpoint what may have caused it?"

Brianna contemplated the events of that evening, uncertain of her ability to label the source of her confusion. Charlie's unexpected visit hadn't really bothered her, and her mom did not seem rattled in the least bit. She had handled herself with the kind of grace befitting a woman who was once known as one of the most prominent Southern belles in the city. It was the usually poised Michelle who had flown off the handle.

Out of nowhere, the light switch turned on. "Michelle responded the way I would have expected my mother to."

"What do you mean?"

Brianna hadn't given it much consideration at the time. The situation had escalated so quickly that she really hadn't had time to think about it. "My mother was calm, eerily calm. She did not seem surprised by Charlie."

Dr. Shepherd nodded her head to signify her understanding. Brianna was hesitant to say it aloud, but the rumbling in the pit of her stomach forced the words up and off the tip of her tongue.

Brianna swallowed hard. The thought left a bitter taste in her mouth. Their relationship was still in the developmental stages, and she didn't want to entertain anything that may threaten it. She had spent twenty-three years without her mother, and she was unwilling to give her up.

"She's keeping something from us."

"Are you certain?"

"Of course not." Brianna stared at Dr. Shepherd. That was an idiotic question. "How could I possibly be certain of anything? All I have are questions. Suspicions. My life has become an elaborate, extensive version of Clue."

"I did not intend to offend you with my question." Dr. Shepherd put her glasses back on, made a note, and decided to move forward.

Brianna rolled her eyes and rubbed her temples. She hated that Dr. Shepherd could so easily get beneath her skin.

"Anything else stand out to you about the evening? Aside from your mother's demeanor?"

Brianna shook her head.

"Speaking of your mother, how is that going?"

"I don't know. I'm on autopilot. I am trying to adjust, but it's awkward."

"What's awkward, exactly?"

"Her melanin deficiency."

"Ah, I see."

"I struggled to love my blackness. My money did not protect me from ignorance. I had to deal with the hate, learned to shoulder it. Being black and female has not been easy. Sometimes having money and being well-spoken made it worse. I didn't belong anywhere. My mother, Lisa, helped me to sort through my pain with that. She had no problem being proud of who she was, and I emulated her."

"Do you feel that embracing your biological mother negates that somehow?"

"I cannot identify with her. I look at her, and I see someone who could not possibly empathize with my path. I see someone whose life profited from a system that consistently tries to destroy me. Her father was one generation removed from the Klan. Her family owned country clubs. She is the embodiment of white privilege."

"She left that life, correct? For you and your sister?"

"That is the story."

"Michelle is your twin, and from what you've shared, she's a strong, emotionally-mature woman. Does she have any problems identifying or relating to black culture?"

"Not that I noticed."

"Does she identify with one more than the other?"

"Talk to Michelle. I cannot tell you."

"In your opinion."

"People tend to center their conversations on things they have in common. So, I really wouldn't know. I don't even know what things white culture would lay claim to. Golf? Country music? What is it?"

Dr. Shepherd stifled a laugh. "I am only asking because I wanted you to see that Michelle is just like you. If she can live as she is, you can do the same."

"Michelle has not known anything else. I have, and I am at a loss. Will Sophie be offended by my black power card? If I tell her I fully support the petition for Assata Shakur to receive a pardon from President Obama, will she have an issue with that? Can she understand my love and adoration for Angela Davis or Nikki Giovanni? Michelle Obama?"

"Brianna, those things have nothing to do with skin color. A black mother could take issue with your decisions, too. I am a white woman, and I admire Michelle Obama."

"That is not the point."

"But it is the point, Brianna. If your issue is with relating to her, that is the point."

"My mother is not supposed to be white. I am a black woman. I don't know how to be anything other than that. Everything I am, who I became, sprang from there. Her family actively discriminated against black people."

"That is your family, too, Brianna."

"Our family. Our family. . . . I keep saying it, but it doesn't make it any easier."

Dr. Shepherd pushed her glasses back up onto her face. "No one says that you have to like it, Brianna. I imagine that your mother is not proud of that truth, either. However, it is a part of who you are, your history."

"This is just a bit much for me. I have a whole other side of myself that I know nothing about. Never felt the need to address my blackness, and now I do, like it's a Girl Scout badge I need to earn. Being more, extra, to compensate for my white blood."

Dr. Shepherd scribbled on her notepad. "There are cultural differences that might come into play here, but you are no different than any other two people trying to establish a relationship."

"I am not following."

"Communication is key. Talk with her. Continue to exchange ideas, common interests, dislikes. In time, you'll start to see her for who she really is and not the image in your mind."

"I never considered the possibility of Michelle's white mother being mine. Not once."

"Shock is normal. Rather than focusing on all you lost, rebuild your life with what you have, old and new."

Brianna closed her eyes, forcing her mind to remain open. She had been more transparent than she intended, but she may as well. She had no choice but to be there and make the time count.

"Are you okay? Any other thoughts about this you'd like to explore?"

Brianna glanced at the analog clock propped on the book shelf and exhaled. There was still a lot of time left in their session. It was enough time to adequately discuss what had been gnawing at her conscience for the last few weeks.

"No, but there is something I'd like to discuss."

Dr. Shepherd shifted in her seat, obviously energized by the prospect of Brianna opening herself up to the therapeutic process without any prodding. "That's great. I'm listening."

"I think I may be in love."

CHAPTER 10

Yet another difficult night with Michelle had left Armand in an uncomfortable space. He could not determine how things had gotten so bad between them. When did loving her become such a chore? He had stopped by Brianna's room on his way to bed, as usual, to check on her, and Michelle flipped on him as soon as he got into their room. What was her issue? Michelle had taught him about opening his heart and showing compassion for others, but it seemed like she had none for her own flesh and blood. Armand couldn't make sense of it. He was doing what Michelle should have been doing, and he didn't mind. They were partners after all. Why couldn't she see that?

Armand pulled into the parking lot of the Bank of America building off Main Street. Choosing a space as close to the building's entrance as possible, he backed his car into a parking spot and killed the engine. Facing the entrance provided him with an unobstructed view of people coming and going. Preparing to people watch, Armand powered down the driver's side window and laid the seat back. He relaxed and contemplated whether it was a good idea for him to be there. Though a small part of him felt like he might be overstepping his boundaries, he couldn't shake the gnawing feeling that he needed to stay close. Michelle would not be pleased if she knew, which meant this moment would be added to the growing list of secrets that made the energy between them uncomfortable.

Maybe he was overreacting and straining their union to satisfy a need he didn't have the words to describe. The bickering seemed to only get worse after she accepted his ring. They had argued more in the last few months than they had in the last few years. He shared the unorthodox nature of *their* origin, and she took it well. She was upset for a moment, but he thought it brought them closer together, strengthened their bond. He was no longer certain if that was the case, or even if their future was probable.

As he was tapping his fingers rhythmically on the steering wheel, debating his next move, the shine of the band on his finger stopped him cold. He stared at the ring as everything it represented clawed at his sensibilities—the man he strove to be, one of integrity, compassion, loving and devoted; the kind of man Michelle could depend on; the kind she deserved.

Michelle was being unreasonable, but it didn't matter much that she was his priority if she didn't feel it.

"Damn it. Why is she making shit so complicated?" he wondered aloud. "I promised her. I am simply making good on that promise."

He could not deny the possibility that in the midst of everything, he had lost sight of that. He didn't want to fight with her, but they needed to hash this out.

"I need to keep them both safe. No way would she forgive me if something happened to Brianna. No way. Argh! This is bullshit." Armand continued venting his frustration, talking himself into either staying or going home. "I'm doing the right thing. Protecting her, them. I am protecting them. . . ."

A twinge of guilt locked his tongue into place. Michelle had not been on his radar, and he knew it. It wasn't because he didn't care. Brianna needed him more.

Still wrestling with his decision, Armand lifted his seat into the upright position, resting his head on the steering wheel face down as he spoke. "Go home, Armand. Just take your ass home. Nothing to see here anyw—"

Turning his key, he opened his eyes and caught sight of something that stopped him midsentence. Opening his door, standing with one leg on the pavement and the other on the car's floorboard, Armand squinted, trying to improve his 20/40 vision, pausing only for a second before deciding to approach for a closer look. "Fuck it. She'll understand."

Squinting again, Armand zeroed in on a gentleman standing a few yards from the entrance. His internal alarm was triggered in an instant. Closing the car door, he casually made his way to the area, moving as quickly as he could without launching into a full-blown sprint.

Roughly ten feet out, the tiny hairs on his arms stood, and his throat felt like he had swallowed a brick. Something was off with this guy. Not only did he seem odd, loitering about in his khaki shorts and T-shirt in the sea of designer suits flanking the walkway, but for some reason, Armand did not *want* him there. He wasn't sure how long he had been standing around, but it was obvious he did not come from inside the building.

As Armand drew nearer to the mystery guy, an eerie feeling swept over him. His vibe was regrettably familiar. The guy's stance and build kicked Armand's instincts into overdrive. Everything in him screamed that he was looking at Javan, but even Armand found it difficult to believe.

Still, Armand needed to be sure, so he perched himself on the side of the building, just a few bodies away from the guy, hoping to steal a glance at his face. The details didn't matter. Armand could only remember his eyes and how the dim light seemed to power the sinister glow he saw in them. They were the eyes of a possessed man.

Armand wanted confirmation of his suspicions, but he also wanted to avoid confrontation. There was a time and a place for everything; this moment was neither.

Turn around. Turn around, you fuck. Come on.

The crowd started to disseminate as the lunch rush neared its end. *Waldo* disappeared around the corner into the construction in progress on the building's north side. *Shit.*

Temporarily frozen in thought, Armand stood, hands covering his curly crown, frustrated that he had missed him. Before he could turn to leave, Armand heard a familiar voice.

"What are you doing here?"

Her curt tone birthed marbles into his muscles. He did not want to mime his way through another argument. Dropping his head, Armand reluctantly turned to meet his foe.

"I'm waiting," she challenged.

"I don't want to do this. I was just leaving."

"Why were you here in the first place? Are you following me?"

Armand took a deep breath, trying to come up with some viable explanation, something other than the truth. "Not exactly. It's not what you think."

"I think you're following me. Unless you have some business here?"

Fuck. I got nothing.

"Fine, Brianna," he mumbled with a hint of defeat.

"Fine? Is that supposed to mean something to me?"

"I am here for you."

"Armand!"

He raised his hands, cutting her thought short. "I didn't follow you, though. I got here a few minutes ago."

"You cannot keep doing this."

"Doing what?"

"Showing up like this. I didn't even tell you I was coming here."

Armand had no response to that. There was no way in hell he was telling her he had snooped through her things to get the info. She would really flip out.

"I'll give you a ride home. Let's go."

Rolling her eyes, Brianna threw her hands up in the air and started walking in circles in front of him. "No, just stop. This is hard enough without you doing this. I got here all by myself, Armand, and I can get home—*alone*. I'm not an invalid."

"I know that, but it's dangerous. I am just trying to keep you safe."

"I appreciate that, but you're doing too much, Armand. I can't handle this. This is too much."

"It's just a ride home, Brianna."

"It's not about the fucking ride, Armand! Holy crap, you are not hearing me!" Brianna pushed past Armand, heading toward the construction area.

He grabbed her arm, pulling her back behind him in an attempt to reason with her. "Stop! Wait, Brianna! Where are you going?"

"Home."

"Let me take you. What is the problem?" Armand stood between her and the small pathway through the construction area. It prevented her, at least for the time being, from taking that route, keeping her from bumping into Javan, who could easily be lying in wait somewhere.

"I'm all over the place, Javan!"

Armand's body instantly tensed. "What did you say?"

Realizing her error, Brianna quickly recovered. "Armand, *this,*" she said, motioning between them, "whatever *this* is . . . is confusing the hell out of me. Let me be. Javan is gone. There's no threat anymo—" Throwing her hand over mouth, Brianna suddenly bent over, holding her stomach.

"Are you okay? What's wrong?"

Brianna slowly straightened back up, wiping her mouth. "I'm fine. I just need you to stop."

Ignoring her answer, Armand kept pressing her. He hadn't really noticed before, but Brianna looked pale and out of sorts. She didn't look well at all. "Is your stomach upset?"

Very slowly, she replied, "No, why?"

"You're holding it," Armand answered, pointing to the hand cradling her midsection.

Brianna quickly moved her hands to her sides. "I didn't realize."

"Just let me take you home."

"I'm not going with you."

Scrunching his face, Armand drew an exasperated breath. "What is the fucking problem?"

"What do you think?"

"Don't do this shit."

"I heard you two last night. I hear you every night."

"And you know Michelle is overreacting. There is nothing going on between us."

Leaning against the wall for support, studying the ground, she spoke in practically a whisper. "Are you sure, Armand? Is this nothing?"

Armand was lying to himself, to Michelle, and to Brianna. It was definitely something, but it was nothing he was prepared to admit. The thought of betraying Michelle was too heavy a weight to have on his mind with all that still needed to be done. He simply could not think that way. It didn't fit his mold.

"I'm sure."

Without warning, Brianna slid down the wall. She looked like the terrified young girl he had found that night at Javan's; nothing like the strong, sensitive, cultural woman he had come to know.

"Brianna, Brianna . . ." Armand bent down, draped an arm around her waist, helping her to her feet. "Let's get you home."

This time, Brianna offered no resistance, barely walking to the car because she was so weak. Something was definitely up, and Armand promised himself that he'd get to the bottom of it.

CHAPTER 11

Since Lisa's surgery, Frank had not left her bedside. The passing hours had provided ample time for him to recollect his previous movements. The picture had not brought him any comfort except to confirm that he had not hurt his wife. His conversation with Charlie pained him like a hangnail in his mind. He sincerely regretted getting involved with her. He never would have guessed that she would deliberately hurt Lisa. That child was not of his loins, and it troubled his spirit to ponder the likelihood of having lost his wife to the grave behind that lie.

He surmised that Lisa and Brianna were the closest he had ever come to experiencing love in its purest form. Shadows reserved for cemeteries mocked his fear during the first twenty-four hours of Lisa's recovery. The thoughts tempted his mind into ominous spaces, but as her survival became evident, his despondent disposition withered away. Regret remained, a weight so indomitable that death still fancied itself as a favorable recourse.

This was day ten of a mind-numbing wait for his precious wife to gain enough strength to speak with him. Words of insight, candor, and repair tumbled needlessly about in his head as he pondered auspicious endings to their condition. The chair, doubling as his bed, reinforced the ache in his back, begging him to change the routine he had embraced with each passing day. He simply sat, recording minutes, only moving to relieve himself in the bathroom or to escape the insensitive, snide remarks of the revolving trio of nurses assigned to tend to Lisa.

He dared not utter a word of complaint, for their work, in her regard, was the best available. Lisa's surgeon and interim medical advisors had advised him as such, and she was his priority. Enduring their nuanced criticisms of his role in what had transpired was a small price to pay for the service they provided. After he owned his failings as a husband, specifically a protector, knifing the carefully-crafted ideal of masculinity he lived his life within, Frank's vulnerability surged to a stifling peak. Cradling the remnants of who he believed he was, juxtaposed with the harsh reality, exposed Frank to suffering he could not yet comprehend.

He had but one measure of solace in all of this: Lisa's recovery. Things were touch and go at first, but after a transfusion, her condition had drastically improved, and she was expected to make a full recovery.

Lisa was not suicidal, but Charlie's news must have had an adverse effect on her. Her strength was something he had come to marvel. None of this felt right; he had to be missing something, but he had no idea what it could be.

"Frank? Where am I?"

The sound of her voice slashed through his thoughts, much to his delight. He quickly moved to the edge of his seat, leaning over the hospital bed, cupping her hand in his with a gentle squeeze. With his free hand, he lovingly pushed the hair out of her face, trying not to shy away from the emptiness he saw in her eyes—a void, he realized, that he alone was responsible for.

"I'm here, baby. I'm right here."

Lisa looked weary as she tried to focus her vision, glancing around the sterile hospital room, straining her eyes under the bright fluorescent light. The bandages from her futile attempt to escape her misery slowly brought the memory of the last few days to the forefront of her mind. Lisa closed her eyes and let a tiny single river of hurt run from its corner.

"Frank?"

Frank's heart dropped so low he didn't know if he would have the guile to lift it again. It took everything he had not to fall to his knees and follow suit, knowing that he had once again failed her so fantastically was difficult to stomach. A stinging sensation spread from his chest throughout his body as he grappled with the weight of his decisions.

"Lisa, please don't. I am so sorry."

"Frank . . ." She shook her head slowly, loosening the words trapped in the air. Tears began to well up in her eyes. Frank continued to hold her hand, caressing it gently as she shared her truth, insisting she lend her pain into the small open space on his shoulders. "Fifteen years. For fifteen years, I tried to have your child. She's having the child that should have been mine."

Shaking his head to deny her claims, Frank wept freely, revealing how vulnerable witnessing Lisa's despair made him.

"Lisa, nothing happened."

Lisa stared at Frank with ruby-frosted eyes, swollen with hurt. His body rocked like he had been hit with a 12-gauge shotgun, sending him crashing to his knees, pleading for her forgiveness.

"Lisa, please."

"Stop lying, Frank! Just don't."

He rested his forehead against the metal railing of the hospital bed, relenting to her request, allowing its cold disposition to ease his growing anxiety. The tension built in his frontal lobe, loosened its grip on his mind as the hurricane wreaking havoc calmed to resemble a large ripple in a small pond. As the pain dissipated, he searched for words to ease her pain, to temper the mood in his favor.

"Lisa, please, try and stay calm. I promise I will answer whatever questions you have."

Lisa jerked her hand away from him, turning her body as best she could toward the window. The ominous sound of her weeping pierced his heart.

"I loved you," she whispered in between sobs. "How could you start a family with someone else?"

Gravity pulled his sullen body lower to the ground as his heart slammed into his rib cage over and over again, taking a little of his manhood each time. Frank dried his face with the back of his hand, stood up, and walked around the bed so that he could look into her eyes. He searched her face for understanding, some inkling that she believed him.

"Lisa, listen to me. That is not my child. I don't know why, but she's lying."

"My heart is hurting so badly, Franklin." Lisa's words were strangled by her tears as she forced them out through her stuffed nasal cavity. "I wasn't perfect, but I never thought you would repay me like this."

Frank maneuvered his head so that his wife could not avoid his stare, visually engaging her while he continued to try to convince her of the truth. "You've got it all wrong." He tried to grab her hand, but she refused to let him touch her, snatching her hand away. Frustration set into his stance as he realized his words were falling on deaf ears.

"*Lisa*, listen to me!" *Clang, clang, clang, clang*! The sound of his hand hitting the metal railing, emphasizing each word, echoed throughout the room. "Just listen! I didn't do this."

Frank's clear agitation raised Lisa's alarm bells, curling her body inward to protect herself. She cried even harder.

Frank stretched his hands in the air. "I would *never* hurt you."

Lisa relaxed enough to launch her verbal assault, every sentence riddled with the pain that kept a fresh set of tears flowing. "You slept with her! You got her pregnant, Franklin!"

"I slept with her, yes, but that child is not mine." Frank repeated himself, but Lisa shook her head in disbelief. "Lisa, I promise you. There is no possible—"

Click.

Frank's sentence was interrupted by the sound of the opening of the large, metallic door of Lisa's private room. Detective Baptiste, his face denoting the grim circumstances of the visit, stood in the doorway, flanked by two uniformed Saint-Martin police officers.

Frank immediately tensed up, fearing the worst.

"Mr. Franklin Mason, ya need to come with me now."

Frank looked to Lisa, whose eyes hinted at the questions she had yet to verbalize. He stood completely still, uncertain of what to make of the situation.

"Mr. Mason, these officers will take ya into custody, if you refuse." Detective Baptiste stared at Frank, reading his body language, willing him to come on his own volition.

Frank, focused on the ground beneath his feet, tried to settle his rapidly increasing heart rate. The sound of shoes shuffling across the ceramic floor brought his gaze upward. The officers were coming toward him. He wanted to move, but his legs weren't listening.

Keeping her eyes on the detective, Lisa rustled her hands through the sheets until she located the remote that controlled her bed. Sensing that something was definitely wrong, she fumbled with the buttons, trying to adjust her bed so that it was in the upright position. Alternating her stare between the detective and Frank, she was waiting for one of them to answer.

"What's going on? What's happening?"

Detective Baptiste spoke first. "Ma'am, we have reason to believe that ya husband tried to hurt you, now. No charges filed right away, but he needs to come with us for further questioning."

Lisa shook her head back and forth, from left to right, dismissing the notion. Lisa's nonverbal claim failed to convince Detective Baptiste of Frank's innocence. The background check had taken a few days to come back, but it revealed that Mr. Mason had been charged with aggravated assault in the States. Though it was not enough to nail him for the attack on his wife, it did show his propensity for violence. He was currently out on bond pending his trial date.

Detective Baptiste walked over to Lisa's bedside. "Ma'am, did ya husband hurt ya? Did he do this to ya, now?"

She hesitated before responding, taken off guard by the question. "No . . . he hasn't."

Detective Baptiste peered into her eyes, weighing her statement against the intuition years on the force had taught him to rely on. Taking note of the fragility of Lisa's mental state, Detective Baptiste interpreted her hesitance as fear, motioning for the officers to cuff Mr. Mason.

"I need to speak with Mrs. Mason alone, please. Take Mr. Mason to the station. Detective Saenz is waiting for you there."

Frank, unable to move, offered no resistance. His limbs remained suspended as the officers placed the metal brace-lets around his wrists and began moving him around the bed and toward the door. Focused on his wife, he seized the moment to plead for her forgiveness once more.

"Lisa, please. I'm sorry. I love you. I didn't do it."

Detective Baptiste gestured for the officers to expedite the removal. Frank continued to plead his case as the officers carted him off.

"Please believe me, Lisa, please."

Detective Baptiste stayed behind, hoping that in her husband's absence, Mrs. Mason would feel comfortable enough to tell the truth.

CHAPTER 12

Things were not progressing as Michelle had expected. The magical, budding new beginning she had hoped would eventually envelop their relationships had yet to happen. Her relationship with Brianna was at a standstill, and she was no closer to forgiving her mother than she had been six weeks ago. If anything, she found herself becoming more distrusting as time ticked away. Making matters worse, Brianna's presence in her home was widening the emotional divide between her and Armand. She felt guilty for blaming Brianna, but she couldn't think of what else it could be. On some level, she admired how tender and thoughtful he had been regarding her sister, but not at her expense.

Brianna's insipid attitude had rubbed her the wrong way, and though admittedly Brianna needed help, Michelle needed it too. The situation, unfortunately, was not alien to her. She understood that people could not see what she did not make visible, but Armand was supposed to be different. Even when she resisted their closeness, her truth had always been detectable. Her fiancé, on numerous occasions, had displayed the ability to recognize her vulnerability, but lately he hadn't noticed, focusing instead on Brianna and seeing to it that her needs were met. It was becoming too much for Michelle to bury.

Michelle stood in the doorway of Brianna's bedroom, her guest room, reflecting on their situation. As much as she adored her sister, the three of them—Armand, Brianna, and herself— would be unable to cohabitate for much longer. Normally, she would have discussed the situation with her mother, but she had not spoken with her since the *will* fiasco. Their conversation made it clear that they still had a long way to go, and it hurt. Michelle missed her mom, her best friend.

For a moment she had thought that perhaps Brianna could help fill that void, but she didn't.

Michelle felt like an orphan, not having any real family ties, and watching Armand drift away was heartbreaking. The isolation trapped her, sealing her spirit inside the pain she was learning to live with. Everything she had lost—her father, her mother . . . in some ways, she had even lost pieces of herself. With no prospect of ever getting any of them back, the reality left a supernova-sized hole in her heart.

She managed her emotions by searching for the answers to the questions still lingering in the air. The truth of her birth was known, but the pathology leading to her mother making such an awful decision was still a mystery. The best place to start was with the maternal grandparents she grew up believing were dead. Taking a break from her business, Michelle had spent her time climbing her family tree. She searched without any help from anyone, assuming any information her mother would give to her would be faulty.

Considering everything that had happened, it was surprisingly easy to trace. Using her mother's maiden name, Freemont, Michelle determined that her maternal grandparents were former Dallas Mayor Richard Freemont and his wife, Katherine. Apparently, the Freemont family name survived generations in Dallas. Sophie Lucille (Freemont)

Lewis had been quite the social butterfly in her heyday, but then had mysteriously disappeared from the scene.

Her father's past was far more difficult to unearth. His father was unknown, and an addiction to methamphetamines had claimed his mother's life when he was a teen. That was as far back as she had been able to go. It was not a complete loss, though. The information was small, but vital, giving Michelle a little insight into the man who raised her, allowing her to reach a place of healing even in his absence.

Even as she found answers, it also created more questions for her. Her father was a survivor, flourishing despite all that had been taken away from him. He was the type of guy who always found a way to push forward. Michelle had found his sudden death difficult to accept, and the information she learned made it even more so. It didn't make sense that he would not have reached out to her beforehand. Their relationship was strained, but in her heart, she always knew that he loved her. She never went without and couldn't imagine him dying or being on the brink of death without informing her of his condition. It did not make sense.

The sound of the front door closing pulled Michelle out of her thoughts. Tapping her hand on the door frame, she turned and leisurely made her way to the front of the house.

"MK?" Dropping his gym bag by the door, Armand hobbled toward the couch. "MK?"

Michelle made it into the living room just as he collapsed onto the sofa. "Were you limping just now?"

Armand grimaced as he carefully lifted his leg, elevating his swollen ankle, placing it on one of the plush pillows gracing the couch. "Yeah. I twisted my ankle on the court today."

Rushing to his side, Michelle inspected the baseball-sized knot. "I'm surprised you were able to walk at all on this."

"I couldn't." Armand laughed lightly. "Didn't you see me hopping?"

"I'll get you some ice, but I think a trip to Care Now would be better." Michelle headed toward the kitchen. "That's a pretty bad sprain. Something could be torn."

"Did I miss you getting your medical degree?"

"Ha ha, very funny. A few basketball injuries make every athlete an expert."

Armand groaned dismissively. With his right foot planted firmly on the ground, reclining on the couch, he laid his head on a pillow similar to the one his swollen left ankle rested on.

"Well, no, I'll be fine in a couple of days."

She shook her head, knowing he would decline the suggestion. Armand had a serious bias against medical facilities. Michelle quickly made her way down the short hall and into the kitchen. The three-bedroom house had belonged to them for a few weeks, and she was still adjusting to living there.

Opening the freezer to grab the blue ice pack, she yelled to Armand, "I'll give you a couple of days and then we're goiiiinnnnng!"

"I doubt that," he said, forcing a smile as he spoke. His eyes shadowed her as she made her way back into the living the room.

Pausing, Michelle eyed the room in search of something.

"What is it?"

"Where is your gym bag?"

"Why?" Armand inquired, apprehension cracking his voice.

Michelle spotted the bag under the table by the door and walked toward it.

"Wait, Michelle. What are you looking for?"

"What's the big deal? Relax." Immediately after opening the gym bag, Michelle was able to answer her own question. "What is this?"

Dropping the ice pack on the floor, she reached into the bag. Pulling out a 9 mm handgun, Michelle turned around to see the agitation shift his features.

Clearing his throat, Armand decisively regained control of the conversation. "Put that down."

Ignoring his request, Michelle leered at him, insisting that he answer. "That wasn't a question."

Michelle kept her cool, despite the cloud of uneasiness circling her waistline. Turning the heavy firearm in her hand, inspecting it, Michelle reiterated her question. "Where did you get this, Armand?"

Armand sat up on the couch, combating the powerlessness he felt, given his current physical limitation. "MK, it's for protection."

"Protection from who? Is there something you're not telling me?" Michelle's voice rose ten notches in alarm.

"What?" Issuing a tepid response, Armand tried to steer their dialogue. He lifted his arms into the air to abdicate his position. "MK, ease off the gas. There's nothing to hide over here."

"Then explain this. Two plus years and I have never seen it." Squirming from side to side, Michelle readied herself for what Armand would say. Neither of them had ventured to discuss the details of what had happened last month, particularly those surrounding the Marx Brothers disappearance or his rescue of Brianna. The miniature volcano erupting within her hinted that this news would not be favorable.

Armand toyed with the platinum band on his finger, stalling before opening the proverbial floodgates. "The manner in which I came into possession of that *particular* gun is not important."

Michelle opened her mouth to protest, but the look in Armand's steely-gray eyes silenced her. He put his hand up, requesting that he be allowed to complete his sentence without interruption.

"I have guns all over this house, easily accessible by me should I need them. I have seen enough to find it necessary, MK."

"I'm not objecting—" Michelle started to interject, but again Armand muted her with a wave of his hand.

The look on his face was unyielding. He took another look at Michelle before he spoke again. "Let this go. I know what you're thinking."

Pursing her lips, Michelle gritted her teeth, keeping her words in her mouth. She had an idea regarding the weapon's origin, and it did not sit well with her. Short of Armand admitting it, she wouldn't know definitively if her hunch was correct. Recalling a minor detail of Brianna's rendition of her captivity, Michelle knew that gun belonged to one of her captors.

"Do you know? What did you do, Armand?"

"I'm not discussing this with you."

Michelle did not back down. "Yes, you are. I want to know."

"Why, MK? Why now? You haven't asked before." Swinging his leg off the couch, Armand scooted to the edge of the couch.

"What does that matter? I'm asking now."

Leaning forward, dropping his hand between his legs, he huffed as he lifted his hands, running them through his short curls. "You've been so damn preoccupied with finding your grandparents."

"Excuse me?"

"You heard me. Never occurred to you how all of this might be affecting me. You weren't the only one going through something!"

"I cannot believe I'm hearing this." Cupping the sides of her face, she felt the cold texture of the gun reminding her of its presence. Caught up in the argument, she had completely forgotten that she was holding it. Placing it on the small table in the foyer, Michelle wondered when the discussion had switched from it to *her*.

"The things I had to do to keep you safe. To get Brianna back." Armand's frustration covered his forehead with beads of sweat. "Jesus, Michelle. What did you think I did? Think my asking politely did the trick?" The intense pain generated from his hurt ankle kept him from vacating the room. Michelle remained silent, weighing his words. "My having a gun should not surprise you."

"Not *a* gun, this one. Looks like the one John had, right down to the chipped handle, Armand!" Walking toward him, Michelle stopped in the center of the room, waiting for an explanation. "How did you get this? Tell me what you did!"

"Stop it, Michelle! Stop it, all right? Let it go. There are more important things that you should concern yourself with."

"Like what? Brianna?" Michelle didn't hide her envy.

"Not this again, MK."

"I'm not the one who needs to be reminded that we all suffered." Her cynicism seasoned her statement, camouflaging the chinks in her armor.

Armand scoffed. "And what is that supposed to mean?"

"All of your focus is on her. Every moment you have to spare is hers."

"Come on, MK! Brianna was kidnapped. *Twice!*"

Michelle shook her head, folding her arms across her chest, and tasted her tears as they descended down her cheeks. She knew what happened to her sister was horrible, but it didn't just happen to her. It happened to all of them.

"I know that, but—"

"But nothing." Armand interrupted. "You're fine. I kept you out of harm's way. Nothing happened to you. You were safe in your little bubble, playing Nancy Drew, while the rest of us were dealing with reality!"

"I lost my father! My mother! He's dead, and she may as well be. Is that the reality you're talking about? Is that real enough?"

"Give me a break. Brianna could have died, and that's on me." Armand sank back into the couch. Covering his eyes with his hand, he let his head rest against the cushion.

"She's not your responsibility. Never was." Michelle calmed down considerably as the fog girding her understanding slowly began to lift.

"She needs me. I cannot abandon her."

Michelle stood still, transfixed by the inexplicable passion behind his words. She stared at the man who had proposed to her barely two weeks ago, confused by the admission. This man, who had spoken with such a deep litany of praise for her that she thought she had dreamt him. This man, who could barely keep his eyes off her, now couldn't even bring himself to return her present gaze.

The guilt that divided his loyalties stretched beyond her understanding. Her heart ached to see him in such anguish, knowing that she was partly to blame, but that was of no consequence at this point. Something was broken between them. Restoration would not happen if Armand couldn't see the ocean filling in their divide.

"I need you, Armand. I need you, too." With that, Michelle returned to the bag, grabbing the towel she had sought earlier. She picked up the ice pack, wrapped the towel around it, and threw it at her impassive fiancé. "Here, ice your own damn ankle."

CHAPTER 13

Frank's wrists were sore from the cuffs that once adorned them. His new chair, in the humid, stank interrogation room of the Saint-Martin Police Department, enriched the twinge in his back. Nothing pained him more, however, than the look on Lisa's face as he was dragged from her hospital room. Her consternation, paralyzing his mental faculties, weighed heavily on his mind. It was all he could think about. The curves of her face, like a curtain hiding a window, prevented him from seeing anything more. He had survived several hours of questioning before earning this small break. The room was without windows, but he suspected the moon's beams were kissing the Caribbean waters by now.

Frustrated, both detectives had abruptly abandoned the previous interrogation, leaving Frank alone with his thoughts. He sat stone-faced in the chair, unwilling to give them anything that would help them to incriminate him. Frank remained immovable, leaving the detective without the answers he sought to force out of him. Lisa did this to herself, and their refusal to accept that was not his fault.

Now, Detective Baptiste and Detective Saenz re-entered the room, forcefully pulling the wooden door closed behind them. Detective Baptiste cast a suspicious eye in Frank's direction as he took the seat nearest Frank.

"May I get you anything?"

"No, I don't need anything." Frank did not want amenities. He wanted to return to his wife, for this nightmare to end.

"We need your help, Franklin." Detective Baptiste kept his eyes on Frank but caught a peripheral view of Detective Saenz, idling in a corner behind Frank, as he spoke. The detective drew his words out to undercut the heavy French accent that showed up in the pronounced *r's* and *k's*, pausing at the end of each sentence to confirm that Frank understood. "Someone hurt your wife; nearly killed her dead. I tink you know who that someone is, Franklin."

Frank stared blankly at the detective, weary at the mere thought of defending himself against his baseless accusations. He shifted in his seat as Detective Saenz suddenly rushed toward him, slamming his fists on the cheap square table, violating Frank's personal space. Frank clasped his hands together in his lap beneath the table, lightly tapping the heel of his foot, pushing the growing rage bubbling in the pit of his stomach into his feet, as far from his heart as was possible—a distance that, he hoped, would help him to manage it.

"I did not hurt my wife."

The detective's eyes traced his mannerisms, heightening his sensibility. Bracing himself for the inevitable questions, Frank summoned his inner child, pulling from the history of the young boy growing up on the East Coast, molded by his father to function as a Manchurian Candidate of sorts.

Gripping one corner of the table and the back of Frank's chair, Detective Saenz injected himself into the interrogation. The lines deepened in his lemon-shaped face as his energy soared to a new plateau. The top of his Hershey-smooth head glistened with sweat, bringing attention to the carefully edged half ring of straggly gray hair holding onto its sides.

"Stop ya lying, now! We know ya did it! Come on! No bullshit! Dis Charlie person is not a real person! Just admit it!" His accent, even more pronounced, stabbed at Frank's patience with each word. Understanding him was difficult in and of itself, but his obvious bias in regard to Frank's guilt equated the act of listening to him with Frank driving an ice pick into his inner ear.

Frank remained silent. His face, expressionless, giving no indication as to which of the detective's claims, if any, were true.

Detective Baptiste cleared his throat, cueing his partner to calm down. "Frank, I am tryin' to help you, but you have got to give me something. Unless attempted murder is okay for you?"

Frank looked at Detective Baptiste and then away again. Distress reddened his hazel eyes. Frank felt weak, exhaustion fracturing his resolve with each passing minute. "Why are you doing this? I need her. Don't you understand? I could never hurt her."

"That's good." Detective Baptiste, who had been slouching in the fold-up chair he occupied, sat up, leaning forward toward Frank. Engineering a false empathic connection. "Then, tell me exactly what happened in dat room." Detective Baptiste tried to sustain a gregarious approach.

"I told you everything I know." Frank grimaced as tension generated fresh knots throughout his body.

Detective Baptiste, deciding to niggle at Frank's apparent frustration, prodded him further. "So what, tell me again, from da start."

Frank slouched his shoulders, preparing to rebirth what laid a constant siege on his mind, the mental picture accompanying his words making him queasy. "I came out of the bathroom and found her laying on the floor, covered in . . . covered in blood. I thought she was gone. I am not sure what happened."

Detective Saenz sat on the corner of the table, leaning in toward Frank's face, nearly brushing his lips against his skin as he spoke. "I heard ya 912 recording. Talkin' 'bout some Charlie person." Saenz rattled off the information, not bothering to mask his agenda. Itsy remnants of the jerk chicken and rice consumed during his lunch, spewing out of his mouth, landed on the exposed layers of Frank's skin. "But there is no Charlie person, and there never was."

"No, Charlie is a real person." Frank looked Saenz directly in the eye.

"You did dis! No Charlie person!" Detective Saenz's words warmed his ears like a lead bullet.

Frank's cheeks reddened as his frustration mounted. He struck his fists on the table in annoyance. "Charlie is a real person but she . . . she isn't here." Frank dropped his head, trying to calm his racing heart. He was losing control of himself. That would not get him back to Lisa any sooner. It would only delay their reunion. He needed to keep it together, regardless of what they said or thought of him.

"Because she does not exist!"

"That's not true! Charlie didn't *physically* hurt Lisa, but she is responsible." Gently raising his head, he peered directly into Saenz's eyes again. Absent from them was any question regarding his guilt or innocence. Saenz was simply gunning for a confession. There would be no convincing him of his innocence. "I didn't touch Lisa. I would never, ever hurt my wife." Frank put his head face-down on the table.

"That is not what the pretty wife said to me, Franklin. She told me that you did dis to her."

Lifting his head, a bug-eyed Frank stared at Detective Baptiste in disbelief. "No, she couldn't have. She wouldn't."

"Come on, Franklin, think about it. Huh? Open your ears and listen to what I am tellin' you."

Detective Baptiste's smug and cavalier tone incensed Frank. His body started to visibly shake as the battle to control his anger ensued.

"The way I see it, she left you, Franklin. Fled your country, *the great Americas*, and come all da way here to get away from you. You followed her here, to *my* island, Saint-Martin, to make her pay for making you feel like a little man, no?"

"That's not what happened!"

"Are you sayin' you didn't follow her here?"

"I did, but it was to bring her home."

"That's right. You stalked her. A couple of days pass by, tension become too much, can't take simply watchin' her no more. So, you sneak into her room and wait."

Frank frantically shook his head from side to side, rejecting Baptiste's story.

"Surprised her in da loo, chased her into da kitchen area. She fought you. Didn't want to go nowhere wit' you. Grabbed a knife to defend herself, but you were too strong. Big man you are, Franklin. Beatin' a little fragile woman."

"You're wrong!"

"She rejected you, and it made you really angry. So angry that you stabbed her with tha knife! Isn't that correct, Franklin?"

"I love her! I would never do what you're accusing me of!"

Detective Saenz jumped in. "Ya record says otherwise. Currently out on bond for aggravated assault."

Frank shook his head, mentally trying to mitigate the effect of the evidence incriminating him. "That has nothing to do with this."

"It has everyt'ing to do with this, Franklin." Detective Saenz hinted at the cards he intended to play. "That tells me that you are a very dangerous, very violent individual. The type of man that nearly beat another man to death."

Frank slammed his hands on the table in frustration. "I did not hurt Lisa!"

Accepting that Frank was not going to change his story, Detective Baptiste decided to conclude their interrogation. "Well, Franklin, I hope for your sake that's true. Trust me, I will find out if you're tellin' me more lies."

Frank was about to stand to leave, but Detective Baptiste held a finger up, stopping him cold. Finding comfort in the fact that although he could not charge him, he did not have to release him, Baptiste stood and began walking toward the door. "Until we confirm whether or not you are in violation of your bond in the States, you will remain here in *my* custody."

"I'm not in violation. I haven't done anything wrong."

"We will see about that, Franklin."

"But I need to see my wife." Frank desperately wanted to get back to Lisa. "You can't hold me without charging me."

Turning his face in Frank's direction, Detective Baptiste did not hide his disgust. "This is my island. I don't care 'bout your money here, or about what it is you want. Only the lady in the hospital now because of you. If it's up to me, Franklin, if and when you leave here, next stop will be Princess Juliana Airport."

Detective Baptiste opened the door and motioned for officers to lead Frank to a holding cell. "But if you want to confess, maybe I could make some'ting happen for you, you know?"

The officers brought Frank to his feet, placing the cuffs on him again, and ushered him out of the room and into a cell. Frank felt empty inside. Things had gone so terribly wrong. Uncertain of where he stood with Lisa, the little fight he had seeped out of him. The money wasn't even important to him anymore. More than anything in the world, he wanted to put his family together again. Time would reveal if he got the chance.

CHAPTER 14

Rachel was running late, and Micah felt his patience waning. This girl was forever behind schedule. If it were left to her, she would be late to her own funeral. Hovering near the door to the front of one of the buildings of North Park Center, a ritzy Dallas mall, Micah groaned in irritation. Nothing pained him more than an inconsiderate woman. Rachel definitely took the cake. Three phone calls and three voicemails equaled three missed opportunities for Rachel to catch a hint. Saturday morning was still fresh on his mind, and he did not want to see her. He wanted to be alone with his thoughts, but she would not take no for an answer, begging him to come pick her up. He had reluctantly agreed to do it at the risk of losing his sanity. This conversation needed to happen. He reasoned his brief suffering would serve the greater good, freeing him from her entirely.

Closing his eyes in acceptance, he reclined his seat and thought back to the motivation behind all of this, the sole reason he had allowed Rachel into his reality. The West End was a far cry from the premier nightlife attraction it was once in its heyday. Reduced to a glorified bus stop and a few run-down food chains, it could no longer boast of its grandeur. Still, the West End station saw plenty of foot traffic. Micah had chosen to ride the train with plans to make the short walk from Main Street and Lamar to

Dealy Plaza. His stint as an architect with Good, Fulton, & Farrell, specifically the 508 Project, had kindled a quiescent fancy for the places of note Dallas offered. The famed patch of grass landed the top spot on his list. Micah, along with a healthy number of tourists, spent hours taking in the remnants of that day, November 22, 1963, a day that changed America. He was completely immersed in his thoughts, preparing to board the train at the conclusion of his trip, when she re-entered his stratosphere.

He thought he was imagining her, as he had on several occasions, but when the shadowy likeness moved, his world came to grinding halt. Butterflies swarmed in his belly, lifting his feet off the ground, granting him access to the moon. His body froze on the platform as he immersed his entire being in their momentary connection. He could scarcely believe his luck and ultimately credited their reunion to fate. Though he did not reclaim her verbally that day, the emotional flood gates were opened once more.

Seeing her at the station, even briefly, had proven to be enough to jar him free of the nightmare he could not stop reliving: the night he lost her. His life had not been the same since that night. He was in mourning and could not be sated by anything or anyone else. Despite the strength of his longing, their last interaction had not ended well, and he did not know how to approach her.

He returned to the West End every day and waited for her to reappear, hopeful that the words would come to him if the opportunity ever presented itself. And she did return, every week. He watched her movements, careful to stay off her radar. It did not take long before he figured out what brought her downtown: therapy. Micah thought he blended in with the L7's frequenting the area, but Rachel noticed him lurking outside the office building and flirtatiously questioned his being there.

His truth slid from his lips effortlessly. He told her about the love he lost, that the building was the last place he had seen her. He confessed that he came back daily, hoping to lay his eyes on her once more. Rachel offered to mend his broken heart, to be the bridge he needed to move on into the next chapter of his life. He accepted her kind gesture, craving a woman's touch. And so began their brittle romance.

Rachel swung open the door, tossing the evidence of her mini shopping spree into the backseat, and plopped down in the passenger seat.

"Thanks for coming, Micah. I wasn't sure you would."

Micah raised his seat upright, staring at her from behind his shades. "Not that you left me much of a choice."

"What do you mean?"

Micah rolled his eyes, discontented with the direction of their chitchat. "You tried to threaten me."

"Whoa! Taking a few liberties?" Rachel laughed lightly. "I believe my government teacher once referred to it as an incentive."

"I doubt that is what he or she had in mind, Rachel."

"Whatever." Flashing a coy smile, Rachel reclined in her seat. "Let's go. I'm starved."

"Are you serious?" Micah had no intention of spending the evening with her.

"Naturally," Rachel quipped, playfully removing the shades from his eyes, prodding his temperament. "We need to talk about what happened the other morning."

Micah knew she would want to discuss the abrupt end to their tango, but he was not in the mood. He didn't feel the need to fix whatever she felt was broken. His mind was on the woman who inhabited the sacred space in his heart. "That's not happening today or ever."

"Why did you come then?"

Micah massaged his temples, considering how best to answer her question, especially since he thought the answer was obvious given the start to this little banter between them. Even if he were willing to mend things, Rachel's confession ushered in a permanent severance.

"Either give me an address or take your bags and catch the bus to wherever you need to go."

"Renaissance Hotel, Room 1123. Not sure what the address is, but . . . I am pretty sure you know how to get there."

Micah shifted into drive, rolling out onto the street, and headed toward the highway. Their presumed destination, his hotel, was a good thirty minutes away, providing him plenty of time to make things clear to Rachel.

"Say what you need to say, Rachel."

"I plan to. Don't worry about that."

"Talk. Now." Micah's voice was stern, like a father coaxing the truth from his child.

"I don't want to talk here." Rachel focused her gaze through the limo-tinted passenger window and out onto the street. "I want your undivided attention."

"This little thing between us is over, Rachel."

Rachel released a long, telling sigh, drawing Micah's attention to her face, then her hand, as she drew a trail from her cherry-red full lips to her egg-size breasts. "But I love you. You can't quit me."

Micah, unfazed by Rachel's clumsy attempt at seduction, reiterated his point. "I don't have time to play this game with you."

Rachel quickly pulled the small lever on the side of her seat, popping up while turning her body toward Micah, quickly deadening her momentary show. "Game? You put my heart through a blender and accuse me of playing games?"

"That sounds like a personal issue. Furthermore, this isn't about me. This is about you."

Rachel's intransigent attitude made reason an improbability. "All of this is about you. Play nice, and I might allow you to keep your freedom."

Micah remained calm, trying to keep his anger under control. "Rachel, you lied to me."

Rachel leaned her head against the dashboard, sighing in frustration as the realization hit her. "Is that the only reason you came?"

"What were you expecting, Rachel?"

"Are you serious? For three weeks, my age never came up. Clearly it didn't matter then, so it shouldn't matter now."

Micah's hands tightened around the steering wheel. "I don't have time for this. Picking you up was a mistake, but I thought I could talk some sense into you."

"Micah, don't do this. I have done everything you asked."

Micah shook his head, tapping his foot impatiently against the floorboard. "Rachel, I am not going to prison behind you or anyone else! Do you understand me?"

"Then I guess we're going to your hotel room?"

Micah tuned into the clicking sound of his turn signal, monitoring the cars to his left and across the light, cautiously making a right turn onto the service road. "I gave you too much credit."

"Excuse me?" Rachel was dogmatic in her retort, feigning a rather passable innocence. "Credit is what I need from you."

Grinding his teeth, Micah swallowed the unsavory bile gathering at the base of his throat, repulsed at the mulish impulse he felt to "take care" of Rachel. It was an impulse he was hard-pressed to deny.

"Micah, all I want is you and a few dollars."

Gunning the engine, he took the nearest entrance, merging onto I-75 South. Micah did not respond immediately. He squeezed his eyes tight. Every muscle in his body contracted as his anger started to best him. He rocked back and forth in the seat, huffing, forcing the air from his lungs.

"Rachel, you and I never happened."

Reaching down between her legs, Rachel rummaged through the contents of her Chanel bag and retrieved her cell phone. Scrolling through her texts messages, she rehashed a few for Micah's pleasure.

"Let's see . . . I HD A GR8T TIME LST NGHT. LET'S DO IT AGN, 2NGHT. CANNOT WAIT 2 C U. -MICAH. Or this one . . . WHERE DID U LRN HW 2 DO WHT U DO? I CNT GET ENGH. XO -MICAH."

Micah pounded the steering wheel, dismissing the relevance of what she read aloud to him. "That proves nothing."

"Wait for it. My favorite is somewhere in here." Rachel continued scrolling. "Ah, here it is. RACHEL, BABY BRNG THT YNG SEXY ASS 2 ME. IT'S BN 2 DAYS, TOO LONG. DINNER, JASPER'S IN PLANO @ 7 PM. BE OUTSIDE @ 6. SEE YA SOON. That was an awesome night, Micah."

"I am not whoever you think I am." Micah stretched his legs, pressing his foot forward on the gas pedal, increasing his speed on the four-lane freeway. "I am not that guy." Brusquely exiting the freeway, he made a U-turn and got back on the highway heading in the opposite direction.

He had a new destination in mind, his abandoned home in Allen.

Rachel swallowed hard, hinting at the uneasiness swirling within her. She sensed a change in Micah but continued, unsure of what to make of it. "I kept everything, Micah. Every message you ever sent, every gift, and any pictures we took. There's no denying us."

Micah pressed harder on the accelerator of his Mercedes, whipping past the few cars in his line of sight. He jumped into the far-left lane, nearly clipping a light-pink Lincoln Town Car in the process.

"Give me that phone."

"Micah! Slow down. What is your problem?"

"Give me the damn phone, Rachel!" Micah weaved in between the cars, darting his gaze from the road to Rachel and back. "Now!"

"No way." Rachel shot Micah an incredulous look, unwilling to give him her only leverage. Her body shook with fear as Micah's erratic driving sent her nervous system into overdrive. "Stop this!"

"Give it to me!" Micah felt his blood curdling in his veins. His breathing intensified as his temper consumed him. Rachel seemed intent on ruining his life, and he was not going to stand by idly. "I'm not playing!"

Rachel stared wide-eyed at Micah, fear muting the monologue vying for stage time. Securing the phone in her purse, Rachel placed it back on the floor between her legs. Confident in her position of power, she issued another denial. "That's not going to happen. Where are we going, anyway?"

Micah was livid. Cars honked their horns as he zipped around them, his pace mimicking the brisk beat of his chary heart. Jail was not an option. It would eradicate any chance for a reunion with the woman he loved. Rachel's obstinate stance clarified, if there was ever a question, her original intention. Easing off the gas, he let the truth permeate his mind. He had been duped. Their brief romance was a ploy to get Micah to fund her lifestyle.

Micah's indignation climbed to new heights as the truth squeezed his intestines, causing him to double over onto the steering wheel in pain. "You little bitch!"

"That's not necessary. Play nice, and everyone wins, Micah."

He slammed his foot on the gas. The Mercedes quickly surpassed its previous speed of seventy-five miles per hour, easily hitting ninety. Rachel, without the safety of her seatbelt, fell forward onto the dashboard with the sudden jolt. Repositioning herself, she rolled her eyes, annoyed with Micah's Grand Theft Auto antics. *He* was not her first wolf; in fact, he was number five in line, and experience had taught her that despite how much they huffed and puffed, if she simply stayed the course, he would come around. He wasn't special.

Laughing hysterically, Micah shook his head in frustration. "I am not asking you again." His voice was low, but it did not mask the rage cinching the soft layers of his epidermis as it blazed a familiar pattern across his psyche. His nerves were unsettled and surging out of control while probable solutions teemed his mind. Gripping the leather circle with one hand, he unsuccessfully reached toward the floorboard between Rachel's legs for her purse. The action sent the vehicle swerving into the lane beside them, causing the car occupying the space to slam its brakes.

"Jeez! Micah, are you trying to kill us?"

Glaring at her while traveling at a speed well in excess of ninety miles per hour, Micah failed to notice a disabled vehicle in their lane until they were seconds away from hitting it. He frantically swerved left, attempting to avoid the inevitable. The car flipped several times, taking Micah's courage hostage. The Benz crumpled like an aluminum can before coming to a stop bottom-side up in the middle of the highway.

His body felt like it had been split in two. His heart pumped furiously behind his broken ribs as images of a revolving landscape powered through his mind. The faint smell of leaking gasoline intensified an already backbreaking migraine. He strained to clear his vision as little sparks of light bounced before his eyes. Disoriented and unable to move, he shifted his thoughts to Rachel, whose screams, which were prevalent before, were notably absent.

Rachel . . . He attempted to call out to her, finding that he was unable to speak. As shock pulled him out of his conscious state, contrasting the urge to sleep, heat emitting from a fresh flame ignited his senses. The cry for help echoed within him, reverberating off the walls of his mind. Rendered silent by the injury resulting from the crash, he felt terror that mocked his mortality.

A Good Samaritan fearlessly pulled Micah from the wreckage, dragging him several feet away to safety. Micah was not awake to see the car engulfed by flames, the horror painted across the faces of the first responders that arrived on scene to assist, nor the drivers, whose commute was interrupted by this moment in his life.

Micah was care-flighted to the nearest hospital, Presbyterian Hospital of Allen. Rachel did not survive, her life extinguished by the fire that nearly claimed his.

CHAPTER 15

The last counseling session had prompted Dr. WonderBra to schedule another session for Brianna later that same week. Brianna was not at all excited about it, but for the first time, she did not mind talking about it. She was curious herself.

"So, Brianna, are you ready to begin?"

"As ready as I ever will be."

"Great. Previously we were able to discuss, for a moment, the prospect of love, or perhaps more specifically, your being in love."

"I remember."

"Good. I would like to delve into that. I think that it is an important development and deserves more than the ten minutes we gave to it earlier."

Brianna noticed that Dr. WonderBra seemed a bit more lively than usual. She was still rocking the bun, though.

"What about it?"

"You stated, 'I think I'm in love.' Expound on the why, please?" Clicking her ball point pen open, Dr. Shepherd prepared to jot down whatever Brianna had to say.

"There's not much to say, really."

"I think there is," Dr. Shepherd countered. "*Indifferent to life* is how you have previously described your emotional state. To move from *in*different to *in* love is a significant change."

Brianna understood what she was saying, even if she felt she was making a big deal out of nothing. "It might not even be that."

"Even if it isn't love that you're experiencing, the fact that you chose that word out of all the adjectives available to you is telling."

"It's a word, four letters. The meaning is subject to interpretation. People do all sorts of things in things in the name of love. Horrible, ghastly things." Brianna's voice trailed off a bit as her thoughts shifted to her father, Frank. Her mother. Love hurt. "My use is only relevant when coupled with my own definition. And I can't give it to you."

Dr. Shepherd's surprise at Brianna's remarks showed in the raised arch of her brow. "True enough. All of what you stated rings true for a lot of people. If you feel that way about love, why the admission?"

Brianna thought for a moment. "I am fluent in French, Spanish, and Japanese. My marketing degree from Pepperdine, the launch of my business and its early success, the lifelong friendships I have with my line sisters, or anything else that I have managed to accomplish means nothing. I literally don't feel anything about it. Things that were once a source of pride no longer mean anything at all. Something has emptied them of their power. My life is gone."

"Brianna, you never cease to be who you are, regardless of how things may change around you. Your resume is incredible, but as impressive as the bullet points are, that's not what truly persuades people to connect, professionally. It is the idea that you had it in you to do those things. People appreciate the tenacity, ambition, the determination, and discipline that it must have taken to do it. Whatever it is that aided you in doing all that you have, will also help you to get through this."

"No, it won't." Brianna sighed deeply, second guessing her decision to speak a tad bit.

"It can and it will. Together, we will find it and learn how to utilize that strength again."

"Not unless you can travel back in time."

"What do you mean, Brianna?"

Her eyes filled to the brim with tears as the moment drowned her. Her mojo, the thing that she had always relied on, had morphed into something unrecognizable, some shape she found too difficult and too painful to embrace. Her eyes could name it, but her heart could not. Rather than wiping the tears away, she let them roll politely down her cheeks.

"I always wanted to make him proud. Never wanted to be categorized as your typical spoiled, rich kid. I worked hard to prove that I was worth more than the money I never went without. To prove that my life was valuable."

"Brianna, are you referring to your father?" She observed as Brianna nodded in confirmation. "What produced that feeling? Did something happen to facilitate this belief that you needed to prove yourself?"

"Nothing specific. My mother, Lisa, was gone much of the time. The only thing she never went without was her American Express Black Card. My dad and I . . . she left us. Didn't need us, not like we needed her. Like I needed her." Brianna dug her fingers into the folds of the couch, steadying her thoughts while she shared her most private feelings with the doctor. "My dad was great. He gave me everything I wanted, but I felt the distance between us. I could tell, even as a young girl, that he was holding back. It was his eyes, you know?"

She gestured toward her eyes to illustrate her point. "There was a longing in his eyes. He was never fully happy.

I blamed my mother; thought she was breaking his heart. Anyway, I never really felt like I could compete."

"Compete with who?"

"Their money. Their finances received more attention than I ever did. Do you know that Lisa gave my dad a weekly bank statement for his review? Every single penny was accounted for. Some nights I would lie in my daybed, pillow covering my face, to muffle their fighting. My dad would blow up over fifty dollars." Relaxing her body, Brianna sank back unto the couch. "Unbelievable. He never addressed her absence, only the money."

"Knowing what you do now about the nature of your adoption, do you still feel it was money that drew a divide, or could it have been something else?"

"It *could* have been any number of things. The *why* does not matter at all to me."

"Sometimes knowing the cause aids in the healing process."

"That may be true, but I don't care. Trust me, I have spun my wheels around this track, and I cannot create a scenario that would make any of this okay. Not one."

Dr. Shepherd nodded her understanding. "Still, some part of you must be curious."

Brianna had considered what Dr. Shepherd was suggesting, and the premise was agreeable. That kind of secret could certainly have been the fault line in their relationship, not only the union between her father and herself, but between them all. The fault line that inevitably shifted, bringing the crack to the surface.

"You don't understand."

"Help me, Brianna."

"The woman I had become was built on untruths. How can I possibly continue to be her? She is not real. There is no explanation that would change that. I have not changed that much since Monday."

"Perhaps you are not the same person you were before you learned about your sister, your mother, before you were kidnapped, but none of us are. We are Silly Putty or Play-Doh in life's hands, and each event in our lives, good or bad, leaves an impression, changing us to some degree. Some alterations are more obvious and feel more pronounced than others, but it's all still part of the same continuous change."

Brianna stared out the window behind the doctor, allowing the emotion to depart from her eyes as she tossed the doctor's words around in her head. It was a rational pathology that she could not deny.

"That makes sense, but I—" Battling the urge to retreat into silence, Brianna squeezed her eyes shut. The throbbing beat of her heart, moving from her chest into her pharynx, threatened to mute her at any moment. "I close my eyes at night, and I'm back on the beach. I'm locked in that room. Terrified, alone, and powerless."

The tiny hairs covering her arms rose, reacting to the slow shot of adrenaline flowing through her body as she revisited the scene of her crime. The beautiful Cancun sunset drifted in and out of the background like a hammock in motion, confusing her emotional palette as the serenity of the picture-perfect landscape gave way to what became her nightmare. It was the calm before the storm. That peaceful, surreal second in time, interrupted by their plans.

"Brianna, you are not alone or powerless. You never were."

"That's funny, because I was held for several days, and I don't remember consenting."

"Michelle was looking for you. Her fiancé was searching."

"I know. I knew it then, too."

"That knowledge had to have helped you in some way. Empowered you, even?"

Brianna puffed out her lips, placing her finger to her temple, expelling the small balloon of air from her lungs. "That's true, it did help. I knew she would find me. I held on long after I felt the urge to give up because of it."

"That brings me back to my original question. Why did you say you were in love?"

Brianna met Dr. Shepherd's gaze, suddenly unable to share her innermost misgivings.

Stripped of a pathway into her own psyche, her mind closed and would not allow her to tape the words together that would explain how his presence made her feel secure like a child in the mother's womb; how sleep evaded her each night until her eyes connected with his. She lacked the power to force them out. Their bond, forged in the face of death, could not be ignored. She could not escape him if she wanted to.

Brianna scrunched her eyes closed as her cheeks suddenly billowed with air. She quickly gulped, sending the acidic fluid back down her throat, attempting to convince her mind that the queasiness percolating in the base of her tummy was nothing more than a figment of its imagination. It was a futile attempt, as Brianna sprinted out of the office, into the bathroom, where she found herself on her knees, reliving her last meal in reverse. It was a scene becoming all too familiar to her.

She walked to the sink, waved her hand in front of the spout to turn on the water. Taking a second to collect herself, she gathered a pool of water in her hands and filled her mouth. Swishing the cool water around, she gargled in an effort to rid it of the bitter residue left behind. Satisfied with her effort, she splashed her face and grabbed a soft paper towel from the wicker basket on the granite countertop. As she dried her face, she studied her reflection in the large mirror, debating whether she wanted to return to her session, which would mean a return to the conversation.

She knew Dr. Shepherd had fifty shades of the same question locked and loaded, probably aimed at her, itching to pull the trigger. Brianna did not mind anymore, honestly. She simply did not have a lot of answers for the good doctor—only questions.

Knock. Knock. Knock.

"Brianna, are you okay?" Dr. Shepherd's voiced eased into the space. She must have come looking for her.

"I am fine. I'll be out in a minute." Brianna could still leave as long as Dr. WonderBra wasn't blocking the sole exit. The private, chic, upscale bathroom provided a small haven for Brianna, if only for a little while. With her stomach knotting up at the prospect of deciding to finish the session, she took a deep breath and opened the door.

Stepping out of the bathroom, Brianna spotted Dr. Shepherd sitting comfortably on the edge of Rachel's desk, presumably waiting for her. Dr. Shepherd's lighthearted demeanor soothed the restless chill crawling up Brianna's spine.

"I thought you might make a run for it."

"Thought about it." Brianna offered a light chuckle as she made her way past the good doctor and into the office, but an eerie feeling swept over her as she passed by the doctor. Something didn't feel quite right. Pausing in the doorway, she gave the reception area a quick once over.

"What is it, Brianna?"

Brianna looked at Dr. Shepherd, ignoring the puzzled expression on her face, realizing that the issue wasn't anything that was there. It was what was missing. Rachel was not there. Brianna had not noticed before. Not her problem really, but she had a strange feeling about her absence.

Brianna resumed her seat on the couch. She waited for Dr. Shepherd to take hers. "I guess I just hadn't realized that your receptionist isn't here today."

"Oh, yes, my niece, Rachel. She didn't come in today. It hadn't dawned on me that you were so accustomed to seeing her."

Brianna laughed uncomfortably. "Surprised me as well."

Dr. Shepherd gracefully walked to her seat across from Brianna. Sitting down in the Italian leather office chair, Dr. Shepherd prepared to dive back into the session. "Are you able to continue, Brianna? If this is too much, we can resume at our regular time next week. Though we concentrate on your emotional and mental health, your overall health is of concern to me."

Brianna shook her head adamantly, admonishing the doctor's supposition. "It didn't make me sick. I have had a stomach bug for a little while now. Off and on. I'm fine."

"A stomach bug? For how long?"

Brianna closed her eyes, trying to pinpoint the first episode. "I don't know. A couple weeks or so. It's nothing, really."

"That is a long time for a virus, Brianna. I think you should see a doctor."

"If I agree to see Dr. Baxter, will you drop it?"

Dr. Shepherd's eyes glazed over at the mention of her unrequited love. Brianna knew Dr. Shepherd had a thing for him. Her swooning made it hard to miss.

"I would." Dr. Shepherd shot Briana a warm, inviting smile.

"Consider it done." Brianna forced her lips to curve upward, reassuring the doctor that she would make the appointment.

"Great. So, shall we continue?"

Pulling her legs up on the couch, stretching out a long its length, Brianna gave her consent.

"Are you in love?"

Brianna took a deep breath, allowing several minutes to pass before responding. "I don't know. I have never been in love."

"What are you attributing love to at this time? There must have been something that warranted the label."

Tears again welled up in her eyes. "I never wanted this."

"This?"

"*This*, to feel like *this*. I was so careful about who I let into my life, in my circle. It didn't matter. Seems like all of that caution was for nothing."

"We often put up walls, intending to decrease the probability of our being hurt by situations beyond our control. We fail to realize that in doing so, we make ourselves susceptible to the very same pain we're trying to avoid. The act itself, feeling pain, is inevitable. It is best to learn mechanisms to cope with it as it comes."

Brianna shook her head in agreement, wiping the tiny puddles covering her eyes. "Well, I cannot ignore anything anymore. The pressure is suffocating me. I move without thinking." Twirling her fingers in the seams of her T-shirt, Brianna continued talking. "I shouldn't, but I miss him. I miss him all the time."

"Who do you miss?"

Muted by the ignominy lingering beneath the interminable surface of fear that flowered her every decision, her lips quivered, her stubbornness denying Shepherd an answer. "I'm too ashamed to say."

"Brianna, this is a safe place. Feel free to speak freely."

Switching her body into an upright position, Brianna inhaled deeply and prepared to welcome the doctor further into her universe.

CHAPTER 16

Scenes spanning the last few days hiked the trails of Frank's mountainous mental terrain. Some disappeared into the caves of memory, never to be seen again. His every thought, like planets around the sun, revolved around his wife. His heart sank deeper into his chest cavity, constricting as it moved. The detective's words hammered at his brittle resolve, dousing his worries with the kind of accelerant destined to kill him.

That is not what the pretty wife said to me, Franklin. She told me that you did dis to her.

The pace quickened as the fleeting tang decorating his rib cage became constant, increasing in severity. Surely Lisa defended his innocence; she wouldn't implicate him. He was not to blame for the physical harm she had done to herself. Her cries echoed in his ears, forcing him to sit upright on the thin cot of his cell. The small metal underwire groaned, shifting to accommodate the change in weight to a concentrated area.

I wasn't perfect, but I never thought you would repay me like this.

Frank, never the vindictive kind, would not seek retribution in that way, especially not from Lisa . . . but would she?

Falling to his knees, he grabbed his chest as the pain steadily increased, the air around him seemed to disappear.

This was not happening again. Glancing a wary eye through the bars of his cell, he searched for a guard to signal but found the narrow hall empty. Recalling a few of his techniques from talk therapy, he attempted to side-swipe his symptoms by replacing his thoughts with less stressful ones. Still gasping for air, Frank sat on his haunches. Lisa would not falsely accuse him. Their marriage, though strained, still meant something to her.

Closing his eyes to the room swirling around him, he fought to clarify his thoughts. Her tear-stained face broke into the frame. Reaching a shaky hand out to wipe her tears, his body seized with tears of his own. Frank's forehead met the cement floor as he doubled over. *I'm so sorry.* Coughing, his body seized, and his eyes popped open like newly formed bubbles. Holding his left hand out in front him, he stretched his fingers, trying to circumvent the numbness encompassing them. Counting backward slowly from twenty, Frank attempted to settle his nerves, to focus his mind enough to regain control of his bodily functions. *Sixteen . . . fifteen . . . fourteen . . .* The tactic proved ineffective as he found himself coughing incessantly, smothering in panic. Realizing he was losing the battle of wills to the reality of his predicament, over and over again, he reassured himself that he was not dying.

Recalling the events of his last episode, Frank thought it best to get help. "Someone please . . ." Crawling toward the narrow, rusted metal poles, he continued to try to get the attention of a guard, but the coughing made it difficult to speak. As his world emptied itself of its color, Frank knew he was losing consciousness. He frantically banged on the bars with his hand, rallying a feeble attempt to draw attention. His energy rapidly depleted, forcing Frank to cease his efforts, lacking the strength to do any more.

As he lay on the floor, completely still, he could not stop his mind from posing the question he had sought to avoid. Would this be the last one? The attack that would kill him? From his angle on the floor, his fingers wrapped around a single bar, the bright peach stucco wall filling his vision—no decorative wall hangings, no windows to the outside, just the wall. Surely fate would not be so cruel as to let that blasted wall be the last thing he saw, not when he so desperately longed to be near his wife.

The morning after his last meeting with the detectives, he had gotten a call from a lawyer. A lawyer whom Frank had not retained. There was insufficient time for Frank to question his origin, and in truth, he did not care. He was grateful for his assistance, especially given the news the lawyer had to share with him. The conversation, however brief, left Frank with a glimmer of promise.

Frank returned to his cell with a smile on his face. There was a chance that his charge would be reduced. Since the threat of prison time no longer loomed in the horizon, he was left with this situation with Lisa. Her implication would certainly complicate things for him back in the States. She was angry, hurt, and rightfully so. He really couldn't blame her if she had lied, but he was almost certain that was not the case. He assumed that Baptiste had issued the insinuation to intentionally upset him. He had caught enough episodes of *SVU* to recognize their tricks. Still, the thought apparently bothered him enough to trigger an attack. It was an attack, unlike the few prior, he could not suppress with his treatment techniques. Now, he lay helpless, praying that a guard would come before he blacked out completely, worried about what it meant for him if they did not.

***

As he flailed his big, burly arms about like helicopter propellers, Detective Saenz's elevated-aged, nicotine-rich tenor sailed throughout the open floor plan of the precinct. Even through the tempered glass of the office, his disdain for their fearless leader's marching orders was evident. Detective Baptiste viewed his mentor's theatrics from his desk. Clearly, the captain had delivered the *good news* to him. Lisa, their star witness in their case against Frank Mason, had completely recanted her story. That *minor* snag, coupled with a phone call from some hot-shot attorney out of New York, crippled their investigation. Frank Mason would be free to go soon. Not unlike his partner, Detective Baptiste was less than enthusiastic about it.

"I cannot believe dis foolishness!" Detective Saenz plopped down in his seat, sliding underneath his part of the adjoining desk he and Baptiste shared. "That bastard is just goin' to walk like da others!"

Detective Baptiste played with the cap on his pen. "We do not have any evidence, Saenz."

"What are ya talkin' 'bout? He was da only one in the room. He story keep a-changin'." Rustling the papers on his desk, Baptiste busied himself in an attempt to avoid the speech he feared would follow. "Don't let ya self be fooled. I see many men like Frank Mason. Rich tourists, tink he can come here, do whatever he want, then leave. Too many have gotten away."

Scooting his chair back away from the desk, Baptiste stood. "Maybe. I need some air."

"Go on, den, but I am right. Never told ya not'ing wrong."

"That is true." Baptiste hustled toward the door of the precinct but decided to look in on Frank. He needed to see his eyes once more. Something did not sit well with him about the entire situation. Frank had seemed genuinely distraught at the crime scene and consistent with the story for the most part. It so happened that the inconsistency, the possibility of another perpetrator, was a huge discrepancy. The evidence was inconclusive at best. The prints on the knife were not discernable. There was nothing to suggest that anyone other than Frank was in the room at the time the altercation occurred. A maid confessed to letting a man in, earlier in the day, but could offer no physical description. Charlie, whom Frank initially accused, was a woman and could not have been the man the maid let into the room. Frank insisted that he only entered the room after Lisa's invitation. Something was missing. Maybe if he spoke to Frank alone, without Saenz, he could get some answers.

Turning down the tight corridor, Baptiste spotted something protruding from the cell where Frank was being held. Squinting his eyes to see, still about seven cells away, he quickened his pace. As he drew closer, he could see that it was not an object but Frank's finger. *That's strange.*

Sprinting back down the narrow hall lined with empty cells, Baptiste screamed from the entrance for help. "Get an ambulance! Get some help, quickly!"

Dashing back to Frank, with an officer in tow, he continued shouting instructions. "Open it up. Unlock this cell! Hurry! Mr. Mason? Franklin!"

The officer, fumbling with the carousel of keys in his hand, unlocked the cell as fast as he could. Shoving the officer to the side once he unlocked it, Baptiste fell to the ground, knees first, at Frank's side. He first laid an ear on Frank's mouth but couldn't tell if he was breathing. Placing two fingers in the shadows under his chin, he checked for a pulse. It was faint, but it was there nonetheless.

Baptiste sighed with relief, grateful he wasn't dead. "Where is that ambulance?"

He looked around the small cell. There was nothing out of place, nothing that Frank could have used to harm himself. At a loss with what to do next, Baptiste, a deeply spiritual man, prayed for his healing. He sat there on the floor beside him, holding his hand until the ambulance arrived to take him to the Hôpital Louis-Constant Fleming.

CHAPTER 17

He couldn't believe it was happening again. He had tried to put it out of his mind, to live like he didn't want it, didn't long for it with every fiber of his being. But the truth hurt—it hurt more than her teeth slightly scraping the soft skin of his shaft. Even more than the slight pinch of her nails digging into his side, reminding him that it should stop. It was a sign that this moment was not truly his. This beautiful woman did not belong to him, but perhaps more importantly, he belonged to another.

His eyes wandered down to the force of nature wreaking havoc on his love jones and watched in awe as her head moved with a rhythm that made his knees weak. *This,* in fact, was something *she* would never do, and on some level, that may be partly to blame for his being there. Still, he knew *she* deserved better.

He had tried to forget the first time he locked lips with *this* woman; the cotton candy–flavored lip gloss he didn't know he'd miss. It began innocently enough, just one moment too many alone together. They shared just one laugh too many—and then it happened, the physical connection that added weight to the fire already smoldering between them. He had tried to forget, but not today. Today, he could not dismiss the wave of pleasure consuming his body as he felt his manhood leave its essence in various places of her mouth. No, not today.

Today, he would not resist her. Taking a handful of her soft, black hair, he drove his piece deeper into that space. He leaned against the desk and steadied himself with his free hand. Matching her beat, he moved with her, racing toward his inevitable finish. He pumped in and out of her mouth, closed his eyes and focused on the feeling. The warmth quickly spread throughout his lower region. He tried to keep his eyes closed. He did not want to see.

He could feel her eyes on him, and just this once, he wanted to leave the memory without blemish. But he couldn't resist. He had to look, to put a face with the feeling. Again, his eyes wandered down to the woman on her knees in front of him, but this time her beautiful brown eyes met his, splintering his heart into a million pieces. Surely someone was playing a cruel joke on him. It was simply not fair. He loved his woman with everything he had and some things he did not.

This woman caught him off guard, and he didn't know she would pull him in like this. Didn't know he would be so vulnerable to her advances. His eyes rolled, and his mouth opened to protest, but his moans were the only audible sounds. Maybe if he could force himself to remember her name and ignore her face, the common trait that she and his wife shared, then he could let go once and for all. Maybe he would finally have the strength to deny his primal urges.

She moved faster, and he knew the end was near. She stopped abruptly and, as if on cue, he pulled her up and bent her over the small table stand that had been supporting his weight and crashed his rocket into her deep space.

"*Shit,*" he whimpered. Flooded with guilt and absolute pleasure, he continued his climb into the atmosphere.

"Armand?" Michelle stood in the hall at the back of the living room, roughly twenty feet from him. Frozen in shock, muted with questions, her legs quit on her.

Startled, Armand pulled out of *her*, his rock-hard wand, now aiming at his fiancée, shining with the juices of another woman. Michelle's eyes widened in horror at the sight, reminding him of his nakedness, confirming the tragedy unfolding. Busted and breathless, Armand snatched the waist of his jeans up, tripping over his own two feet in his haste to reach her, landing face down on the carpet.

"Michelle, I can explain."

"What in the fuck is going on, Armand?"

Standing, knees slightly bent, with his hands in front of him, palms out, Armand attempted to erase the image out of Michelle's mind. "MK . . . it's not what you think."

"It isn't? Please tell me that you weren't fucking some bitch in my house."

His legs nearly gave out as his mind rattled off empty explanations, none of which he offered to her because it would only make things worse. "Okay, I'm not going to lie to you. I . . . I messed up, MK. I am so, so sorry."

Tears slowly filled the brims of Michelle's eyes. Waves of pain and panic washed over her as her mind toggled between the two emotions. Her fists clenched and unclenched near her sides. The room spun around her so violently that it made her queasy. *She* did not utter a word but had quietly pulled her sweat pants up above her waist, sliding into the corner by the front door, choosing to look there instead of in Michelle's direction. Armand's eyes darted from *her* to his fiancée. Fear turned his insides into pudding.

"Michelle, I can explain." His words liquefied the cement that had set in her legs. He shrunk a little as she started to move in his direction.

"How could you!"

Armand, still nursing his sprained ankle, staggered backward, leaning on the front door for support. Michelle's calm demeanor only increased Armand's anxiety, the anger and hurt in her eyes cracking his bones the longer she stared.

"Michelle . . . I—"

"You what, Armand? You what?"

Their living room, a major selling point for Armand, had always seemed massive, until now. Now, that room felt like the backseat of a cab. Gulping, he cursed himself for having been so damn stupid. This was the very last thing any of them needed. *Shit.* He was unclear whether Michelle had noticed *her.* If she hadn't, perhaps he could get *her* out the front door before she did. Their relationship would not be the same, their love changed forever, but he wanted to protect however much of her heart was left.

He hobbled forward, with his arms reaching out toward Michelle, blocking *her* body with his tall, muscular form. "MK, I am so sorry. Please hear me out." Silently, he prayed that some telepathic ability would manifest in him, instructing *her* to quickly open the door and run like hell up out of there. That didn't happen.

Armand's plea paused Michelle's movement, at least temporarily, near the center of the room. While he racked his mind, trying to figure out how to prevent any more casualties, he continued to try to keep her calm. "You got every right to be pissed. How can I make this better?"

Michelle started toward him again. Her steps were unsteady. As she got closer to him, the look in her eyes sent a chill down his spine.

"Michelle . . . tell me what to do."

Michelle, inches away from him, never broke their stare. "Move."

Disregarding her request, he presented a counter offer. "Can we go in the kitchen and talk?"

Payment for his insolence was swift and immediate. Unleashing the fury hinted in her eyes, Michelle exploded. "Fuck you!"

Michelle swung wildly. The first hit caught him by surprise.

Maneuvering his head, he quickly tried to gain control of her arms. Armand put his hands up, gesturing surrender, but she didn't ease up.

"Michelle, stop. Wait."

"I trusted you!"

"I fucked up." Taking her into his arms, he absorbed her blows as they decreased with frequency until they eventually ceased.

"I hate you," she sobbed into the folds of his T-shirt.

"I know." The fact that *she* was still behind him was not lost on Armand. Preventing a clash was priority. Before he could make his move, Michelle made hers, taking advantage of his bum ankle as she pushed him to the side. Realizing his error, Armand braced himself for the inevitable. Michelle's vulnerability, though honest, was a ploy to get him to relax. To give her access to *her*.

"Michelle, this is my fault. Let me explain."

"Brianna?" Michelle's usually soothing, smooth Southern tone was broken by betrayal. "Bria, look at me. Look at me!"

Brianna slowly turned around to face her twin, shrinking into the corner as much as she could, trying to disappear. "Michelle . . . I don't know what to say. I can't make you understand *this*. It's . . . complicated."

Michelle was livid. Her body shook with anger, tears streamed down her cheeks. She was shaking her head in disbelief but accepting it all the same. "Make me understand, Bria? That's all you have to say?"

"I can see that you're hurt. . . ."

"Can you? That's my fiancé!" Pointing to Armand, Michelle shot a disgusted eye in his direction. "*Was* my fiancé. You're my sister . . . or so I thought."

Armand cringed, hearing all the things he had aimed to avoid. Their relationship was still fresh, and he knew Michelle. This would be difficult for her to stomach. She was all he had before this thing with Brianna began. Family was precious, and he sincerely regretted ripping into hers like this.

"MK, blame me, okay? Don't hold this against her."

"Are you taking up for her? Defending her?" Massaging her temples, Michelle backpedaled away from them. "I cannot do this right now."

Brianna remained silent, and Armand felt that was best. Her statements were complicating things even more so. "Don't go. I'll leave. Stay here and talk this out with . . . your sister. This was a terrible mistake."

"You broke . . . my . . . heart. I can't breathe. I can't be here." Michelle turned and left, presumably back out the way she came, out the French doors in their bedroom leading onto their private porch. Earlier, his moans muted the soft purr of her engine; now, the sound echoed throughout the house.

He sank to the floor, burying his face in his hands. Brianna stood in the corner a moment longer before disappearing into the guest room.

How did he let this happen? MK was his partner, his friend, all the family he had. He looked at the silver band on his finger and removed it. His mother deserved a better son; Michelle, a better man. He had shamed his mother's memory and himself. Pocketing the ring, he pledged to make things right.

CHAPTER 18

"Peter?" Sophie stood, leaning against the kitchen sink, estimating how long it would be before he realized she had asked a question. Peter sat on a bar stool on the far side of the island, facing her. She could tell from the dreamy look in his eyes that he hadn't heard one single word. "Peter?"

"Yes, I'm sorry. I didn't hear you." Peter flashed a big, bright smile.

"Dinner plans?"

"I made us reservations, but before we get to that . . . I think we need to talk."

Sophie continued leaning against the counter, tapping her fingers along its surface, uncertain if she was ready to have this conversation. Before she made up her mind, Peter swiftly took control of their discourse.

"This is a little awkward, I guess."

As her stomach knotted up, Sophie forced herself to speak. "Peter, this should have happened a week ago."

"I know."

"If you don't want to be here because of what happened before . . ."

"Sophie, if I didn't want to be here, I wouldn't be."

"Then, what is it?"

"We need to address what happened that night. That's all."

The gentle hue of his words offered very little comfort. Her fear did not seem rational, but her body slowly gave way to the mild tremors of apprehension nevertheless.

"This last week has been amazing, but I want more than this, Luce." His eyes were soft and inviting.

Sophie tried to relax a little. "That was a long time ago."

"Not to me. Not after what we've shared."

"What do you want me to say?"

Peter looked at the woman who'd held his soul hostage for over two decades, the tenderness in her eyes caressing the sensitive strings of his heart. He spoke gently to her, almost in a whisper. "Nothing. I don't want you to say anything. I want you to listen."

"Let's go sit over there," Sophie suggested, pointing to the breakfast area of the kitchen.

Peter followed the sway of her shoulders as she walked to the little nook area, sitting down in one of the chairs. Soon, he joined her, sitting in one of the adjoining chairs. As she pulled her legs into the chair, folding them beneath her, he waited for Sophie to get comfortable before speaking.

"I tried really hard to find someone to love. To love someone else. Each time a relationship failed, I blamed you a little more."

Sophie sank deeper into the ranch-style wicker chair. "Peter, I don't think I want to do this."

Lifting his hand, he paused her thought. "Let me finish, Luce. It was irrational, I know, but the way you left . . . you just disappeared."

"I was sixteen."

"That never mattered, so don't give me that."

Sophie chuckled uncomfortably. "Peter . . ."

"I was eighteen, but so what? I knew what I wanted. You turned your back on me. Rejected me."

"That's not what happened."

"Luce that is *exactly* what happened." Peter's eyes lowered like anvils into his ocean of truth. His tone echoed his assurance in the accuracy of his interpretation. It was almost like his bravado was made visible to her at that moment; like it colored his naked forearms, blanketed the hairless chest she knew rested beneath his Polo top, and seared itself into the bottom lip he could not keep his perfect set of white teeth from sinking into.

"I am not going to sit and let you put all of this on me, Peter. Seven months went by before I moved. Seven months. You left *me* that night. You walked away."

"I gave you a ring. You broke our promise."

Switching positions in the chair, Sophie fastened her emotions into place. "That was not my decision, Peter. I mean, I did it, but . . . I did not have a choice."

"If we are going to move from here. I'll need more than that."

"What more do you want, Peter? I didn't break our promise. You did!" Her face flushed a cherry red as she lost control. "You left me, and I never heard from you again! I didn't leave! I never left you! Never!"

Peter remained calm. If her outburst had upset him, his face did not let on. Sophie inhaled deeply, trying to reign herself back in. She did not want to argue with Peter about something that happened so long ago. He had abandoned her, but she had long since forgiven him. Why did he insist on discussing it now?

"Luce, what did you expect me to do? That ring cost me everything. It wasn't just some little trinket. It was a symbol of my love, my commitment to you. It meant something to me."

"It meant something to me, too!"

"Then what happened, huh? Explain it to me."

Sophie did not utter a word. Standing abruptly, she scurried off, disappearing out of his view, power-walking down the hallway to the other side of her home. She brusquely pushed open the French doors leading into her bedroom, pausing only a moment to collect herself. She made a beeline for her vanity area, a setup very similar to the one she'd had in her father's house.

Opening the slim drawer in the center, she pushed her silk scarves to the side and wrapped her fingers around what was hidden there. Taking the small band into her hand, she took a deep breath and swiftly walked back into the kitchen where Peter awaited her.

"Luce, you cannot keep running. I'm not going to make it easy for you this time." He didn't even let her get into the kitchen before unloading on her. "I won't go away quietly. You shouldn't expect me to, either. Not after this last week. Not after what I have told you."

Sophie gingerly took her seat like it pained her to do so. Curling her body inward, Sophie tried to find comfort in the little distance between her and Peter. The silver band felt warm in the palm of her hand. She stared at her closed fists, contemplating if this was something she was really prepared to do. Technically, that door had opened a week ago, but somehow she knew that after this moment, there would be no going back.

"Luce, talk to me." Slamming his hand onto the table, Peter aired his frustration. His nostrils flared, tension squaring his shoulders. "Stop with the silent treatment! It's not going to work. If you want me to go, fine, but communicate that. Be woman enough to say so!"

Sophie didn't flinch. She met his stare, opened her hand, and let the diamond ring fall to the table. As it clattered about, swiveling into a resting place, Peter couldn't help but fixate on it. It still glistened as it had that night under the moonlight.

He swallowed the lump in his throat. "You have kept it all these years?"

Sophie nodded her confirmation, keeping her eyes on the ring, the only piece of jewelry she had kept from the life she forfeited when she walked out of her father's house. Though it was the smallest piece of jewelry she had ever owned, it held the most the value. She could not have left it behind.

"Why did you keep it?"

Closing her eyes, Sophie prepped herself for the moment she had rehearsed too many times to count. Chill bumps covered her arms and legs as she embraced their presence. For the first time in a very long time, she was going to speak her truth. She took a deep breath and sent a prayer out into the universe to precede her admission.

"I never stopped loving you, Peter. Not ever. That ring was my connection to you."

"Do you honestly expect me to believe that?" Peter cast a doubtful eye at Sophie, tapping his fingers impatiently on the table's surface, struggling to keep calm while he awaited a more suitable answer.

She winced as the venom from his words corrugated in her center, easily penetrating both flesh and bone to find the softest, most intimate part of her. She squeezed her eyes closed until her tears understood they would not reach her face. This conversation was not going at all as she had envisioned it would. She never dreamt of having her truth met with such disdain, and as vulnerable as she felt . . . this man would not see that tender side of her, not this time.

"I did love you, but I was afraid."

Peter sprang from his chair in a fit of frustration, causing its wicker base to scrape the tile floor. "Afraid? What did you have to fear, Luce? I was the one risking everything!"

Her body shook involuntarily with the sudden movement, her lips quivering as her soul absorbed the impact of his words. Their courtship had not been without trial. Peter was aware of her father's antics to some degree. He did not know everything, but she thought he knew enough to understand. Clearly, she had been mistaken.

"You don't understand."

Pensively pacing the floor in front of the island, Peter threw a dismissive hand in her direction. He stopped to look at her before he spoke. "Sure I do. Daddy's money, was it? Scared to give up that lifestyle for me. Freemont told me you wouldn't let it go."

Sophie stiffened at the mention of her father. Sophie shuddered as an imaginary wind whistled by. "Peter! Is that really what you think of me?"

Peter slumped against one of the bar stools with his face downcast, his hands on either side.

"Money? Really, Peter?" Sophie picked up the ring, twirling it in her fingers as she spoke. "The mirror never regarded you as a friend."

"What are you talking about?"

Rising to her feet, cradling the ring in her fist, she slid across the tile toward Peter. Taking residence on the stool nearest him, she grazed his leg with her knee as she turned her body inward, resting her arms on the island's marble surface.

The quiet dispelled the air, suffocating them both as they tried to maneuver through it into the perfect words. Sophie peeked at Peter from the corner of her eye and caught him staring at her. Sensing his urge to turn away, she swiveled her body into his gaze, gently requesting he follow suit with a dubious hand on his thigh. Honoring her request, Peter faced her, adjusting his long frame into a more comfortable position.

Holding time, Sophie waited until she had his undivided attention before speaking. Running a manicured finger along his profile, Sophie released the last of her anxiety, pushing the tension into the thin layer of air between her skin and his, losing it to the comfort gained from their contact.

Turning into her touch, he covered her hand with his, briefly kissing her palm. He inhaled her scent and lifted his gaze to meet hers.

"Oh, Peter. I never saw the poor boy the mirror reflected back to you. Not once. You meant everything to me."

The energy in the room shifted once more as Peter stewed on her words. Swallowing a bit of truth, Sophie fell silent. She was no longer that little girl he left swaying under the moonlight all those years ago. Life had matured her, changed her in even the most basic ways. Peter may have elevated himself socially, catapulting himself into the successful doctor he was, but there was still some very important part of him trapped inside that young boy.

"Many times I picked up the phone to call." Peter carried his gaze up into hers, holding her thoughts captive. Pulling her hand down into his lap, he held it, caressing her skin. "Seemed like you had moved on overnight. It was like we didn't even happen."

"Peter, it isn't what you think. That's not what happened." Corralling her body into his space, she rested her forehead against his. "You were my champion. I loved you."

"The ridicule before *us* hurt, but after . . . I was the guy that lost you to *him*. I couldn't handle it. I ran, found refuge on the East Coast. Returned with something to prove."

Mingling her fingers in his hair, eventually grasping his profile, she brought his face up meet hers. "To prove to whom?"

Tension filled the room and funneled inward, swirling between them. Peter's face grew warm in her hands. A dubious smile crept into his face. As he parted his lips to respond, Sophie covered his lips with hers.

CHAPTER 19

Her legs stopped at the door. It was not a graceful, organic stop, but the kind of stop a brick wall provides when some poor, inattentive soul crashes into it running full speed. If her heart had not already suffered a break beyond repair, this scene would have certainly done the trick. Dozens of frames flowed through her mind, none of them quite as shocking as the one playing out before her eyes.

The slight rattling of the slender brass knob she held in her hand echoed in her ears, expediting the countdown that had begun the minute she pulled into the driveway. She took long, gulping breaths like a sprinter at the end of the race for an Olympic gold. Her eyes fluttered like the shutter of a camera's eye, capturing every heartbreaking detail. She descended into the fury percolating around her midsection, and she feared there was little she could do to stop it.

But perhaps it was not too late to change directions, to stop the bomb from exploding. Her presence had not yet been detected. Departing seemed like a plausible solution, but as the images multiplied, crowding out all other thoughts, she knew she couldn't. The obscene photograph of her fiancé forking her sister hung unhinged, frozen in her mind, baiting her. She had walked away from that situation; she could not walk away from this one.

The rage swirled around her, enveloping her into a cyclic whirlwind. Her lips quivered as the hurt and anger mangled within. Erupting, snatching the French door open with a thunderous bang as it slammed into the house, she stormed inside.

"Michelle!" Abruptly breaking their kiss, Sophie stumbled backward away from Peter, sending her stool crashing to the floor with her on top of it. *Ouch, goodness.* Grunting, Sophie waved off Peter's assistance, using the island's edge to return to her feet. Clumsily brushing the imaginary dirt from her blouse, Sophie shot a quick, tattered glance at Peter. "This is quite a surprise. I wasn't expecting you, but it's . . . uh, good to see you."

Michelle ignored her mother's futile attempts at conversation, not seeing the need for pleasantries. "Who is this?"

Sophie hesitated with her answer, briefly looking to Peter.

"Why are you looking at him? I asked the question!"

Stretching her hands towards the high ceiling in her kitchen in her defense of herself, Sophie launched into an explanation of sorts, trying her best to appease Michelle yet keep her business to herself. "I will be happy to explain all of this to you." Mindlessly fiddling with her blouse and tugging at her leggings, Sophie was not like the calm mother Michelle was accustomed to seeing.

Michelle tried to quiet the storm brewing in her mind, but if her mother provided anything other than the truth, she knew she'd explode. "I'm listening."

Swinging her twitching eyes from Michelle to Peter, Sophie took an audible breath before speaking again. "Great. Go pull the door closed."

Michelle did not move.

"Sit down there." Sophie motioned to the breakfast nook area. "Or over here by the island, wherever is fine. Let me get a glass of lemonade for you. I have a fresh pitcher."

Michelle felt any patience she might have had dissipating with each step her mother took toward the cabinets where the cups were kept. It was not lost on her that she took the scenic route either. If her intention was to pull Michelle's attention away from this man, she had failed miserably. Michelle could not be distracted. If anything, this song and dance only made this situation less tolerable.

"Mom?" Rolling her eyes and wiping her hands on her face, Michelle wrestled her swirling emotions. She wished her mother would get to the point.

"Just sit down," Sophie retorted.

Despite the urgency sprinkled into her tone, Sophie continued moving about as if Peter were not sitting there, infuriating Michelle even more so. She closed her eyes, seeking some infinitesimal measure of peace, something that would stretch her patience a bit more, only to be bombarded with mental images of Armand and Brianna, then her mother and this man. Images morphed into a compilation of kissing, touching, and thrusting, and she wanted to beat the shit out of everyone in the picture. Her thoughts were jumbled, adding to her frustration, as fire coursed through her limbs.

"Gawd! Just answer the damn question! Who is that?" Michelle screamed, pointing at Peter.

"Michelle Kaye! I understand that you're upset, but I will not allow you to speak to me that way. You give me the respect and decency I deserve."

Michelle imploded as her temper escalated. "The respect you deserve? Are you kidding me? Twenty-three years! Twenty-three gotdamn years you lied! So save that decency and respect speech for someone who doesn't know you auctioned off your kid!"

Sophie froze, dropping the glass she held in her hand. It shattered as it hit the floor, cracking the silence. She looked at Michelle with eyes so big that Michelle could see each word of the rebuttal her mother opted not to speak marching around her cornea. Peter looked sheepishly at Sophie, too embarrassed to face him.

Tiring of her mother's shenanigans, opting to deal with Peter directly, she charged toward him as he stood with his back pressed against the island. Noting his bare feet, loosely buttoned shirt, and the ruby tint of her mother's lipstick on his lips, she wagered that this visit was not his first.

"Who are you!"

Peter shifted uncomfortably under her intense stare. The shock of having witnessed the events transpiring in front of him, and perhaps a twinge of fear, forced the pink in his cheeks to spread all over his face. Peter drummed his fingers on the island's marble surface, not certain if or how he should respond. Rattled and very uncomfortable, Peter threw a quick glance in Sophie's direction, hoping to absorb some moral support, only to find she was no longer standing there.

"Umm . . . I am a friend of your mother's."

"Direct your questions to me!" Sophie appeared by Peter's side, catching him before he slipped off the stool, startled by her sudden proximity. "He is my guest and has nothing to do with any of this. Leave him out of it."

"It's too late for that," Michelle fumed. "Maybe you should have kept your tongue out of his mouth! Or better yet . . . kept him out of you!"

Sophie gasped, grabbing the neck of her blouse with one hand and slapping Michelle across the face with the other. She pulled her hand back into her body, cupping it near her chest, surprised at herself. Never before had she struck Michelle in such a manner.

Michelle touched her face, where her mother's imprint burned a deep red, not quite willing to believe her mother had hit her. She smothered the need to defend herself as the ache of her soul bubbled up, saturating her anger. Hot tears dripped from the corners of her eyes.

"What is wrong with you people? You're all so fucked up!"

"Michelle, I . . . I . . ." Sophie did not know what to say. Things had gotten completely out of hand.

"I asked you one question." Michelle stood just out of Sophie's reach.

Sophie, no longer upset, released her words gently. "Michelle, this is complicated."

"The question was simple." Michelle kept her eyes on her mother even as tears continued filling them, wetting her cheeks. "I needed an answer, Mom."

Their discourse drifted into deeper waters, and everyone in the room felt the change. The residue of her mother's betrayal resonated with each syllable she uttered. "After everything you've taken from me, why couldn't you give me that?"

"Michelle, I am so very sorry. I cannot undo—"

"I hate you," Michelle interrupted. Sophie reached for Michelle's hand, but she jerked it away. "Don't touch me."

Backpedaling toward the open door, Michelle swung her eyes toward Peter for one last look when something caught her eye—a small, shiny something on the island, in between the stools where she remembered seeing her mother and *this friend* when she first arrived. Curious, she paused, squinting to determine what she was seeing.

"You cannot be serious!" she exclaimed as she realized what it was. "A ring? You gave my mother a ring?" Michelle tried to steady herself as the room began spinning around her.

Peter raised his hands as he attempted to excuse himself. "Perhaps I should leave and let you two talk."

"No, no, I'm leaving," Michelle barked, stumbling again toward the door.

"Michelle, wait. We need to talk about this."

Braking just beyond the door's threshold, Michelle turned to speak, looking Sophie directly in her eyes. "I need some time. Space to clear my head."

"Sure, as long as we can deal with this. I don't like the way things have been between us. How long do you need?" Sophie questioned, hope floating around her words.

Michelle stood in the doorway, finding it increasingly difficult to look at the woman she loved with everything she had, the woman who had been more than a parent, but had been an excellent friend. Michelle never would have guessed that the malice and disdain reserved for her father would ever shine in her mother's direction.

As impossibility stretched and transformed their dynamic while she stood, the painful truth oozing steel into her veins. Michelle was ready to go, but before she exited, she wanted to do for her mother what Sophie had failed to do for her: answer her question.

"Four weeks."

Sophie dropped her head. "Oh, Michelle . . ."

Michelle closed the door behind her.

CHAPTER 20

Sophie watched her daughter disappear around the corner of the house into the fading light of day. Her departure, inked with a touch of permanence, hurt Sophie more than anything ever had. That was her *Number One*, her eldest daughter, and for the first time, she feared that the bond she had once shared with her was gone forever.

"Luce?"

She faced Peter, her eyes leaking with shame. She could not discern his thoughts from the expression he wore. This was the worst possible way for Peter to discover some of the horrible things she had done. Michelle's admonishment forced her into a conversation she was not sure she wanted to have with him.

"Peter . . . I know what you're thinking."

Drawing a short breath, with a raised brow, he replied, "I doubt that very seriously."

"Peter, I don't want to talk about any of this."

"I understand that, but—"

"I need some time alone," she interrupted.

"I understand that, and I *will* honor your wishes, but if you plan to see me again, I'll need an answer from you."

Sophie sighed deeply. These questions were certain to be her undoing. "What is it, Peter?"

"Is *Michelle* your only child?"

Relieved, Sophie quickly answered, "No, she isn't. Michelle is not my only child." As she spoke, fragments of the last conversation she'd had with Lewis sprang to mind. *That night, when you didn't bother coming to the hospital, I gave birth to twins.*

"Michelle is a . . . twin."

Sophie looked back out toward the open French doors where Michelle had stormed out.

Tears began to fill her eyes when a figure suddenly appeared at the base of the porch. Fear gripped her heart; shock emptied the scream erupting from her throat. She couldn't be seeing what she thought she was. It was not possible. They had buried him.

Peter grabbed her as her body sank to the ground, her eyes glued wide with panic. "Luce, are you all right? Luce?"

Sophie could not respond. Her lips wouldn't form any words. Mumbling, she attempted to answer him. "He just . . . I . . . he . . . did you . . . he . . ."

"Luce, look at me." Peter tried to get Sophie's attention. "Luce, hey, can you hear me?" Grabbing a mini flashlight from his pocket, he shined it in her eyes, examining her pupils. "Luce, does anything hurt?"

The soft-white beam from the flashlight hurt her eyes a tad but helped to bring Sophie out of her stupor. Still feeling a bit panicked, she looked back at the bottom of the porch where she thought she saw Lewis, but she found the space empty. Nestling herself in the breast of Peter's shirt, she allowed her body to return to its normal state.

"Luce, are you okay? What happened?"

"I don't know, Peter. I am just glad you were here."

"Me, too. Come here." Peter squeezed her tightly, and she rested there in his arms, sitting on the floor of her kitchen.

She had not been completely honest, but it was not the first time. Besides, she could not tell Peter that she thought she saw the ghost of her dead husband without sounding a little cuckoo. "I am sorry if I scared you."

"It's fine, Luce. Really. This has been a lot for you. Maybe you are feeling overwhelmed by it all."

"Maybe." Sophie wished that were true, but she feared something more dire was happening. She was losing her mind, literally. Lewis had been showing up in random places around the house, always outside but present still. It freaked her out each and every time. She didn't feel guilty about choosing to save her own life, so why was the universe punishing her? Why was Lewis haunting her?

CHAPTER 21

Brianna removed every article of clothing hiding her physique. Stripping until she donned nothing but her birthday suit, she dropped to the ground, creating a static electric map of her body's dimensions across the floor of her bedroom. She didn't flinch as the thick, ruby-red carpet fibers tickled her bare backside. Only the work of her lungs negated her mannequin-like state. Knowing Armand would not dare enter into the room after their sexual tryst had been uncovered, she felt free to be as she was—nude.

Vulnerable and exposed, Brianna struggled with her personal discomfort, her inner turmoil, desiring to somehow force herself to mirror the sentiments on an emotional level, to get to the truth of who she was in the *present*, gain some clarity and perspective on things. Something twisted and ugly had driven her into the arms of her sister's fiancé, and she needed to label it, not only for herself, but for Michelle, whose pain-stricken face lit the darkness like a constellation in the night sky.

Special microfiber eclipse curtains covered the bedroom's only set of windows, installed by Armand at her request, preventing any natural light from seeping in. The annoying red flash of the useless digital alarm clock in the far corner served as the only source of light. Usually the rhythmic flash would help her relax, but not tonight. The twentieth-century relic aggravated her. It, like everything else in the room, belonged to Michelle. Her guilt would not allow her to unplug it or change anything aside from the curtains over the window. Absurdity not-withstanding, given the erroneous nature of her involve-ment with Armand, Brianna felt obligated to deal with the minor irritation.

This moment did not mark the first time she had contem-plated her motivations. She had not had any luck before, but this time would be different. It had to be. Things had been strained between her and Michelle. If there was any chance at mending fences, the truth in its entirety would be a basic requirement. *I don't know* wouldn't be sufficient.

Concentrating on her breathing, Brianna tried to turn her mind into a blank canvas to allow her thoughts to flow in a more natural manner. The darkness in the space embodied the loneliness she felt. Logic dictated that some deep, resounding, unrequited love must exist between her and Armand for something this trifling to have happened, but that was not the case. His loyalty to Michelle was never in question. Brianna did not desire *that* from him. Her relationship with Armand had honest beginnings. She couldn't really isolate when it had turned a corner, but she accepted that it had. Perhaps if she could determine what he gave her, she could find some other way to get *it*.

The catalyst for all of this seemed to be the unraveling of their respective families. Michelle's insistence on finding the truth stripped Brianna of everything she could call her own—her parents, her sense of security, her self-confidence. Michelle left her world without color, merit. Brianna could not function without a sense of purpose or some direction for her life. The truth had caused her world to implode, and it could not be repaired. Maybe Brianna could have handled it all better if she had more time to adjust, but Michelle was relentless.

Armand was not revenge, more like a consolation prize, if there could be one. Brianna needed someone to confide in, and Armand lent his ear, sharing his heart with her. Michelle hadn't even bothered to offer her assistance. Their blossoming bond flamed out in the midst of all the revelations. Michelle was not the same Michelle she had grown to know in the last couple of months, but Brianna supposed she was not the same person either. Who would be, after all they had been through? Brianna felt the brunt of the responsibility and rightfully so, but it was not entirely her fault. Once their parental search concluded, the closeness Brianna felt with Michelle, *her* eagerness to bond, had evaporated into the air.

Sophie's stellar performance as the regretful mom was not strong enough to erase the image Brianna saw when she looked at her, the woman who had sold her for five million dollars to a guy without even bothering to learn his name. Brianna had been fortunate that Frank and Lisa were decent people. The fact that she could have been auctioned off into the lucrative world of sex trafficking was not lost on her.

Brianna had been guarded before her world turned upside down, and the level of trust she required to be transparent did not exist between them. The people that raised her, Frank and Lisa, were not Stateside, but even if they were, she didn't know if she wanted to talk to them. They had enough lies circulating between the two of them to put the Central Intelligence Agency to shame. She wanted to reach out to a few of her line sisters, but she felt awkward. The Brianna they knew was gone, and she hadn't figured out how to get back to her.

She was relieved when Armand made it clear that he was available. She knew she wouldn't have to explain what had transpired between her and Javan. He was there and saw him for himself. The craze in Javan's eyes, it was as if he were some other person, possessed with a rage beyond his control. Armand never asked her anything about that night. Everything he had to say was in his eyes. She appreciated that about him.

The sexual nature of their bond happened almost accidentally. They had been talking one night, as usual, discussing her therapy session, laughing about her suspicions about Dr. WonderBra's clandestine meetings after work, when the tension between them squeezed itself into something more profound. The pull was magnetic. When their lips met, she knew she could not go back. Things would be different. The sudden rainfall between her legs was proof.

Armand left immediately, leaving her to deal with an avalanche of emotions the *innocent* kiss ignited. Things escalated over time, but they had been very careful until today. Armand met her at the door of the house, grabbed her, and kissed her like he had something to prove. The moment was so intense they didn't even venture beyond the doorway. By the time he started to resist, momentum had catapulted them past the point of no return.

Brianna was not thinking of anything beyond what was emerging between them in that instant. *Stopping* never entered her mind. For her, nothing existed but the two of them. Michelle, her parents, the pieces of her life she tried to salvage, those things were fantasy. Brianna had vacated her body and delved into the act. Anyone could have replaced Armand to that extent. Michelle's arrival had quickly put things into perspective.

The cracking in her voice clawed at Brianna's heart. She knew that sexing Armand was an awful thing for her to do, but the urge was stronger than her resistance. With him, she shed her zombie motif. She felt alive, even if the feeling couldn't stretch beyond a few minutes. She hungered for it like a junkie chasing a high. She kept opening her legs to him, tasting him until he became her preferred flavor. She auditioned to be the star in his private porn, and he hired her for the role.

Much to her surprise and delight, he needed her as much as she needed him. Brianna knew she should regret this, but the truth was, she didn't. She hated that Michelle was in pain and hoped that they could find a way out of this with everyone intact, but if not, it didn't matter much. She had nothing left to lose. Michelle had her mother, the life she lived with her, her career, and she still had Armand. Brianna was all alone. She had nothing.

Fluttering in her belly forced her into an upright position. Instinctively, she placed a hand on her stomach. She might not be alone after all. No time better than the present to make good on her promise to Dr. WonderBra. Crawling to the bed, noting how tender her breasts felt, she reached for her cell. Pressing 6-4-2-2-4, unlocking her phone, she quickly found Dr. Baxter's number and hit TALK before she changed her mind.

"Dr. Baxter? Evening. This is Brianna. I need to make an appointment. . . . I'm sorry, are you busy? I feel like I'm interrupting something. The sooner, the better. Tomorrow afternoon would be fine. Thank you."

That was weird. She had definitely detected high levels of anxiety in Dr. Baxter's voice, although he insisted that he was fine. The usually long-winded Dr. Baxter was polite but short. Something was definitely going on, but that was none of her business and not her problem. One thing did seem particularly crazy, though: she could have sworn she heard her mother's voice, but how could that be possible? He didn't even know her. Nah, she must have been hearing things, and that was even more reason to see him. Better yet, she figured, she'd better call Dr. WonderBra too. She would want to hear about this latest crash into madness.

CHAPTER 22

Michelle knew it was too late to go to the gym. The eighty-two-year-old owner, Doug Eiid, had locked the doors over an hour ago. Still, she found herself parked on Commerce Street in downtown Dallas, across from the large white stone municipal building, parallel to the entrance of her small slice of heaven, staring at the singular glass door bearing the gym's operating hours: Monday–Friday, 11–8 p.m. and Saturday, 11–6 p.m.

On a regular day, Michelle had no issues with the hours but *this Friday*, she wished 9:30 would allow her inside. She desperately needed to punch something, and there was a heavy bag with her name on it.

Established in 1962, Doug's Gym was the oldest gym in the nation, and it looked the part, too. Just beyond the plain glass door was a long, tattered but sturdy wooden staircase leading upstairs to the one-room gym with a beautiful aged wood floor to match. The gym, with equipment older than Michelle, offered very few of the amenities that a modern fitness center would: no central air, no flat screens mounted on the wall, no refreshment area. Some of the machines were probably the first generation of their kind, and some might not even be in production anymore, but that was the beauty of the gym.

Michelle loved the austerity, the simplicity of it. Portions of the walls were transformed into Doug's personal scrapbooks, with old Polaroid photographs taped to its blotchy, brown covering. Nothing had changed in the fifty years the gym had been in operation, and anyone that ventured to join appreciated its history.

The people who joined Doug's gym understood immediately that it was much more than a gym, easily ingratiating themselves into its familial atmosphere. Though Doug personally trained each of his members using fundamental weight lifting and cardio techniques, they also supported one another. There was one person who Michelle worked out with fairly often, a young jazz musician by the name of Grayson Hines. The atmosphere at Doug's didn't really allow for any two people to remain strangers for long. It fostered connectivity. The fact that they were the same age and both shared a love for jazz gave life to their blooming friendship.

As she sat there in front of Doug's Gym, craving a good workout, his name sprang to her mind. A training session was not possible, but Michelle figured some company would be nice. The two had never had a conversation outside of the gym, and Michelle was not certain if he would even come. This would be the first test of their friendship, revealing whether its legs were strong enough to tread into deeper waters.

Her anger had subsided not long after she left her mother's, but she did not want to speak to any of them. Armand had been calling and texting non-stop since she left him at their house. His efforts to communicate with her were so incessant that Michelle turned her phone off, removing the battery and chucking it into the backseat of the Audi.

By the time she had reached her childhood home, her nerves were vapors, making the craziness that ensued even more likely. Climbing into the backseat, she fished for her the slim piece of lithium. She needed a distraction, and Grayson was on her short list of friends. The only name on the list, as a matter of fact.

Capitalizing on the few minutes lost fumbling in the dark for the battery, Michelle powered her cell on and placed the call. Rather than the usual burr of a ringing phone, a sample of a common jazz standard, "Naima," rang in her ears. Michelle was pleasantly surprised and reclined in the seat, resting her cranium on the headrest, allowing the smooth tunes to massage her mental while she anticipated his answering. He played beautifully, and even though her car's Bluetooth pushed the notes out of her factory speakers, they did not do it justice. The basic sound system failed to capture the essence and unmistakable brilliance of her most beloved jazz ballad.

"This is Grayson Hines."

Startled by the interruption of her groove session, Michelle sat up in her seat, botching her opening as she failed to do both at once. "Gray . . . Gray . . . Grayson, hi. . . . This is Michelle."

Grayson's jovial demeanor marked his tone. "Michelle, my belle, this is a pleasant surprise. Everything okay?"

"Yes and *no*. That is kind of why I'm calling."

"My interest is piqued. What's up?"

"Do you think you could come up here?"

"*Here*?"

"The gym."

"The gym is closed. Doug locked up already."

"I know. I just . . . I had a really rough night, and I could use someone to talk to."

Grayson waited before answering. Michelle bit her lip, afraid of what the silence might indicate. She really didn't want to be alone right now.

"Where are you?"

"Sitting outside."

"What made you call me? I mean, I'm flattered that you would think of me, but . . ."

Michelle was having second thoughts, but she *made* the call. As nauseating as she found the idea of opening her life up to a virtual stranger, it was necessary. Michelle, the loner, was trading her emotional solitude for the rawness of the human connection.

"I have never felt so alone in my life, Grayson. Ever. So if you could just . . ."

"I'm on my way."

Sighing with relief, Michelle wiped the tears collecting on her face, whispering, "Thank you," into the empty phone line. Michelle was on the verge of a dramatic shift in consciousness. It was too early to tell whether it would lead her down a better path or send her flying off a cliff with no chute. Either way, it was happening, and she decided that leaning into the curve rather than fighting the transition would be more beneficial.

The sharp blue lettering of the sign for the neighboring Oqua Lounge caught her eye for the millionth time. Michelle did not venture out very much, but seeing it with each visit to the gym tempted her to break her rules. Exhaling, she closed her eyes and relaxed again, hoping Grayson arrived before she lost her nerve.

Roughly thirty minutes later, Michelle peeped Grayson walking toward her car in her rearview mirror. Readying herself for his arrival, she hit the switch to unlock the doors and lifted her seat to the upright position. He lightly tapped on the passenger window with his knuckle, requesting permission to join her. Michelle waved him in and offered a half smile.

"Thank you. I wasn't sure if you would come."

"I told you I would."

Michelle took a deep breath. An awkward situation grew into an uncomfortable one while she struggled with her decision to open up. She looked at her trembling hands and couldn't recall the last time her nerves had gotten to her like this. Oxygen imbued with her indecision chafed her lips, drying her throat as it traveled to her lungs. Rendered mute by her embarrassment, Michelle directed her attention outside the small quarters of the car.

Grayson gently grabbed hold of Michelle's hand. "It's okay."

With tears streaming down her face, she examined the truth resting in his chestnut-colored eyes. Satisfied with what she saw there, Michelle hastily dried her eyes, embarrassed by her inability to control her emotions.

Noting her state, Grayson took it upon himself to generate conversation. "I usually take a stroll through the park around this time."

Michelle checked his dark-gray men's skinny jeans, loosely laced red-and-white vintage Chucks, fresh white cotton V-neck tee, and doubted that very seriously.

Grayson caught the question in her once-over. "My family recently expanded to include a puppy in need of a home."

Michelle raised her eyes in surprise. "You don't seem like the dog type."

"I'm not really certain what that means, but *Common* is the child I feared having too soon."

Michelle cringed a little, thinking about how young her mother was when she and her sister were conceived.

Grayson kept talking. "He was a rescue effort. Police raided a house, trashed the place, and arrested a handful of people, including his owner."

That tidbit snatched Michelle out of her head and forced her into their dialogue. "That sounds like a fascinating story."

"I mean, it is pretty incredible, *but* I can share it at another time." Patting her on the knee, he reminded her of why he was there. "I came here for you."

"I would appreciate your sharing it with me *now*," Michelle stated, figuring it might give her the time required to gather her thoughts. "I could use a good story."

"No problem. As you know, I do a lot of community service type of activities."

"I am aware."

"Well, I used to visit this neighborhood in South Dallas near Rosewood and Hatcher. Tried to be of some service to the people there. Gentrification is slowly making its way through the area, and the people are getting pushed out. I went to this particular neighborhood to see if there was anything I could do to help them prepare for what was coming."

"Did the city ask you to do that?"

Grayson shook his head. "Nothing like that. I just wanted to help."

"That is commendable, but how did you know that was happening?"

"I'm resourceful."

Realizing she had started to interrogate him a bit, she muted the last of her questions.

"SWAT swooped in pretty deep with an armored truck and a Humvee. It was like something out of a film, and you could see it all from up the street. The commotion got my attention, and I tiptoed in that direction to get a closer look. I recognized this old guy, and my heart kinda sunk." Grayson shook his head as he spoke. "He was a decent guy, not any trouble, but unfortunately he loved that pipe better than he loved himself."

Michelle watched his eyes dart about as he traveled into that moment.

"Sad situation. I was standing on the sidewalk, watching the badges move, when I heard a faint whimpering sound. I couldn't really make it out at first, but when I closed my eyes, I recognized it easily. I searched the yard. Everyone was stretched out like dominoes, flat on their stomachs, cuffed with the plastic wire, baking in the Texas sun, but I didn't see any animals. The whimpering stopped, so I leaned against a tree near the front of the house and waited. The old man looked up at me, *into me* with a look so intense it literally pulled me. My legs moved toward him before I could object. It was as if he and I were the only ones there. Before I knew it, an officer shoved me hard toward the sidewalk, ordering me to keep my distance."

"What was your plan, Grayson? Walking into a yard swarming with officers?"

Grayson shrugged his shoulders. "I wanted to comfort him, I guess. He deserved better than that."

"What are you talking about? You said he was on drugs. That's what happens."

Grayson looked at Michelle, taken aback by her rush to judgment, but didn't respond to it. "Not long afterwards, the barking started up again, and I look up to see an officer coming from the back of the house with this puppy. He had the most beautiful ocean blue eyes I had ever seen. This may sound corny, but I think he noticed me at the same time I noticed him. The old man started grunting a little bit and moving around. The puppy started barking frantically. I told the officer the puppy belonged to me."

"You lied?"

"I did. I couldn't leave him there. The old man stopped moving, and I took it as a symbol of his support. Felt like it was the right thing to do, so I said it again with more authority this time: *'I have been looking for him all day. I came into the yard because I thought I heard him. May I have him, please?'*

'This is your dog? What's your name, young man?'

'Grayson, but if I could just have my dog, I'd like to get home.'

'What's his name?'

'Excuse me?'

'The dog. What is his name?'

"I looked at the old man lying there like a piece of wood, helpless and stripped of his dignity, and felt a deep, soulful connection to him. He felt familiar, and I figured the puppy was his, so I said, *'Common. His name is Common.'*"

"That is a beautiful story." The untruth slipped from her lips before she could stop it. What else could she say after a tale like that? It had everything in it. Her inner journalist was mildly impressed with his impromptu storytelling skills. Besides, fact or fiction, the story had lifted her spirit.

"Thanks. He catches a little cabin fever when he's left alone during the day. We try to go for a walk every night."

"I am sorry. My mess interrupted your routine."

"Stop that, Michelle. I could have said no. I wanted to be here for you."

Michelle did not respond.

"So, how about that walk?"

Michelle remained silent. Grayson's pleasantness refreshed her, and she was no longer sure if she needed to talk anymore.

"I don't know what's going on, Michelle, but you can talk to me about whatever it is. I wouldn't betray your confidence."

Michelle shifted in her seat and glanced over at Grayson. "I'm not that dude."

She had no reason to doubt his words, except for the fact that everyone she loved had done the opposite—people she never would have thought would be capable of such things. Each memory reactivated the pain, elevating it as it passed through her mind and waged war on her heart. Michelle wished she could forget it all.

"I am not going to pretend like this is easy for me. It isn't."

"Focus on the walking aspect. No pressure to open up."

"I don't want you feeling like you wasted your time coming."

"You missed our workout this afternoon," Grayson stated playfully nudging her arm with his finger. "Walk with me to make up for it?"

Any fear lingering within her evaporated with that question. Instinctively she knew, deep down in her gut, that she was safe with him. That her thoughts would be safe. Like the gentleman he had always presented himself to be, his gentle prodding eased her anxiety, pulling her away from her own thoughts and forcing her to focus on his words.

"Sure. Where do you walk?"

"I usually take him to Belo Garden Park up the street, but I was thinking that Klyde Warren might be a nice change. It's a little bigger."

"That park off of Woodall Rogers? The one that used to be a parking lot?"

"That is the one."

"That's cool, but do you think we'll be able to find parking in the mass exodus of people that seem to always be there?"

Grayson chuckled. "Yeah, there are a lot of events there, but it's really beautiful, especially at night. If you don't want to drive, we can take my Vespa."

"You have a Vespa?" Michelle asked in surprise. "In Dallas?"

"I'll pretend like your astonishment wasn't a blow to my ego at all." Grayson laughed a little harder this time. "A summer in Paris, France was a graduation gift from my parents. I fell in love with the city, the culture, and the Vespa. I couldn't take the city with me, so I took a piece of it."

Michelle nodded her head in acknowledgement. "*I think I understand that, but I don't mind driving. We're already in the car, but I definitely want to see your Vespa—*"

"Steely," Grayson interrupted. "His name is Steely."

Michelle shook her head in amusement. "Steely. I would like to see Steely one day. The closest I have come to a Vespa was a scene in the remake of *2000 Alfie*."

"We can make that happen, captain."

Grayson buckled his seatbelt as Michelle pulled out onto Commerce, heading north toward Cesar Chavez Boulevard.

"So, did you ever find out what happened to the old man?"

"I did, actually. He died in custody not too long after the arrest. Massive heart failure."

"That is awful. I am so sorry, Grayson."

"It's okay really. I didn't even know his name at the time."

"Then how did you find out?"

Grayson was silent for an uncomfortable period of time. Michelle, navigating down Elm Street, could not see the slight tears forming in his eyes. She simply kept driving and hoped he would respond without her having to pose the question a second time.

"Obituary. I saw a blurb in the paper."

Michelle didn't quite understand why, after everything else he had shared, that seemed to be the most difficult, but she decided to let it go as they neared the park. Grayson was the compassionate, kind guy she imagined him to be. Michelle took a deep breath as she eased into a parking spot, preparing to ease into the next phase of her life.

CHAPTER 23

"Thank you for being here."

Shifting uncomfortably in her seat, Lisa did not rush to respond, signaling to Frank, despite the obvious, that *here* was not a favorable space. The thought hurt but had no merit. Not only had she come of her own volition, but she also petitioned hospital staff to be allowed to do so. Though he longed to see her, he had yet to verbalize his desire. Either fear of legal punitive measures or emotional trappings kept him silent.

Surprised was too small a word to describe his reaction to her coming. Elation filled him after opening his eyes and finding her bedside, but it steadily dissipated in the subsequent hours of silence. Five days of muted communication—his words could not provoke even *one word* from her, causing him to postulate that her goal was not to support him, but rather to punish him with her presence. If so, it was working.

"Lisa, will you please say something? Anything. Curse me out. Scream. Something."

Frank's bed was in the center of the room. Lisa sat to his right, close enough to touch him if she felt compelled to do so, but she never did. The chair she had occupied for the last few days screeched as she stood.

"Wait, please. I don't want you to leave. I won't push, okay? If you don't want to talk to me, that's fine, but please stay. All I could think about was getting back to you. Your face replaced the bars of the cell that caged me. So, please. Stay."

Pausing, Lisa circled the room with her eyes, resting them on everything but Frank. After a few painful minutes, she slowly lowered herself back into her seat. He wanted to thank her but kept his mouth closed. The pensive look on her face spoke volumes about the things he imagined flowing through her mind. Part of him feared what may come out if she did speak to him.

"I have been trying to understand, Frank."

Frank braced himself for the worst and prayed that he didn't say anything stupid. "Understand what?"

"Our last conversation at the house. The day I left. I told you everything. Why didn't you?"

"I did. I mean, there was nothing else to tell."

"A baby is something, Frank. A really big, live, life-altering something."

"Paging Dr. Natii, paging Dr. Natii. Please report to the OR immediately." A voice rang out over the intercom, pausing their interlude for just a moment.

"That is not my child, Lisa." He drilled his eyes into hers, emphasizing his point. "That is not possible."

"Condoms are not absolute," Lisa quipped, not buying his show of confidence.

"Well, a vasectomy is." He had not meant to say it. There it was . . . something stupid had made its way out of his mouth. The tears on Lisa's face were proof that the information about his procedure was something he should have taken to the grave.

"What? What are you talking about, Frank?"

Frank closed his eyes, cursing himself, knowing that he had probably just blown any chance he had to get Lisa back. *Shit.* "I cannot father children, Lisa. I had a vasectomy long ago, so I know that her child could not possibly be mine. She is lying."

Lisa wiped the tears from her eyes. "Fifteen years, Frank. Fifteen years you allowed me to think that something was wrong with me."

"I didn't *allow* anything. Never once did I mislead you."

Lisa kept talking as if she hadn't heard him. "You knew I wanted to give you a child. The fertility treatments . . . the rituals . . . I tried everything."

"You what?"

Lisa shook her head dismissively, trying to free herself from the thought.

"Lisa, what are you talking about, rituals and fertility treatments?" Frank inquired, pressing the button on the remote, lifting himself up. Seeing that he still had not garnered her attention, he continued calling her name. "Lisa . . . Lisa . . . hello . . . *Lisa?*"

Clank, clank, clank! Banging his hand on the plastic railing, he called out to her still.

"Lisa!"

That broke her trance.

"What are you talking about? What fertility treatments? Rituals? What did you do?"

Lisa looked at Frank, confused and fearful.

"What are you talking about?"

"I wanted a baby. My family. You shut me out, and I thought a baby would let me in again."

Frank grabbed the sides of his face, massaging his eyes. The skin on his face felt so tight it might rip open. "Fertility treatments? Why didn't you say anything to me?"

"Shame. Fear. I don't know."

"You don't think that you might have wanted to discuss any of that with me?"

"You mean how you might have thought it was a good idea to tell me about the procedure?"

Frank had no rebuttal. She was correct. Had he been honest with her about it, she would not have suffered in silence. "Lisa, I cannot believe you went through that stuff by yourself." Frank felt sick inside. He had truly failed her in every way possible.

"You shut me out, Franklin. You and Bria shared something so special, and I could see it. I just wanted that for us. I tried everything. I even went to a witch doctor."

Frank felt dejected. He could do nothing but stare at his wife, a woman he apparently did not know much about. "Is that what you were doing all those trips?"

Lisa looked away from him before she answered. "Most of the time."

Tears steadily ran from her eyes. Frank fought the urge to wipe them away.

"I thought you were cheating on me."

Lisa's eyes opened wide, and she looked at him for what felt like the first time. He could see her surprise. "What? Are you serious?"

Frank nodded yes, lowering his head in shame.

"But you never questioned me. Why?"

Frank inhaled deeply. "Guilt, I guess. I was so consumed with guilt about Brianna. I kind of felt like I deserved it. That maybe I needed to let you have that. I knew I was not giving you everything you needed. I wanted to, Lisa, I really did, but I did not know how."

Lisa lowered her head back on the chair, wiping her eyes with the back of her hands. "Wow." Lisa spoke in between sniffles. "This is probably the most honest conversation we have ever had."

"Well, being naked under this sheet thing doesn't leave me with a lot of room to hide anything." Frank laughed, happy to hear Lisa join him.

"Too bad it took all of this."

"I really am sorry, Lisa. I should have told you about the procedure, but I was too busy dreaming. Everything I ever wanted was happening. I found love with a beautiful woman, married, and I was a signature away from securing my financial future."

"I deserved a chance to make my own decision, Franklin."

"I know, and trust—"

Lisa cut her eyes so hard Frank thought they might have whiplash.

Stuttering a bit, he continued. "Trust me, I was going to tell you."

"When?"

"That day we met with Jacob."

Lisa relaxed, softening her stance. "Oh. Why didn't you?"

"Kids were not really on my mind until that moment. Everything was going according to plan. When we got that news, it felt like Mount Everest landed on me. I felt like the biggest ass ever. How could I tell you that we could never get the money because I couldn't father a kid? I could barely process the news."

Frank briefly turned his attention to the small television mounted in the far corner. Footage from a leaked police cam showing the murder of an unarmed black man sprawled across the screen in silence. Frank's stomach turned, recalling the previous four or five cases that had made the front page—no convictions, no indictments, no concern over the loss of life. It disgusted him. With each name added to the ever-growing list, Frank thanked the heavens that Brianna was female. Her odds of surviving were a little better.

"I understand you were fearful, but . . . damn, Frank. Really?" Her words verbally rebuked him for allowing his attention to sway away from her. "We never discussed kids, and then we had Brianna."

Frank shrugged his shoulders. "I thought having her fixed things."

"You were wrong."

"I know."

Lisa sprang to her feet, briefly locking eyes with Frank. She slid toward the television, giving Frank a clear view of her nude bottom peeking through the slit of her hospital gown. Watching the coverage, Lisa asked the question that had been leering at her from the shadows.

"Did you try and kill me?"

Frank sat up straight in bed, waited for Lisa to face him. "I have made some horrible decisions. I have been an asshole, a liar, and in some ways a thief." Taking a deep breath, he spoke from his heart. "I did not do this to you. I love you in my own imperfect way. I love you more than anything in this world. I need you to believe that."

"I believe you, Franklin. I believe you."

Feeling somewhat relieved that she accepted his answer, he shared his commentary on the moment. "I thought you tried to hurt yourself because of me. Because of that baby."

"How did you know?"

Frank scoffed. "Charlie kept calling over and over again. I excused myself to the restroom—"

"To take her call."

Frank could see the wheels spinning in Lisa's mind. "Yeah, and she warned me about the messages. I ran out and—" Frank fought back his tears. The image of his wife still hurt. "I found you lying there."

Lisa sauntered back to her seat beside his bed. She climbed back through the moment when she had found him lying on the floor. She knew exactly how he felt.

"I lost it. Anyway, I don't even know how she found you."

"Full disclosure: Charlie and I have stayed at the hotel a few times."

Frank remained neutral in his reaction to the news. He did not want to regress. Besides, he could not be upset with anything she did. He had vacated their marriage, leaving her to fend for herself.

"You and Charlie were pretty serious, huh?" he asked.

"That relationship met a need. I won't belittle it to soothe your ego. There were moments when I craved to be with her, in her presence."

"Why? What was it about her?" Fear crept into Frank's heart, chipping away at his ability to be enough for the woman he loved.

"She made me feel like I was the only thing in the universe that mattered at all to her. The planets revolving, galaxies exploding, she put me in the center of her world. I came second to nothing."

Even with his eyes closed, Frank could see what Charlie gave that he had not. His wife felt ignored, unimportant, and that feeling left her vulnerable, in need. He would not make that mistake again. "And now? How do you feel now?"

"That was a lie."

"About me. How do you feel about us?"

"You scare me."

Frank swallowed his words, unsure of how to process that. "I would never hurt you, Lisa."

"I don't trust people, Frank. Nothing personal against you, though your record definitely hasn't helped, but in general, I don't trust people. I am not sure I know how to do that."

"One decision at a time."

Lisa did not say anything. He could see her contemplating his offer.

"I am a better man than I have been. Let me prove that to you."

"I don't know, Frank. I love you, but I don't know."

Frank's heart sank, but he wasn't giving up yet. "Treat yourself, Lisa. You stuck around through all of my bullshit. Suffered with me. Don't bail now that I am finally the man you always needed me to be."

"I don't need you to be him for me. I am good by myself. Always have been."

"I don't doubt that. Maybe you don't need me, but I need you."

Lisa looked down at her hand; Frank still had hold of it. A subtle smile washed over her. "If we are staying in our marriage, we are in it forever, Frank."

"That was always the plan."

Lisa smiled a huge, genuine smile this time. "Great, because I hate divorce."

"Thank you for giving me another chance, Lisa. I'll never fail you again."

"You better not. I am in your corner, too."

Frank leaned over the bed, pausing inches away from Lisa's face. She closed the space, planting a kiss on his lips, sealing their reunion. Lisa tried to break it, but Frank was not having it. He pulled her face closer with the palm of his hand, deepening their connection, rekindling a part of them that had been dead for decades.

"I love you, Lisa Raine Mason," Frank whispered as he reluctantly released her.

"So, you are in this no matter what?" Lisa inquired.

"No matter what."

"I have plenty to share with you."

"I'm ready."

"Someone tried to kill me."

"I know."

"That needs to be resolved."

Frank nodded in confirmation. "Details are sketchy. Happened really quickly. Played it over and over in my mind. What do you remember?"

Frank stared in wonder as Lisa's aura seemed to shift before his eyes. Emotion disappeared from her eyes, her voice. It was like she had flipped an internal switch.

"Masculine energy. Must have been hiding somewhere in the kitchen. Happened really quickly. Heard the voicemail, turned to the stove, upset, distracted, and he attacked me at the precise moment. One hand over my mouth, the other pushed a knife into my chest. Motion was fluid. Over in seconds."

Lisa recounted the incident like it was a minor traffic accident. This woman was made of steel. Her speech was not that of a victim. There was little, if any, detectable emotion, only the facts as she remembered them to be.

"My chest erupted in flames. Tried to scream, but I couldn't for some reason."

Frank interjected. "The knife punctured your lung, instantly filling it with blood." Swallowing his discomfort, he continued. "Consequently, you started choking on your blood until you lost consciousness."

Lisa stared at Frank but did not reveal if his words had affected her. She seemed to be processing the information objectively, as if it had happened to someone else.

"What are you thinking?" he asked.

"Trying to think of who would have the skill set, the gall, and the intellect to pull something like this off. And how that person may be connected to Charlie."

Frank drew back, surprised that Lisa would think Charlie capable. "I blamed her initially, but I was upset. Distraught. She isn't capable of doing this."

"You don't know her, Frank."

"Come on, Lisa. Murder? I just can't see that."

"Just because your dick got familiar with the walls of her pussy does not mean you know her. It certainly shouldn't option you for her defense, seeing as though she is, at the very least, trying to pin a baby on you."

"Point taken." He lifted his hands to indicate he had no intention of pressing the issue. "Just never heard you speak of her that way."

"You have not heard me refer to her at all."

"True enough. Why do you think she would do this?"

"Charlene believes I don't remember her, but I do."

Frank perked up. This sounded promising. Lisa was finally letting him in, taking him into her past, a place she refused to visit.

"From the start, there was something familiar about her, but I couldn't name it. Her features weren't distinct. She looked like plenty of other women I knew. I had no clue until her letter . . ."

"Letter?"

"She confessed her sin in a letter before she abandoned me at the hotel. Told me about her deal with Lewis and where we met."

Frank bit his question, deciding to let her tell the story uninterrupted.

"Leaving Indiana was necessary. I buried her and everything related to it once I crossed the state line into . . . Never looked back. I still couldn't remember who she was, but during our last phone call, she said something that struck a chord: '*We weren't in your future. We were only in mine.*'"

Frank was flabbergasted. Charlie really wanted his wife for herself. She was out of her fucking mind. "I cannot believe I am hearing any of this."

"I have had women *love me,* but not like her. Her infatuation blinded her to the point where she would do anything I asked. Anything at all, without question or protest. She met a need, and I didn't mind using her desire to my advantage, but she was becoming unmanageable. Required too much of me, and I knew our season was ending. It took a few days, but that phrase came back to me, punching me in the gut and ultimately nailing down my decision to leave, recoup. Prepare . . ."

"Prepare for what?"

"For her. Charlene Grae, aka the psychotic bitch from hell. She's been searching the country for years, trying to find me. Hunting me is more like it. I left Indiana because of her."

"Wait a minute." Frank fell back onto his pillow, staring up at this large tiled ceiling of the hospital room, trying to wrap his mind around what he had heard. "What? She hunted you?"

"Her mind is fucked up. Obsessed with me even in high school. I'd find letters, poems, and random gifts in my locker. She would show up to parties uninvited. She wouldn't interact. Just sat in a corner, watching me."

Shaking his head in disbelief, Frank did not know what to say.

"I let it go because she just seemed . . . off and harmless for the most part. But one night, I lost it, confronted her. She freaked out, ran away humiliated. She quit coming after that, and I thought maybe it was over. Then I got home one day, found my parents sitting in the living room. My very abusive, sadistic father had letters in his hand. I don't know where he got them. I didn't have time to ask. All I remember is the sight of his closed fist rushing toward me. I don't know when it stopped, but I woke up in bed. Could barely open my eyes, missed nearly two weeks of school."

"I don't understand."

"No daughter of his was going to be no damn lesbian."

Frank's heart ached knowing Lisa had endured so much so young. No wonder she didn't want to talk about it. The pain on her face showed how she was clearly still bothered by it.

"Started partying pretty hard. Didn't want to be home. He beat me every time he thought about those damn letters."

"I thought your dad . . . you know . . ."

"The last night I was there. The last party. I got home, pretty intoxicated. My dad was pretty lit, too. He helped me to into my room. Turned on the light, and . . . there were pictures, letters, flowers all over the place. Somehow she had gained access into my room and *decorated* it. My dad went ape shit, destroying everything in his sight, cursing the whole time. I should have run, but I couldn't think of one place to go. So, I stood there in the doorway, braced myself for the beating I knew was coming. But when he turned around, I saw a monster standing there. His eyes were black like coal. He was heaving, saliva dripping from the corners of his mouth." Lisa closed her eyes, shook her head, trying to force herself to finish.

"Lisa, you don't have to do this. This is clearly upsetting you. You're shaking like a leaf."

"Fear is a sobering thing. I was so fucking afraid in that moment. I wished my mother would come this once, but I knew she wouldn't. He was going to kill me. I tried to fight back, but . . . it was useless. He threw me around that room like a rag doll. Every part of my body hurt, but when he threw me on the bed . . . I wished he had killed me. I prayed to the Most High to let me die. I left after that. Minutes later. Never looked back."

Frank wiped the tears cascading down Lisa's face with the palm of his hand. "I am so sorry." He didn't know what else to say. Nothing would undo what was done then. Lisa covered his hand with hers, cradling it to her face, while she wept softly. "No one will ever hurt you again."

She gently kissed the inside of his palm before letting his hand drop to his lap. "I am okay. That hurt, and I admit that it has affected my decisions, but I feel free now that I have shared it with you. This space between us feels . . . safer than it did before."

"I feel it, too. Lies kept us apart; painful truths are bringing us closer. We are not going back to how things were. We can never go back there. When I thought Jacob had hurt you, something came over me. I barely remember driving to his office, but I remember swinging, the altercation, but it was not his face I saw."

Lisa gazed upon him, eyes full of understanding.

"It was mine. I was beating myself up that day, punishing myself for my ignorance, how insensitive I had been. For how badly I had failed the only woman I ever loved. I wanted to protect you, but somewhere deep inside I knew that attacking him wouldn't accomplish that. I couldn't admit it until later, but that's the truth."

"We both have to take responsibility for what transpired. I am not innocent in all of this either. Let's just deal with what is on the table right now. Charlie. She is dangerous."

"Well, it's unlikely she is going to try anything more here, if it is her behind this. We don't know that for certain. I have a few enemies as well, people capable of hurting you to get to me. I did almost go down for attempted murder."

"That's right. How did you get out of that?" Lisa inquired with a kind of peculiar look on her face.

"Some lawyer from up north took my case and forced their hand. They really didn't have enough to charge me, so they had to release me. Jacob handled the legal situation Stateside, and so that's done, too. Still have to make a court appearance for it to be official, but that's it."

"I really am sorry about that."

"Not your fault, Lisa, all right? Don't do that. I made an emotional decision. Predicated on a lie, but it was still my decision. I understand." Frank held Lisa's hands as he spoke, sincerity dripping from his words. He truly understood her. He had cornered her, and she did whatever was necessary to free herself. "That is my bag. He was my friend." Frank looked off into the distance as his mind raced back to that day.

"What is it?" she asked.

"I am not sure, but he was calm when I got there, like he was expecting me or something."

"I didn't call him or anything."

Frank waved her off. "I am not saying that, but I think that perhaps there is something else he expected me to be angry about. He didn't even bother trying to defend himself."

"What do you mean?"

"I got the feeling that he was anticipating my rage. At the time, I thought he was being smug, but now I think there may be something else . . . some secret he's keeping from me."

"Interesting. From my vantage point, all roads lead back to the States."

"Indeed, my love," he said. "This time next week, we should be Texas bound."

CHAPTER 24

Straining to transform the funeral palette of colors into the shapes he knew they were, Micah focused his wandering eyes, ignoring the slight stinging sensation it caused. It was a gift to his irises left by the smoke that still smothered his nightmares. The morphine drip was nearing its end and death's dance rushed him, expanding his cranium, pummeling his chest, performing an un-choreographed number with the pieces left of his ribs.

The faint touch of burning gas decorated every breath he drew, completing his trifecta of torment. The nurse's button was not within reach. The morphine trip, a flight through space, a conglomerate of everything beautiful, would soon be over. Soon, he would be lost to the thing he had come to hate more than anything in his life, the inevitable pain awaiting him. He gripped the hard, white plastic railing of his hospital bed, failing to limit his movement, as the brittle bones' recital caused his body to convulse violently.

A short, plump, elderly woman walked into the room. Too deep into the recesses of his personal hell, Micah did not notice her. In less than a minute's time, she replaced his morphine bag with the one of the fresh pints she'd brought into the room with her.

"That simpleton never listens to a single thing I tell her. Good English is simply wasted on some people. That is the third time in two days. She is fortunate her father has deep pockets." She rested her hand on Micah's forearm, waiting for a visual cue that his pain had subsided. The writhing ceased within seconds as the liquid medicine cooled his veins, sending his pain into some far distant place. "Darling, are you okay? Hmm . . . does that feel better?"

Opening his eyes, Micah found Ms. Vida, the night charge, with her full head of misty white hair pulled back into a polite bun and cinnamon-brown eyes staring down at him from his bedside.

"Can you speak?" Prompted by his calm, she busied herself fluffing the pillow around his head and re-adjusting the thin hospital blanket. Micah, distracted by the sudden cloud of freshly picked strawberries, did not respond immediately.

"Are your ears functioning? Is your tongue swollen, preventing you from answering my question?"

Micah smirked, enjoying Ms. Vida's sarcastic humor. "Yes, ma'am. I feel much better."

"Well, good, I am relieved your lips still work," Ms. Vida joked while she stocked his cabinet with fresh blankets and sheets.

Puckering his lips and scrunching his nose, Micah inhaled, pretending to suck in an exaggerated amount of air. He purposely posed the question so that it came out more suggestive. "Did you put on some *special* fragrance for me, Ms. Vida?"

Not missing a beat, Ms. Vida, answered, "Darling, if you are trying to get an extra cheesecake or something, you need only ask. This little flirt thing you are trying is not a good use of your oral skills. As it is, I consider you more like a son than anything else. Furthermore, it is not necessary."

"Ms. Vida, I was merely commenting on how pleasant your perfume is."

"Darling, that is nothing but lotion. Ms. Vida does not wear perfume."

"Oh." Micah cleared his throat, feigning embarrassment. "It's really nice. Perfect for you. And you don't need any cheap perfume anyway," he stated, punctuating his sentence with a wink.

"Thank you, darling. As long as I do not smell like my garlic-loving mother, or those dreadful mothballs, I count it a victory. *But,* if I were to wear some perfume, it would not be anything cheap."

Micah burst into laughter again. "I think we all would count that as a win. Somehow, though, I think you could make us love that, too."

"Darling, if I did not know any better, I would think you were a little sweet on Ms. Vida."

"Better believe it. I must admit, though, those Mother Goose glasses took some getting used to."

"Excuse me, young man?"

Smiling, Micah continued, "I didn't even know they still made those. Where did you find them? Did Ms. Muffett have a garage sale?"

Pressing her palm against her bosom, Ms. Vida exclaimed in between bouts of laughter, "Mother Goose glasses? There is nothing wrong with my bifocals. These Mother Goose glasses keep me from mistaking your eye for an arm."

Micah laughed until tears streamed down his face. Ms. Vida had quite an effect on him. Her presence disarmed him and empowered him simultaneously. Her daily visits gave him something to look forward to, and she had yet to miss a day. She poured so much of her life into him that he couldn't help but love her. The medals she acquired from living glistened in the pictures she painted. Her Nina Simone tune seemed to put him at ease with her every utterance.

Ms. Vida reminded Micah of his fourth foster home. The lady of the house spoke plainly as she did, but that was where the parallel ended. That woman wielded her whit like a weapon, bringing many grown men to their knees, especially her husband; but he did not believe that Ms. Vida had the heart to be so cruel.

"I am only kidding with you, Ms. Vida."

"How is your pain level now, darling? On a scale of one to ten?"

"What pain?"

"That is what I like to hear," she stated, shaking her head, acknowledging the mistake that was made. "That never should have happened. I apologize about that. I should have checked your vitals and liquid levels myself. It will not happen again."

Struck by the sincerity in her eyes, Micah didn't doubt her words. He was not certain who had dropped the ball, but he was confident that Ms. Vida had nothing at all to do with it.

"Promises, promises," he joked. "Seriously, I don't blame you. You have been looking out for me ever since I arrived."

"That is my job, darling, *and* my pleasure."

"Not all of it."

She slowed her movement but did not stop.

"I appreciate what you did," he said.

Ms. Vida stopped working to peer into Micah as she spoke. He felt her eyes climbing into his mind, searching for a space to land. "Darling, you were scaling the slopes of eternity. That crash scrambled your brain, took out a few ribs, almost crushed your leg, punctured a lung, and I imagine it gave your soul a good lashing. I was not even certain about your ability to heed my words or comprehend enough to retain the information."

"But I did hear you, and I thank you for telling me. For talking to me."

"Prayer is a powerful tool. It was not my place to say anything, necessarily, but I thought you should know about the person in the accident with you. My mother kept raving about some horrible accident she saw on the news. The timing fit perfectly with yours, but they did not release any names. One night, you started screaming for a Rachel. I rushed in, but you were not coherent. That confirmed what I had suspected about that accident being yours, and I decided to tell you about her. It only seemed fair since you kept asking for her."

"I just wish I could remember what happened—or *her,* for that matter. I cannot remember anything."

"I know, but there is no need to stress yourself about it. You are lucky to be alive."

"I am not lucky; I'm blessed. I could have been stretched out on the highway. I'm in pain"—Pausing for effect, he then continued—"but at least I'm here."

"Darling, that is nothing but the truth. Thank God for that, and count your blessings."

"I do, with every breath." That was only a partial lie. Gratitude hit the nearest exit whenever the pain hit. He supposed he hadn't evolved to the point where he could appreciate it yet. "Did you reach Brianna, Ms. Vida?"

Ms. Vida smiled, grabbing the clipboard at the foot of his bed, giving it a quick once over.

"Ms. Vida? Did you reach Brianna? I know she must be worried about me."

"I did not want to tell you. It may not mean anything, but that number you gave me is no longer in service, chile."

"What? What do you mean? It could not have been that long ago when we last spoke."

"Micah, she has not looked for you. You have been in this hospital for nearly three weeks. That is ample time for her to have located you if she so desired."

"Ms. Vida, Brianna is . . . special. Our relationship is a very complicated, intense game of cat-and-mouse. She is probably waiting for me to find her, not thinking that something is wrong."

"After three weeks, Micah?"

"Each time we get close, she pulls away. She's terrified of what our being together would open her up to receive. I love her dearly, and she wants that, but the potential pain is too much for her to risk. She won't let me in completely. It would take some extremely traumatic event for that wall to come down."

"Like an accident that nearly sent you to the grave?"

"Probably. I just want to see her."

"Well, I'll see what I can do about finding her for you. Okay?"

"Thank you, Ms. Vida."

"Have you had your medication today?"

Micah weighed his options before answering. He really didn't want to take the medication. The nothingness he experienced once it took effect seemed worse than the symptoms of his condition to him. Besides, he had done fine all this time without that blasted medication and figured he didn't need it now, either. Still, Ms. Vida more than likely could see from the clipboard that he hadn't taken it today. There was no sense in lying to his favorite nurse.

"No, ma'am. I have not."

"I know. I did not see any notation for today. I swear that girl is good for absolutely nothing. I am going to send someone in here with them."

"Okay."

"You need to *take* the medicine, darling. Do not roll your eyes to dismiss my request, either. We all have a little bit of crazy in us, some more than others. Just be glad yours can be helped with some medicine. There is no hope for some folks."

"I know. I just hate the way it makes me feel."

"Feelings fluctuate. Emotions are not concrete. They are subject to change. Happy one minute and wanting to end it all the next. That is life, darling. With your situation, the natural shift is intensified and even more sensitive."

"That's the problem. I kinda don't *feel* anything but a numbness I can't shake."

Lightly patting the foot of his bed, Ms. Vida responded, "Darling, I will not pretend to know the details of who you are and how you came to be this way. However, I will share with you my opinion on the subject in question." Lowering her glasses, giving him greater access to her eyes, she continued. "There are different levels of crazy. Refusing to utilize every medical advantage available to you in regards to your health is the worst kind. The results are not favorable for the patient and devastating because it is one hundred percent preventable. Now, maybe you do not like the pills, and I sympathize with you. My diabetes got me swallowing cylinder blocks, too, and I do not care for it much myself. But those pills are putting distance between myself and that funeral plot I purchased when I got my diagnosis two years ago. I cannot make the choice for you, Micah. I cannot force you to choose to save your own life, you must decide to do that on your own."

"Ms. Vida . . ."

"Death is not prejudiced, Micah. This is serious. We have been back and forth all week about this medication.

We all have an expiration date, but some of us rot long before." Pointing her finger at him, she offered, "I don't know how you turned that Benz into a piece of scrap metal, but someone died, Micah. Records show you have been off your meds for a very long time. Maybe that had something to do with it, or maybe not. It is impossible to know for certain since you cannot recall the events leading up to the crash, but chances are it did. It was an accident, but that does not mean that it could not have been prevented. I do not believe in coincidence or bad luck. Some things are the result of bad decisions. Karma keeps an impeccable record."

Micah lifted his hand. "Ms. Vida, I was going to say that I'll take them. *For you*, I will take the meds. The speech wasn't really necessary."

"I will never know, and neither will you. Nothing is for nothing. Perhaps you had long ago decided to comply, but something I said may be of benefit to you some other time."

"Yes, ma'am."

"Besides, you could be deceiving me. Biblically, your name means 'the deceiver.'"

That took Micah by surprise. "That is interesting. Well, I'm not."

"Well, I hope that is true. I know that it does not seem fair, but fairness is irrelevant when it comes to living. The vital aspects of your life rest in your hands. The single most important thing is your ability to make a decision. From where I am standing, your choices have been questionable, but it is not too late to change."

"I won't lie to you, Ms. Vida, ever." He meant every word. He felt a connection to Ms. Vida that he had not felt with anyone. She made him feel safe, protected.

"I believe you, darling. Enough of that. I need to run before my other patients think I have abandoned them."

Micah scoffed, "You mean I'm not your only patient, Ms. Vida?"

"Now, you know better than that. Besides, you have a visitor."

CHAPTER 25

Micah peered around Ms. Vida's bubbly frame and into the hallway. The confusion in his eyes was evident. He had no idea who would be visiting him. Mike, maybe? Brianna was a long shot.

"I didn't hear anyone knock."

"Oh, I had him wait at the nurse's station."

Micah's eyes widened in shock. "All of this time, Ms. Vida? Why didn't you tell me when you first walked in?"

"Well, you were shaking and perspiring like fire ants had a tight grip of your coconuts. I got sidetracked a bit."

Micah shook his head. "But a lot of time passed, Ms. Vida. What if they left without seeing me? I have no idea who it could be."

"I doubt that. He did not seem like the type to leave without what he wanted."

"*He*? How so?"

"The fact that we are well beyond visiting hours and the hospital director contacted me personally, advising me to allow him in to see you. He must have done some Olympic-style maneuvering to get in here this late. Especially since he could have come tomorrow without any hoopla."

Micah's interest was extraordinarily piqued at the last comment. "What is his name?"

"Apparently, that information is above my paygrade, but his cufflinks had the initials *R.S.* on them. Does that mean anything to you?"

Micah could not think of anything offhand. "I don't think so."

"I will send him in—and remember to take your medication, Micah. I will be by later."

"Yes, ma'am."

Ms. Vida closed the door behind her and headed toward the nurse's desk.

Micah leaned back in the bed, closing his eyes, trying to conjure some idea of who the mystery man could be. He could not think of anyone with the credentials required to manage what Ms. Vida had suggested happened, but before his thoughts traveled too far, the door opened, and a deep tenor halted his trip.

"Micah Javan Harrison . . . or is it Harris now?"

Micah's eyes sprang open and settled on the man to whom the voice belonged. His face warmed as his emotions went into a frenzy.

"That was a typo on my insurance card."

How could he have known where he was? Micah had calculated this moment happening under very different circumstances. He was not prepared, and the thought angered him a bit. None of that mattered, he surmised, as an undeniable truth simmered around the tips of his trembling fingers.

Filling his lungs with a deep breath of the cold air of his hospital room, Micah focused on the nasty, sterile taste it left on his tongue to calm his nerves. If things went south, he could always hit the nurse's button and have him carted away. He could handle him. He could manage this.

"What are you doing here, Dad?"

Mr. Sterling smiled at his son. He removed his gloves, top hat, and dress coat, laying them neatly across the chair before taking his seat. "*Dad*? Humph. Isn't that the word that won you a residency in that boarding school?"

Micah's intestines tightened as his anxiety twisted them into knots. The moment to which his father was referring had hardened into his mind over the years; an innocent moment that changed his world. Years passed before he could speak the one syllable word again: *dad.* He had blamed himself for what happened, but not anymore. Looking at the man who fathered him sitting so smugly in the chair at the foot of his bed, he knew to whom the fault belonged.

"A girl called me asking about you one night. Had me wondering, thinking I may never see you again, but here we are." Richard grinned widely at his son.

Micah could have sworn he saw love in his eyes, but he knew his father was not capable of it. "What do you want?"

"I have come to take you home."

Ignoring his father's baseless statement, Micah posed his next question. "How did you know I was here?"

"That isn't important. Did you hear what I said? I am here to take you home."

Micah rolled his eyes. "It is important to me, and we both know that is not true."

"I suppose you are right about that. You made certain of that, didn't you, son?"

Micah remained silent for a moment. "How did you know?"

"Things were great for all of us, but you had to ruin it. Do you remember, son?"

Micah tried to keep the tears slowly blurring his vision from painting his cheeks. His face shook, the veins in his temple throbbed as they swelled, making themselves visible.

"Rushed into my office without knocking as was customary for you. How many times had I instructed you to knock? But you didn't, did you?"

"No."

"Correct, you did not. Rushed in there calling me. *Dad, Dad, Dad!* But I was not alone, Micah. My wife sat in there with me. She hated you as soon as she saw you, son. My twin, the son she could never give me. I couldn't have you or your mother around anymore. Elizabeth would have destroyed me. I had to make a difficult choice."

"And you chose your wife."

"I chose myself, Micah. I chose me. I always do."

Sniffling, Micah wiped the base of his nose with the back of his hand. "I was so excited that day." He laughed a little thinking about it. "My teacher added me to the team that would compete in the U.S. Chess Federation national championship. I raced in to tell you because I thought you'd be proud of me. He said that he thought I could be a grandmaster one day. It meant everything to me."

Richard did not respond for a few moments. He shifted in his seat in preparation for his rebuttal. "Yes, well, let's be serious, Micah. Your mother's half would have crippled you, preventing you from doing anything worthwhile. I always thought that, and your life has proved me correct."

Micah was inured to his father's callous disregard of his emotional well-being, so he steered the conversation in a direction favorable to him. Micah despised the man and hated how badly he desired to be loved by him. "What do you want, Dad?"

"I came to see about you."

"I am no concern of yours."

"Why would you say that? I love you, Micah . . . *in my way*."

Micah let his eyes drift up into his head, letting his father's words disappear into the air. "I wanted your love for a long time. Not anymore. As of right now, I don't want anything from you. I don't need your approval, your acceptance. I ruined my life trying to be like you."

"You were always so dramatic. Your being a screw-up has nothing to do with me. I fixed that little situation for you a while back with that girl. Did I even get a thank you? Who do you think stopped the investigation, Micah?"

Micah clenched and unclenched his fists in his lap, turning them in and out, admiring the change in color in his melanin. "Why are you here?"

"How did you fool these people into thinking you have some mental disorder? That is incredible. Mental disorders are nothing but excuses for people to throw their lives away, to be lazy, living off the government. Bipolar disorder. Ha! No such thing. Mental disorders are a farce!"

This rant was not new to Micah. He had heard it many times before. His father could not accept his mental disorder. It had first appeared while he was away at boarding school, and his father had refused to pay for treatment. His mother never contacted him, and weary of Richard's criticisms, Micah fled the school and ended up in the system. He traded in the real version of his mother for the one that lived in his dreams. That mother did not abandon him or let anyone take him away from her. No one came looking for him. No one but Mike.

"Go away."

"Listen, if you plan on storming into my house like that whore that birthed you, be prepared for what you'll find there."

Micah glared at Richard, his eyes blazing. "Get out!"

"Not until I am done! Save your words for someone that cares about them."

Micah seethed, his heart racing a mile a minute. Beads of sweat bonded together, streaming down his face, mixing with his tears.

"I don't know if this whole accident is a ruse to get your hands on my money or not, but it isn't going to work. You cannot extort me, son."

Micah gently bit the inside of his lip, squeezing his eyes closed to fight off his anger. He looked at the man whose eyes mirrored his own. "Noted. Message received, and you are free to get the fuck out of my room!"

Richard remained as a cool as the other side of the pillow, unfettered by Micah's explosion. "Fine. I am glad you understand. I am doing this for you, for all of us."

"Just get the hell out!"

Mr. Sterling grabbed his things and headed for the door. "I really do love you, son. One day, you'll understand why things need to be this way." With that, he closed the door behind him.

Micah did not bother wiping the tears from his eyes. He had exhausted himself devoting nearly all of his life trying to win his father's affection. Richard Sterling had made it painfully clear that he was incapable of being the father Micah deserved. Micah would have to look within himself and affirm his value, not to the man he once idolized. He didn't want or need validation from him anymore. Much like Ms. Vida had advised, his life was under his control.

It mattered not that his father had chosen to not be a part of it. That was his father's choice and had nothing to do with Micah. For the first time, Micah decided to concentrate on *Micah*. He had become the same selfish, manipulative bastard his father was, and it infuriated him. It was time for a brand-new Micah.

He eyed the nurse's aide as she walked in with the medication Ms. Vida promised to send and a little cup of water. "Thank you," he stated as he threw the pills into his mouth, flushing them down with the water.

Here's to the new me, he thought as the medicine made its way down his trachea. *Here's to the new Micah Javan Harris.*

CHAPTER 26

"Step onto the scale, please."

Brianna eased her bare feet onto the frigid metal of the scale.

"Thank you." Noting her current weight on his pad, Dr. Baxter motioned for her to stand against the wall. "This will only take a moment. I need to get an accurate height for you."

"Sure, no problem." Brianna skimmed the walls of the small corridor. Dr. Baxter shared the practice with three other doctors, but the suite was empty tonight. Brianna had requested that Dr. Baxter see her alone, and much to her surprise, he eagerly obliged. The space was decent as far as private medical facilities went. The waiting area housed the standard floral paintings and patterned seating. Nothing out of the ordinary.

"The bathroom is the last door on the left, there." Dr. Baxter pointed down the hall about three doors away from where they were standing. "I need to test your urine. Standard procedure. Just follow the instructions on the bottle and join me in examination room one."

"Is that where I changed earlier?"

"It's actually the room next to it. I need to give you a physical exam, and that room is a little bigger."

Brianna watched Dr. Baxter disappear around the corner into the nurse's area. Once alone, she began having second thoughts about the visit. Briefly staring at the glowing EXIT sign at the opposite end of the hall, she considered ditching Dr. Baxter. Perhaps she had not yet passed the point of no return, where it would be unconscionable even for her to recuse herself, but the thought left her as soon as it came. Dr. Baxter had inconvenienced himself at her behest, and as much as it pained her, she needed to follow through, despite the probability of her finding his news unfavorable. Not knowing would only bolster a false reality, and there was no real comfort to be had living that way.

Locating the bathroom with ease, Brianna spotted the cup sitting on a silver tray on top of a straw hamper as soon as she walked in. It had all sorts of feminine hygiene products on display: travel size lotions, soaps, sanitary napkins, single tampons, and three or four different types of air freshener. Brianna bypassed the assortment of toiletries and grabbed one of the cups. The instructions were simple enough: pee in the cup, close the lid. As if on cue, her bladder did the two-step. Pulling her pants down, Brianna snatched a mini package of cleansing wipes and straddled the toilet seat. She wiped her vaginal area with the antibacterial wipes, trying to avoid an accident before she had the stupid plastic cup in place. *Damn it!* The task, a complicated dance between balance and aim, proved to be much more difficult than Brianna remembered. The teasingly wide-rimmed cup magically shrank in size, forcing her to bust out an original yoga move to get the job done. *Shit.*

"That was harder than it needed to be."

Brianna cleaned herself up, locked and labeled the cup, and shuffled back down the hall to Exam Room 1 where Dr. Baxter was waiting.

"All done?"

The question was absurd. Of course she was done. Why else would she be there? Brianna nodded in confirmation.

"Good. I'll go run the tests on that in a minute, but before we get to that." Noticing Brianna was still standing in the door, Dr. Baxter pointed her toward the examination table near the center of the room. Once she was seated, he continued. "Before I go do that, I wanted to be sure that I have a clear picture of your symptoms."

"I have been nauseous, lethargic. Appetite is all over the place, but Dr. Shepherd said that those things are normal considering what happened."

"That is probable, but we can run a few tests to rule out anything else." Dr. Baxter, who had been resting against the counter, made his way toward Brianna. Grabbing the blood pressure pump, he wrapped it around Brianna's arm to check her levels.

She squirmed uncomfortably as the suction on her arm increased. Javan ran across her mind, nearly sending her crashing to the floor. Dr. Baxter caught her before she slid completely off.

"Brianna? Are you okay?" he asked, concern etched on his face.

Brianna felt uneasy, felt her heart beating erratically. "I'm sorry. I'm not sure what happened. I don't . . . I'm sorry."

Dr. Baxter carefully pushed her back onto the examination table, removed the cuff, and sat in front her. Using his foot to pull the rolling stool closer to him, Dr. Baxter took a seat on it. The stool was no more than a foot or so off the ground. Brianna's elevated position gave her comfort for some reason. She felt her body relaxing again as she looked down at him, waiting for him to speak.

"How are you feeling, Brianna?"

"I'm okay. Honestly. I don't know what happened."

Dr. Baxter squeezed his eyes closed, opened them, and forced a smile. He knew she was lying; the truth was in her eyes.

"I think you do know and you don't want to tell me. If you aren't honest with me, I can't really help you."

Brianna tried to resist sharing herself, but something in the oval rim of his eye compelled her to spill her tea. Something stronger, deeper than her fear of what may come, coaxed her into creating a divide in her wall wide enough to let him in, urging her to trust him.

"Javan."

Dr. Baxter nodded. "Feared that might be the case. I trust Dr. Shepherd's work and her process. I admit that I'd hoped you'd be further along. I have no gauge, really, since I didn't know you before, but you don't seem like yourself, if I may."

Brianna remained silent.

"I'm worried over the physical nature of what needed to be done tonight. Though I hope you know I'd never hurt you in any way, I am still a man. We are alone here, and I don't want to undo any of the progress you've made."

"I am fine, really. It was just a second. Happens sometimes," Brianna stated, shrugging her shoulders. "Provocateur isn't a determinant or necessary."

"I'm sorry, Brianna. I don't want to ever make you uncomfortable. Let me know if something is too much. Okay?"

"Sure."

"Do you have anything you want to talk to me about? I am your doctor, but I like to think we are a bit more. I think there was a reason I found you that night."

Brianna was not sure of how to take his statement, but the thought of anything sexual happening between them made her even more nauseous than she already was. There had to be some rule against doctors getting romantically involved with their patients, wasn't there? Wasn't that what the Hippocratic Oath was for? Wait . . . no, that was for saving patients, not *fucking them*.

Interrupting her thoughts, Dr. Baxter temporarily derailed her suspicions. "I am going to go ahead and run the tests on your urine. I won't be long. The TV is not functional, I'm afraid."

Brianna followed his eyes to the flat screen hanging on the wall to the right behind her, wondering why she hadn't noticed it before.

"We are switching service providers, so unfortunately we have thirty channels, and they are all variations of static. Not that entertaining."

Brianna laughed at his attempt at a joke. Regardless of whatever weird vibe he was giving her, one thing she could attest to was his pleasant personality. She could see why he was so popular. People want to be treated, but being personable can take you places an excellent skill set alone cannot. Dr. Baxter came off like a really sweet man.

"I'll be fine."

"Great." Dr. Baxter stood so quickly the stool rolled away from him. Paying it no mind, he turned and exited the room.

Brianna casually let her eyes rove around the room. Her urge to inspect her surroundings lasted all of thirty seconds. She scooted up toward the crest of the table until she felt she might be able to lay comfortably. Lying on her left side, giving her visual access to the doorway, she tried to rest. Less than two minutes passed before Michelle crept back into her mind. Brianna did not want to think about Michelle; that situation was such a mess.

It had been nearly a week, and Michelle still would not accept her calls. God created the universe in seven days, so surely that was enough time for Michelle to calm down. Brianna was not entirely sure what she would say to her, but that shouldn't matter. They were twins, and that should count for something. What did Michelle expect her to do?

On a lighter note, she noted that she had not felt like she was being stalked as of late. Maybe the sessions were actually working and the paranoia was subsiding a bit. Then again, she had not heard from Sophie lately, either. Maybe that helped, too. Sighing, she hated that this system of inaccurate guesses had become her life. Fighting the sadness tempting her tears to flow, she answered the question she dreaded asking.

"Yes, Brianna, you will get back to yourself. You'll get there." *Hopefully within this century.*

Knocking lightly on the door, Dr. Baxter drew her eyes to him before entering into the room. "I didn't want to startle you."

"Oh, thanks. We know what happened last time you surprised me."

Dr. Baxter laughed, holding his hands, pretending to protect himself. "I think I am still *feeling* that one." Brianna sat up on the table. "Actually, if you wouldn't mind lying on your back for me, please, I want to examine your torso."

Brianna did as he asked, resting on her back, giving Dr. Baxter access to her stomach. Dr. Baxter walked beside her, blocking her view of the useless television. "Forgive me. My hands might be a little cold."

That was the understatement of the year. His hands felt like sticks of ice against her skin. She couldn't suppress the squeals that slipped from her as she concentrated on her best statue imitation while he pressed his fingers into her six-pack's last resting place.

"Humph." Pausing, Dr. Baxter leaned in to get a closer look at her side, and Brianna had a good idea of what he was looking at.

"What is it?"

"It looks like an angel or butterfly maybe? Did you try and get a tattoo removed or something?"

Her birthmark had gotten his attention. She was not surprised. It was pretty unique, and the few that had seen it all had the same reaction. "That's my birthmark."

"Really?" The energy in the room shifted dramatically, and the change made Brianna very uncomfortable.

"Yes, it is. Not typical, I guess." Brianna watched an emotion take shape in his face that she couldn't label. His mouth hung open a bit, forcing him to take a big gulp of nothing. Dr. Baxter was not breathing, and Brianna could see the color draining from his face.

"Dr. Baxter, are *you* okay?" She gave him a slight nudge, trying to pull him back from wherever he was. "Dr. Baxter." The movement jarred his thoughts loose.

"Yes, I am sorry. That is very . . . umm . . . interesting. Not a very common tattoo." His voice trailed off as he spoke, and Brianna excused his error. He was obviously distracted.

"*Right*, did you find anything?"

With her question, Dr. Baxter walked to the counter and grabbed the paperwork from the urine test he had performed.

"You are awfully quiet, Dr. Baxter." Brianna sat uneasily on the examination table, swinging her legs back and forth, watching Dr. Baxter review her chart.

"Excuse me?" He briefly made eye contact with her before returning his full attention to the tablet in his hand. Hospitals and doctor's offices alike were converting their systems to the web service that would house all current and future patient medical records. It was part of a green initiative to promote both the patient's health and the environment. Brianna did not have extensive medical history and could not imagine what had rattled Dr. Baxter.

"This visit turned a corner, and I would like to go back. This street is awkward."

Placing the tablet in his lap, Dr. Baxter cracked a smile and met her gaze. She had only seen Dr. Baxter once since that night at Javan's, but they had spoken over the phone on several occasions since then. Dr. Baxter, like Armand, made himself available to her if she needed to unload, but she didn't feel comfortable disclosing too much to him. Despite all the good he had done for her, he was still a stranger.

"I apologize, Brianna. This is not like myself, I admit." Clearing his throat, Dr. Baxter stood and walked to the sink behind him. After carefully placing the tablet on the counter, he turned back around to speak with Brianna. Leaning casually against the counter's edge, arms folded and legs crossed, he sucked his bottom lip pensively.

Brianna's heart sped up a bit. A few weeks of nausea had prompted this visit, but she hadn't expected anything serious. What could it be? She had no other symptoms. Squinting her eyes, Brianna looked quizzically at Dr. Baxter.

"What's wrong? I figured I just had a little stomach bug or something. It's just nausea, right?"

Shifting positions, Dr. Baxter lightly tapped his hands on the counter. "Brianna how long have you been feeling this nausea?"

"I am not sure, really. That incident changed everything for me. Nothing felt like it did before. Nothing functioned quite the same. I guess a month maybe."

Dr. Baxter took a deep breath, closed his eyes, and took a seat on the stool. Offering Brianna a reassuring look, he rolled to the examination table where she sat.

Brianna fought the urge to flee the space before he could fill it with whatever he had to say. Nothing about this felt right. She did not know if she could handle any more bad news. What kind of fatal illness starts with nausea? That's just what she needed—a disease that would kill her.

Dr. Baxter grabbed a hold of her shaking hands. "Brianna, this news may or may not be favorable."

Now she was really confused. What news could be good or bad?

"I am here, and I will be here in any capacity you see fit. You are not alone here."

She appreciated the kind words, but she wished he would just come out with it.

"Nausea, exhaustion, fluctuating appetite, and hormonal . . ."

Brianna could see the writing on the wall but hoped he was not going to say what she feared he would.

"You're pregnant, Brianna."

Brianna began shaking her head in laughter. "No, this is not happening. I cannot believe this. Wow. I just . . ."

Dr. Baxter waited patiently for Brianna to process the news. "I know this is a lot and may come as a shock. We can take a break before proceeding if you'd like."

"I don't need a break."

"Are you sure?" Dr. Baxter asked, wiping tears from her eyes with the palm of his hand.

Brianna shook her head, pushing his arm away from her face. "I'm sure." Brianna did not like the physical affection or the dreamy look she saw in his eyes. He was crossing every line in the book, and she was beyond uncomfortable. "Do it before I lose my nerve."

Dr. Baxter launched himself from the stool, washed his hands, and stood on the side of Brianna where the ultrasound equipment was. She laid down again, trying to prepare her speech for Armand, thinking that Michelle would likely never speak to her again.

How could this happen?

Dr. Baxter rolled her shirt up, exposing the stuffed carry-on that housed most of her internal organs. Applying the warm gel in a circular motion, he wasted no time running the smooth, round surface of the fetal monitor across her stomach.

She stared wide-eyed at the monitor, still in disbelief that the moment was even occurring. Dr. Baxter looked on, made notes, took pictures, arbitrarily identifying parts of the fetus he could easily determine, but Brianna did not hear him. Her mind was running in a thousand directions. She could not believe this was what her life had come to. Sixty hard fought days ago, her life was everything she had designed it to be. The long nights at school and the *fun* she had sacrificed to ensure that she could set herself up for success were paying dividends. Though her father would gladly bankroll her lifestyle, self-sufficiency was important to her. People assumed that she worked for nothing, and so she had worked hard for everything. She refused to embrace the notion of being a pampered princess, even if it were true to some degree. She wanted to be valued for more than her finances; more for the things she accomplished.

She had a bourgeoning career, decent personal life, and, perhaps most importantly, she had herself. She knew who Brianna was, and she loved her. Who was she now? Somebody's baby momma? Was she the girl that fucked her sister's fiancé? Shamefully dependent on others to color her life.

Dr. Baxter finished, passed her a towel to wipe her abdomen clean, and then proceeded to put his equipment away in silence. "Brianna, you are roughly seven weeks, possibly more."

"Excuse me?"

"Do you know who . . . fathered your child?

Brianna curled into a little ball as the math added up to her very worst fear. This was even worse than she thought initially. Tears streamed from her eyes as her reality swallowed her up whole. She didn't want it to be true, but she knew it had to be.

"Javan's. The baby is Javan's."

CHAPTER 27

Boom, boom, boom!

The sound traveled through the large wooden front door, echoing off the walls of her home. Sophie was just down the hall, sitting in the den, nursing her second vodka tonic when the noise interrupted the quiet quell of her buzz.

Boom, boom, boom!

She placed her drink on the stand and slowly rose to her feet.

Boom, boom, boom!

She took her time walking to the door. She was not expecting company, and anyone she cared to see had a key to let themselves in.

Boom, boom, boom!

"I am coming!" Pausing in the door frame to gather herself, Sophie made the right toward the door.

Boom, boom, boom!

"Why are you knocking on my door that way?" she bellowed, fiddling with the locks, trying to get it open.

Boom!

"Stop! I am here. I . . . am . . . here."

Sophie stared at the Seymore Krelborn imitation standing in her doorway. "What can I do for you?"

"Are you Sophie Lucille Lewis?"

"Who's asking?"

Suddenly "Seymore" shoved the manila envelope he held in his hands into Sophie's chest, causing her to stumble backward into the house. Then the *Little Shop of Horrors* understudy told her, "You have been served. Evening." With that, he turned and walked brusquely out of the drive. Though she thought it strange that he didn't have a vehicle, it did explain his ability to remain innocuous before those obnoxious knocks.

Now, with the envelope firmly in hand, Sophie closed the door and ambled back into the den. Taking her seat, she grudgingly opened the package. Much to her dismay, her lawyer had finally gotten something correct. As she read the notice, dread inched its way through her veins, clotting them, filling her with an uneasiness she hadn't felt in a long time.

This was not possible. No one knew the situation, but, more importantly, no one, at least, that she was aware of, had the authority to do something like this. The funeral was over, and she waited long enough, a respectable amount of time to move on to the next phase: cremation. She had not shared her plans with anyone. Clearly, someone knew, and that *someone* had hired a lawyer, involving the courts. This stupid little piece of paper could undo everything.

Her life's reflection was not at all what she had envisioned. She thought she had been careful, planned meticulously. It was flawless. But her plan was now in shambles, and this notice was proof. Michelle was still not speaking with her and, oddly, neither was Brianna. She was even powerless to ease the tension between herself and the one person who wanted to be there for her—Peter. Her nerves were raw with everything going on, and this amplified it all. Sophie did not make these types of mistakes. She rarely made an uncalculated decision to avoid ever feeling like this. Steven Sheffeld, her less-than-inept lawyer, had contacted her earlier to prepare her for this moment. He used some legal jargon to comfort her; she chose to self-medicate with a couple of vodka tonics. Neither approach helped much, but the latter felt better.

Sophie grabbed the cordless, walked to the window, and after several failed tries, managed to dial her lawyer.

"Steeeevvveeennnnn . . ." Her words slurred far more than the drinks would encourage. The slur actually confused her. Her buzz didn't feel that heavy.

"Sophie?"

"Steven, I received the paperwork. I don't want it," she stated very matter-of-factly.

"Don't worry about this. I'm taking care of it."

"Steven, I *neeeeed* this to go *away*. Time to move on. My girls are ready to move forward and this—"

"This is just a little stumbling block," Steven interjected.

Snatching the phone from her ear, Sophie stared at it in disbelief, like Steven could see her. "A *little* stumbling block? This is the . . . Mauna Kea of stumbling blocks! Find some legal, important, legal precedent thingy that overrides this ugly paper!" Sophie screamed, shaking the paper emphatically in her hand. "Twenty-three years I sucked his dick . . . *and* it was nasty, *sometimes*. I didn't always like it, Steven!"

"Sophie, please . . ."

"I didn't, and I cooked every night, all of the nights, and in exchange, he gave me all of the diseases," Sophie spewed, laughing at how truly pathetic her existence had been. "That bastard."

"Sophie, please, stop."

The setting sun filled the horizon with beautiful layers or orange, violet, and lemon. Sophie admired the view a bit before pulling the curtain closed until only a small slit remained open to the impending night. Thinking of the sun setting, the sky appeared inflamed, triggering Sophie to issue more orders to Steven.

"Tell them that! I want to burn him!"

"Sophie, you don't mean that."

A soft voice whispered for her to shut up, harping on the inevitably of her saying something she'd later regret, but she couldn't stop. Her words leapt from her mouth like vomit.

"Why not? He can't feel it, Steven! He's dead! *Dead, dead, dead.*" Her voice trailed off as her thoughts landed in the base of her empty glass. Her emotional pendulum swung from sadness to hurt as her buzz subsided.

"I am working on taking care of this for you, Sophie," Steven stated again.

"Steven, now we both know you're *working* on something, but that's not it."

"I understand your frustration, Sophie, but there is no—"

"Oh, *shut up!*" Sophie shouted. Steven did not respond. "Just stop talking. Give your lips a rest. Save your factory-made empathy." Sophie blew air in complete frustration. Having this conversation sober was making her ill. She didn't want to utter another word to him.

"I am your lawyer. I am on your side. Perhaps I can't understand exactly what you're feeling, but I need time to work."

"Well, Steven, no one can accuse you of being an over-achiever, that's for sure."

"There is no need to be ugly, Sophie. I am doing everything I can."

"It *is not* enough. I am on the brink of losing my family! Everybody is gone! I will never get them back if you don't fix this!"

Steven was too green for this job. Sophie should have known better, but her friend at the coroner's office had suggested him. It was a lesson for her: never take advice of people who spend the majority of their time with the deceased.

"If you had told me about the provision, I could have prepared a case for it ahead of time."

Sophie headed toward the mini bar. She needed another drink to finish this conversation. "It isn't a *provision*." *Fucking dumbass.* "Lewis, apparently, gave this pain-in-my-ass lawyer power of attorney over his remains. Information that I was not privy to. *That* is strange in and of itself. I never gave him a reason not to . . . *trust me*."

Steven picked up on the hesitation in her voice and jumped at the opening. "What crossed your mind?"

Sophie thought about the pictures she had received from an anonymous *friend*. She recalled how Lewis had refused to believe her when she told him that she didn't know where they came from. She rolled her eyes, realizing that *that* was probably why he had made the change.

"Sophie? Is there something you need to tell me?"

"Nope." Opening the cabinet, she selected a bottle of Brandy. "Nothing at all."

"I see."

"Did you see this coming?"

"No, I did not. But *that* is what I pay you to do, Steven! To foresee this type of situation. I trusted you, Steven. I trusted that everything was in order."

"I know, and I will fix it."

"Stevie Wonder could have seen this!" Slamming the bottle on the bar, she scooped a few cubes of ice from the ice tray and threw them into her glass. Snatching the top off the bottle, she filled the glass. "What is your plan, little Stevie?" Sophie brought the glass to her lips, inhaling the sweet liquor, before emptying the glass down her throat. "What do you plan to do?"

"It has only been a few hours, Sophie. I am working on a way to get around this, but the power of attorney seems pretty iron-clad."

Sophie quickly poured herself another drink. Then another. This could not be happening. How could a fictitious burial be easier to pull off than a cremation? She had no problems arranging the funeral and did not expect any for this last leg of her run. She was not even sure how the lawyer had found out. The coroner was the only person who had knowledge of her intention, and she doubted he would say anything. It was his brainchild.

"Find something."

"Why not just leave him buried?"

"I value my life, Steven. I *value* my life." Slamming the phone down, Sophie guzzled the fourth glass of bourbon, sixth drink of the evening. Feeling the burn of the bourbon as it escaped her mouth, coating her trachea and disappearing into the part of herself that needed to breathe, Sophie traipsed back over to the window. Veering out the slit into the absence of day, Sophie took a mental picture of the peace she saw there, secretly wishing she could have some it for herself.

"Richard, I guess you were right. I can't have it all." Sophie swung around, feeling the effects of the alcohol, nearly falling to the ground. She shook her head, denying the tears that wanted to join her pity party. She was in no crying mood.

Deciding to drag herself to bed, Sophie parted the curtain for one last look. Fear seized her nervous system, paralyzing her for a second, trapped by an impossible reality as she found herself staring into the eyes of Leonard Lewis.

Logic told her that it could not be real; her own memory of that fateful day prickled her mind, substantiating that truth. But she had to deal with what was in front of her, literally. A dead Leonard Lewis leered at her from the outside. His eyes were like embers in a fireplace, burning a hole into her soul, stripping her of all her sensibility, leaving her naked and afraid.

She must have indulged a little too much in the alcohol. It was the only reasonable explanation. She had seen him before, but not like this, not this close or for this long. *This must be a hallucination*. Confusion swept over her as the bourbon sent her further into the clouds, while fear forced her back down. The internal war raged on while those eyes held hers captive. She was projecting, she convinced herself, and that was why she couldn't move. Her *mind* kept her there.

As soon as the thought occurred, she felt free to move again, and satisfied with her pathology, no longer felt the urge to run. She chided herself for drinking so much and smiled faintly at the reflection, knowing that he was merely a figment of her overly concerned conscience. Nothing changed, and so she smiled again. Then he returned her smile—an awkward, crooked, *knowing* smile.

Sophie screamed so loudly that she unwittingly initiated her own movement. With either foot sprinting in two different directions, Sophie plummeted to the ground. She began crawling as fast as she could toward the hallway, mentally moving at the speed of light. In reality, Sophie could still feel the weight of his stare. Too afraid to look back, still holding the drink in her hand, she scooted on her belly toward the door.

The door was a lot farther away than she remembered. She gathered her courage and glanced back. Lewis waved with the tips of his fingers.

Oh, hell no! She tried to stand but kept falling all over herself, stumbling, crawling, skipping, and rolling toward a doorway she couldn't seem to reach.

"Luce?"

Hurling her glass in the direction of the voice, Sophie covered her head with her hands, lying with her face buried in the carpet.

Crash!

The glass shattered into pieces as it hit the wall, missing Peter by inches.

Peter ducked, crouching low in the doorway, and spoke in a loud whisper. "Luce? What is going on?"

"Peter!" Lifting her head from the carpet, she tried to focus enough to make a positive identification.

"Did you throw a glass at me?" Peter stood, staring at Sophie as she lay sprawled out in the middle of the floor.

"No . . . yes, I didn't know it was you." Slowly unlocking her body, Sophie stretched her limbs as far as she could to release the tension.

"What are you doing? Are you okay? I heard you screaming, so I used the spare."

Moving herself into a sitting position, Sophie's head felt heavy. Her attempt to find balance made her resemble a bobble head doll. The constant movement only served to increase her dizziness. She quit and resigned to lay down, back against the carpet, ceasing all movement.

"The devil is at the window," she uttered very calmly.

Peter walked cautiously into the room, elevating his body a bit while he looked out the window. "Luce, I don't see anything."

Sophie was adamant. "He issss . . . out . . . there."

"There is nothing but the night out there." Peter joined her on the floor. "Was it your husband again?"

"Mm-hmm," Sophie mumbled, unable to speak, ensnared on the merry-go-round moving at hyper speed, created by her mixing liquors coupled with overall consumption. That was such a rookie move.

"You should see a doctor or something, Luce. That is not healthy."

She shook her head to contest, or at least she hoped she did. Everything moved in slow motion as her adrenaline lost its zeal and the liquor mixed in her abdomen. The night turned into a black hole as her cognitive functions ceased. The perfect ending to her less than stellar day. Tears were coming. She felt the sobs swelling in her chest like ash clouds over a volcano. The temperature in the room dropped without notice. The floor felt like a bed of feathers lined with concrete. Everything hurt, even inhaling. She didn't want to take a breath.

"Hold on, Luce." Peter departed the room, leaving her to contemplate his words in his absence.

What did he mean, hold on? Hold on to what? That was exactly what she was trying to do, *hold on*. Her sanity was slipping away, and the only true cure could cost her everything she loved. So, what did Peter want her to hold on to, she wondered. To him? Would he leave her if he knew the truth? If he knew who she really was?

"Okay, here you go." He lifted the circular rock hiding behind the flesh of her face, sliding her pillow underneath it. She recognized the scent of her strawberry shampoo; it was nauseating.

Peter. This pillow stinks. She opened her mouth to speak, but nothing came out. Screw it. She didn't realize how badly she was shaking until she felt his arm draped over her. She was in the midst of a personal spin cycle, but Peter held her firm. Her bones felt like ice; she was so cold. Then, like an answer to her prayer, Peter draped a blanket over them. Between the blanket and the warmth of his body, Sophie started to feel a bit better.

"It's okay, Luce. Calm down. It's okay."

I'm not crazy, she thought to herself, cursing her conscience for tormenting her with the ghost of husbands past. She felt herself being lured into dreamland. *Wait, what was Peter even doing here in the first place?* It was a question she'd have to ask later. She was already a few stages into a deep, alcohol-driven, coma type of sleep. Sophie needed to rest her mind, recuperate. Tomorrow would be the start of a new day.

CHAPTER 28

"I can't undo the shit I did."

"Damn right."

"But you know me, Jacob."

Jacob scoffed but did not respond.

"J, if I could walk that back—"

"Keep that shit, Frank."

"You're pissed. I get it, but damn."

"Bullshit. Did you forget who you're talking to? I know you!"

"Then you should know that I'd do anything to defend my fuckin' family! Anything! No one is safe, J. Not you. No one."

"Defend them from who, Frank? Me? Me, Frank? Huh? I threatened your family? When did that shit go down?"

"Jacob, I . . ." Frank scammed his mind for a viable excuse, anything but the truth. There was no need to bring Lisa into this mess. "I fucked up, all right? I fucked up."

"We were family, Frank. Before that bitch fucked your mind up. I knew you when you were shopping for a degree at NYU. Back when your dad issued a weekly and your brother stiffed you for more than half. I shared my grub to keep you from starving when you blew the rest flossing, trying not to be the piece of shit you were. I considered you my brother. And you came into my office throwing jabs. Didn't care about what I may have had to say about the shit."

Frank took a deep, calming breath. He didn't need to get into a pissing match with Jacob about who had been the better friend. "J, look, man. I was wrong."

"Whatever you needed, I handled for you. No questions asked."

Frank muted himself, deciding to let Jacob get it all out.

"All the shit I did for you, and you just rush me in my spot? No conversation. No explanation. Nothing."

Frank stood on the balcony, leaning against its frame, enjoying the view for the last time. Both he and Lisa had been released from the hospital and were preparing to return home. The plane would not leave for several hours, and as much as he would have preferred to have this conversation in person, this phone call could not wait.

"That wasn't me, man. Something came over me and I snapped. I lost it."

"You spat in my fuckin' face, Frank! Shitted on me, man."

"I blacked out." Dropping his head, Frank steadied his gaze on the peeling paint of the balcony beneath his feet. "My mind was gone. I wasn't thinking."

"Tuh, you never do. Always doing shit without considering the outcome. Judging everyone around you like your shit ain't equally, if not more, fucked. Took weeks for me to even process what happened."

Frank was remorseful, but he didn't know how many more verbal blows he could withstand. He knew he was dangerously close to his limit. "Look, man, I hear you, but I didn't call for this. I got enough going on right now."

"You are a piece of fuckin' work. What did you expect, Frank? Want to just chop it up like old times?"

"I wanted to apologize. I know what I did was fucked. No excuses for it." Frank took a big whiff of the island breeze. Someone had a nice fade working nearby. "I don't expect things to go back to NYU, but maybe something like that."

"You are a selfish, arrogant bastard."

"I'll take that."

Jacob let loose a hearty laugh. Frank knew Jacob well enough to know that his laughing was not an indication that he found anything humorous.

"Huge fucking balls. Are you serious? I haven't talked to you in damn near two months."

"Jacob, you know I couldn't reach out to you with the charge, but I checked in on you."

"Fuck you, man. Fuck you."

Momentarily giving into the frustration flirting near the tip of his patience, Frank barked. "Dropping the charges, lobbying the judge, and getting the case thrown out meant what?"

"It meant that I am still cleaning up your fucking messes. It means that despite the fact that you beat me into a fucking coma, I still don't want to see nothing happen to your ignorant, stubborn, selfish, pompous ass."

"Jacob."

"Nah, fuck you. Fuck you and that inflated, worthless-ass ego. You ain't shit, Frank."

"If it's like that, let's just cut this shit short then."

"Not before I get this shit off my chest."

"Talk to that reflection in the mirror. I'm done with this. I called to apologize, and you ain't did shit but drag my ass."

"You broke bones in my muthafuckin' face, son! Three ribs! Fuck what you called to say! The least you can do is listen."

"Fuck that shit. You said enough."

"You could be sittin' in jail right now, Frank. Jail."

Frank seethed, heat radiating throughout his body. Jacob was right and he knew it, but he didn't care at the moment. He didn't want to spend one more minute listening to Jacob attack his character.

"What in the fuck do you want from me? Gotdamn. I have apologized."

"Nothing. I don't want shit from you."

"If you are so pissed about it, why play Mr. Fix it?"

"Cuz that's what I do. I fix shit. Even for society's least deserving."

Filling his lungs with the coping mechanism wafting through the air, choking on its potency, Frank swallowed his infant pride. "Thank you, Jacob. For everything."

Jacob was silent a moment before he spoke. "I ain't accepting that shit from you."

Frank shook his head. "Look, I can't lie. That shit hurts to hear, but I understand."

"Maybe one day. I just don't know. That shit is damn near unforgivable."

"Why did you really help me?"

"Brianna."

His shoulders dropped as his muscles began the process of releasing the tension, hardening his heart. "Oh, I see."

"She adores you, and despite everything that transpired between us, *I* don't want to be the thing that takes you away from her."

Frank's heart sank. He had not spoken with his daughter in several weeks. She wanted nothing to do with him, and he had no one but himself to blame. "I appreciate that. She deserves a better man than me. Always has."

"I still think you're a piece of shit, but Brianna could do worse."

Frank chuckled. "I don't know about that, but I appreciate it. Thanks for reaching out to the lawyer up north, too. He straightened everything out here."

"I didn't contact him."

"So, who did?"

"Griffin."

"You called my brother, J?"

"Chill. Yeah, I hit your brother. I don't know of anyone more connected than he is. You needed more help than I could give you. I didn't have a choice."

"I'm good. Thank you for persuading him to make a few phone calls for me."

"I only asked. Didn't need any convincing. You need to call him. He is your brother."

"Nah, I'm straight. He disowned me, not the other way around."

"That was a long fuckin' time ago, and he came through for you, Frank. Doesn't that warrant something from you?"

"Stop pushing this reunion shit. He is not who you think he is."

"Yeah, all right. Coming this way solo or what?"

That question brought a smile to his face. "Lisa and I are coming back, *together.*"

"No shit?"

Despite the conversation's murky beginning, Frank relished talking to his friend. He hadn't realized how much he needed to talk to someone. "I know. I know. She is doing much better. Still sore, but the doctors are pleased enough with her progress to let her fly."

"That is good news. Great news." His relief rang in his voice. "So, what happened?"

"Still tryin' to figure that out."

"Was she shot or stabbed?"

"Someone pushed a knife into her chest. Tried to take her from me, man."

"Damn . . . you're having a rough stretch here."

Frank felt a pang in his stomach. "Lisa has had it far worse than me."

"Can't argue with that. Any prospects?"

"A few." Having knowledge of Jacob's relationship with Charlie, Frank opted to keep his suspicion to himself.

"It's not Charlie."

Frank smiled. Leave it to Jacob to cut through. "I don't know that."

"I do. I know her. She's a little loose, but attempted murder? Too far."

"She called minutes before. Timing is perfect. The whole setup. I took her call in another room. She warns me about Lisa, and I run out to find Lisa . . . laid out."

"I don't know about that, but I don't think she got this in her. She might hate your ass, but she wouldn't hurt Lisa."

"I'll find out."

"Well, let me know if I can help."

"Thanks."

"Where is Bria?"

Frank's stomach twisted into a knot at the mention of her name. "Dallas. She didn't make the trip. Have you tried calling her? I'm sure she'd love to hear from you."

"I tried, but her number is disconnected. Does she have a new one?"

Frank swallowed the lump in his throat. "Damn, I had it, but you know it was in my cell, and it got lost in all the commotion over here."

"You don't know it by heart?"

The surprise in Jacob's voice served as a tacit reminder of the closeness he once enjoyed with his daughter, forcing

Frank to deal with Brianna's decision to exclude him. Brianna was his world, but his actions had severed her faith in him. She no longer wanted anything to do with him, and as reality sank in, the impact of the loss overwhelmed him. He had been so preoccupied with Lisa that he hadn't even had time to try calling Brianna in the last few weeks.

He had no idea she had changed her number. For the first time in twenty-four years, Frank had no way to contact his only child; no clue as to her whereabouts, activity, or who she was with. It was a fact that broke him down so swiftly that his legs wobbled beneath him.

Frank chortled uncomfortably. "Come on, man, no one remembers numbers anymore."

"That shit don't even make sense. This isn't like you or her, frankly. What's going on?"

Frank attempted to speed through this line of questioning. "Nothing I can fix from here."

"Is she all right?"

"Honestly, I don't know, man. Like I said, there is not a damn thing I can do from here."

"When are you coming Stateside?"

"Soon. We have to stop through New York first, but—"

"You fuckin' kiddin me?"

Frank rolled his eyes, seeing where this was circling back to.

"New York, and you won't see your brother? Even after he freed your ass?" Jacob asked.

"That was the plan. Not interested in seeing him."

"Fuckin' joke, man."

Frank was ready to end this call, especially with the love fest Jacob was putting up with regard to his brother. "Jacob, leave the shit alone. You don't know him."

"What in the fuck are you talkin' about, Frank? He was tight with your cash. You were irresponsible as shit! I can't blame him!"

Frank shook his head, disgusted and frustrated. His brother was a fucking monster, and Jacob couldn't see it then, and he clearly still had blinders on. "Why do you think I pressed you to move to Dallas with me, Jacob? Ever think about that?"

"What?"

"Never mind. I'm not going."

"Either you go, or I'm reinstating the fucking charges. That's it. No more runnin', Frank. Deal with your shit. I'm done. Be a fuckin man for once!"

"Oh, it's like that? For my brother, J?"

"It's like that. Deal with your shit."

Jacob's campaign infuriated Frank. He had never imagined Jacob would threaten him over his brother, but he couldn't disregard him at this point. His demons were ruining his life, and he suspected that if he kept pretending otherwise, the casualties would outnumber the living soon. Still, he was reluctant to pull out his white flag.

"Jacob, you have no fuckin' clue about what kind of guy my brother is. No idea what the fuck you doing. You think you're schooling me on humility? On the virtues of responsibility? You're not."

"Is that supposed to change my mind? Everything you have you either schemed your way into or you stole the shit outright. Enough is enough."

"This is bullshit. It's not going to be what you think, Jacob."

"We'll see."

"You are out of your fucking mind." Frank had an inkling Jacob was not telling him something, but he was in no position to push the issue. He needed the possibility of going to jail completely off the table. "I do this and we're square? Everything's good?"

"We'll be good."

"Fine, I'll do it."

"Cool, call me when you touch down at LaGuardia."

"No problem."

Frank ended the call. He was perplexed to say the least. This shit from Jacob was a definite curve ball, and Frank was not quite sure how to handle it. Something felt off about Jacob's insistence on him reaching out to his brother. He hadn't spoken with him for years. Why press him now? Something had changed, and he had no idea what it could be. Maybe the near-fatal beatdown was the catalyst. Only time would tell. It was possible.

The real issue was his brother. Frank never knew what to expect from him, and he was not looking forward to the visit.

CHAPTER 29

"Franklin?" Lisa stepped softly, subtly aggravating her healing body, and ventured out onto the balcony.

Frank pulled his eyes away from the beachfront view to the voice of his beloved. "I'm here." His conversation with Jacob left him with a sadness that claimed his smile, but he was determined to find a way back to it. Things were far from what he desired, but he had this woman. The love in her eyes revived him, sustained him.

"What are you doing out here?"

"Needed to make a phone call. Didn't want to disturb your rest."

"Haven't slept like that in a long while."

Frank gingerly pulled Lisa into his embrace. Wrapping her arms around his waist, he enveloped her in a bear hug. His six-foot-four-inch frame effortlessly eclipsed her scrunching body. Burying his face in the top of her head, Frank took a deep breath.

"Franklin . . . I love you."

"I love you, too." Frank let the bitter conversation drift away as a sweet peace replaced it. His life was a total and complete mess, but at least he had her. For now, that had to be enough.

Pulling slightly away from him, Lisa peered up into his dreamy gaze. Frank lovingly covered her lips with his.

"Please." Lisa pouted between kisses. "More of that."

Savoring the hint of apple cider coating her lips. Frank ran the tip of his tongue along the contour of her mouth, enjoying every second spent tasting her. "I'll be whatever you need me to be, Lisa." Frank witnessed the change in her eyes, confirmation that she believed him. He had never felt more powerful than he did in that instant.

"I guess we have to finish packing before our flight?"

"Unfortunately. I like this space. No beauty is comparable to yours, Lisa. I am so sorry for my part in all of this."

"This is enough, Frank. Just last month, I stood in this spot, missing you, longing for you, lamenting our marriage, mourning what could have been. But look at us now. We are here."

"I thought you were . . . my life was over."

"I know the feeling. How about we agree to avoid near-death experiences from this moment on?"

"I like that plan." Frank visually roamed the shoreline, drinking in every little detail.

"Only missing Brianna."

"We will get our family back, Lisa. I promise."

"Don't wager those types of guarantees, Frank."

"Trust me."

Lisa pecked his chest through his polo top. "Packing."

"Right behind you."

Frank followed Lisa into the room, walking behind her in case she were to fall. "Why don't you let me pack your things?"

"Are you sure?" Lisa inquired as she hobbled toward the couch.

"I'll take care of things here, and then I'll go to my room and pack my things up as well. I don't think it should take too much time." Frank hurried to Lisa's side, taking hold of her hand while she lowered her body onto the couch.

"I should be back with plenty of time left for us to partake in a *little island fun*."

Twisting the corner of her mouth into a half smile and offering a little wink, Lisa stretched out on the couch. "I don't know how much fun I'll be right now."

"No worries. I don't need you to do anything. Let me take care of you. These last few weeks have been stressful for us both. I just want these last few hours to be stress free. So many have taken so much from you, including me. I won't let this amazing space be taken as well."

"That is really sweet, Frank. This *you* is a pleasant change."

"This me isn't going anywhere. You deserve this. Always have."

Click, Click, Click, Click.

"Mrs. Mason, Detective Baptiste here. I need to speak with you. Open the door, please."

Frank braced himself for what this visit could mean. Neither he nor Lisa had been expecting it, and as far as he knew, there was no reason for it. There were no charges pending against him on the island. He and Lisa exchanged looks of surprise before he left her to answer the door. Swallowing the lump in his throat, Frank twisted the metal handle before he lost his nerve.

"Detective."

Baptiste's eyes widened in slight shock at Frank's presence.

"Please, come in. Lisa is right over there," Frank stated, motioning toward the living room area. "She's lying on the couch."

"Thanks." Detective Baptiste eased past Frank and made his way into the living area. He wasted no time diving into the purpose of his visit. "Mrs. Mason, I can see that you are resting. I only came by to update you on the progress in your case. If I may have a minute of your time?"

"Sure, please. Do you need me to—"

"No, Lisa. Rest your body. I am sure the detective does not need you sitting up to speak with you. Do you, Detective Baptiste?"

"No, please, no need to move."

"See? So, rest and listen."

Following a stint of awkward silence, the detective continued. "Well, ya husband has been officially cleared. We got partial prints off the knife used, and his was not a match. Phone records, financial transactions don't show any suspicious activity that would connect him. I no longer believe ya husband had anything to do with this crime."

Frank breathed a sigh of relief, grateful that the detective reaffirmed his innocence to Lisa. Though she told him that she believed he was innocent, there was no disputing the evidence.

"Wait. You had the weapon all this time?" Frank asked.

Detective Baptiste looked at Frank, meeting his obligatory accusation. "We tend not to share our evidence with the primary suspect. Since you are no longer under suspicion, I tell you."

"What does the partial print mean? What type of knife was it?" Lisa questioned.

"Print would mean more if we had a suspect."

Frank could feel his face warming as his frustration over the situation rose to the surface. "Whoever it was probably got away while you were wasting time trying to pin it on me!"

"Mr. Mason, I had a job to do. There was no conspiracy." Detective Baptiste squared his shoulders, facing Frank, but kept his voice even.

"But I told you I didn't do it! I would never hurt her." Frank began pacing, trying to calm himself down. Visions of the interrogation room, the cell, and the feel of the handcuffs ran through his mind. Hours wasted on him.

"Every guilty person is innocent until the evidence convicts them," Baptiste said.

"It does not change the fact that you let the son of a bitch get away! Whoever it was. They are gone because of you and your vigilante partner!"

"We follow the evidence."

"Is that what your partner was doing? Following the evidence?" Frank stared at Detective Baptiste, daring him to disagree, to deny that his partner's behavior was completely unprofessional.

"Right or wrong, the goal was to get justice for ya wife. His heart was in the right place."

"His goal was to lock me up. He was not interested in getting justice and you know it."

"I did not come here to discuss him."

"Frank, please. Come sit." Lisa waved Frank to her side, patting the floor in front of her. "Come on. Here. I need you here."

Frank did not protest, obliging her request immediately. He sat on the floor near her head as she casually draped the arm closest to him over his shoulder, offering her hand to him. He grabbed it and closed his eyes. Lisa picked up the conversation.

"What type of knife was it?"

"Military grade. USMC. Nothing that ya would find 'round here."

"So, whoever did this brought it with them?"

"I believe so, yes."

Frank raised her hand to his lips, kissing her palm, trying to communicate what his silence may have not, that he was behind her. He was present and listening.

"What other clues do you have? Anything?" Lisa asked.

"Not really. Mistaking him for your husband, a maid let him in. Much earlier. He waited a long time for you. Another maid, a different worker, witnessed someone fleeing the room around the time of the incident."

Frank felt his body growing tense again. He could not believe the detectives had been so careless. "Someone ran from the room and you didn't think that clue was worth investigating?"

"We had a suspect with motive, means, and opportunity covered in the victim's blood. No, we did not find it necessary at the time. Obviously, that is no longer the case."

"I cannot believe this bullshit. Fuckin' negligent bullshit."

"There was a lot of confusion in the beginning. Witnesses are not always reliable. Mrs. Mason, please understand that we took all the necessary steps to get justice for you."

Removing her hand from Frank's, Lisa gently squeezed his shoulder. Frank understood.

"Well, thank you, Detective Baptiste, for the update, but it's been a long few weeks, and she needs to rest before our flight."

"Oh, you're leaving? So soon?"

"No offense, but my wife was nearly killed. I was arrested and jailed."

"Point taken, but I do hope ya will return one day. Don't let this memory be the last ya have of this place."

Frank stood to walk the detective to the door. "We will see, I guess."

"I suppose. I did not want to say this in front of her, but—"

"This is her room. If this is another tactic to intimidate me . . ."

"No, I was coming to visit you next."

Frank shifted his weight, leaning on the door frame for support. "What is it?"

"I am not going to stop until I find out who did this."

"Why wouldn't you want to tell her that?"

"I don't need to tell her. You are the one that needed to hear it."

Frank responded defensively. "Are you saying that I am still a suspect?" Frank shouted in a whisper. "Are you serious? After what you just said in there?"

"I am saying that I will never stop looking. No matter how long it takes."

"We appreciate you being zealous in your pursuit of the truth," Frank retorted, his statement dripping with sarcasm.

"I am."

"Yeah, well, you do that. Let *us* know what you find."

Frank watched the detective walk down the hall toward the elevators before quietly closing the door. He returned to the living area to find Lisa fast asleep. He walked over to her, careful not to wake her, kissing her on the forehead before he proceeded to pack her things.

Uncertain of the detective's angle, Frank knew he needed to watch his step. Regardless of what he may think, there was a very real threat to Lisa's safety out there, and it was Frank's duty to protect her. Nothing would hurt Lisa ever again if he had any say in the matter.

CHAPTER 30

Waking up on the floor of her den, Sophie scrunched her nose as the lingering scent of bourbon assaulted her senses, turning her stomach. Unable to decipher whether the scent was self-inflicted or coming from the walls, Sophie buried her face in her pillow to get some "fresh air." The strawberries ironed out her temporary abdominal complications but highlighted the dust storm living in her throat.

She looked around warily, searching for something to fuse the fragmented pieces of her memory. Her head hurt like she'd slept in a rehearsal hall with a heavy metal band. A cacophony of every kind of unpleasant sound rang out, sending waves of pain out from her cranium like a boomerang sealed in the hardest sediment known to man. Peter was gone but had left her a glass of water and two aspirin a few inches from her head. Rolling over onto her stomach, she tossed the pills into her mouth and drank the water. Thankfully, the curtains were pulled close, protecting her fragile blues from the high noon sun.

The aspirin immediately began relieving her headache. She stood very slowly and surveyed the room. He had wiped the bourbon from the wall and cleaned up the broken glass. She shuffled to her favorite chair in the corner of the room, took a seat, and grabbed the phone. The ringer was off. No wonder she had been able to sleep uninterrupted. Peter was so thoughtful.

She'd contact him later. Business first. She needed a new plan. Hoping he'd have good news for her, she decided to make Steven her first call.

"Steven, this is Mrs. Lewis."

"Afternoon, *Mrs. Lewis* . . ." Steven replied, uncertain what to make of her formal speak.

"I am *Mrs. Lewis* to you until you prove that you are worth my money," Sophie retorted, responding to the question hidden in his greeting. She toyed with the possibility of this entire ordeal being an elaborate scam in order to drain her account. She needed to micromanage until she received some assurance that her fear was unfounded. Being in the shadow of R. Freemont had taught her that sophisticated people aren't more decent than others; they are simply better at hiding.

"What can you tell me about the Charlie situation?" she asked.

"She has not filed a case with the court yet. No word from her or any legal representation either. Maybe she decided to cut her losses and leave."

Sophie knew that was not the case. She was definitely still around, but she couldn't figure out why Charlie hadn't gotten legal representation. Given everything Sophie knew, she could concoct a reasonably good case. There was no way Sophie was going to allow her a victory, but still, she could try.

"She is here. I don't know why she is quiet right now, but she's here. She's waiting for something."

"I suppose you want me to find her." His tone reflected his distress and irritation.

Sophie did not care how he felt about what she asked of him. "I may have said some things in poor taste last night.

Drunks don't always say the most politically correct things, especially when speaking in anger."

"You don't have to apologize, Mrs. Lewis."

Sophie scoffed. "I had not intended to. You are paid for your services. If you're sensitive to somewhat *harsh language,* then perhaps you need to look at another line of work. Otherwise, compose yourself. Stop complaining and do the work that I am paying you to do."

"Of course. I am more than capable of doing my work."

"Glad to hear it. I trust I'll hear from you later with good news?"

"That's the plan."

Sophie disconnected the call feeling even less certain about Steven's ability to maneuver. This was a gross oversight and could be very costly for her. If her desire to cremate him should come to Michelle's attention, Sophie would be without an explanation for her. Michelle's inquisitive nature would certainly send her digging into Sophie's cave of wonder. It was the absolute last thing she needed to happen. No. Steven needed to figure this out or Sophie would be forced to call in the reserves. Richard was old and senile, but still very connected. She had no desire to speak with him, but if it came to that, she knew exactly what to say.

Baaadinnng, baaading . . . baaading. The phone rang in her hand.

"Hello?"

"Luce? Finally up?"

Sophie could hear the hustle and bustle of the hospital in the background. "Yes, and thank you for everything."

"I told you that I would take care of you. Many years ago."

"That you did."

There was an uncomfortable pause before he went on. "I only have a few minutes. I am actually at work. Checking in with you. I have been calling off and on."

"The ringer was off."

"I thought you needed some rest. You were pretty worked up last night."

"I am sorry about that. Rough day."

"Do you want to talk about it later on?"

"Maybe. We'll see." Sophie was not certain if she could trust Peter, and even if she could, she didn't think it would be fair to burden him with her misdeeds.

"I left a number for a therapist friend of mine. Did you see it on the table?"

Sophie looked at the table again and saw the small note written on the back of a receipt for the first time. Picking it up, she read aloud, "Dr. Miya Shepherd?" For some reason, the name sounded familiar, but Sophie knew she had never crossed paths with any doctors in that profession.

"You need to talk to someone. I somewhat understand your resistance in regards to being completely open with me. I highly recommend you see someone soon. Your episodes are getting worse, Luce. I can't watch you fall apart like this."

If only you knew the half of it, Sophie thought. "I shouldn't have involved you in this, Peter."

"No, you should have told me what was going on the day I asked after the blow-up with Michelle. Instead, you lied, and they have progressed since then. You have been through a lot. You can't keep trying to do it all alone."

"I know."

"Listen, I am being paged. I have to go, but we'll talk later."

"Sure. Just call."

Sophie sat in silence for a long while after that, pondering his offer. Perhaps he was correct and she needed help. She needed to tell someone, and Peter seemed best suited for the role. He had waited twenty-plus years to be with her. If that did not show his commitment, she did not know what would.

She rose, aiming to retreat to her master bath to shower. By the time she arrived at her master suite on the other side of her home, she had made a very important decision. She would confess her truth—the whole naked, ugly truth. Hopefully he could handle it.

CHAPTER 31

Michelle emerged from the shower feeling new, believing the piping hot stream spouting from the rainfall-style shower head to have possessed baptismal powers. Pushing her feet across the square earth-tone stone tiles, Michelle felt a plenitude of strength. It was not unlike surges of hope that had surfaced before, tempting her to believe that she could possibly survive this moment, until the mirror, which consistently proved itself to be a sobering agent, suggested otherwise. As she extended her arm, carving an oval out of the fog on the mirror's face with the palm of her hand, she suspected this moment would be no different.

Michelle studied the misty image before her and felt the pulse of a thousand prayers ossifying her spirit, anchoring her feet. It was a stark contrast to her swollen eyes, giving credence to the bottomless pit her life had become. Her emotions tumbled about like shoes in a dryer. The movement provided an audible record for her ears alone, echoing the unceasing cramping of her heart, the rhythm of her hurt. Nothing could soothe the ache of knowing all that was lost to her. She knew that she needed to move from this moment, but she didn't know how. She felt cemented, trapped between what was and what could have been.

Armand had blindsided her. Their relationship, in the midst of transition, had its fair share of uncomfortable moments, but she had not expected this. After everything that had transpired in the last few months, she had finally released herself to him, unlocking her heart completely when she accepted his proposal, giving him full access to all of who she was. He had proven himself to be a man of action, willfully putting himself in danger to save both her and her sister. She had no reason to question his devotion, no reason to suspect that he thought so little of the promise they had made to one another.

The longer Michelle planted herself in front of the waist-length mirror, admiring her imperfections, the more at peace she found herself. Slowly, her psyche began to heal, finding jolts of courage in the scars she could not ignore. This chapter would end eventually, and she'd start the next. The thought invigorated her, peeling back her layers, exposing her most vulnerable parts.

Michelle struggled to hold steady her trembling body as mobs of tears attacked her. Why had Armand done this to her? To them? She could not wrap her mind around it. Yet here she was, standing in the mirror, staring at her feminine form, questioning what she lacked that loosed her of the love she once counted herself among the few lucky souls to have found.

Her brow scrunched in frustration. Starting with her head, Michelle gently wiggled her body free, frustrated that these types of thoughts were even entering her head. She knew she was not to blame, but her search for answers forced her there.

Sauntering into the bedroom, Michelle, preoccupied with her mental ramblings, did not notice Grayson lurking in the door. She took her time clothing her naked body, enjoying the layer of cool air disseminating from the whirring fan overhead, covering her as it removed the last traces of her shower. She plopped down on the side of the bed, nearest the bag that housed her toiletries.

She still had not noticed Grayson.

She reached into the bag and pulled out her lotion, powder, deodorant, and a hair tie, throwing them on the bed. Her breath caught in a lump in her throat, frozen; her body shivered as she found herself locking eyes with a gawking Grayson perched in the frame of the bedroom door. Judging by the look on his face, *she* had caught him, too. Seeing her nakedness locked him into the room with her.

Emboldened by the longing she saw in his eyes, Michelle entertained the call of her ravenous libido. The warmth between her legs spread like wildfire, surging from somewhere deep within her feminine well, sending her sweet tea rushing from between her swollen lips like the falls of Niagara. She bathed in the energy she so desperately craved, her body ablaze, tormented by a need she hoped he would be obliged to fulfill.

He could not, nor did he refuse to leave. She didn't want him to, either. She didn't run for cover at the sight of his six-foot frame darkening the doorway. Instead, she sashayed to the bed, sticking her plump ass into the air as she went. She dangled her body like a treat before him, tempting him to devour her whole. He licked his lips, pleased with the show.

The bed conformed to her frame as she made herself comfortable, lying naked atop the dark navy-blue spread. It did not matter that Grayson had not yet joined her. Her need was so great that, at least for the moment, knowledge of his desire was enough to occupy her thoughts.

Once she made it to the bed and he still hadn't joined her, she sat down, facing him. Intent on seducing him, she leaned back, resting on her elbows, and opened her legs as wide as she could, giving him a clear, unobstructed view of her bald love hole. *Still,* he took his time coming to her, admiring her design from a distance.

The wait nearly killed her, but he finally joined her on the bed. She sat up and waited for him to make his move. He never uttered a word, but his lips looked so good, she didn't need him to speak. They were like magnets, pulling her closer to him, even though she hadn't moved a muscle.

An eternity passed by while they sat, staring into one another. Michelle's resolve grew weaker with each passing second. Her body was so sensitive that a gust of wind against her nipple could have made her orgasm. Her body succumbed to involuntarily jerking as the anticipation overpowered her. Just when she thought she couldn't last a second longer, Grayson leaned in to kiss her.

She had no choice but to return his kiss. Their chemistry was off the charts, and this moment was inevitable. This moment had taken over her dreams. So, when he leaned in, grazing his lips against hers, teasing her to the point where it felt unnatural not to give in, she . . . *gave in*.

The moment was bigger than her, the energy between them easily defeating the slightest resistance her mind offered. *So,* when he leaned in to kiss her, there was no doubt that he was what she wanted. What she needed. She kissed him like the she had something to lose. Bomb after bomb ignited within her; the earth straightened up and quit its rotation. Every corny love song ever written played in her ears all at the same damn time. That kiss was every fucking thing.

Months of pent-up sexual aggression evaporated with that kiss. His lips were the softest she'd ever felt. Tasting the vanilla ice cream she'd caught him sneaking earlier only increased her hunger. Vanilla was now her favorite flavor. His tongue explored her mouth, dancing with hers, exciting her even more. Craving the feel of his fingers against her skin, his breath on the nape of her neck, she covered her bare breast with his hand.

Michelle swallowed the hue of his chestnut eyes while they connected for just a moment before he found that *one* spot on her neck; that *one* spot that drove her libido into overdrive. She purred as he gently molded her hardened pearls, rolling them ever so slowly between his fingers.

Gasping as her erect nipples stretched and spread to fill his mouth, he toggled between the two, tonguing them as if they were one of his instruments. Michelle writhed in pleasure as her desire grew to an uncontrollable height. Why did he have to be so damn perfect?

Thrusting her hand in between her open legs, she ran her fingers over her enlarged clit, dipping them into her soaking wet hole, dousing her fingers in her natural juices. She couldn't help herself. His touch made her clitoris throb with need. She had never behaved this way before, never been this starved for anyone in her life.

And it was wrong. All of this was wrong. She was engaged to another man, a man she loved, but none of that seemed to matter. Those truths failed to cool the flame burning for Grayson, and he wanted her just as badly. She felt her back hit the comforter as he continued to explore her body with his lips, caressing her breasts with his hands.

She closed her eyes and embraced the immense pleasure awaiting her, tossing aside all thought that did not pertain to the artist's work. He painted her bare shoulders, arms, the palms of her hands, her stomach, and the inside of her thighs. Michelle braced herself for what she anticipated would happen next, removing her hand to make way for the prize.

He neared her *womanness*. She could feel his breath on her throbbing lips. It took all of her strength not take his head and jump start the party. Again, he made her wait, tormenting her by hovering just above her, barely brushing his lips across her clitoris and massaging her inner thigh with his hands. Michelle thought she'd go into cardiac arrest at any moment.

Without warning, he French kissed her, forcing his tongue deep into her wet space. Michelle drew a deep breath. She couldn't even scream. Wave after wave after wave of bliss rocketed through her body.

He lifted his head, only to start all over again, tracing the form of her swollen lips with his tongue before suckling on the very tip of her clit. Michelle screamed with delight when he again put his mouth on her, flicking her clit with the very tip of his tongue. He felt so amazing. She could feel the orgasm coming. She just needed him to stay there. Right there. She couldn't breathe until it happened. Any movement slowed it down, and she didn't want to slow it down. She didn't want to stop. Grayson kept suckling her clit. He didn't move an inch. His moans intensified her pleasure as she felt herself closing in on the peak.

Oh my gawd, don't stop, Grayson. Oh my gawd . . . I'm cumming . . . I'm cumming . . . I'm cum—

Wake . . . Up!

Laurence Fishburne's tenor ripped through the air.

Wake . . . Up!

Dap, played by Fishburne, stood seemingly suspended in white space, megaphone in hand, screaming the phrase at the top of his lungs.

Wake . . . Up!

What in the hell?

Wake . . . Up!

Startled, Michelle popped up in bed, looking wearily around the room. Dap had disappeared, but his battle cry still rang.

Wake . . . Up!

The last line of legendary filmmaker Spike Lee's 1988 classic, *School Daze*, sounded on a loop, announcing the end of Michelle's date with the stars. There was no sign of Grayson, and the tank top she threw on before sinking into his king feather mattress was still intact.

Wake . . . Up!

The call to consciousness sounded again. Michelle rolled around the bed, frantically combing through the thick comforter in search of her cell phone. Finding it trapped in her pillow case, she picked it up and swiped left, dismissing the alarm.

She watched the doorway for a moment to see if her alarm had wakened him. Satisfied that he wasn't there, she shook her head, relieved. That was the fourth wet dream she'd had about him since he offered to let her stay with him just a little over a week ago. This was the most intense of the four, and she was a little concerned with what it might implicate. She climbed out of bed, stuck her head into the hall, and sure enough, Grayson was still fast asleep on the couch with Common on the floor nearby.

She rarely ever had sexually explicit dreams, at least not with anyone she actually had a chance with. Grayson was clearly different. He was attractive and kind, but he hadn't hinted at harboring any romantic feelings for her. This notion of them *coming* together came out of nowhere. She guessed it would be nice to attach herself to such a beautiful person, but this was much too soon to even consider dating. She needed to sort things out with Armand first. Grayson was definitely worth more than a romp session, even if it would be an incredibly satisfying, mind-blowing romp session.

She checked the sheets for any remnants of her dream, and they were good, this time. Michelle had been fortunate enough to make use of the on-site laundry room before Grayson would see anything the last time. She could not imagine trying to explain that to him. In fact, she probably wouldn't. That was one of those situations where you simply leave.

Michelle rummaged through her duffle bag for her toiletries. She was in desperate need of a cold shower. *Unbelievable.*

Whether she wanted to admit it or not, there was definitely some chemistry between her and Grayson. He was a very handsome guy, and she'd have to be blind not to see that. Complicating things even further was the fact that she and Armand were doing more arguing than anything else over the last several months. She could use a little *sexual healing,* but that was not a priority. It couldn't be.

Michelle could hear Grayson start to move around in the living room. Snatching her clothes out of her suitcase, she made a mad dash to the bathroom for a quick shower.

CHAPTER 32

"What do you mean you cannot see me?" *Pins and needles, needles and pins. This is not how the story ends. Breathe, Brianna. Breathe.*

"I am taking some personal time."

"This doesn't make sense. Sessions are mandatory. How can you just quit?"

"It is not that simple, Brianna. There are extenuating circumstances."

"But you are my fucking therapist." *Keep it together.* "I need to talk to you."

"I can arrange for someone—"

"I don't want to talk to someone else!"

"It cannot be avoided."

"This is bullshit." Being thrust into the realm of mothers had pushed Brianna into an emotional minefield. Everything about life and living aggravated her to no end. She spared no one, issued no IOUs. Even the poor train attendant got an earful after he gently reminded her to pay before taking her seat. Snapping had become so commonplace that even she was bothered by it. Taking it upon herself, she had reached out to Dr. WonderBra to request an emergency session, and apparently her state-mandated therapist would not be available to do her fucking job.

"I just cannot do it, Brianna."

"I am not trying to be unreasonable, but I really need a session. I spoke with Dr. Baxter as you suggested, and it didn't end well. I assumed we would discuss it at some point, and now you're telling me that you can't see me at all?"

"I usually don't do this, Brianna, but I can hear the distress in your voice, and I imagine you can detect it in mine."

Brianna plopped down on her bed, grabbed her pillow, released her frustration into the cotton, and took a deep breath. She pried her mind open so that she could listen without bias.

"There is a familial situation that warrants my immediate attention, and I am taking a personal leave to do that. Due to the nature of the emergency, I honestly am uncertain of how much time I'll need. I would be happy to recommend another doctor, as I have with my other clients."

"What is the emergency?" Perhaps it was not her business to inquire, but Brianna didn't care at this point. She was not too broken to request the explanation she felt was due to her.

"Rachel is missing. No one has seen her in over two weeks, and her mother is worried that something might have happened to her."

Distracted with her own trifles, Brianna had not noted her absence beyond the day she mentioned it to Dr. Shepherd. The thought of Rachel in danger made her very nervous, rekindling her own horrific experience.

"Two weeks? Why are you just now looking?!"

"Brianna, do not project. We have discussed this before. Similar is not synonymous. It is okay for you to identify with her, but she is not you."

"I never said she was."

"The tone of your question implied as much."

"Nonsense."

"I'm sorry?"

"You're wrong. The tone of my question reflects my disdain for your cavalier attitude about your missing niece—a niece I assume you have some sort of a relationship with that's worth something, since she works with you on a daily basis. That niece disappears, and you don't bat an eye. What educated, civilized person responds that way when someone they love goes missing?"

"Brianna . . ."

"How can you help me when you're so obviously fucked up?"

"Brianna! Stop. Stop this."

"She should mean something to you! Her life should matter!"

"Brianna! She is not you! Stop! I have not stated that I believe any of what you have accused me of. What gave birth to those thoughts? It was not me, Brianna."

Brianna squeezed her eyes closed and rolled over onto her stomach. The movement forced the tension from her body, shifting the energy surrounding her. She screamed into the soft folds of her comforter. Dr. Shepherd was correct. Brianna was truly angry with herself, upset for not realizing that Rachel may be trapped in the same hell she once found herself in.

"Brianna?"

"I'm here."

"Rachel has run off like this previously. Not quite this long, but I personally am not alarmed by it. My sister is, however, and that is the only reason I am taking this time. My sister, Bella, has lupus, and this stress is not good for her. I have never seen her this distraught, and I must make myself available. Do you understand?"

"I do, and I apologize. I didn't mean to come off so harshly. There's a lot going on, and I'm not sure how to feel about it any of it."

"I would love to help you right now, really I would, but I just don't have the time. Would you like a referral?"

"No, I am not going to talk to another counselor. I'll just wait until you come back and try and figure this out on my own in the meantime."

"I strongly urge you to continue counseling. I suppose the courts could amend your time under the circumstances, but that isn't a certainty."

"I don't want to start over with another counselor."

"How do you feel about Dr. Baxter? I know that you said your visit did not end well, but how do you feel about talking with him? He is licensed, though this isn't his specialty. Seeing him could probably satisfy the probation requirement. He is insightful, communicative, and that might prove to be of even greater benefit since you already have a relationship with him."

"I'll try. Don't worry about me. Good luck with finding your niece. I hope she's okay. She was always nice to me when I saw her."

"Thank you, Brianna. Talk to Dr. Baxter."

Brianna ended the call worried about Rachel. She could imagine all the horrible things that could be happening to her at that moment. She felt so powerless and frustrated that there wasn't anything she could do about it. It didn't seem fair. Then it hit her—she was probably feeling a small fraction of what Michelle felt while she was gone.

Michelle had the great misfortune of literally seeing Brianna snatched right off the beach. She remembered the pain in Michelle's voice as she yelled her name, running as fast as she could to save her. Even after it was evident that Brianna would be taken, she never saw Michelle stop running. She kept running and screaming anyway. Michelle's screams were the last thing Brianna heard as the van she was thrown into sped away. Michelle had never stopped looking for her.

Brianna had stupidly focused on Armand, when Michelle had been there all along. It was the image of Michelle running down the beach that had sustained Brianna during some of the more difficult moments of her captivity. It was Michelle's voice on the other line, picking up every bread crumb Brianna left while she was at Javan's. Michelle put her nerves to the side, focused, and continued the search for their parents. Not only did she find them, but she rushed outside to pass along the news before Brianna got the shock of the century inside the house. Since the moment they met, Michelle had treated her like a sister.

Something told Brianna that it was not Michelle who had made some drastic change. *She* had shifted the dynamic in their relationship, and all the attention Armand gave her just made it worse.

"What do I do now?"

The house was empty. Armand had not been there for several days, and Michelle had not come back since she left that infamous day. She needed to get Michelle to talk to her. She knew it was unlikely that Michelle would want to hear anything she had to say, but it was her time to try. Motherhood was etched into her future now, and she needed to try to put her life back together. She doubted if she could get it back to what it was, but she would give one hell of an effort.

Tell the truth/Tell the truth/Tell the truth/Everyone has a closet/In the night, they wear disguises.

Brianna laughed at how appropriate her ring tone, a snippet of the song "Tell the Truth" from Fox's hit show *Empire*, was at this junction in her life. Things would be completely different if just one person in her circle would have been honest.

"Morning, Dr. Baxter."

"Good morning, Brianna. How are you?"

"I could be worse."

"I suppose that's true."

Brianna didn't bother hiding her irritation. She didn't mind Dr. Baxter calling. After all, he was her doctor, but calling this soon after she had hung up with Dr. WonderBra could only mean one thing.

"Let me guess. Dr. Shepherd called you?"

"Yes, she wants to make sure that you are being taken care of."

"I was going to call you. I assumed you were at work at this time of the day."

"I am. Well, I was. I am taking a personal day."

Brianna was relieved but also alarmed to hear that. Seemed like everybody was in the trenches. "Oh, is everything okay?"

"I'm fine, but I thought maybe you and I could talk?"

Brianna still was not totally at ease discussing her personal life with Dr. Baxter, but he was the only person that knew of this latest development. She needed to discuss that with someone. "I would like that. Can you come get me?"

"Sure, I'll be there shortly."

"Sounds good."

Brianna rolled off her daybed, making sure she had everything she needed together before Dr. Baxter made it to get her. She hated making anyone wait if it was something she could have prevented. She was about as dressed up as she was accustomed to being these days—a comfortable pair of blue jeans, T-shirt, and flats. The only other thing she consistently traveled with was her cell phone, so she was prepared.

She was straightening up a few more things in her room when she heard her phone ringing again.

Tell the truth/Tell the truth/Tell the truth/Everyone has a closet/In the night, they wear disguises.

"Dr. Baxter?" Brianna couldn't squeeze the shock out of her tone. Neither his practice nor the hospital was remotely close to her. She was not sure how he arrived so fast.

"I'm here, Brianna. Are you ready?"

"Uh, sure. Let me lock up and I'll be right there." Brianna surveyed the room once more. She was proud. Her room must not have been as bad as she thought. She had not been cleaning for very long, but she was confident that the result would have satisfied Michelle's OCD. She closed her door and walked out the front door, securing it behind her, walking toward where Dr. Baxter was waiting.

Brianna lit up when she saw him, carefully opening the door and sliding into the custom leather seats. "Is this a vintage 1962 Shelby Cobra?"

Dr. Baxter smiled, mildly impressed with her knowledge. "Indeed it is. I collect vintage cars, and I felt like taking her out for a spin today."

"She is beautiful. The black suits her." Brianna didn't tell him outright, but she had a fascination with vintage cars as well.

"I didn't think you would know anything about that."

"I don't collect or anything, but I can appreciate the beauty in just about anything."

Dr. Baxter nodded in agreement. "That makes perfect sense to me."

"Where are we going?"

"I'm not sure, honestly. I guess I didn't really think this through," Dr. Baxter admitted, laughing. "I didn't think you'd agree to speak with me."

Dr. Baxter flashed her a look that made her uncomfortable. He had an angle, and Brianna started to get that uneasy feeling again. She just hoped that he wouldn't say anything inappropriate, because she would hate for the ride to end. She was truly enjoying the car.

"Well, what if we just ride a bit until you think of something better?"

"Plenty of gas. Let's do it."

CHAPTER 33

Dr. Baxter eased onto the 67N, presumably headed toward Dallas. Traffic was light around this time of day. Parents were still at work, and schools were still in session out in Cedar Hill, where they were in a ghost town compared to other parts of the city.

"What did you want to speak with me about?"

Dr. Baxter glanced at her before countering with his own question. "What did you want to speak with *me* about?"

"Simple question with a complicated answer." Brianna reclined the seat, enjoying the breeze as it kissed her face. The sun shone brightly, but the day was cool with a high of 70 degrees.

"*Un*complicate it," he said.

"Ha, I wish it were as simple as that."

"Think it over. I'll go first, and maybe it'll help you as well."

"Please."

"Pregnancy," he said.

Brianna rubbed her hand across her forehead. "Figured."

"Suffering from a mild case of PTSD, maybe a little Stockholm syndrome. Support system is questionable. I'm worried."

Brianna was worried, too. How did he know all those things about her? They were details that she was certain fell under the patient/doctor privacy umbrella.

"Haven't been to your apartment, driven your car. Those things should not be dismissed as trivial. I think they are important things to consider."

The more he talked, the more convinced Brianna was that Dr. WonderBra had been running her mouth to her #mancrush. That woman had it so bad for him that Brianna wouldn't have been surprised to find that she provided him a transcript of their sessions.

"I see Dr. Shepherd does not care much about patient/ doctor confidentiality."

"Cliff notes only." Dr. Baxter chortled.

Brianna did not find the situation funny.

"I may have taken advantage of a particular *fondness* she has for me to get more information than I should have, but I did it for you. I just wanted to make sure you were okay."

"That does not help as much as you'd think."

"I promise we didn't violate your privacy."

"Seems like you did, Dr. B. How do you know those things?"

"She only shared very basic information. These things are typical for someone that has been through something traumatic as you have," Dr. Baxter tried to reason.

"Never mind. It's not headline-worthy I guess." Brianna really didn't care so much about Dr. Shepherd sharing her clinical observations. They were both her doctors, and she considered them colleagues. The more important part of all this for her was why. Why did he feel so obligated to help her?

"Why do you care?"

Dr. Baxter exhaled audibly. "I know your mother," he blurted.

Brianna adjusted her seat into an upright position. Perhaps she had heard him incorrectly. The wind could have distorted the words or something. "What did you say?"

"It's true. I was afraid to tell you because I didn't want you to think I was using you to get to her, but I know her."

Something was not adding up. "If you know her, why would you need me to get to her?"

"I haven't been in touch with her for years. When I saw you at Javan's that night . . . it felt like fate. You looked so much like her. I just knew you had to be her daughter."

"So, you were using me?"

Raising his shoulders and shaking his head slightly to the left then to the right, Dr. Baxter responded honestly. "Yes, I was, but in my defense . . . believing that you belonged to her did create a genuine desire for me to make sure you were all right."

Brianna could tell that he still cared a great deal about her mom. Even though he wasn't smiling, she could hear the smile in his voice when he spoke of her.

"How long had it been?" she asked.

"Over twenty years."

The open air kept the vibration free. The conversation was serious, but being so close to the vast blue sky kept everything in perspective. Highway 67 turned into Interstate 35, and as they rounded the curve passing the Dallas Zoo, downtown trickled into view.

"And you still wanted to see her? That is a long time to hold a torch."

"I didn't spend all of those years alone, but your mother was . . ." He glanced at Brianna. ". . . is very special. So, you are very special to me also."

That explained his creepy behavior. He wasn't trying to sleep with her, but trying to get in good with her mom. Brianna could not remember the last time she had been so wrong about someone. *Oh, wait.* As her mind flashed back to Javan, maybe she could. Something was still missing from the narrative. If his main goal was to reconnect with Sophie, why hadn't he asked anything about her?

"Have you contacted her?"

"Contacted who?"

Brianna scoffed. "You know who."

"I have."

"And?"

"And I believe that is something to discuss with your mother."

Blowing her cheeks up like a puffer fish, Brianna considered pushing him for answers but decided against it. "Maybe I will."

"Back to your child. Have you told her?"

Fear sent her voice up a few octaves. "No, of course not. I have not said anything to anyone."

Dr. Baxter activated his turn signal and exited the freeway. Brianna had not really been paying much attention to where they were going. She was immersed in the peace of the ride, but after the exit, her curiosity grew.

"No Cliff Notes?" Brianna asked, laughing at her quip.

Dr. Baxter laughed, too. "No, I promise. I would not do that. It isn't my place."

"That's a relief."

"How are you feeling?"

Brianna allowed herself to be distracted by the hustle and bustle of downtown Dallas for a moment. That part of the city was allergic to quiet—bumper to bumper traffic regardless of the time of day or night. Construction was a constant part of the scene, even more prevalent then the buildings themselves.

"Brianna?"

"I am an emotional mess. Feeling everything all at once. Guilt. Pain. Hurt. Happiness. Fear. It's overwhelming."

"I can imagine. I never had . . . a child, but it can't be easy." Dr. Baxter empathized.

"Where are we going?" Brianna inquired as they rolled to a stoplight.

"There is a renowned photographer, resident of Dallas, Richard Andrew Sharum. He's doing an exhibition called *Observe Dallas 2015*. He selected eight photographs, each several stories tall, and essentially turned downtown Dallas into his personal art gallery."

"I had no idea. That sounds like an enormous undertaking."

"I'm sure it was. I haven't gotten an opportunity to see his work in person, but I thought, since you 'appreciate the beauty in just about in anything,' that you would enjoy it as well."

"Touché. Where is the first print?"

"The first print is at 211 South Ervay, but the one I have been wanting to see is around the corner from here at 500 South Ervay," Dr. Baxter stated, rounding the corner onto South Ervay. Spotting an available parking meter, he pulled over and parked. "It's just up here."

"I can tell that something is hanging there." Brianna got out of the car and waited while Dr. Baxter fed the meter. Looking around the square, she realized that she knew the area. "Isn't that City Hall over there?"

"Yes, it is. Sharum insisted that this and the photo that will eventually replace this one be hung here to protest homelessness."

"Why?" Brianna asked as they crossed the street onto City Hall Plaza. They walked for a few minutes before turning to view the print. Muted initially by the sheer size of the photograph, Brianna stood speechless. It was truly breathtaking. She had never seen anything like it.

"This is amazing. He was able to capture the brilliance of humanity in his lens. That is remarkable."

Dr. Baxter shared her sentiment, standing at her side, beaming with pride as if he had taken the picture himself. "His hope for *Ronnie* and for the others is that people will empathize and celebrate the ordinary."

Brianna could not help but feel encouraged by that. It spoke to her on so many levels that she could not possibly explain them all. She just felt it in her soul, moving her spirit. Celebrating the ordinary was exactly what she needed to do.

"This is the piece you looked forward to seeing the most?"

"We were *Ronnie*. My father and I were homeless for a few weeks. There aren't many shelters for single fathers, so he did what he could. I still remember the stares. There is nothing more painful than to witness someone looking through you."

Brianna stuck her hands in pockets, continuing to admire Sharum's brave accusation, thinking of the statements she was making in her own life.

"Nothing has been the same for me. I couldn't figure out how to get back to where I was before. *She* feels like a stranger. I am surrounded by these people that knew her, and I feel strange because I don't feel like I do."

"Families are not trained to deal with victims, and sometimes that ignorance leads to inappropriate interaction with the victim. I advise the families of victims who have survived a difficult pregnancy or labor to seek counseling along with my patients. Oftentimes our support systems need support, too. The victim needs help, but the wrong kind can have devastating consequences. We tend to overlook the fact that when someone close to us is hurt in some way, we are hurt as well. We all suffer."

"Victim. I don't even know how to be a *victim*. Am I supposed to be feeling a certain way? Am I supposed to look a certain way? Is there a manual for dummies somewhere I can read? I don't look like the victims depicted in film and on television. I can't mark off everything listed in the Diagnostic Manual. Where do I fit?"

"Healing is not about being able to fit perfectly into a category. Those things are not absolute. They are meant to serve as a spring board. Concentrate on just being present. Not in the future, not in the past, but right here."

"I'm terrified," she said.

"I know, but you can't let a moment, or even a series of moments, in your life define the rest. Time exists in fractions—hours, minutes, seconds—and those spaces are opportunities for you to change your life. It does not have to be a Broadway production."

Brianna remained silent while she pondered his words. This was the best she had felt in weeks, and it had all started with her saying yes to his offer to talk. There was some truth to his words. Dr. Shepherd had been correct; his advice was spot on.

Rubbing her belly, Brianna came to a decision. She did not know how to go about repairing her relationship with Michelle, but there was something she wanted to do that she was certain Dr. Baxter could help her with.

"Are you sure you are willing to help me through this?" she asked.

"I am positive. Whatever you need."

Brianna knew her request would sound odd considering everything that had happened, but it was what she wanted. Being present, for her, meant facing the past.

"Help me find Javan."

CHAPTER 34

"Ms. Vida, you know I love you, but I am not eating anything off that tray," Micah stated. His discharge papers, crumpled and torn, rested at the base of the sink. He sat, slouching in the wheelchair, a despairing look chiseled into the soft lines of his face. He was finally being released from the hospital, but the moment arrived minus the pleasantries he had expected.

"Micah, you have not eaten today, and you will do so immediately."

Micah's appetite had abandoned him hours before. For two weeks, his bat signal had failed to beckon Brianna to the door of his hospital room, and her elusiveness plagued him. Even after considering every solecism he had made with her, he believed not one warranted this iceberg-sized shoulder she forced him to contend with. Compounding the problem, thoughts of Rachel impeded his mind. His leaving reinforced the reality that she never would. Call it a moment of rectitude or a splash of regret; either way, Micah found himself trapped in a serious case of survivor's remorse with no visible path to freedom.

"I am not hungry. Besides, the only edible thing on there is the Jell-O."

Ms. Vida stood, casting her shadow over him, preparing his tray for the last time. "Yes, you are. This is the *ne plus ultra* of hospital cuisine, and you will eat."

Micah looked up at Ms. Vida, meeting her unwavering stare, and doubled over in laughter. "Those glasses, Ms. Vida. I cannot take you seriously with the magnifiers on."

"At least you came out of your gloom for a moment." Ms. Vida pushed the tray to the other side of where he sat in the wheelchair. After parking it between him and the counter, she sat down on the bed and lightly tapped his knee. "I cannot absolve you of the guilt you feel, not with any substantial degree of certainty."

Sighing, Micah dropped his gaze. Lifting his chin with the tip of her finger, Ms. Vida locked eyes with him. "This guilt you are exhibiting seems like the morally responsible thing to do. I know that it feels right to you to behave this way. You were speeding, off of your meds, and to that extent you are responsible, but I have news for you, young man."

Micah held eye contact with Ms. Vida, awaiting whatever wisdom she had to share with him. He hoped that it would be more endearing than what had been stated thus far.

"Being remorseful because you have an opportunity to live your life is the quintessence of selfishness."

Micah turned his head in disgust, unable to believe that something so profoundly ignorant could come from his beloved Ms. Vida. He was not even sure of how to respond. How could feeling guilty be selfish? That did not even make sense.

Pulling his face back to her, she continued. "Nothing you *feel* has any bearing on her or where she is at this time. Your *feelings* are about you, Micah, not her." Ms. Vida released him but continued speaking, seeing that she again had his attention. "There is no way to determine, definitively, that your actions led directly to her death."

Micah opened his mouth to speak but changed his mind. The look on Ms. Vida's face let him know that interrupting her would be a bad idea.

"Stop mourning your miracle."

"What are you talking about, Ms. Vida?" Micah inquired. His foot rattled the square piece of metal it rested on. His leg jumped around involuntarily as his annoyance started to best him.

"Did you intentionally crash?"

"Of course not, Ms.—"

"Were you also in the accident, or was she alone in the vehicle?"

"Why are you asking me this stuff?" Gesturing to his wheelchair and his various injuries, he exclaimed, "Clearly, I was in the car."

Ms. Vida maintained her calm demeanor. "Were you trying to kill yourself and failed?"

"No, ma'am."

"Then stop mourning your miracle. Somehow, you lived and she did not. Neither of those things were under your control. Her death could have been a blessing for her just as your living is one for you. Those answers are not for you to know."

Micah understood the point Ms. Vida was trying to make. He didn't know if he agreed with all of it, but he could see where she was going. "I'm being ungrateful. It just really sunk in when I saw those papers. She was really young, Ms. Vida. Who knows what kind of woman she could have been? I have no memory of her. She could have been an engineer, a nurse, or an architect like me. I hate to think that my actions shortchanged her."

"Somehow, you must find a way to forgive yourself. I cannot tell you how to do that, but I trust that in time you will figure it out."

"I'll have to take your word for it. I cannot remember a time I felt this low."

"I do not doubt that, but you must move forward. Live. If nothing else, you should have a greater appreciation for the fragility of life. Enjoy the time you have, Micah."

"What am I going to do without you, Ms. Vida? I wish I could take you with me to rehab."

Ms. Vida lowered her glasses and winked at Micah. "I am not going anywhere, Micah. Do not worry about that."

"I don't understand. Do you moonlight at the rehab facility or something?" Micah questioned jokingly.

"I am officially retired."

Micah leaned back in his chair, genuinely surprised. "Really? Why didn't you say anything?"

"I had planned to do so, but I was waiting."

"Waiting for what?"

"For this moment. I loved being a nurse, and I do not regret one minute I spent on the job," Ms. Vida offered, looking around the room until she rested her eyes again on Micah. "But I think I finally found something that I may love a little more."

"*Ah ha*! Ms. Vida, I knew you loved me!" Micah stated playfully. "I love you, too. I am glad I won't have to say goodbye to you. I am tired of losing people I love. Let's do this, Ms. Vida!"

Ms. Vida smiled, flashing her perfect pearls. "Let us do this."

Knock, knock, knock.

Dr. Ramvi, the physician in charge of Micah's care, strolled into the room. Closing the door gently behind him, he turned to face Ms. Vida and Micah, tucking his large hands into the pockets of his white coat. "Ms. Vida, I heard you're leaving us?" Ms. Vida nodded. "Do I have you, Micah, to blame for losing this jewel?"'

"It was news to me as well, but I'm grateful."

"As you should be. Not every day that happens."

"I am fortunate."

"I suppose it is fitting, all things considered. I came by just to recap and check on you before transport arrives."

"I am feeling better. I am see-sawing emotionally, but physically I feel okay. I guess. Soreness, hurts to breathe a little."

Dr. Ramvi furrowed his brow, unifying his thick eyebrows, creating one long line across the bottom of his forehead. Placing a fist under his chin, Dr. Ramvi gave Micah his undivided attention, supplying a range of *um-hmm's*, and *I see's* while he spoke.

"Micah, the next phase of your recovery will not be easy. Your injuries were pretty significant, but I have seen much worse. You were still very fortunate. I reviewed your most recent CT scans, and the swelling from your TBI has gone down considerably. You were unconscious for several hours, suffered memory loss around the event and likely time extending beyond those few days, but without any family, it was just too difficult for us to verify that. The soreness in your chest area will fade as the lung puncture heals. Fortunately, you didn't suffer any broken bones, but you will experience some weakness in your limbs, primarily the lower part of your right leg where you had some significant tissue damage. I propose that a few weeks of physical therapy will fix that. Do you have any questions for me?"

"I know you removed a rib. I'm still not sure what I should expect from that."

"It's different for everyone. Mobility will be limited during recovery, but that isn't out of the ordinary. Patients have reported some discomfort when that space where the rib was is touched, but I don't expect anything beyond that. The facility knows to contact me immediately if a complication should arise. We will proceed accordingly, and that goes for your leg as well."

"I suppose we are hoping nothing goes wrong."

"Unfortunately, the uniqueness of our bodies prohibits any guarantees, but optimism is a key component in healing. Hope heals too."

Micah stole a glance at Ms. Vida, feeling more confident in his ability to invest productively into his future. It was something he had not felt since he first took on the 508 Park Avenue Project. After several phone calls, he was no closer to recovering the time he was missing than he had been before them.

"How long before my memory returns? I contacted my employer—my ex-employer, that is—and I was informed that I had tendered my resignation almost two months ago. I have no recollection of doing that. My girlfriend has not contacted me, and her number is no longer in service. I don't remember anything happening there, either."

"Micah, these things vary. To be frank, your memory may not return at all. Results vary. Your condition is very rare, Micah. The fact that you are able to speak in such a concise manner, your cognitive ability at this stage is phenomenal, even with the memory loss. You should consider yourself very lucky."

"I do. I just . . . I do."

"Don't worry. You will have an excellent team of therapists around you and one of the best nurses that I have ever had the pleasure to work with. You, my man, are in great hands."

CHAPTER 35

Michelle caught a glimpse of Armand standing in the kitchen as soon as she stepped inside the house. *Damn it.* She had hoped to avoid him. His normal schedule had him elsewhere.

"Michelle?"

Pausing in the doorway, Michelle contemplated doing her best Misty Copeland impersonation, pulling a half-pirouette and exiting back out the door. She was running low on clothes and had come by to widen her current selection. There was only so much she had been able squeeze into her duffle bag when she stopped by a few days after the *incident*, but this morning Grayson had graciously cleared a drawer for her. It was a gesture that prompted her to make this impromptu clothes snatch.

"MK?" Armand's voice, with the whistle's power, dizzied her senses, smacking her with the comfort of a mother's kiss intermingled with the disappointment of a hard-fought loss.

Her mind shifted as her location sank in. Brianna had been on her left, ass up, bent over the table. Armand was behind her, fucking their future away. *This* was the spot where she had witnessed her life explode. Hurt attacked her brittle defenses, nearly sending her to her knees. Wobbling, she moved forward with a new mission: to get everything she could, fully intending to avoid ever having to come back.

"Michelle, can we talk?" Armand asked as vacated the kitchen, walking toward her.

"I have nothing to say to you." *I probably could have come in through the back door, gotten my things, and managed to leave undetected*, she thought. Hindsight was fucking stupid.

"Michelle, please, I am only asking for a minute."

An avalanche of pain descended upon Michelle, freezing her limbs. Under its weight, she struggled to keep her shaky legs beneath her. She stared at the carpet, avoiding the brokenness etched in his eyes. Regret strained his voice, twisting his sound like a wet towel, wringing it out, leaving it ragged with tears. His rasp tugged at her will, prodding her to open up to him, but Michelle could not. She was unable to tear the love from the hurt; the promise from the betrayal. They were intimately linked in her mind, and she didn't want to hear from him.

"Go away." Making use of her legs again, Michelle trudged toward the hall.

Stepping in front of her, Armand temporarily blocked her path. "I have been trying to reach you for nearly two weeks."

Pushing Armand to the side, Michelle stormed past him, heading for the bedroom. Each word he spoke felt like a direct hit to her heart, like he'd taken his fist and punched her with all his might. His sound, the inflection, the love in his tone that she'd learned to depend on—a tune so familiar that she could pick his cough out of a crowd—now replayed as a twisted part of her worst nightmare come true. His moans filled her ears. She couldn't hear anything else, and she wasn't sure how much longer she could stand to hear him speak.

"I can't talk to you. Just leave me alone."

Armand, following closely behind her, persisted. "Michelle, tell me what to do."

Snatching open the nearest drawer, Michelle grabbed a fistful of clothes and threw them in the bag. She kept most of her grooming items atop the dresser. In one sweeping motion, she pushed everything into the duffle bag she held in a shaky hand.

"Please, just tell me how to fix this. Fix us, please!"

Tears clouded her vision as she lost her composure to the fury that had been building since she turned her key in the front door. Mindlessly grabbing clothes out of various drawers and chucking them into the bag, Michelle hadn't even noticed that she was on Armand's side of the dresser they shared. The clothes were his.

"That's my shit. What are you doing? Wait!" Armand yelled, reaching his hand to stop her.

Swiping his hand, pushing him back on his heels, Michelle ignored him. "Leave me alone!" she spouted in between breaths, desperate for this exchange to end.

"MK! Stop! Damn it! I am fuckin' sorry!" Armand hollered.

Michelle pulled open the next drawer, throwing those clothes in the duffle, too. "I hate you." She wished he would go away and let her get her things in peace. Being in his presence brought everything back—the love she couldn't release and the pain of his betrayal. It was like being given your favorite dessert along with electric shock, over and over again.

"No, you don't."

Halting her efforts, she dropped her duffle as she turned to address her ex-fiancé. "Don't tell me how I feel! You fucked my sister!"

"Michelle . . . I . . ."

"My fuckin' sister! My sister! Twin sister! Out of all the bitches available to you, bitches I have seen you with . . . you chose my twin?"

"It's not that simple, Michelle! It . . . wasn't like that. It's not what you think. Just . . . wait!"

"I cannot un-see it! It's like a fuckin' tattoo on my eyes, Armand! I can't run! Everywhere I look, I see my heart breaking over and over again!"

"Just let me explain."

"Explain what? Explain how you are going to return the last two years of my life you stole from me? Explain how this ring I accepted belongs at the bottom of a Cracker Jack box? Explain what? What, Armand?"

"Michelle Kaye . . . just . . . please, I love you."

"I fuckin' hate you! The both of you are dead to me!" Michelle fumed.

He moved closer to her, filling her lungs with his signature Polo Double Black cologne. "It was messed up what we did. What I did. It was a mistake. A mistake, Michelle," Armand insisted, reaching out for her hand.

"Don't touch me! Don't you ever fuckin' touch me! Just go away, Armand!" Michelle shrieked, shrinking away from his grasp. Her body shook so badly she felt a migraine coming on. Her hands vibrated before her eyes. The room began to spin around her.

"I love you, MK. I love you. Let me fix it. Let me try, please."

Tears continuously streamed down her face. She couldn't do this with him. Every second she stood there increased her hurt. Her head felt heavy, her chest tightening like someone was winding it. This was too much. Her thoughts traveled as Armand continued rattling a flimsy defense of his actions. His lips were moving for several minutes, but Michelle was no longer listening. Deciding to leave, she abruptly tuned back into him.

"I put Brianna out. She isn't here anymore. Come home."

Disgust framed her face. "Putting my sister out in the street is supposed to make me feel better? Is that it? The fuck is wrong with you?"

Armand narrowed his eyes, clenching his teeth as he exploded. "Fuck this shit! You mad when I bring her in, mad when I put her out. I can't win you with you!" Shaking a finger at her, he continued, "I can't ever fuckin' do shit right!"

Michelle's body shook as she absorbed his words.

"Tell me what to fuckin' do, Michelle! What the fuck do you want from me?"

Matching his intensity, Michelle shouted back, "Die! Just fuckin' die! Take that fuckin' gun and blow your mutha-fuckin' brains out!" Blistering tears coated her cheeks.

The request zapped whatever air was left out of the room. Armand shrank into the hurt he couldn't hide. Her words had wounded him. That hurt, too.

"I need to go." Not bothering to pick her bag up from the floor, she walked briskly out the back door leading to their private patio. Michelle, on the verge of completely falling apart, sprang into a full-blown sprint when she realized Armand was still following her. Reclaiming her days as a track star in the 200-meter dash, she hugged the curve, rounding the corner of her house toward her idling Audi.

Grayson, who had been waiting in the car, spotted her coming around the corner and quickly exited the car to help her. Michelle ran as fast as she could into Grayson's open arms. He held her until her heart slowed down to a normal speed. Then Grayson, paying no attention to Armand, led Michelle the short distance to the car and placed her in the passenger seat.

Grayson tried to comfort her, but Michelle was inconsolable. Pain ripped through her body, her mind, her soul. She couldn't think of what she had done to deserve to be betrayed by everyone she loved. Did any of them truly love her? Her words were indiscernible, sobs transforming her words into an infant's attempt at communication.

Kissing her forehead, Grayson wiped her tears with the inside of his hand, offering her some assurance. Satisfied that she was calm for the moment, Grayson closed the door, rising to his feet, only to turn to find a seething Armand standing a few feet away.

Armand shifted his weight from one foot to the other, sizing him up. He didn't know what to make of the situation other than what he saw in front of him. He didn't like what he saw one bit. He continued to move in Grayson's direction, intent on getting the answers to the questions in his head.

Grayson did not cower in fear or show any weakness at all, sensing his vibe shift into something else, something cold, steely. Michelle attempted to peer around him but could not. Grayson stood in front of her door. His frame blocked her view of Armand and prevented her from using that door to exit the vehicle. Her gut told her that by standing there, he intended to send a message to Armand. There was no reason for them to still be there. He could have put her in the car and driven away, but he didn't. He took his time, kneeling before her, kissing her, offering her comfort, all while Armand watched.

She hadn't told Grayson the specifics of everything, but he knew that Armand had been unfaithful to her, and his response to the news had not been *pleasant*. She would not be surprised if Grayson used the moment to taunt Armand. He spoke often about "teaching guys like him a lesson." As much as she fancied the idea of her ex-fiancé being clobbered by the hands of a former Golden Gloves champion, she didn't want Grayson getting into any trouble. Her hysterics were replaced with silent prayers for a peaceful end to the standoff as she looked on from the car.

Her apathy for Armand's well-being only worsened when he finally broke the silence.

"What the fuck are you lookin' at?"

Michelle rolled her eyes, irritated with Armand's antics. She wanted to leave, but as usual, he expected her to put her feelings aside and tend to his. She had no room in her life for his opinions on her business and could not care less about what Armand thought of her relationship with Grayson. She hadn't so much as looked at another man in nearly three years. Grayson sprang from circumstance, but Armand had been casually screwing her sister for who knows how long—right under her nose, no less. He made all the right moves to save Brianna, but he was making all the wrong ones trying to save their relationship. She needed space, and he seemed hell-bent on not giving her any.

"Michelle is upset. She is my priority. Understand?" Grayson stated. "I don't want any problems here."

"You are not driving off with my fiancée," Armand growled, flexing the muscles in his neck as he spoke.

Grayson reaffirmed his position. "I *am* leaving." He lowered his voice a few registers. "She does not want to be here, and you cannot keep her here."

Armand took a few steps toward Grayson. Grayson raised a hand to stop him.

"Now, I would like to do this peacefully. Michelle is under enough strain. This is unnecessary. Think about her. Consider her."

Armand arrested his movement, pondering his next move. "Michelle, I just wanted to talk to you. That's all. Two years cannot end like this."

Michelle remained silent.

"Try another day, all right? She doesn't want this today. If you love her, you won't upset her any more than you already have," Grayson said.

"No offense to you, but this is between me and Michelle. This is not your business."

"*This* is between you and me. You are talking to me."

"Fuck you."

Grayson laughed lightly. "That is the problem with dudes like you. No respect."

"I don't know you."

"That's right. You *don't* know me, so do both of us a favor and step the fuck back."

Michelle's mouth dropped in shock. She had never heard Grayson speak that way before. She couldn't say that she wasn't enjoying it, though. Too bad she couldn't see Armand's face or Grayson's.

"I ain't got to do shit."

Michelle felt the situation getting worse. Sticking her hand out of the window, she pushed her fingertips into the small of Grayson's back and instantly felt his body soften. Turning his body to the side, keeping a watchful eye on Armand, he looked at Michelle. Choosing not to speak, she made a plea to him with her eyes. It was a message he must have received because he gave Armand one last look and hastily made his way around to the driver's seat. Michelle refused to look at Armand.

"Michelle! Wait, Michelle!"

She could hear him calling for her as they drove away. Tears sprang from her eyes, forming a basin near the base of her throat. This transition would be even harder than she had anticipated. She knew she would need to speak with him at some point, but after today, she was not sure when she would be able to. It hurt like hell just being in the room with him. Hearing his voice was literally painful. She had no idea how they would move forward from this.

"Michelle, are you okay?"

Michelle looked at Grayson through her tears and attempted to speak. She couldn't say anything, but managed to shake her head no.

He ran his hand across the top of his dome. "You don't have to go back there if you don't want to. I can help you get new clothes. My couch is pretty comfortable. I prefer to sleep there anyway. Sleeping in that big bed by myself is . . . a *little* depressing. My room is yours as long as you need it."

Michelle could hardly believe what she was hearing. She knew Grayson was a good guy, but what he was offering was above and beyond. She cried even harder. She hadn't done anything to deserve how well he treated her, the type of friend he was being to her, but she was grateful. She angled herself in the seat, resting her head on his shoulder, a gesture of thanks. They could discuss what would or wouldn't happen later, but for now, she was headed back to her temporary home, a place where no one could find her. Not her sister, Armand, or her mother. Maybe being separated from them what just what the doctor ordered.

CHAPTER 36

Sophie and Peter sat across from each other in the breakfast nook. Timidity circled around them, squeezing their throats closed. Neither had found a way to begin the conversation. Sweat coated the inside of her palms, her nerves frayed and raw. Fear kept her mute. The moment of truth had arrived. Peter already looked pensive and on edge. This could potentially push him over.

"This is not awkward at all," Peter stated, breaking the silence.

Sophie offered him a half-smile. "I am searching for the perfect way to say what needs to be said."

"Luce, this is you and me. We will never have a *perfect* version of anything, and we don't need it. I have made my share of mistakes."

Sophie smiled genuinely, but she was still nervous about what she needed to share with him. "You just seem tense, and—"

"I am tense. This has been pretty stressful, Luce. We still have not discussed in detail what happened a couple weeks ago. Haven't gotten any closure about what really happened twenty years ago, but that doesn't mean that I don't love you. I expected the rugged terrain."

"I did, too, but I didn't know it would be all of this," Sophie confessed.

"Luce, I can't stop thinking about you. I don't want to be away from you. What am I supposed to do with this? I don't even know what you want."

Sophie took deep breath. "I love you, Peter. I do, but I have a lot going on, and I don't know if bringing you into my mess is fair."

"Why won't you let me make my own decisions? I am a grown man, and I am very capable of making choices. I know I had mommy issues in high school, but I have long since put those to rest. I don't need you to be *her*."

"I know."

"So, why don't you go ahead and tell me what's going on, Sophie? For once."

Sophie watched his Adam's apple rise and fall as he spoke, pulling her energy in order to force the words out. "Fine. I will start with what happened that night, twenty years ago."

Peter straightened up in the wicker chair, placed both arms in his lap and closed his eyes.

"Richard did not want me with you. He never did, but earlier that year, he told me that I had to break things off by the end of the summer. It didn't make sense to me. I had done everything he wanted me to do without any questions. Everything."

"What do you mean?"

"That is not important. I had followed orders, and I didn't understand why he wanted to take this one thing from me. Like he just didn't want me to be happy, ever."

Scrunching his face, Peter was visibly angry, trading in his tan hue for a redder tone. "Why didn't you tell me, Luce?" he asked between clenched teeth.

Sophie smothered her tears, determined to get this out once for and for all. "If I failed, he was not going to let you graduate. He told me he would ruin everything for you."

"What?"

"I knew he could do it. I had seen him do it to others, and I couldn't let that happen to you."

Peter bit his bottom lip, took some deep breaths, and stared out the window, trying to rein in his anger.

Sophie felt like a child again, helpless and afraid. "I'm sorry, Peter. I just didn't know what else to do. I had to do what he said. I had to."

Peter stood, reached over the table, and grabbed hold of her hands. "Luce, don't cry. Stop crying." He slumped into his seat, still holding on to her hands.

Shame took her words. Sophie waited for Peter to speak again. She couldn't bring herself to say another word. She was terrified, not because of what she said, but because of what she had left to say. Her confessional was not over. She had more to share, much more.

"Luce, I don't like that you didn't tell me, but I understand. We were young. He's your father. I have no right to be upset with you for being obedient to him. You were still a child. I forgive you."

Sophie saw a calmness color his eyes and knew he was telling the truth. She sighed with relief, glad that part of their past was behind her.

"Thank you, Peter. I was afraid you wouldn't understand."

"Of course I do. I do have a question, though."

Sophie's breath caught in her chest. Perhaps she had celebrated too soon.

"You met your husband while we were together?"

Sophie swallowed the lump in her throat. "Yes, I did. My father arranged it. Political reasons. We only hung out a few times, and nothing ever happened."

Peter released her hands and brushed his own against his thighs, drying them of the sweat that had accumulated. "So, how did you end up pregnant so quickly? If nothing happened?" His tone changed again, taking on a more accusatory tone.

Sophie hesitated before answering him, uncertain of what he would make of her truth. "Letting you go was one of the hardest things I have ever had to do in my life. I still cannot compare anything to that pain. I hated my father for that. I felt that I would never be free, no matter what I did. He would just keep using me, manipulating and controlling me."

Peter waited patiently while she spoke.

"When you left, I saw him on the porch."

Peter's eyes widened in shock. The question lingered on his lips.

"He had been watching the entire time. I couldn't believe it. I felt humiliated. I slept outside. Couldn't even go in the house. Nan came and fetched me early the next morning. There was a function later that night. I remember sitting in front of my vanity, looking at the mirror but seeing his shadow on the porch. I could not shake the image."

Sophie shook her head, sorting through her emotions at the time. "Nan was giving one of her pep talks, and I had a thought. I needed to make myself useless. If I did that, then he'd get rid of me, like he did my sister. I used to think she was crazy, but at that moment, I understood. It was the only way to get away from him."

Peter remained silent, listening intently.

"I knew what I needed to do, and then Nan said something that got my attention." Peter gave her an inquisitive look. *"Watch what happens,"* Sophie said, mimicking Nan.

"Something clicked when she said that, and I knew exactly how I would get him."

"What did you do, Luce?"

"I slept with Lewis that night."

Peter looked like he might collapse, his mouth opened in disbelief. "What?"

"I had sex with Lewis. My chess move. Found out I was pregnant later. Shared the news with Richard." Sophie reflected back on the moment with a fondness she could not hide from Peter. "He was so pissed. I wish I could have recorded it. Katherine was so upset she went to bed."

"So, you never loved the guy?"

Sophie looked up at Peter, confused by his question. One had nothing to do with the other. "Eventually, yes, we did grow to love each other, but I think our beginning hurt us."

"What do you mean?"

"He was distant. Aloof. Numerous affairs. I practically raised Michelle alone. Finances were not an issue, but the love between us never fully developed in a healthy way."

She could see Peter's mind moving, working, piecing things together. He had a question but did not pose it. She thought this was as good a time as she was going to get to segue into the rest of what she wanted to get off her chest today.

"Why did you stay with him if it was that bad?"

"I didn't go to college. I forfeited my inheritance. I didn't know how to function outside the world I had created for myself. I couldn't go back to the Freemont Estate, so I stayed. It wasn't very comfortable, but I had Michelle and this home."

That pensive look flashed across Peter's face again. It seemed to happen whenever she mentioned Michelle's name, but she wasn't certain. "I dealt with it until . . ."

"Until what?"

Sophie slowed down, choosing her words very carefully. "Until Michelle . . ."

There was that look again; it was Michelle that was bothering him.

"Michelle had graduated from college, living on her own. I was here by myself. One night, he came home, and we had a really vicious argument. Things got physical." Sophie watched the change in Peter's demeanor as she got emotional. "He beat me pretty badly. Michelle called, and I had to lie to her. You know? I didn't want her to see me that way."

Peter's mouth hung slightly agape while he listened. She knew she had him, but she had to do this just right.

"He didn't leave the house for several days after that night. I was so afraid. Every day he tormented me. He said mean, nasty things, and he . . . and he beat me constantly. I thought he was going to kill me."

"Luce, why didn't you call the police?"

"I couldn't. He had complete control over me. Plus, I knew that if I got away, he would just find me. He had connections. I was alone." Sophie burst into tears.

"I am so sorry you were going through that." Peter stretched across the table to comfort her, but Sophie raised her hand, stopping him.

"Oh gawd, Peter, I did something terrible, but you have to understand. I didn't have a choice! He would have killed me!"

"Luce, what did you do? What happened?"

"Oh, Peter, I killed him!" Sophie began wailing uncontrollably, falling onto the table, burying her face in her hands.

Peter jumped from his seat and quickly wrapped his arms around her. "Luce, I don't understand."

"I killed him, Peter," she confessed in between sobs. "I put cyanide in his drink and . . . and . . . it all happened so fast. I was just so afraid." Sophie tried to pull herself out of his hold to look him in the eyes. "He would have killed me, Peter!" Erupting into sobs all over again, Sophie continued to plead her case. "I just know he would have killed me. I had to do it, Peter! I had to!"

Peter held her while she cried. Sophie curled up, snuggling as close as she could to him. "Please, don't leave me, Peter. I love you. I never stopped." Sophie was not sure what would happen, but she was grateful that, at least for the moment, he was still there.

"It's okay, Luce. He can't hurt you anymore. He can't hurt you anymore."

CHAPTER 37

Frank and Lisa arrived in New York much later than expected—a week and two days later than expected. After the unexpected visit from Detective Baptiste, they had decided to hang around and see if the officers came across information relevant to the case. Even if the investigators did not find it helpful, it could be of use to the duo in the course of their personal search in the States. The decision proved prudent. Lisa started to feel worse and used those days to improve. Unfortunately, nothing more was acquired, but they did get another week of relaxation, courtesy of the hotel. Lisa could not move very fast, but they got out and enjoyed the beach, even did a little shopping for tax-free jewelry. Frank came to better understand what Lisa loved about the island.

LaGuardia was busy, noisy, and congested, with people milling about. Frank hated airports. He felt overstimulated, and it made him antsy. He feared the time it would take to get their things, but thirty minutes after their plane landed, they had their luggage and were waiting for the car service Frank's brother had sent to get them. Frank could not believe he had let Jacob muscle him into doing this. His brother, Griffin, was one of his least favorite people in the world. He had not seen him since he made that fateful trip to Dallas.

"I think that's the car there." Lisa interrupted his thoughts.

"I'm sorry. What did you say?" Frank asked.

Pointing to the charcoal Mercedes Benz S550, Lisa reiterated, "I think that may be the car right there."

Frank followed her finger and stared at the Mercedes. "Why did you—" Before he could finish the question, he spotted a hand slide through a small opening in the window, beckoning them forward. "I think you're right. I know we spoke about him briefly, but I just want to remind you. Please follow my lead with him."

"I know, Frank. Don't worry. I'm sure it will be fine, and if not, we can handle it." Lisa gave Frank a reassuring glance.

He hoped she was right. He had no idea what to expect from his brother. He was like night and day. Growing up, they had been pretty close. They shared the same hatred for their father, and they pitied their mother. Everything Frank knew about the art of finances, he had learned it from his big brother. Their father probably knew about the money they "borrowed," but he didn't seem very bothered by it. In fact, Frank thought he was proud of them. But one day, his brother suddenly had a change of heart.

Frank had accepted an invitation to join his brother for lunch. Curiosity had persuaded him to agree to join his brother at his Manhattan apartment, but Frank felt uneasy about it. Griffin had been horrible to him over the last several months, and Frank took a chance to receive an unlikely apology.

His instincts were correct. His brother had not contacted him to apologize, nor was he interested in rekindling their broken bond. He cornered Frank in the living room, trapping him between the fireplace and a window overlooking Central Park, demanding that Frank repay every penny he had taken from their father, spouting some nonsense about morality and birthrights. Frank dismissed Griffin, punched him in the face, and ran out of the apartment. It was the first time he could remember fearing his brother. The look in his eyes that day sent Frank on plane to the South. He booked a flight that night to Dallas and had not spoken with his brother since.

The car was not very far away, but the passenger pickup area was so crowded that it still took several minutes to slither through the crowd. Frank braced himself for what awaited.

"Here we go."

The doorman nodded, acknowledging Frank, and smiled at Lisa. "Afternoon, sir, ma'am." He opened the door, and Frank's mouth dropped open. He could not believe his eyes.

"Hello, Franklin."

Frank looked to Lisa, incredulous over what he saw once he stared back into the car. The muscles in his face froze in complete shock.

"Griffin?" Frank was not sure what to think or what was going on.

Lisa hit his arm with her hand, pushing him away, before gripping him hard enough to break his skin. He could feel her body grow rigid as she stood beside him. Tapping her arm in reassurance, he ushered her into the car, never taking his eyes off his brother. Frank did not know what to think as he climbed into the car behind Lisa, but one thing he knew for certain: Jacob had some serious explaining to do.

"Franklin, as I am sure you can guess, there are a few things I think we need to discuss."

Frank rode in silence, holding tightly to Lisa's hand, staring in bewilderment. His brother was right. A conversation was definitely needed, but Frank wasn't sure if he wanted to be a part of it. He glanced at the gentlemen seated beside his brother, his eyes finding Lisa again. She refused to look at either of them, noticeably bothered by the situation. Frank wasn't too keen on it, either, but it was too late to retreat.

Squeezing Lisa's hand, managing to get a quick glance from her, he gave her a peck on her cheek and smiled. She returned a half-smile, he could see the unease in her eyes. He needed some answers.

Clearing his throat, he turned to his brother and inquired, "Griffin, what in the hell is going on here?"

"All of your questions will be answered soon enough. Hold tight." It was not his brother who answered his question, but the familiar stranger seated beside him.

Frank looked at him, trying to decide if, and how, he should address him. Something felt wrong about his presence there. Frank could not put his finger on what it was, but something was definitely off with this guy.

"Who are you?"

Ruffling the hem of his long pea coat, the gentleman tilted his head slightly forward, giving Frank an obstructed view of his face. "My friends call me Henry."

CHAPTER 38

Brianna lay sprawled across her mother's bed, curiously awaiting the conclusion of the war of whispers Sophie was engaged in on the phone in the hall, a nail's length beyond the door frame. Following a particularly intense exchange with Armand, Brianna had taken a cab to her mother's home, seeking refuge.

Armand's antics were tinkering with her fragile grip on sanity. Her nerves were already stretched to capacity trying to manage her feelings about the probability of seeing Javan again, the man who haunted her thoughts. It seemed like he was chasing her underneath a cloak of invisibility, spying on her through her bedroom walls, and left his inescapable essence nearly everywhere she went. The thought of driving herself to the Terrell State Hospital crossed her mind several times since she had roped Dr. Baxter into her quest for a reunion.

She was extraordinarily confident that he would come through for her and, according to their last conversation, he was getting close. *That* little tidbit popped the last guitar string on the instrument playing a tune for her and Armand, stripping her of any patience she had left to deal with him.

He had been invading her privacy as usual, an unnerving practice that guilt coerced her into accepting, as he pressed her for details she was unwilling to share. His attitude soured by the second, and she had to get out of there. The argument drifted away from her conversation to whatever random nonsense rattled around in his mind. He kept rambling about some Grayson guy who Brianna had never heard of.

Her expectation for change following the incident had weakened into nothingness with the passing of that first awkward week. Initially, Armand quelled his urge to smother her, but something had changed in the last couple of days. His larks and erratic behavior had worsened substantially. He began interrogating her after phone calls and demanding to know her every move. Brianna thought she might snap if she didn't get some relief.

Sophie had been very hospitable and lulled Brianna into the comfortable space she craved. Their conversation had been reasonably pleasant, despite the incessant interruptions from her lawyer. Brianna's growing curiosity easily eclipsed her annoyance. Sophie barely even ventured to take bathroom breaks when they were together. She so desperately wanted them to bond that Brianna was sure she would hold her breath if she felt it would interfere. Her mother taking a call, let alone multiple calls, indicated the importance of the matter being discussed. Something was up, and Brianna wanted to know what.

The flickering in her belly fueled her desire to snoop, reminding her that she had someone else to consider, to protect. Since Sophie took each call out into the hall, out of earshot, Brianna assumed it had nothing to do with the will and was most likely something Sophie didn't want her to have any knowledge of. Unfortunately for Sophie, Brianna's hearing had greatly improved since she mastered the art of quieting her mind. Her mother's hushed tone amplified as she concentrated on it. Stretching across the large, king-size bed, listening to every word, she made a mental record of her mother's half of the conversation.

"I don't want to give her anything. That is unequivocally off the table. Take care of it." Sophie shifted her weight from one side to the other, sighing audibly in frustration. Brianna caught the subtle shades of panic in her mother's blue eyes, casting a worry line in her direction.

Noticing Brianna, Sophie waved in greeting, rolling her fingers across intangible ivories, offered a weak smile; but she continued talking, incorrectly assuming her words were private. "I thought the payment was all that was needed, Steven. Why isn't he being moved?"

Who was the *he* her mother was referring to? The only person Brianna could think of was Dr. Baxter, but she could not create a scenario that would make that question applicable.

"One thing at a time. Focus on the grounds and getting that motion dismissed. I will take care of Charlie. . . . It does not matter. I can handle her. Just do as I say, Steven."

Charlie? Nothing involving that woman could lead to any good place, and Brianna couldn't fathom what business her mother had with her. She could only hope that it would not adversely affect her or her child.

Her child. It still felt a little weird, that notion. Still, she couldn't persuade her lips to part for the request for parental advice to emerge. This part of her mother, the murky water she lived in, persistently worked against reconciliation. Trusting a person, especially this person, her mother, who intentionally left so much of herself shrouded in darkness, fictionalized the idea of a tangible relationship. The reality of being birthed, then sold on a whim, consistently thrashed its fiendish edges, slicing through every reasonable argument that might allow for a bridge connecting their cliffs to be borne, reducing her mother's delineation of what transpired to nothing more than an excuse, unworthy of any space on her mental landscape.

Prior to this period in her life, where she now found herself trying to navigate the intricate dynamics of the complexity of motherhood, empathy was not possible. Feeling her own seed fluttering about in her belly was the single driving force behind her newfound ability to gradually accept that her mother had acted out of hopelessness and desperation—two things Brianna could certainly identify with at the moment.

"Sorry about that," Sophie stated, rejoining Brianna in the room. Rolling over on the bed, Brianna made room for her mother to sit beside her. "So, where were we?"

Brianna wanted to ask her about her conversation but decided not to. She had enough going on without inviting her mother's issues to her party. Besides, she was in no hurry to recreate the tension that had brought her there in the first place.

"You were telling me about Dr. Baxter."

"Ah, yes, Peter. He didn't tell me that he knew you. I wondered how he got my number, but . . ."

"I didn't give it to him. Up until a few days ago, I didn't know he knew you, either."

"Humph . . . well, anyway, we went to school together. I have known him for a very, very long time."

"Has he contacted you?"

Sophie didn't sprint off, but she got the *crap, the police are behind me* look in her eyes.

"What was the nature of your relationship with him?"

Sophie scooted to the edge of the bed, surgically increasing the space between herself and Brianna. "Why does that matter?"

"Is telling me a problem?"

Cupping the back of her neck with her hand, an uncomfortable Sophie danced her way to answer. "We were high school sweethearts. Circumstances stifled what could have been. I broke things off with him. Met your father and never looked back."

"Must have been pretty intense."

"Excuse me?" Sophie looked back at Brianna, still lying on the bed.

"Serious?"

"Between your father and me?"

"*Peter*."

Sophie shook her head. "Oh, whatever was between us evaporated centuries ago and is as valuable as a silver dollar now."

Brianna doubted that. "Are you sure about that?"

"I have a lot going on right now. Building our relationship. Mending things with Michelle. I cannot even think about Peter."

"Well, I guess it's just my luck that he saw me that night, or *your luck* rather."

"My luck?"

"I have not been on his mind for twenty something years. He isn't chasing me." Brianna pretended not to see the coy smile that crept into her mother's face.

"Brianna, Peter thinks everything happens for a reason, you know? So, he may feel responsible for you or something. Given the situation."

Brianna had picked that up from him.

"You aren't curious about your father at all?" Sophie asked.

"I guess I am. I don't really feel one way or the other." Thoughts of Frank ran through her mind. "I grew up with a great dad, and I never knew Lewis. I guess I didn't miss him."

Turning over on her back, she admired the artwork on the high ceiling, deciding, after careful study, that it looked like an illustration of randomness. It was the type of art the untrained eye would credit a child with. Brianna did not recognize anything in particular, but the massive mash of colors was breathtaking.

Sophie lay down beside her. "If anything changes, I'm here," Sophie stated, giving her a hand a quick squeeze.

Brianna continued looking at the painting, bathing in its energy.

"I had this done about a month after we moved into this house. Needed the color. Your father and I, Lewis, were falling apart. This reminded me to live each day. To smile."

Placing an invisible hand over her mouth, Brianna stuffed her inappropriate humorous quip about Sophie's need to have *color* in her bed being the catalyst for her suffering back into her dungeon of forgotten funnies, swallowing her words until the urge to speak them had passed.

"How so?"

"The curve is so high that you can only see the painting from this position," Sophie offered, illustrating the high point of the curved ceiling with her finger as she spoke. "Life is similar in that it does not matter how much you have or lack. Happiness, peace, joy are all about perspective. Things might look pretty bleak, but if you find the right position, you'll see the beauty in your situation."

Brianna meditated on her words for a minute. "I cannot stop looking at it." Brianna gasped as she felt her belly flutter, much more dramatically than before. She unconsciously draped a protective hand over her stomach. "A bowl of passion and energy. Simple, but exquisite. Reminds me a little of Charles Alston's work."

"Who?"

"He's an African-American painter. Mentored Jacob Lawrence." Glancing at her mother's expression, she continued. "I assume you are familiar with Lawrence."

Sophie didn't give an indication one way or the other.

"Maybe not." Of course she didn't know. Her mother seemed educated, knowledgeable about many things, but she was white. It wasn't surprising that she wouldn't know about the brilliant gems polished during the Harlem Renaissance.

Brianna took in the subdued look on Sophie's face from her profile. "Maybe we can go see some of his work at the African American Museum."

"Alston?"

"They have a few pieces by Lawrence. Beautiful pieces."

"I'd like that. Did you study art in school? College?"

"Not more than what my degree required. Traveled a lot. I guess my eye developed from seeing the Creator's artwork in nature. Cultivated my appreciation for the artists' eyes. Of course, their gifts are remarkable, but their vision is what I am most impressed with. The why behind the production. Lawrence is one of my favorites, and I am well-versed in everything that has anything to do with him."

Sophie's mellow tone livened up. "Really? I would love to hear about him."

"Sure thing," Brianna offered, mentally withdrawing from their current dialogue and disappearing again into the painting above her. "Back to you and *Peter*."

Sophie laughed uncomfortably. "Why the interest in him?"

"His interest in me."

"What do you mean?" Sophie asked, concerned.

"He has gone out of his way to help me. I haven't always been the most agreeable person, but he hung in there anyway. Not sure what his angle is, and I don't want any more surprises."

Sophie flipped over on her side, facing Brianna. "Peter is a very decent person. He doesn't move with hidden agendas. I don't know how credible an endorsement *from me* is, but if it has any weight with you, you can trust him."

Brianna felt her chest tightening. She sank her teeth into her lips to break the numbness ensuing. She didn't want to have this *talk,* yet it was one she knew she could no longer avoid. Her mother's last remark foretold their direction.

"Brianna, I cannot—"

"Mom, please don't." Brianna focused more on the painting above her, picking pieces to concentrate on in an effort to keep her emotions under control. Knowledge of pregnancy seemed to have turned her into an emotional mess, subject to burst into tears over anything.

"I made a horrible mistake, and I appreciate you giving us a chance to breathe."

"Mom . . ."

"I know that this had been very difficult for you. Maybe I am not what you expected."

"Stop, please," Brianna begged.

"Brianna . . . no! You will talk to me. Right now!" Sophie screeched, bordering an emotional dam herself as her frustration took over. "I am no mother at all if I let us stay this way."

"You're barely a mother now!" Brianna retorted.

Sophie gasped, tears pooling in the corners of her eyes. "Maybe I deserve that."

Closing her eyes, Brianna took a deep breath. "I didn't mean that, Mom."

"Yes, you did, and that's okay, Brianna." Sophie took her forefinger and wiped the tears streaming down Brianna's face. "You are my daughter, and I love you. Nothing I did changes that. I know my decisions don't speak to that, but I do. Very much. Hate me. Loathe me. I'll still love you." Sophie was barely audible, her words like a soft falsetto. "Feel whatever you feel, just let me in, please. You can say to me whatever you need to say. Share your heart. I am not going anywhere."

Brianna inched closer to her mom, scooting down in the bed to nuzzle her face in the soft fabric of her chiffon blouse. "Passed me off to a stranger," she mumbled. "People keep pennies longer than you kept me."

"I promise. I'm never letting you go again." Sophie cradled her in her arms.

Brianna allowed her mind to simmer, trying to pry herself loose of her fear so that she could fully receive what had been missing. "My life is nothing like it was and it never will be again. I don't know how to trust you, but I need someone. I cannot do this alone."

Sophie pulled Brianna closer. "It is okay, Brianna. We will get through this. No matter what happens, I'm never letting you go again."

Brianna felt the dampness of her mother's shirt and wept even more. Sophie held her tighter, offering Brianna comfort that only a mother could. Though she had only recently learned of Sophie's existence, she had felt her absence for quite some time, rooting itself in the distance between herself and Lisa, an invisible chasm weakening their ability to make a genuine connection as she grew older.

The unexplained loomed in front of her, embedded in the half-smile her mother wore that mirrored her own. Perhaps the space between herself and Lisa had been Sophie in a very real, tangible way. For the first time in months, Brianna did not have to rely on rationale to escape the solitude that seemed to follow her closer than a shadow. There, in her mother's arms, she felt protected and loved.

CHAPTER 39

"Come on. We really need to get inside," Frank urged as he stood leaning against the door of the cab.

"My pain is getting worse by the minute. Moving is a . . . bit of a challenge."

Dropping the bags on the curb, Frank reached down to assist Lisa. He felt his nerves fraying as her turtle pace increased the inevitably of their capture. "Griffin probably sent him after us."

Lisa offered little to no support as he tried to help her stand, effectively replacing his apprehension with dread. This was not a good scenario. Now her slow pace shone like gold in comparison to her not moving at all.

"This isn't going to work. Hold on. Sit a sec." He gently placed her back inside the cab while his mind drafted a new plan to accommodate the change. He kept constant vigil of his surroundings, searching for a plausible solution.

"Frank . . ." Her face contorted as she struggled to breathe through the pain. "It hurts."

Bending slightly into the cab, Frank yanked the duffle bag from the floor behind the passenger seat. Lisa whimpered in pain while Frank sorted through its contents to retrieve the OxyContin prescribed to her.

"Please hurry, Frank. It's . . . worse." Lisa sat with her back to the driver's side passenger door, feet dangling toward the sidewalk. Her gelatin frame shook with each pang emanating from her wound. Seeing Lisa leaning against the backseat, whimpering in pain, was enough to send Frank over the edge. He was not accustomed to seeing her so defenseless, and it struck a nerve.

"I am. Hang in there." Frank had the medicine but nothing for her to take it with. "Simmy, my man, got anything to drink in here? Water bottle?"

The cabbie peered at Frank through the rearview mirror, observing as he opened the bottle and counted out the amount of pills Lisa needed to take. "Not a free one."

"I'll pay for it."

The cabbie handed Frank the water bottle over his shoulder, keeping an eye on him through the mirror. "Say, is she all right? I can't have nobody dyin' in my cab."

"No one is dying."

"That's good, 'cause I hit a cat once. Well, technically, the cat hit me . . . well, the cab. Anyway, I couldn't sleep for weeks. Kept seeing that Cheshire cat from that *Alice in Wonderland* joint. Like he was haunting me on behalf of his dead homie. I'on know, son. I think a person would be worse, though."

Paying no attention to the cabbie, Frank twisted the cap off the bottle, placed the pills on Lisa's tongue, and lifted her head while she drank them down. "Should be better soon."

He was relieved that she would not be in pain, but the pills usually made her very drowsy. He definitely would need help with her. They needed to get back to Dallas as soon as possible.

"Did you know them dudes was high as shit when they wrote that joint? I found that out and was like, yo . . . that makes so much fuckin' sense!"

Frank scanned the loading/unloading zone for a familiar car and was relieved to find none. "Listen, my

man, Simmy . . ." Frank peered into the front seat, finding Simmy's gaze locked on him in the rearview mirror.
"'Preciate you driving us out here. And the water."

"It's yo' money. Don't know why you want to come to
Newark Liberty International Airport over LGA, but mo'
money for me, so it's yo' play."

Frank laughed lightly, constantly scoping their scene.
"This is an excellent airport, Simmy. The first in this area."

"The first in the area? Sounds like a plane museum to
me."

"Ha, maybe it is. Listen, I got another job if you're
interested."

"I'on know 'bout dat. I barely want this one. Plus, the
way you looking around all nervous and shit, that job don't
hardly seem legal."

"Trust me, it's legal. Two stacks in it for you."

The cabbie turned his nose up in disbelief. Frank rummaged through his duffle bag and pulled out two stacks of
fresh hundred-dollar bills. "They are yours, if you accept."

"Frank . . ."

Frank glanced down at Lisa and noticed the blood seeping through her blouse. *Fuck.*

"What happened? Was it the bag?"

Lisa's head rolled slowly from left to right, but Frank
couldn't discern her answer. Not that it mattered. The damage was done, leaving Frank to hope that it was something
minor, within his scope of medicinal practice. Departing
his parents' home, the residence that his brother assumed
ownership of, had not been difficult, but Lisa insisted on
doing something useful. Frank failed to dissuade her, resulting in that *something* materializing as her carrying the
duffle bag, the lightest in their possession, to the cab.

"Lisa . . . Lisa . . ."

Lisa did not verbally respond, but the somersaults her face was doing indicated the pain she was in.

"Shit." Even more desperate than before, Frank looked at the driver again. "Come on. My wife needs medical attention. I could really use a hand."

"Say, son, that ain't none of my business right there."

"Two stacks to carry the damn bags. That is all I need you to do."

"I don't know, son. You look like you into some shit that I want no parts of."

"I don't have time for this shit. Take the fuckin' money."

"Nope, not me. Not Simmy."

Frank diverted his eyes away from the mirror, breaking contact, took a deep breath, and looked again. "I'll throw in another stack."

"I'm saying, though, my grandma need this operation . . ."

Frank wanted to wrap his hands around Simmy's neck and shake that snarky grin off his face. He couldn't believe he was being extorted by the fucking cabbie. Frank bent his knees, hovering in the door, and looked up at Lisa, his anger quelled by the sight. Her honey cover was flavored with different shades of cherry, and her eyes were wet with tears. The medicine still had not kicked in. He needed to get her inside.

"Five stacks! Five thousand dollars to grab my fuckin' bags!"

"Cool. I got yo' bags."

"Thank you." Frank rose to his feet and shoved his hand in the duffle.

"No prob, son."

"Fuckin' Republican."

"I'll carry them to the gate." Simmy turned the car off, removed the keys, and hit the button, turning on his hazard lights. "This can't take too long, though, 'cause I ain't tryin' to lose the cab."

"Here." Frank passed him two stacks. "Get the rest at the gate. Don't try and fuckin' run with that cash. It's nothin' to send the guy after me in your direction."

"It's not even like that, son. Man of my word. Scout's honor and shit."

"Are you a Scout?"

"I could be the fuckin' King of Zamunda. Don't matter."

Frank, without options, had to trust Simmy. Worst case scenario: he'd be out of his luggage and two thousand dollars, things he could replace. Truth was, he needed Simmy to accompany them to Dallas. He did not know who he could trust there and would need help with Lisa, presumably having impeded her healing. The move was risky, but if Frank's assumption was correct, Simmy would be of great benefit to him.

"Guess it doesn't," he said.

"Cool, but yo' cab fare is separate."

"Are you fuckin' serious?"

Unfazed, Simmy replied, "I ain't 'bout to pay my job out of my ends. Not to mention the meter has been running this whole time, so don't try and stiff me."

Frank stifled a laugh. Simmy hustled him for five thousand dollars to carry some bags, and he was yelling about getting stiffed on a cab fare. If anything, Simmy was audacious. "Five thou and you still chargin' fare. Un-fuckin-believable."

"That is a separate job. Two jobs, two payments, yo'."

Frank rolled his eyes, slamming the door closed with a swift kick. "Grab the bags. Let's go."

"I ain't no Republican, neither. I'm a Black Panther."

Halting his movement, Frank threw Simmy a quizzical look. "What?" Frank had completely forgotten about his Republican comment.

Simmy elaborated. "It's a political party."

Frank cocked his head at an angle, eyeing Simmy with an exaggerated squint.

"You know . . . the Black Panther *Party*?"

Shaking his head, Frank turned toward the entrance, stepping away from Simmy, who continued, determined to complete his thought. Frank had knowledge of Panthers. He didn't know of anyone he grew up with that didn't. Simmy bringing them up in the manner that he did was what confused him, and that was something he could not undo.

"You know, the Black Panther *Party*, like the rest of 'em—Democrat, Green, Tea. Only difference is they actually care about black folk. So, I fucks with them."

Frank had no words. He dared not pause to look at Simmy. "Just come on." Simmy's youthful ignorance filtered through his tough-guy speak a little more with each word. Frank figured he was not too far beyond the legal drinking age, counting it as an advantage. However, Simmy's mouth threatened to force Frank into pulling the plug on his exit strategy altogether.

With the duffle on his shoulder, Frank scooped Lisa up into his arms, carrying her like an infant. She held on, with an arm around his neck, as best she could.

"Frank, I think I'm losing a lot . . . of . . . blo . . . blood."

"Stop talking, babe. Save your energy. It's probably the medicine taking effect. I'll take a look once we find a secure space inside." Frank tried to keep her as still as possible, concerned about the stitches in her chest, but he couldn't prevent her from shuffling in his arms.

Her speaking pattern reflected as much. "Do you . . . rea . . . lly think your . . . brother would . . . send for us?"

"I know it. He hasn't changed. Still wants to control everything, control me."

"But does he . . . even know we're gone?"

"Yeah, son, who are you running from at three in the morning?"

Ignoring Simmy, Frank answered his wife. "Babe, I don't know if he knows yet, but I'm not taking any chances."

"Wait . . . you running from some dude who don't know if he chasing you? Is he into Voodoo or something?"

"Simmy, stay out of this." Simmy had found the perfect set of chords to strum Frank into an asylum. He could not recall a person who had annoyed him with such tenacity.

"I don't play with that Voodoo-hex-type shit. Fuck that. Nope. Not Simmy."

"What are you talking about? No one said anything about Voodoo."

"Well, no one said Voodoo was off the table until you said it right then, so I was forced to prepare for a Voodoo priestess bitch to pop up."

"Something is wrong with your fuckin' mind."

"What? I can't ask no questions. Got me carrying yo' heavy-ass bags through this big-ass airport. It's like a whole otha city in here."

"Please. Shut the fuck up. Damn. Give your lips a fuckin' rest. Shit."

"I picked you up, yo. If this dude got you sneaking out in the middle of the night, am I safe? Maybe I need to come with'chu."

"Come with me where?" Frank had no idea how he was carrying Lisa and engaging in this weird-ass conversation. He noticed Simmy took to scanning their surroundings as well and would have found some comfort in that if he had any clue as to who he needed to look out for. Sure as hell wasn't no damn Voodoo priestess or whomever else had entered Simmy's mangled mind.

"I don't know. Where you going?"

"Nowhere."

"Then why in the fuck are you powerwalking through the airport?"

"You are not coming with us." Frank's adrenaline was pumping fast. His muscles strained under Lisa's weight, but he refused to falter. He pushed through it, holding her as high as he could.

"Do you really want me here with the crazy dude that might or might not be chasing you?"

"Fra . . ." Lisa started drifting into La La land, her medicine lulling her to sleep, wafting on the edges. "Le . . ."

"Shhh. We're almost there." Frank searched for a semi-secluded seating area. The airport was bustling with people even at this late hour, making the task a difficult one.

"Over there." Simmy spoke from behind Frank, pointing over his shoulder to the left. Not bothering to wait for Frank, Simmy headed that way.

Frank followed the kid around the corner to a few clusters of chairs, each holding four or five chairs, nestled behind a few artificial trees. The spot was not bad. It was out of sight but still allowed Frank to keep an eye on the main floor of the airport. Frank settled a sleeping Lisa into one of the chairs, propping her into what he hoped would be deemed a comfortable sleeping position if she were awake.

"She doesn't look hot, yo."

"That fee doesn't cover unsolicited medical advice."

"No worries. That's for free. She look ill."

"Thanks, but my wife is not your concern." Frank sat beside Lisa to peek at her stitches. The bleeding had stopped, but the fact that she had been hemorrhaging at all was troublesome. He didn't want to disrobe her in view of Simmy, but from what he was able to see, the stitches looked intact. He surmised it was the strain of her aggressive movement that had caused the bleed.

"Yeah, but if she drop cold, then you'll be looking at me like, *why you didn't say something?*"

"I told you, no one is dying."

"You also offered me five Gs to drag some bags through the airport."

"I did, and I'm questioning my decision."

Simmy lifted his hands, waving them in front of his chest. "No need for that. *I'mmm* not tryin' to question yo' judgment or nothin'."

"I need to hit the teller, purchase our tickets." Frank stood to leave.

"Our? You mean one for me, too?"

"Your cab is parked outside in a no park zone."

"I'on care about my uncle's cab."

Frank did not respond to his admission. From the moment they entered the cab, Frank had determined Simmy was either new to the profession or posing. He didn't even turn the meter on until Frank prompted him.

"Are you serious about coming with us?"

"As a trail of gas near an open flame."

"Why?"

"Always wanted to go to Texas."

"Who said anything about Texas?"

Patting the top of one of the suitcases, Simmy replied, "These expired airport tags."

Frank was mildly impressed. Simmy was literate, resourceful. So far things had gone in accordance with what Frank had envisioned.

"Those don't mean I am headed there now."

"I'on care where you goin', yo. I can take the money and fly myself wherever, but I'd rather roll into yo' city."

"What's in it for you?"

"The duffle. Yo, you pay, I'm there. Nothin' poppin' here."

Frank stood in silence, pretending to mull the decision.

"Yo, you might want to hurry up."

"Got somewhere to be?"

"Nah, but I think dude in the black trench got a brick for you."

Turning to see who Simmy was referring to, Frank slid behind one of the trees, peeping through the branches, and spotted the black trench coat. He breathed a sigh of relief when the guy turned, confirming that he wasn't Ghost.

"He's just another patron. No problem."

"Yeah, but clearly dude got you shook, yo. I'm a loyal dude. I can help you, yo."

Frank made him wait a few more seconds, baiting him, checking to see if he would make another push. Simmy held his peace, and Frank liked that. Maybe there was some hope that Simmy wouldn't constantly be yappin'.

"I'll be back. Watch her." Frank left Simmy sitting there without an answer. He made his way to the main desk to purchase three tickets on the next flight headed to DFW. If Simmy was still there upon his return, the last ticket belonged to him.

CHAPTER 40

Aiyana Jones, say her name, Aiyana Jones, say her name, Aiyana Jones, say her name, won't you say her name. Sandra Bland, say her name . . .

As the chant sprinted forward, she felt her center plummeting, forcing a hole through her gut, landing in the inches between her feet. She felt paralyzed by the Afrikaans' drums dancing behind Janelle Monet's anguished cry for justice. The moment again rose like tiny speed bumps, recreating the horror in her mind.

Hellll yoouuu talmbouuttt? Hell you talkin' 'bout? . . .

Leaning forward with her head cemented to the door, smearing her DNA across its surface, Michelle pleaded with her body to move. Her fist was poised to request entry, grappling with her inability to maintain her indifference, the necessary space she had created to hold on to her sanity in the turbulent social climate the country had revealed itself to exist in.

There was too much life happening for her to keep up with it all. Death had been a recurring theme lately. Black Death all over the Internet. All over the country. Over and over, story after story. Unarmed black bodies dropping to be resurrected with hashtags, protests, and T-shirts. She couldn't help but see her father in their sullen faces, and that hurt. She, too, longed for justice, for something to ease the ache, erase the fear, but she didn't have the energy to lend to the street. She did not have anything to offer anyone.

The beat vibrating through the air, massaging the minds, anchoring the spirits of the oppressed and the weary in its rhythm, had claimed her hero. The Black Lives Matter movement, birthed from a collective pain, swallowed many, night after night. Michelle, too broken to dance, felt the angst of resisting the urge. Residents in Ferguson, Missouri took to the streets while a mother's son lay sprawled out in the hot Missouri sun for four-plus hours. Michael Brown was not special, not unlike other sons who have fallen victim to violence. Not special, not unlike other sons who had been forced to eat lead from department-issued handguns, except this time, the people said *enough*.

Maybe it was the callous disregard for the boy's humanity on behalf of the officers involved, their fellow brethren, and eventually the city of Ferguson, Missouri that changed the hearts and minds of the people there. The horror of seeing his broken body on display that set ablaze a spirit of resistance that swept the nation and spread all over the world. Michelle couldn't know, but what followed was the unleashing of a constant Polaroid of unarmed black bodies taken by police violence. No black body was safe; not man, woman, or child.

Back then, Michelle had Brianna to rescue, her parents to find. There was plenty to keep her attention. But now, she had nothing—no energy to do anything, not even cry for herself. Grayson had been a godsend to her, removing her reservations and permitting her to grieve in whatever way felt proper. The vicious cycle of the constant exposure to state violence through social media had not radicalized her or Grayson during the year following Brown's murder, but things had changed. Grayson was not the same man from even two weeks prior to this moment. He had left her to do his part. The movement, as necessary as it was, had taken her sole confidant into its grasp.

And Michelle knew exactly when it happened. It almost took her, too. Sandra Bland, a woman twenty-eight years young, just a few years away from Michelle; a woman very much like her was found dead in a Texas cell following an illegal arrest originating from a routine traffic stop. Nothing made sense to Michelle. She couldn't see how a woman so vibrant, intelligent, and determined could take her own life as the authorities claimed she had. No one could accept it.

She didn't get her information from the news. Twitter was her source, preferring to see and hear from people like herself on the ground, but it was Grayson who had relayed the awful details about Sandra Bland, creator of Sandy Speaks, an inspirational vlog geared toward encouraging black youth.

Michelle had not been on social media. The unraveling of her relationship with Armand had forced her mind closed to the world. Grayson had been considerate of this, until that moment. She could still see the look in his eyes, a mixture of anger and despair. It was a look that failed to leave him for days. Sandra was too close to home, too close for Grayson to continue being the man she needed him to be for her. A new light shone in his eyes. His energy, his attitude, had changed overnight.

Amadou Diallo, say his name. Amadou Diallo, say his name. Amdou Diallo, say his name, say his name, won't you say his name. . . .

The song continued to play. Name after name rang out, adding to her pain, punishing her for listening, for hearing, for knowing and pretending otherwise. Some part of her yearned to put her journalistic skills to use, lending her eye, her gift to narrating the truth often ignored or misconstrued by mainstream media. Some part of her wanted to do something, but what good was a car with no gas? Where could it go? That was how she felt, empty. Her life was in shambles, and she had not a clue of how to change that. Searching for a solution took everything from her. Some days, showering felt akin to standing atop Mount Everest. She was barely of any of use to herself, let alone others.

She smiled at the irony of it all. As long as she could remember, she had longed to live without inhibition, but the safety of her existence precluded her from doing so. The injustices piling up before her eyes, stacked with bodies too high for her comfort, should have been a great propeller. Ordinarily, she imagined, it would be more than enough to send her to the front lines, where she would gladly sacrifice her body in the name of freedom. She knew she would be with Grayson, fighting alongside him and others, exposing the hypocrisy within the system. It was a system she watched break her father down, one she became familiar with during her time at Rice. But this was no ordinary time for her. Michelle was already in a fight for her life.

Grayson's preoccupation with the movement, however noble, had created a wedge between them that she could no longer ignore. So, she stood outside the door, waiting for the song to conclude, hoping to avoid the disappointment this tune brought to his eyes. It invigorated him, and when she didn't return his energy, the rejection cut both ways. The conversation she needed to have would be painful enough.

The mystic chant concluded, with the sound of Michelle's knuckles drumming against the polished oak providing the only sound. Grayson opened the door in an unexpected burst. Her mouth hung slightly agape in surprise.

"Finally decided to come in," he stated as he moved to the side, allowing her entry.

She didn't ask him how he knew. It was not important. She felt his eyes shadowing her movement, drawing her into him as she made her way to the couch. Common scurried from the bedroom, his paws clawing the floor as he ran. Plopping down on the couch, she smiled at him, rubbing the top of his head, scratching behind his ear the way he liked. He licked her fingers in gratitude before taking up residence around the back of her bare ankles.

"Have I become that insufferable, Michelle?" Grayson slowly made his way to the couch, dragging his feet as he went, not hiding how painful each step seemed to be. He walked like a man journeying toward something he was not quite ready to face. "It's ten in the morning. You've been gone for hours. Where have you been? Why did you go without me?"

Grayson was not suggesting that he needed to monitor her comings or goings or suggesting that he should accompany her at all times. He was inquiring about the change in their dynamic, wondering if the distance bothered her, too.

"Nowhere."

He sat down on the couch but gave her the space he felt she wanted. There was room enough for two people to sit comfortably between them. "What does that mean?"

Michelle swallowed the timidity threatening to silence her. She knew she needed to speak, but she was not disillusioned about what was at stake, either. These past few weeks with Grayson had revealed a side of him that she had honestly grown to love. His patience and attentiveness proved to be a kind of balm for her spirit. He had not made a move of any kind on her, yet the tension was ever present.

She knew he wanted her; his eyes couldn't lie, and she could not deny that she yearned for him as well.

The timing was horrible. She couldn't be sure of anything, and the last thing she wanted to do was hurt him, this man who had been nothing but kind to her. He had opened his home and his heart, offering her a safe space to heal. He protected her in a way that no one ever had. That was why this conversation frightened her so. It was why she dreaded what may come about as a result of it.

"Have I done something to lose your trust?" His question was sincere.

"I am not sure where I am, Grayson. I don't know what . . . *this* . . . is or what it could it be."

Tension lines shown across her forehead. His shoulders squared defensively. "I have not pressured you into anything. I mean . . . I care about you. You have become one of my closest friends."

"Amazing, Grayson, is what you have been. Perfect even." Michelle's eyes began to water, and her lips trembled. "Something is happening, and I don't know that it should."

Grayson slumped against the couch, inhaling deeply. He ran his hands over his freshly shaved dome, around the left side of his neck over the *Himnuta*, a word meaning *faith* in Aramaic, he'd had inked on the eve of his eighteenth birthday.

"I don't want you to leave, Michelle."

"I don't want to leave, either."

"So why don't—"

"I think that's why I should. Maybe I never should have stayed in the first place."

"It's too late to second-guess yourself now."

"Not too late to change my mind."

"Michelle, you needed someone. I saw that, and I see that. Let me be here."

"I will. I want you to . . . just not like this." Michelle broke eye contact with Grayson, too ashamed to admit what she saw to be true. "We are in different places, Grayson."

"I have to do this work."

"I know."

"I cannot believe you're doubting me after all I have done until this point."

"I am not doubting you. I just . . . I need more, and it isn't fair of me to ask that of you. It never was. You were my workout partner at the gym, and now . . ."

"And now we are more than that, Michelle. We are more. You don't need to go back to him. You and I don't have to cross any lines that you aren't comfortable with, but don't go back there. If you could have seen your face when you came tearing out of that house. Heard the pain in your voice. Your hurt got me out of the car. Don't go back there."

Michelle sighed. That day had changed things, pushed their friendship just beyond the boundaries designated for relationships like theirs. That was the first day she knew that this moment would eventually come to pass; that this conversation would be necessary.

"I'll go to my mother's. Not to . . . not there."

"But what about your mother's fiancé? Are you certain you want to be around that?"

"I have not spoken with her since that day. I could be overreacting. Misread the situation." Tears lazily fell from her eyes. "I had rushed over there after catching . . ." Michelle couldn't bring herself to finish the sentence. "I was emotional."

"Still, that's a possibility. Tellin' me that being here is worse than that?"

"No, Grayson, but—"

"Then stay here. I'll do whatever. Tell me."

"Stop, Grayson. I am leaving. Nothing you will say is going to change that."

Grayson looked dejected. "Fine. I wish you would change your mind."

Michelle did not respond. She closed her eyes and counted backward from ten, trying to calm her nerves, beckon her tears back from the wells of her eyes.

"I want to—"

She locked into his gaze, deleting the rest of his sentence. It did not need to be said. She knew, as he knew, what was brewing between them. He had saved her, but if any of what they felt was true, she needed to leave, to exit this space and see if it could survive the separation. To see if anything would change in her absence.

"I cannot keep hiding, Grayson. You know that I cannot do that."

"I don't want to see you get hurt. I don't know how to protect you from here."

"That is not your job, Mr. Hines. I appreciate you, but a month is long enough. I have definitely overstayed my welcome."

"That is not possible."

"Besides, reality has caught up with us."

"I don't like this, but I respect your decision. I guess I knew this day would come eventually."

"We both did." Michelle patted the space next to her.

Grayson slid down the sofa until his thigh brushed hers. Throwing his arm around her shoulders, he drew her into him. Michelle rested her head against his chest, listening to his lungs fill with air, release, and repeat.

"I know you're confused. I know you loved and had that love stolen from you. That pain is not easy to circumvent. I cannot change any of that. But we have something here, Michelle."

Michelle didn't respond. Instead, she sat up, turning slightly to her right to face him. His smoky gray eyes had hypnotic powers even as the light of midday poured in through the skylights above them. She saw in them what she had seen before: the truth. It was the truth of this moment and the past month, and it scared her, overwhelmed her.

"I won't let you forget. I am not going anywhere."

Michelle could not force a word out from her lips, trapped in place by the depth of her longing. She could not be this person, could not be the woman who leaves one man for another. She could not be her mother.

CHAPTER 41

Three hours into the last half of an average work day, Sophie found herself parked in front of Michelle's home, fretting a bit over her decision to try to force a truce of sorts. Her grand knowledge of her daughter reminded her that Michelle was famously stubborn with these types of things. Texas had a better chance of getting snow on Christmas day than she had with coaxing Michelle into doing something she didn't want to do. Still, she had to try. Failing would confirm her fear: Michelle wanted nothing to do with her. She missed her daughter terribly and hoped that the explanation she had prepared would suffice.

Her bond with Brianna had strengthened significantly after their last visit. and she credited that change to Brianna's decision not to hide behind pleasantries. Though Michelle had never done that, Sophie felt that to a degree, the same type of frank speak could also help their relationship. So, maybe she was there hoping that *this* would not be something she could not repair, unlike the other parts of her life, specifically the situation with the deal she longed to close with her husband.

The injunction was a benign tumor, with all the marks of turning into a malignant one. Five p.m. would mark the passing of the forty-eighth hour since her last conversation with Steven. Her numerous calls had gone unanswered, and it did not sit well with her at all. She could only hope that the silence meant that he was working feverishly on getting the injunction thrown out. He was due in court in the early morning hours, and Sophie thought she would have heard from him by now. She was not certain of what to make of his behavior. She promised herself that *he* would be the last favor she honored. She would have preferred someone more competent, but the situation required that she relax her standards to employ him, a fact she regretted more and more with each passing minute. Neither of them had anticipated all that had unfolded, but still . . . this was his job.

Opening the car door, Sophie pushed her bare feet into the grass and stepped out of the car. Normally she would not travel without shoes, but she felt it was time to try to do things differently. This change was small enough to manage with everything she had going on. The act had actually proven to be quite liberating for her, suggesting that her life fell inside the lines more than she suspected after having run away from her previous life of financial religion and countryside celebrity. Perhaps she had not left so much behind after all.

Michelle's home was modest by Sophie's standards, but it still worried her a bit. She knew Michelle was unemployed. Between the car, her old loft, and this new home, she was certain Michelle must have been nearing the end of her graduation gift. She hoped her daughter was being fiscally responsible.

She made her way to the door and rang the bell. The sound of scuffling brought her ear to the door. She heard no arguing, but a lot of bumping around. Sophie pounded the door with her fist and rang the doorbell incessantly. She knew Brianna was not home, and fearing Michelle would ignore her outright, she decided not to announce herself. More racket seeped from within the house.

"Shit. Fuck."

The tenor belonged to Armand, her son-in law. Sophie scraped her bare feet across the rough fabric of their welcome mat, crashing her fist once more into the door. The door opened abruptly.

"Mich—" Armand started to say but stopped when he saw Sophie standing in front of him.

"Armand? Is everything all right?"

His eyes were bloodshot. His tight curls, usually kept low and tapered, now fell lazily about his head. He wore a pair of basketball shorts, a T-shirt from his high school alma mater, and one lonely sock. From the limited view of the living room behind him, it did not appear to be in much better shape.

"May I come in, please?"

Armand shook his head. "I don't think now is a good time, Mrs. Lewis."

Sophie's face grew warm, briefly visiting her turbulent past with Lewis. She would be damned if her daughter suffered in that way. "I insist," she stated as she pushed past him and into the living room area.

Several things caught her attention immediately, sounding her internal alarm. The couch was flipped over on its side, the table beside it was in pieces, joining the shattered lamp on the floor. Clothes were strewn about, pictures smashed. Someone had taken a pair of scissors to some of the art pieces from Michelle's treasured Harlem Renaissance collection. The space was in complete disarray.

Armand stood near the door while Sophie walked about, inspecting the room. She could not hear anything beyond her breathing. Her heart was racing, but she was practiced at hiding her panic.

She calmly addressed Armand. "Where is my daughter?"

Armand shrugged his shoulders but did not answer.

Sophie felt herself losing her patience. Something had happened there, and she did not want to assume that Michelle was involved in any way.

"Where is Michelle, Armand?"

"Anywhere." Dragging his legs toward the hall, where Sophie stood nearby, he looked like he planned to exit the room. Sophie was not going to allow that.

"Armand, I have only known you this last month or so, but I believe that time is sufficient enough for you to know that I will do anything for my girls. I am going to ask you again. Where is Michelle?"

"Mrs. Lewis, I told you this was not a good time. No disrespect to you or nothing, but I already told you. She could be anywhere."

"What happened here?"

Armand slouched against the left wall near the hall's opening, Sophie stood across from him.

"Something is wrong, and you need to tell me what it is."

"Look, I don't have to tell you nothin'. You ain't my momma, Mrs. Lewis. You have two children, and I'm not one of them."

Armand reeked of alcohol. Sophie's stomach twisted into knots.

"Is she hurt?"

Armand did not answer. This child was fraying her nerves. Armand had seemed decent enough, but she couldn't take any chances. She never would have pegged Lewis to use his fists as weapons against her, either.

"I need to know where my daughter is, Armand."

"I cannot help you. You need to get out."

Sophie relaxed against the wall. She closed her eyes and took a deep breath, trying to push any thoughts of Michelle's body lying somewhere out of her mind. Surely Armand had not done anything so heinous. Surely not. They were in love. He was the hero in their family, one of the main reasons they were all alive to tell their stories.

"I cannot do that. Not until I know where Michelle is."

"This is my house, Mrs. Lewis."

"This is my daughter's house, and I am not leaving until I see her standing in it."

"Well, good luck with that."

Sophie slammed into his face before she processed her next thought. She found her hands wrapped around his throat. She was not a strong woman, but he did not resist. Sophie did not notice at first; her rage consumed her. All she could think about was Michelle and what he may have done to her. She aimed to squeeze the truth out of him like toothpaste from a tube. Then she noticed his eyes, the puffiness underneath them. She looked down, noticing his hands dangling by his sides in submission.

"Just do it," he pleaded.

Sophie, confused by his behavior, loosened her grip but did not release him. Something terrible must have happened to break him like this. He was not the same young man who had pulled into her driveway after rescuing Brianna. This man had no fight in him.

"Please," he begged again, "just do it."

Sophie removed her hands, watching his body slide down to the floor. Armand sat with his long legs open, his head bent between them. She could not explain it, but something told her that he needed to be handled with delicate hands. He was fragile. If she went in too hard, he'd break, and she'd never get the answers she sought. She sat down across from him.

"Armand, I apologize. I should not have touched you."

"I deserve it. I deserve all of this. I failed."

Sophie continued to study him, counting the tears as they fell from his eyes. "No, you didn't. My fear drove me to that, and—"

"I failed her." Armand's voice was soft, barely above a whisper. "I broke her."

Sophie tried to remain calm. "What do you mean, Armand?"

He never looked up at Sophie. His voice traveled through the curls that hung blocking his face from view. "It's so fucked up. I just . . . I loved her. I didn't mean to . . . I didn't mean it."

Sophie's body started trembling uncontrollably as her mind inserted Michelle into every scene in every episode of *SVU* she had ever seen. "What did you do, Armand?"

"I wasn't trying to hurt her. I swear." Armand was unraveling—if he ever really had it together.

This visit had revealed a different side of him, introduced her into a part of Michelle's life that she hated to admit was new to her. That was her fault. She had lied to protect herself, though she reasoned at the time it was for Michelle. Now, trying to unpack whatever horror her daughter may have suffered through another person was humbling. She had to admit that it had been about her. Not telling Michelle about Brianna had more to do with her inability to speak about her shame, to address the guilt she lived with, than anything else.

Armand was a reflection of her. She understood his pain, the remorse she saw in his eyes, heard in his tone. She looked out into the living room, searching for something to indicate that Michelle could have been hurt there. She was looking for evidence of a struggle between two people but found nothing. There was no blood anywhere, no scratches on Armand. If there were a scuffle between them, Armand might have been on the losing end of it. She still needed him to say it, though. The words needed to leave his lips before she could leave this house.

"I don't know what you did, but you're not beyond redemption. None of us ever are. It isn't too late to make this right, Armand. Tell me where she is."

Armand sniffled. "I can't. I can't tell you that."

"Why?"

"I don't know. She's gone."

CHAPTER 42

Temporarily relocating to the center provided Micah with a unique opportunity to exercise his bourgeoning perspective. Setting the stage for the next phase in his life, Ms. Vida's presence was lively, indicative of how very different this span of time would be. Before her, he had no one but his fickle love, Brianna.

The first day at the center was simple enough. After briefly meeting with his team of professionals to discuss his therapeutic plan, he spent the remainder of the day acclimating himself to his new surroundings. His room was about the size of the average private hospital room, fitted with the latest in medical equipment, a 32-inch flat screen mounted on the wall, positioned so that he may view it easily from his bed, and a few items Ms. Vida brought to make the space feel a bit more like home.

There was a large window on the longest wall, separating him from the parking lot outside. The view of the parking lot was nothing to marvel at, but he was glad to see the sun rise and set each day. This routine quickly became a favorite of his. The natural light refreshed him, as did counting the handful of stars visible in the night's sky, an activity he fell in love with. Staring into the vastness of the sky settled his mind, offering time for him to reflect on how fortunate he was to still have his life. He could have easily died, and perhaps he should have. Some very brave bystanders had pulled him to safety, and he didn't even know their names. For a spell each night, he descended into a gratuitous space as a way of paying homage to them, sending his thank-you into the universe in hopes that it would reach them.

Each morning, he woke before the rooster crowed, excited to start his day. This was a completely new Micah. Even he was surprised by the degree to which his attitude had improved since leaving the hospital. The center's staff embraced him from the onset. He knew that his condition was not nearly as bad as some of the other patients there, but he was not made to feel any less important. Everyone had an encouraging word, a smile, and made it clear that they were rooting for him. He did not know if their niceties were a matter of policy or if they emerged from a genuine place, but he didn't care. The daily chorus of voices offered him a high-octane energy that propelled him far beyond the mental limitations he had lived with for so long. He could not recall a moment in his life when he had worked so fervently toward achieving one singular goal.

Ms. Vida, his "hype (wo)man," did not stay overnight, but returned each day, presiding over his sessions and hounding him about taking his medication, just as she had during his hospital stay, bringing her vibrant spirit and no-nonsense demeanor right along with her. It was not lost on him the profound affect she had on him.

Micah, no longer shirking his responsibilities to himself, took his bipolar medication without coercion and without shame. This shift in his perception was solely thanks to her. His father had taught him that needing medication meant that he was weak, convincing him that acknowledging his disorder signified cowardice, but his father had been wrong. Ms. Vida helped him to see and understand. His disorder was no fault of his, but pretending like he did not have it had left him susceptible. Refusing to embrace all of himself had poisoned his psyche and left a fatal imprint on everything he did. Nothing good in his life had ever lasted for long—not that it was not a possibility, but his attitude had precluded him from holding on to those memories. Embracing what some would perceive as flaws, imperfections, was an essential part of learning to love himself, a vital step in his recovery. Possibly for the first time in several years, Micah was in a healthy space.

Team Harrison, his therapists, were each at the top of their respective fields, in his opinion. With no major physical impairments, Micah had already completed his work with Jimmy Keith, whom he saw for physical therapy, after only one week. The first few days were grueling, when his attempts to corral his gelatin legs to hold his weight proved frivolous, but it wasn't long before he regained his strength. He walked with a noticeable limp from the injury to his leg, but Jimmy was satisfied with his progress. His chest still hurt like he had worked out for the first time in a decade, but he considered it a minor irritation compared to the alternative. With the first hurdle firmly in his rearview, Micah figured that the worst of it was behind him.

The majority of his time belonged to Hannah Nguyen, his eccentric occupational therapist. Together they traveled through what would amount to an ordinary day of life on his own, so that she could assess his independence. Early on, he had balance issues, but even that had improved to a significant degree. The importance of having the ability to stand upright without wavering to the left or the right had been lost on him, until he realized how truly difficult it was to do even the simplest of things without it. Moving around was one thing, but even a task as thoughtless as washing dishes, wiping a table, or putting groceries away after shopping were exhaustive. If she was not satisfied with his progress by the projected discharge date, she had the power to retain him. Micah was not necessarily concerned with this, but he did not want to disappoint Ms. Vida. She had rearranged her life for him, and he wanted to continue to make that decision a bright spot for her.

Mayesha Stills, cognitive therapist, made pulling his memories out of storage the focal point of their time together. Since the accident had remarkably left his speech and, for the most part, his mental processes intact, she could forgo the need to help him relearn the complicated mechanics of speaking and delve directly into the commission of his memory. To Micah's dismay, Dr. Ramvi's foreboding rang true. Each day of his demanding schedule exhausted him physically, mentally, and emotionally. Nevertheless, Micah was progressing well ahead of schedule, and much of that he credited to Team Harris.

Things had moved relatively smoothly until yesterday. Admittedly, the time with his speech therapist was the most challenging, mostly because the task felt improbable to him. That had changed yesterday. Near the end of their time, something had returned to him. It was one sliver of a memory, a glimpse into his past, revealing Brianna expressing her desire to slow things down between them. He could only remember that moment, something he was certain that he must have taken to mean she wanted to part ways.

He deduced this to be true. It was the exact feeling that swallowed him after the memory surfaced. Brianna had a lot of rules, and he abided by them, hoping to earn a place in her life, but even before her admission, he had started feeling the distance between them. Needless to say, the memory was not a pleasant one, but it did explain her absence.

Mayesha highlighted that, although the news hurt, its recovery meant that he stood an excellent chance of full restoration over time. The news was intended to encourage him, but Micah was not sure if he wanted to remember. Maybe not knowing was better. He went to sleep with these things on his mind and awoke in this morning, greeted by the same sadness.

He continued his work and powered through. He tried to stay upbeat, but he couldn't deny how the news had zapped much of his energy. He loved Brianna and missed her. He really thought they could have had something special, and it hurt to know that he was wrong. He couldn't even be certain how much time had passed. Even if he could find her, it may be far too late to win her heart.

Some part of him hoped that she would seek him out, but he fully understood how unlikely this was. He had not fallen to pieces or slipped into the same kind of numbness that had caged him his last day as a resident of the hospital, but he worried about his proximity to doing so. It was easy to put his grief to the side while he was working by focusing on the task, but in moments like these, when he was alone in his room, the sadness reached through his rib cage and pummeled his heart.

The sunlight of midday poured into his room, making everything on his left visually off limits to him. The plasma was on, but no sound escaped the speakers. The quiet was necessary. The turkey sandwich had lost its fresh appeal, as the Dijon mustard turned the ciabatta bread into some mushy matter, steadily pushing its flavor into his nostrils. The sandwich was made at his request, fuel for his body, but he could not eat. The aroma turned his stomach into knots. He forced the fruit portions to go down, and he hoped that would be enough to soften the blow to Ms. Vida's expectations. Surely, she would understand the hurt he was feeling. His appetite simply was not there.

"Micaaahhh?" Ms. Vida sang, drawing his eyes to her peppered bun and Mother Goose glasses as she entered the room, allowing the large, wooded door to close with a loud clang behind her. "Micah Harris, what are you doing?"

"Thinking, Ms. Vida." Micah watched her grab the rolling chair, covered in cloth, stained with a floral design from the seventeenth century, and push it to her "area," the space where she sat each day, beside his bed.

"Just thinking."

"Not eating, I see." She spoke plainly, but with a hint of tenderness, speaking like she knew he needed her to be gentle.

"I ate some. I cannot . . ." Micah did not finish his sentence. Her eyes silenced him. He knew that look. She knew he was hurting but did not care to hear any excuses. She left no room in his world for them, and he wouldn't force one on her.

"Why aren't you eating?"

Micah shrugged his shoulders and took a deep breath, readying himself for what he knew was coming.

"Are you quitting? Are you throwing your progress into the abyss? Undoing all of the changes you have made?"

He winced as her demands packaged in these questions sliced into his pain. "No ma'am. It's just a sandwich."

"No, Micah, it is not just a sandwich. This is your *life*. This is about the commitment you have to make in order for this *new Micah* to find permanent residency within your heart, your mind. You cannot do this." She motioned toward his half-eaten meal. "You cannot leave work undone and expect to win. Halfway will not get it done. Just *enough* is *never* enough, Micah."

Her indictment of his manhood, of his desire to heal, hurt like cool water on scorched skin. He shrugged off the sting as one last visage of resistance scurried to his lips. "Ms. Vida—"

"Listen to what I am telling you. Pull yourself together. I understand you received unfavorable news yesterday, but this is a new day. This new day requires all of you. All of you, Micah. Do not lose out on what is available in your present, harboring sentiment from your past." Pointing to the sandwich, she said, "Take that and eat."

"Ms. Vida, the last thing I want to do is disappoint you, but—" The glare in her stare paused his thought, sent him scrambling for a new angle. "I ate the fruit. Isn't that enough?"

"No, it is not enough because you still have a sandwich there. If you lack the discipline to eat a measly sandwich, how do you expect to face real obstacles? Consider this practice: you are creating mental muscle memory intended to help you finish any and every task before you. Developing an attitude consistent with a drive to finish what you begin. To finish."

Micah did not respond. He picked up the sandwich and ate it quickly. Even if he failed to comprehend all of what Ms. Vida said, one thing was perfectly clear: she was unwilling to let this pass without his compliance. He felt like a child in her presence from time to time, but he liked that. She lavished upon him the kind of mothering the hurt little boy living within him needed. Ms. Vida helped to heal him one lecture at a time, and he could feel it.

"Good. Now clean yourself up as much as you can. I spoke with Ms. Nguyen, and she shared, with mild enthusiasm, that she was impressed with your progress. If you continue at this pace, you could be released to my care as soon as two weeks from now."

Micah perked up a bit. That was good news. "What does that have to do with me cleaning myself up?"

"It does not have a thing to do with it."

Micah raised his brow in confusion. "Well . . .?"

"You have a visitor. Two, actually, and you should not be seen like this."

"Who is it?"

"Please keep your questions and do as I have asked. I probably cannot answer them anyway."

"Of course, Ms. Vida, but—"

"No buts. Do not ask for my help with the mundane. As I told you, I spoke with Hannah. I want to see for myself what you are able to do. I will provide assistance if I feel you need it."

Micah chuckled. He was going to let her know that there was not much for him to do. He worked out first thing in the morning, showered, and dressed after. He was only in bed because he preferred the semi-softness of the mattress over the hard leather backing of the only other chair in the room. Micah pushed the tray out of his way and tossed the covers back, revealing his navy-blue basketball shorts and white T-shirt. "Ta da!" He stated as he swung his legs off the bed's edge.

"Comedy does not suit you," Ms. Vida replied with a wide grin on her face. "I am going to retrieve your guests. While I am gone, please find your smile and a more pleasant demeanor."

"Yes, ma'am."

Ms. Vida stood and hurried out of the door. Micah tried to gather his bearings. He was in no mood to receive company, and faking it would be difficult. Nonetheless, when the shadows graced his doorway, he plastered a smile on his face. Looking up from the floor, he greeted them.

"Hello, I—"

Micah could not believe his eyes. If Ms. Vida had not been standing there, he would have discounted it all as a dream. Excitement bellowed within him like clouds of smoke over the mouth of a volcano. He wanted to break into a gospel number, a ridiculously difficult dance piece, and morph into the most expensive fireworks display ever, all at once. And just like that, the whole world opened up to him once again.

CHAPTER 43

Fear gripped her heart. She may have run away were it not for Dr. Baxter. His eyes reassured her that she was safe. Javan could not hurt her. This nurse spoke very kindly of Javan, but she called him Micah. Micah did not sound anything like the Javan who had forced her to flee in the night from his home. This Micah did not even seem real. Yet there he was, sitting on his bed, staring at her with eyes brimming with questions. She could only imagine the things roaming through his mind. Dr. Baxter nudged her back with his forefinger, pushing her out of her head.

"Please have a seat, child."

Ms. Vida's voice was kind, inviting. She instantly felt at ease with her. Ms. Vida spoke with an eloquence Brianna could appreciate. She found it peculiar that she didn't use any contractions, but for some reason, the odd fact made her even fonder of her. It was a sentiment that Brianna did not hand out to many.

"Sure, thank you." Brianna made her way to the floral-patterned chair Ms. Vida ushered her into. She could feel Micah's eyes recording her every move.

"Micah, do not be rude to your guests. Speak."

"Oh, yes. Forgive me. I'm just . . . shocked. I cannot believe you are really here. I didn't think that I would ever see you again, Brianna."

"Trust me. That makes two of us." Brianna watched his eyes shift from her to Dr. Baxter and then back. "You remember Dr. Baxter, Javan? I mean, Micah."

He took a moment, squinting his eyes in thought. "You were my neighbor at a house I purchased in Allen. Some kind of special obstetrician?"

Dr. Baxter ventured away from the sink area where he had been standing and conversing quietly with Ms. Vida. "Maternal medicine, and it's . . . nice to . . . good to see you again. Too bad it's under these circumstances but . . . at least you . . . survived." Dr. Baxter laughed uncomfortably, cleared his throat, and retreated back into his previous position.

"That is very true. I am fortunate," Micah stated, settling his eyes again on her. "Where did the two of you meet? I can't . . . don't remember introducing you."

She did not want to be as uncomfortable as she was. Clasping her shaky hands together tightly between her legs, she fought through her fear, reminding herself of why she was there.

"Javan—I mean, Micah, that is a long story, but he helped me to find you." Brianna tried to laugh as she spoke, removing the sting of ambiguity.

"Oh, okay. I'm glad for that. I'd like to hear about it someday. If you . . . if you are up for it. I mean, you don't have to tell me—"

"Micah, may we speak privately?" Brianna noted the relief on his face after her interruption. He was fumbling over his words, perspiring, fidgeting. He seemed even more nervous about this than she was.

"Of course. Whatever you want." Micah looked over her head, behind her body, to where Ms. Vida and Dr. Baxter stood. "Ms. Vida, can we get a moment?"

Brianna did not look back, but she felt a hand on her shoulder. Dr. Baxter spoke softly in her ear. "I'll be just outside the door."

Squeezing his hand to reassure him, she released him to exit. A private conversation had been a part of the plan. Though Ms. Vida had been pleasant in their phone communication, she was a stranger. Brianna did not want to discuss this with anyone else in the room. The fright that had blanketed her upon their arrival was unexpected. Dr. Baxter was reacting to that change in her, offering her a chance to call an audible. She had been convinced, and so convinced him, that she was no longer afraid, that she had healed from the experience enough to be alone with him. She was no longer certain, but still determined to do what she came to do.

She locked her body to keep from jumping at the sound of the door closing behind them. Swallowing hard, Brianna was visibly shaken. Finding herself alone with Javan again sent her back into their last moments together. Her mouth was so dry she couldn't speak.

"Brianna, are you okay?" Micah inquired. Narrowing his eyes in confusion, he asked again. "Brianna, is everything all right?" He did not move from his seat on the bed, but he leaned toward her a just a bit.

She spoke reflexively. "I'm fine." The words rang out to create distance. She did not want him closer. In her mind before her, a monster stood, covering her with his shadow—an angry, vengeful monster. These images collided with the man who sat before her now. Her emotions were all over the place. Taking a deep breath, she once more focused on the task at hand.

"Can I get you some water? I can call for something," he said.

"No, I am . . . good. Thank you," Brianna stated, offering a half-smile. She was not good, but resting her hand on her stomach gave her some peace, calmed her nerves.

"I need to say something to you," he stated.

"I'm listening. Please."

"Look, it's obvious to me that you're still upset with me. The last thing I remember you telling me was that you were done with us, with me."

"Micah, I'd rather not—" Brianna's nerves had just barely settled, and she did not see the direction of their conversation being very beneficial.

"Just . . . I was not a nice person then."

Brianna relaxed again.

"Whatever I did to make you feel that way about us . . . I apologize, sincerely. I am not that person anymore. I am a different man."

"Micah . . ." She did not need or require an apology. She only wanted to share this news and go back to her life.

"Brianna, please. I am going to share something with you that I have not said aloud to anyone in my adult life."

Her interest was piqued. "Oooo . . . kay."

"I have bipolar disorder. Diagnosed at boarding school when I was a teen." Micah stared at his feet as he spoke, glancing up every few words or so. "Never really consistent with taking my medication. Ashamed to have . . . needed it. Thought it made me weak, worthless." With that, he met her eyes and held them. "A few months had passed without them when I met you. You made me incredibly happy, and I thought . . . maybe you could cure me, could save me. I wanted that so badly, Brianna. I am so very sorry. You were never responsible for me, and if you . . . felt pressure . . . I was wrong. I was wrong."

Brianna had never seen him so vulnerable. Perhaps something within had truly changed for the better. "Micah, you could have told me." She had sat with the reality of his disorder for a few days. It was one of the things that Dr. Baxter had made it a point to share with her prior to their visit.

"I couldn't even admit it to myself."

Brianna believed him. She believed every word.

"But it's different. The accident, Ms. Vida . . . my perspective and approach to living is not like it was. I am working on many things, but my mind is clear. I am regularly taking my medication, and I know for certain that I am a better man for doing so."

"I don't know what to say, honestly. I am very happy to see that you are doing as well as you are. When I first heard of your accident, I wasn't sure of what to expect."

"I hoped every day that you would come, and here you are. I am glad that I could at least get the opportunity to apologize to you for my behavior. Maybe if you're willing to allow me to prove to you that I am better . . . that we could give us another shot. We had something very special, Brianna, and I don't want my—"

"Micah, we're having a child," Brianna blurted.

Micah's eyes opened wide. "What?"

"I am pregnant with your child."

"Uh . . . how? I mean . . . when? Wow. A baby?"

Knock, knock, knock.

Ms. Vida poked her head in the door. "Is everything okay in here?"

"Yes! I mean . . . we are fine. Just a few more minutes please."

"Sure." Ms. Vida closed the door to give them more time to finish the conversation.

"Brianna?"

"I haven't known very long, but it's why I needed to find you," Brianna explained.

Micah looked slightly dejected with that comment, but it was the truth.

"I wanted give you a chance to be a part of our child's life. I have to live knowing my father was not given a choice. I did not want that for our child."

Micah still stared on in his disbelief. "This is unbelievable."

"If this is too much and you need time to think, I understand."

"I don't. I don't need any time to think. I want to be there for my child, and for you . . . if you'll let me. I know what it feels like to grow up without a father. I won't abandon my child. This just gives me more motivation to get better and stay better."

Brianna was taken aback by his eagerness. Given all that he was dealing with, she had not been sure how he would respond. "I am not sure how I feel about . . . us, but I am encouraged by the probability of our child having us both. That means a lot to me."

"Take all the time you need. I am not going anywhere."

The corners of her mouth curved up into a genuine full smile. This Micah showed restraint, unlike the Javan of old. "Good. So, what were you doing before the accident? We have not spoken in nearly two months."

"Really?" Micah's eyebrows rose in surprise. "I don't remember. I don't remember anything about the last few months, I think."

"But you remember my telling you that I wanted a break from us?"

Micah nodded in agreement. "That is all I remember, and I don't even have a timeframe for it. It's strange and uncomfortable to have a memory floating in space like that."

"Well, I told you that about two months ago. Right before I left for—" Brianna hesitated to mention Cancun, not only because of the pain it triggered, but because she was not sure if she wanted him to remember any of that time, if she ever wanted to discuss it with him at all. He seemed to be a different person, and maybe this *clean slate* was a cosmic gift to their family. "Right before I left for . . . a convention . . . in California." She lied, but she didn't want to risk triggering a memory. She felt good about her decision to keep that horrible tale to herself. For once, it could live in her mind as the nightmare it truly was. *This,* this was reality.

"Two months? Well, that gives me some sort of timeframe. Thank you. I am sure Mayesha, my cognitive therapist, will appreciate that."

"No problem."

Micah slid toward her again, but Brianna did not shrink away or try to stop him. He put a hand over her tummy. "I cannot believe my child is in there. This is amazing."

Brianna closed her eyes, covered his hand with hers, permitting the love she'd sought to suppress to bloom and live in this moment. She had missed him more than she wanted to admit. She had been grappling with the truth of her situation ever since she confessed to Dr. Shepherd that she loved him despite all that had transpired.

WonderBra thought she might be suffering a bit from Stockholm syndrome, but Brianna disagreed. She had always loved Micah, but her familial issues would not allow her to do anything with those feelings. She simply did not trust them, but things had changed. Her family was a sham, and her life nearly ruined by lies. She needed to be honest with herself about everything, including this. Their child fluttered in her belly to consecrate the reunion. This felt right. The monster she saw for a moment that night was a psychosis; it was not who he truly was, and he had it under control now. She deserved this and wanted it more than anything else.

"I love you."

He looked up into her eyes. "I love you, too."

Knock, knock, knock.

"Come in!" Micah screamed, briefly checking her eyes for permission. Brianna smiled. "We're having a baby!"

Ms. Vida squealed in delight and rushed toward Brianna. "Congratulations, child!"

Dr. Baxter grabbed Brianna's hand and gave it a tight squeeze. As she looked around at the smiling faces, a joyous energy filled the room.

This just might work, she thought. *This just might work out after all.*

CHAPTER 44

"Everything is fine. I don't want to go into any details right now, but I am handling the situation. This is a non-issue."

Beep . . . beep.

Frank pulled the phone away from his ear, glancing at the number flashing across the screen. "I need to go, but keep this between us. Speak to no one about this. Trust me." He abruptly ended the call, switching to the incoming call before it rolled to voicemail.

"This is Frank Mason."

"Mr. Mason, this is Dr. Brunti of the Hôpital Louis-Constant Fleming in Saint-Martin. You left several messages for me. I would normally delegate this type of thing to a nurse, but your matter seemed urgent in nature. What can I do for you, sir?"

"Thank you so much for returning my call, Dr. Brunti. I won't keep you long, but this situation is delicate and time-sensitive. For those reasons, I am hoping that you can handle this personally, for a nominal fee, of course."

"I am not sure what this is concerning, Mr. Mason, but as a medical professional, I can assure you that money is no guarantor of favorable results."

"It isn't anything like that. My wife, Lisa Mason, was a patient under your care. She was released from the hospital about a week ago. Knife victim."

"I did not operate on anyone."

"No, I know that. You checked on her frequently during her post-op care. I only spoke with her surgeon once, but I saw you nearly every day until . . . I just had hoped that since you were familiar with us, you could assist me."

"I apologize, Mr. Mason, but I am not sure of what you are referring, sir."

"I imagine you have direct access to her medical records from her stay at your hospital. Her condition has gotten worse, and for security reasons, I have chosen to hire a private doctor for her. We are back home in the States and so, for obvious reasons, I cannot just swing by the hospital, but I need her medical information to give to the doctor."

"Well, Mr. Mason, any medical records can be retrieved through the proper channels, sir."

"I reached out to you specifically so that you could send them to me. My wife is dying. I don't have time to surf channels. It was just last week. I am sure you remember us. She was a knife victim, needed a blood transfusion during surgery. I sat by her bed every day. I spoke with you every day she was there. You commented about her beauty, her resilience. Stated that she was lucky compared to others who had been in a similar situation, died under similar circumstances."

"Mr. Mason, I am afraid there has been some misunderstanding, sir."

"What do you mean?"

"I have only returned to work this morning from vacation. Nearly a month I was gone. I have not seen you nor your wife or any patients during that time."

The room lost its color as Frank struggled to process Dr. Brunti's statement. Nothing in his world moved for several seconds. "That is not possible. I met you."

"I am afraid that is incorrect. I have never met you or your wife, sir."

Dr. Brunti's words ricocheted off the walls of his mind, causing a series of mini-explosions as they tumbled around. The room began a slow spin, whirling around him until he felt sick inside. Stumbling toward his desk, he tried to maintain some control over his body.

"How is . . . this . . . po–possible?"

"It is a very serious security matter for our hospital. If what you say is true, this person, whoever it was, will be caught and punished. I will have our security team look into this immediately."

Frank was not listening to Dr. Brunti. Lisa was his only concern, and none of what he rambled about had anything to do with saving her. Suddenly, Frank started coughing uncontrollably, so hard his stomach ached with the movement. Gasping for air, he leaned over his desk, looking for something to distract his mind. He needed to focus. His eyes landed on a photo of Lisa and Brianna. The picture took him back a decade, permitting him to visit a simpler time, before it all began to fall apart. His heart rate regressed, leveling out at a pace typical for him. His coughing ceased.

"Listen, I couldn't care less about any of what you're talking about. My wife is in trouble. Someone is trying to kill her, and you are telling me that your hospital gave this person access to her. I want—"

"Mr. Mason, I can—"

"Don't interrupt me."

"Mr. Mason, I apologize. If this thing happened, I can understand how upsetting it is."

"What do you mean, *if* it happened? I am telling you that someone disguised as you pumped my wife full of who knows what. If you aren't going to do anything about this, put someone on the phone who will. My wife is very sick and—"

"I am only saying that the hospital has a procedure in place to verify such things. It is a very serious accusation. Believe me, I will personally look into this. Other patients may have been at risk as well."

Frank restrained himself. He could not afford to lose his patience. Plopping down in his chair, he massaged his temple with his free hand. "My wife has gotten worse since she was deemed well enough to leave. What am I supposed to do here? How can I help her?"

Dr. Brunti audibly sighed over the phone. "Mr. Mason, I would advise you to have your wife screened for toxins as soon as possible. I don't know anything beyond what they show in movies about killers, but I know medicine. Sometimes medicines can be killers themselves. If your wife was released, then it is likely that whatever was given to her by this person took longer to affect her. Do you remember when she started feeling worse? Any particular time?"

Frank thought back, mentally combing through the days before they left the island. "Maybe after she first took her pain medication? We had a bit of a scare a few days after she was discharged, and it delayed our leaving for about a week, but she got better and was cleared to fly."

"Ah, so I would think that perhaps whatever was given to her interacted negatively with her medication. Maybe the break from it allowed her system to recover, but once you started administering it again regularly, it resumed its original course."

"This is insane. She is in pain. There is nothing else to give her."

"Sir, that prescription may be killing her. I cannot tell you what to do with your wife, but if it were my Rhonda, I would seek medical advice."

"That is what I'm doing now."

"From someone who can tend to her. I am not knowledgeable enough about her to be of any further use to you."

"Fine. What about her medical records?"

"I will do what I can to fast track getting the records to you. I have your written request here, along with the required identification. I don't anticipate that being a problem, but as an insurance, I suggest you contact the police. An officer has scissors to cut political tape that I do not."

"I cannot believe this."

"I am very sorry, Mr. Mason. Good luck to you and your wife. I hope that she gets better."

Frank was angry, dejected, but this Dr. Brunti was not at fault. "Thank you. A detective will be in touch."

"I don't know how helpful I can be, but I'll expect the call. Good day."

"Yep." Frank ended the call, chucking his cell phone across the room. "Fuck! Son of a bitch!"

Simmy came barreling through the door. "Frank, yo . . . is you cool, bro?"

Frank stood, ramming his chair into the wall behind him. "Close the door!"

Simmy closed the door behind him. "Yo, bro. A'ight. You good?"

Frank clenched his fists until his knuckles turned red. "No, I am not cool."

"Tell me what to do, yo."

"My cell is on the floor over there." He gestured with his hand in the general vicinity of where he thought his phone had landed.

Simmy walked to the wall farthest from them. He bent his knees to inspect the damage. "Yo, this phone is smashed to shit."

"Then just pick a phone in the house, Simmy."

With six steps, Simmy reached Frank's desk, placing a hand on his office phone. Frank rolled his eyes.

"Not that one."

Simmy shuffled back, awaiting further instruction.

"Pick some other phone in the house. Contact the Saint-Martin Police Department, ask for Detective Baptiste. Tell him that Frank Mason said to get his ass on the first flight here."

"Saint-Martin? Like the island where the good rum is?"

Frank's mind whirled as he came to grips with the magnitude of this problem. This person, trying to kill his wife, was not some random hire. This person was a professional.

"Yo, what's going on?"

"What in the fuck did I tell you about asking so many got-damn questions, Simmy?"

"No disrespect. I'm just sayin', what kind of shit you into that you need to fly in police? You already got the Men in Black patrolling like this house is Fort Knox or something."

"Simmy."

"Yo, it's like twenty dudes. You got four bedrooms in this house. . . ." Squinting, Simmy stared at the ceiling while he did the math. "That's like five dudes per room. We can't even breathe in here at the same time."

"Make the fuckin' call, Simmy."

"I'm sayin', don't you think I need to know?"

"Simmy, now is not the fuckin' time for this!"

"When is the time, yo? I followed you from New York, yo. You ain't told me shit. First you runnin' from trench coats in the Apple, your wife in there sick as fuck. Now you flying in cops from other countries? What the fuck, yo?"

"How long have we been here, Simmy?"

"Like four or five days."

"So, for four or five days, you've been safe."

Simmy twisted his face in confusion. "What are you talking about, yo?"

Frank turned to him, fire in his eyes. "I know, Simmy. I know who you are. I know what you did. I know why you were so anxious to come with me."

Simmy straightened up, shifting his wiry frame into a defensive posture. "Oh, yeah?"

Frank nodded.

"So, what you sayin', yo?"

"Shut the fuck up. Find a got-damn phone and call Baptiste. Stop talkin' like you're doin' me some fuckin' favor by bein' here."

"I'm not even sayin' all that—"

"Stop fuckin' talkin' and go do what I'm tellin' you to do."

"My life is in danger, too, yo."

Frank lost it. He rushed at Simmy, slamming him hard into the door. "I don't care about you, or me. Understand? We don't matter. She does. I thought I was clear at the airport."

"I got it but, yo, you runnin' round like Sonny on the *Godfather*, yo. That little money you payin' me ain't shit if I can't spend it."

"I need to save her, Simmy. I need to save her. Either you are going to help me, or you're not. The decision is yours." Frank released Simmy and walked back to his desk.

"Baptiste, right? I'll get him here, yo."

Frank nodded in gratitude. Simmy continued rambling something Frank could not understand as he left the room.

"Aye, come here."

Simmy turned around, popping his head in the entrance of Frank's office.

"Lisa does not need to hear about any of this from you. Understood?"

"Yeah, whatever, yo. I ain't sayin' nothing." Simmy snailed his way down the hall to the kitchen.

The concierge doctor would be arriving within the hour. Lisa's health had continued to deteriorate with each passing day. He checked her stitches daily, and they looked fine, normal. Frank's conversation with Dr. Brunti had reaffirmed for him that hiring a private doctor, as opposed to taking her to a hospital, was the right call. The hospital posed too many variables with so much beyond his control. She would be too vulnerable there, and Frank refused to make the same mistake twice.

He had ramped up security at the house with a security team and a state-of-the-art alarm system. Simmy may have thought it all to be a bit excessive, but Frank wanted to keep Lisa safe. His actions were not borne of logic, but were those of a frightened, desperate man. He thought the measures he took would be enough, but they were no match for the attack her body had launched from within. He didn't know how to fight that, and considering the lengths to which this killer went to take Lisa from him, he was not as confident in his personal army.

Despite Simmy's assessment, Frank was no mobster. He could only pull from film and flashes of his father's dealings. He sat at his desk, pondering these things, agonizing over the truth his heart punctured his pride with. He needed reinforcements. The one advantage he had was the killer's face etched into his mind. He had seen him every day for at least a week, and he remembered every single detail. Game on.

CHAPTER 45

She heard the door open and close. Her mother's feet shuffled across the tile before they made the transition to the wooded floorboards that paved the way to the room where she now sat, waiting patiently. Seconds passed while she sat in the evening light, see-sawing over her decision to move back, temporarily, into her old room. The light flipped on.

"Oh my gawd!" Sophie gasped, drawing her hand to her heart in surprise. "Michelle Kaye! I didn't know you were here." Sophie relaxed and entered the den, making a beeline for the mini bar. "Where have you been?"

Michelle watched as her mother thoughtlessly grabbed a few ice cubes and threw them in a glass, covering them with vodka. "It doesn't matter really."

She downed it effortlessly like it was something far less acidic, like it was water. Sophie poured another glass, quickly emptying its contents down her throat. Sophie gulped down a third glass before forcefully placing it on the mini-bar's marble surface. The sound sliced through the silence. "It matters to me."

"I have been nowhere, Mom." Michelle did not want to talk about Grayson, especially not while her mother was drinking like this. She watched Sophie erase a fifth shot and wondered how she managed to stand. It pained her to see her this way. Michelle had only seen her mother indulge a handful of times in her life before her father's funeral. She guessed the behavior could be an expression of grief, which manifested in different ways, but this felt like something else.

As she watched her mother pour a sixth drink, it occurred to Michelle what else she might be seeing. There was only one other thing that she believed could inspire a love for liquor so quickly: guilt. Her mother behaved like a woman whose conscience berated her so that libation offered the only plausible escape. Michelle could not know the exact date, but she knew that it had not been so prevalent a notion before.

"Nowhere, huh? Well, I just left your house." Sophie waddled over to her favorite chair in the corner by the small round table, falling into its embrace as the alcohol she consumed started to have its way with her.

"You what?" Michelle stood in alarm.

"That's right. Your house. Where you left your fiancé, apparently."

"Mom, you are drunk. We shouldn't have this conversation right now."

"Who is this guy you ran away with?"

Michelle felt her anger rising to the surface. This was already starting off very badly. Perhaps this was not such a good idea. "I did not run away, and I don't want to talk about it."

"So, that's who you are now? You just cheat on your fiancé?"

Michelle let her browns roll into the back of her head. "Mom . . ."

"What's the plan? To ride off into the sunset without any explanation? Live happily ever after?" Sophie slurred her words. "Disney isn't real. Can't run from life, Michelle. Traipsing around with, with random men."

"Mom, stop this."

"That boy saved your sister! You, me, the whole world! And you repay him by cheating? For what?"

"You don't know what you're talking about!"

"I didn't raise a whore!"

Michelle flinched as the label her mother hurled at her landed. Tears immediately gathered in the corners of her eyes, but she refused to cry. "I cannot believe you just said that to me."

Sophie did not grasp what she had just done. She kept on badgering Michelle with her words. "You can't do that to people, Michelle! Armand is a mess! I have never seen him like that."

"Mom, you barely know him! You only met him a few days before he brought—" Michelle could not finish her thought. Images of Brianna and Armand flashed through her mind.

"Brought your sister home? That's right, he did. He saved her because he loves you! Do you know what I would give to have someone love me like that? To put it all on the line for me? What is wrong with you?"

"Fuck him! I don't care!"

"Michelle Kaye Lewis! You will not—"

"I'm serious. You need to let this go. You don't know what you're talking about."

"I would know if you told me, but you don't talk to me anymore. I hardly hear from you."

"Save your tears, Mom. I cannot do this with you."

"Michelle . . ."

"This is your fault! All of this is your fault! I don't even know why I came here! This was a mistake." Michelle stormed toward the doorway of the den. Sophie raced after her. Michelle could hear her bumping her way down the hall.

"Take responsibility! I didn't make all the right decisions. That is true, but that is no excuse for you to start whoring yourself out! For you to start . . . behaving this way!"

Michelle made an about face in the middle of the kitchen. "My father is dead! I didn't even get to say goodbye to him. Do you have any idea what that feels like?"

Sophie, with very careful steps, made her way to Michelle. She grabbed Michelle's hand. "I am so sorry about that. Can we just talk?"

Michelle snatched it away. "Talk about what? About how my father has barely been in the ground a full month and you've already moved on? Talk about how you never reached out to your parents, my grandparents, like you stated you would? How many lies have you told, Mother? How many more do I have to uncover before you volunteer the truth?"

"Michelle, I am not denying that I haven't made some questionable choices, but I love you. You are my daughter. I raised you."

"You used me. You used me to appear far less morally corrupt than you are. You cannot hide behind me anymore. Face yourself, Mom. I see you, and I have never been more disappointed." Michelle stormed out of the kitchen, leaving Sophie to bathe in her tears.

CHAPTER 46

Pain rippled through her body. Every fiber of her being seized and convulsed. She could not believe what had just happened. Michelle was gone, *really gone*. She did not say that she would never return, but if felt that way.

Forever hurt. Regret rained from Sophie's eyes without pause. This was far from the first argument that she'd had with her daughter, but none had ever felt like this. The words she had let escape from her lips tore her soul from her. Michelle was no whore, never was, and Sophie could not believe she had spoken that way.

Michelle may never forgive her this, and she couldn't blame her. How many mistakes could any one person be expected to forgive in such a short period of time? Why didn't she just tell her that she was happy to see her? Explain how relieved she was to see that she was safe and back home? She did not do those things. Finding her fear to be completely, utterly unnecessary had allowed rage to assume its place.

Frustration, stemming from the emotional distance between her and Michelle, mixed with the guilt of having betrayed her, scripted Sophie's part in their dialogue. The softness Sophie needed to invoke to open the lines of communication with Michelle to even enter into their conversation seemed sabotaged from the first words out of her mouth. Sophie rarely lost control, but lately it did not seem as though she had any at all.

She had not seen *Lewis's ghost* in a week or so, and she wanted to claim that as a sign of things to come. The promise of second chances had washed over her situation, bringing a tide of change, resulting in a momentous shift upward. The morning sent her to find a disheveled Armand, wallowing in filth, faulting the loss of his love to another. She did not know what to make of that, but she could personally attest to how different her daughter seemed to be.

Michelle had not really dealt with everything as far as she could tell. She had buried her head in work as usual and ignored the world shifting around her. Sophie watched Michelle carry on this way all her life. Any attempts to force Michelle into dealing with things before she was ready had always ended in catastrophe. Sophie was prepared to offer friendship to her daughter, to give counsel. She had learned it was the most effective way to assist Michelle, but she did not do those things. She attacked her, viciously and ruthlessly, like she was some stranger on the street and Armand had been her child.

Ding dong, boomp, boomp, boomp . . . Ding dong, boomp, boomp, boomp . . .

Sophie pulled herself up from the floor, dragging her body through the hall to the front door. Her eyes were too puffy to see anything through the peephole. She didn't bother looking.

"Who is it?" she whimpered.

"Police, ma'am. Please open the door. We need to ask you a few questions."

Sophie gulped. Wiping her blue eyes with the back of her hand, she opened the door. "What can I help you with, officer?"

"Step aside, ma'am. We are executing a warrant to search your home."

Sophie expertly disguised her increasing panic as innocent confusion. "Search my home, but why?" She laughed. "What is this about? May I see a copy of the warrant, please?"

While the officer produced a copy of the warrant, she looked beyond him to see Michelle's car leaving the driveway. She fought the urge to burst into tears all over again. The officer handed her the warrant. As she looked over the details, the scales tipped as the pain of possibly losing Michelle forever was eclipsed by the very real probability of prison. Her house was being searched as part of an investigation into a potential homicide. It did not name her nor Lewis, but it was not hard to deduce what was going on here.

She couldn't think straight. The foyer started collapsing around her. She sped toward the den, grabbed the phone, and dialed the first number that came to mind.

"Hello, Peter? Peter . . ." Sophie whispered, cradling the base of the phone in her hand to amplify her voice into the receiver. "Peter, I need you to come here, now."

"Luce?"

"Yes, it's me. Can you come over?"

"I cannot come right now. What's wrong?"

"*Peter*. Peter . . . this is urgent."

"I have a few errands to run. Might be able to come by later."

"But the police are here. I need you."

"The police? What's going on?"

"I don't know. They're looking for something. I don't want to be alone, Peter."

"Luce, just stay calm. I'll be there as soon I can."

"Please hurry."

"Sure."

"Okay . . ."

An officer opened the door, ventured in, and began to sift through her things. She took that as a cue to leave. She couldn't stand to watch them dismantle her home, violating her privacy. She walked swiftly to her room, softly closing the door behind her. The search had not ventured into that part of the house yet, and she was certain it would not be long.

She walked to her dresser, retrieved the ring, Peter's ring, hidden amongst her undergarments, and slid it on her finger. She wondered what Peter needed to do that could possibly be more important than being here for her, but she did not have long to ponder an answer. Peter was correct. She needed to calm down and think her way through this.

She took a deep breath to let her mind work. Slipping into her bathroom, she fished out the manila envelope taped underneath the bathroom sink and slid it sideways into her pants. Checking herself in the mirror, she noticed her bottom looked unnaturally flat. The folder was obvious. She slid it around the side, rubbing its sides until it took on the shape of her thighs.

Satisfied with the results, she threw some water on her face, grabbed a towel, and began patting her face with a towel as she emerged from the bathroom.

"Ma'am, what were you doing in there?"

Sophie smiled uncomfortably. "Oh, I just needed to brush my teeth, wash up. My daughter and I had a horrible fight. I had a few drinks before you came. I wasn't expecting you."

"Of course. That was your daughter leaving?"

Sophie looked down sheepishly. "Yes. She didn't even come back to check on her mother. So, I guess you can imagine how bad the argument was."

"Yes, ma'am. I need to look around in here."

"Yes, I am leaving." On her way out of the room, she rested her hand on the young officer's arm. "Please, be sensitive. These are my most intimate items."

"Yes, ma'am."

Sophie slithered through the sea of officers, through the French doors of the kitchen, and into her car. She sat there for a minute contemplating her next move. She really did not have anywhere to go. She wanted to pay Ernest, the medical examiner, a visit but couldn't imagine how that would help her defense. He was the only other person with knowledge that something other than suicide had happened that night, but the ruling was his decision. She had not asked that of him and doubted very seriously that he would venture any information that would earn him an orange jumpsuit. Besides, she hadn't told him everything, either.

Her weasel of a lawyer probably had some hand in this. His absence now made perfect sense. She had not been able to reach him prior to him informing her about the date for the hearing. She could not even be certain there ever was a hearing scheduled. Who knows when they may have gotten to him? Something about him did not bode well with her from the start, and fortunately, he did not have any information that would incriminate her. He only knew that she desired cremation following the funeral services. The request was unorthodox but one she could easily explain. She had not entertained a detective or fielded any questions from the police department beyond the initial report taken the day the coroner came to retrieve Lewis's body.

From that day until her lawyer called to inform her of the injunction stopping the cremation, things had gone as expected. This search, though it would not uncover anything, was a very serious hiccup. It alluded to the fact that there were variables that she had not accounted for. It was possible that her lawyer embellished, creating suspicion where there was none, offering his own fictional account of what had happened. She could not determine why he would have done that, though. Breaching the lawyer/client privilege would mean the end of his career and possible jail time. What advantage was it to him to create an issue for her?

But what else could it be? A judge had signed off on a search warrant, granting the police access into her home. There had to be sufficient reason to support that decision—something to suggest that a homicide had occurred. The only other person who knew the truth besides her was cold, waiting to travel through the coroner's oven. No, someone else was in play here, but who?

CHAPTER 47

Peter put his phone on silent mode. His nerves were bad enough without adding any more interruptions, least of all from Sophie. He did not know what kind of crisis she had managed to get herself into, but after the confession she had made the last time he was there, he had to guess that it probably had something to do with that. She would be fine until he could get there. She had lived with her decisions for twenty-something years; a few hours weren't going to kill her.

He pulled up in front of the apartment he *gave* to Brianna. Peter had done quite well for himself. Not only was he one of the few doctors with his specialty in the area, but he was also the owner of several rental properties, one of which was an apartment building in Plano. It was not upscale by any means, but his managers kept it up, and he was able to provide homes at an affordable price in an otherwise pricey residential area.

He had been surprised when Brianna called him a few days ago asking if he could help her find a residence. She would not go into details, but she no longer wished to stay at her sister's and did not feel comfortable at her mother's. Peter was happy to help her. He made a few phone calls and found that he had a vacant apartment. If she had declined, he would have paid for her to stay elsewhere, but she accepted his offer.

She did not have much to move, other than a few clothing items. Within a few hours, the apartment was fully furnished with a new living room suite, bedroom furniture, brand new appliances, and he brought in a home interior designer to give it that "model house" look. Brianna resisted initially but conceded after Peter explained that he could use it to attract future residents. The thought put her at ease with things. Peter knew that she had a difficult time accepting help or trusting any assistance offered to her, and he knew what she needed to hear. The idea was not a complete lie, but the truth was . . . he did it for her.

He parked, got out of his car, and knocked on Brianna's door. The papers shook in his hand, but he forced his nerves to be still once she opened the door.

"Dr. Baxter?"

He knew Brianna had not been expecting him. In his haste to get to her, he had neglected to call before arriving. "I know . . . I didn't call, and I hope my visit isn't intrusive, but I would like to talk to you if I may have a minute."

Brianna stepped away from the door, waving him in. "Of course. This is your place."

"Brianna, please, this is your space, and I intend to respect and honor your privacy. Don't allow my relationship with the property to excuse my violating your rights here." Dr. Baxter headed to the couch while he talked. "How have you been? Feeling okay with the baby and everything?"

Brianna plopped down on the couch near him, folding her legs Indian-style on the couch. In a pair of cotton warm-up pants and a slightly oversized T-shirt, Brianna looked comfortable. He noticed a slight change in her after their visit with Javan.

"I feel good. Better than I have felt in a long while. I'm actually glad you came by."

"Oh?"

"I was thinking about Dr. Shepherd. Did they find her niece, Rachel? Have you heard anything?"

"We chatted briefly the other day, and they still don't have any leads. It's like she just up and disappeared into thin air. She was using a prepaid phone, so they can't even say where she was last. Dr. Shepherd is hoping no news is good news."

"I keep thinking about her. She's been gone a long time. Seeing Javan triggered a few memories I need to purge from my mind. I almost didn't get away from him and could have easily been her. You know? Missing without a trace."

"I understand. That sentiment is natural. I worried what seeing him would do, but you seem to have handled it well."

"I did. Thanks to you. I mean seriously, thank you for all of your help. I mean for this," she chimed, sweeping her arms across the invisible space holding the room. "And for Javan—I mean Micah."

"Micah."

"Micah, Micah, Micah. I have got to get used to that I guess."

"I guess so. We have discussed it numerous times. I won't question your decision, but if you change your mind about this . . . *him,* it's okay. It's noble what you want, but no one could blame you for pulling back."

"I appreciate that, Dr. Baxter. I cannot explain it, but I feel very strongly about it. It's what's right for us, for my family."

Peter saw that as the perfect segue into what he needed to speak with her about. "Speaking of family: have you spoken with your mother lately?"

"No, why?"

"Just curious. I have been thinking a lot about what you said regarding the importance of a child knowing their father. I had an excellent example of a man in my father, and I completely agree with you. That bond is vital and more important than I think people realize. Not just for the child, but for the dad, too. It changes you."

"Frank was a great dad, and I was devastated when I learned the truth. It was like the best part of me was stolen. I could not understand how he could do something so foul. I still can't really. I haven't talked to him since . . ."

"Believe me when I say that I know exactly how you feel."

"Then, seconds later, I found out that my biological father had died. I never even met him. I felt robbed, twice. I cannot describe it."

Peter felt his heart racing. His palms were sweaty. He was not sure how Brianna was going to take his news, but Sophie had left him no choice. "No need to. You have been through quite a lot, and your present mindset is a testament to your strength. You are doing great. Especially over the last few weeks. I am very proud of you."

"Thank you for saying that. I, for once, am pretty proud of me too."

"Well, there is something . . . something that I . . . uh . . . wanted to talk you a–about." He watched as her smile faded as the rattling of the papers he held drew her attention. Placing them on the table, he grinned to comfort her, and checked his nerves. "Uh, do you remember the night we found out about your little bundle of joy?"

"Of course. I doubt I will ever forget that night."

"Me either. Special night. I was honored to be a part it. Something else . . . stuck out to me that night."

"Bigger than my being pregnant?" Brianna asked, laughing.

"I mean, that was big, but . . . I was thinking about your birthmark. The blurry butterfly."

Brianna drew her legs close, causing Peter to put his hands up in a defensive posture. "No, no, no. It's nothing like that." She laughed uncomfortably as he continued to explain himself. "It's just that . . . it was familiar to me. See, my mother had one, as did her mother, my grandmother, and my great-grandmother, too."

Peter stared intently into Brianna's eyes to see if any of his words were registering. She just looked confused. "That's cool, I guess, but what does that have to do with me?"

Peter slid the papers toward Brianna. Tapping them for effect, he attempted to elaborate. "Brianna, as you stated, family is important, and that is the primary reason I feel it necessary to tell you."

"Tell me what, exactly?"

Peter braced himself for the worst, the papers sitting there, nearly tormenting him. He took a deep breath and rolled the dice. "Brianna, I am your father."

Brianna was incredulous. "Are you serious?"

Peter picked up the papers and handed them to Brianna. "I hope you don't mind, but I used a DNA sample from your visit to test against mine, and . . . well, as you can see for yourself, ninety-nine percent."

Brianna stared wide-eyed at the papers. "How is this possible? I mean . . . you're white."

"Actually, my mother was—I'm biracial." Peter still couldn't tell how Brianna felt about the news, but he was relieved. He had gotten the results from his lab and rushed over to her place as fast as he could. He could not keep it to himself. "I hope . . . I mean, are you okay?"

Brianna looked up at him, her eyes round like her mother's. "So, my father isn't dead?"

Peter's eyes filled with tears. He didn't bother wiping them away. He loved her with an encompassing love. He knew that he would do anything, anything in the world for her. He knew without a shadow of doubt that he was looking into the eyes of the most important person in his world. He could not believe Sophie would keep this from him. Would keep Brianna from him.

"No, he isn't. I am right here. If you'll have me."

"This is . . . Did you know?"

"I came here as soon as I confirmed it. I don't know if your mother knows, but I am glad that I do. I hope you are, too."

"Wow. You're my father. My real . . . father." Tears flowed freely down her face. "I dreamt about you. I had accepted that I'd never meet you, but . . ."

"I promise I'll never leave you. You are the best thing that has ever happened to me."

"Do you mind if I give you hug?" she asked innocently.

"Are you kidding me? Come here." He took another deep breath as Brianna crashed into his body; felt his heart growing inside his chest as he wrapped his arms around his daughter for the first time.

"I cannot believe this." Brianna pulled away from him. "Oh my goodness, you helped me so much and you hardly knew me. I didn't know what to think of that at first. I was suspicious of you, your intentions, but at some point, I realized that you were just a good person. That touched me. No one in my family had done that. Honestly, this is . . . I'm not sure how it is. I feel something, not sure what to call it."

"You are my daughter, my family. We will get through this together. I had planned to be here anyway, but now there is no way I could let you leave my life." Peter took a hold of her hands. "Take your time. I know this is a lot and we still have a lot to unpack, but I'm not worried. You don't have to worry either. I'm here."

"I knew it. . . . Everything is going to be fine. Just fine."

"I'm going to be a grandfather!"

"Yes, you are!" Brianna exclaimed. "I have so much to tell you! Where should I start?"

"The beginning sounds good. I want to hear everything." Peter sat mesmerized by the pure delight that lit her face. He knew there were questions that still needed answers, but for now, this was exactly where he needed to be. Sophie wasn't going anywhere. He could deal with her later.

CHAPTER 48

"Grayson, I cannot do this right now." Michelle eyes burned red. She didn't know if she could handle anymore knives in her back. The proverbial edge was far behind her. She had fallen off it many decisions ago, but it had never been clearer to her than in this moment.

Swerving her Audi onto the road connecting her to what she once thought would be home, Michelle felt her sanity evaporating, and it was just as real as the screeching of her tires gripping the tarred path.

"Michelle, where are you? Let me come get you."

An ominous feeling bloomed in the pit of her stomach. She feared what she might do once she reached her destination. This fear dialed Grayson's number, hoping his mellifluous tenor could dampen the potency of the fire that warmed her from within, sending liters of sweat spilling out of her pores. "I'm fine, Grayson. I am sorry I called and pulled you into my drama again. This never-ending fuckin' cycle."

"You are not fine. Your voice is elevated. You're talking on the phone while you're driving. You never do that. Something is going on. Talk to me."

"I can't. I need to face this, face him."

"You made a promise, Michelle. One promise. To me."

"I tried, but I can't avoid it. I have to deal with it, Grayson."

"You are too upset to do this right now."

"I cannot put it off anymore."

"Just come here. We can talk, scream, cry, or whatever you want. Whatever you need to do. But you need to come here."

"The phone is going to disconnect."

"Michelle!"

Michelle slammed on the brakes and threw her car into the park.

"Michelle, wait before—"

Michelle killed the engine and swung open the driver-side door, disconnecting the Bluetooth. She did not have the capacity to welcome a reasonable calm into her space. She was too raw, too tired of being betrayed by those who were supposed to love her. Her life was in shambles, and she had yet to find anything to ease the pain of having lost everything. Her family, her fiancé, the promise of a life worth living had all been snatched by the same evils that currently held some intimate part of her hostage. She, too, found herself shackled by bad decisions, one in particular, and hated the skewed timeline that sprouted from it. She did not want to be *her*.

Each person she professed to love had been washed from her presence by hurricane deception, leaving her no one but Grayson, a confusing blend of Prince Charming and El-Hajj Malik El-Shabazz, sprinkled with the familiarity of the bank teller whose line you seem to routinely find yourself standing in, to help her repair the damage. Calling him was a kneejerk reaction after the fight she'd had with her mother. She hoped that he could reach into her soul and soothe her anger as he had done with her hurt.

Ordinarily, his words were like her own personal bonsai tree, shifting her energy into something as calm and peaceful as a wave-less ocean. That was not the case today. She hopped out of her car, slamming the door hard enough to make her Audi seize with fright.

Adrenaline pumped through her system as she sprinted to the front door.

BAM! BAM! BAM!

"Open the door, LaCroix! Open this muthafuckin' door!" She heard a lot of commotion inside, only serving to exacerbate her anger. "LaCroix!"

BAM! BAM! BAM!

Grayson had her house key. She had given it to him to put him at ease about her leaving. It was something like an assurance that she would not come to this house, but things had changed. Again. Her life had survived so many alterations that change itself had become her only constant.

"Open the door, LaCroix! Now!" Her body shook with anger. She could not believe Armand had run his mouth to her mother. She could hear him fumbling around inside, making his way to the door. Anxiety kept her moving, bouncing from side to side like a boxer waiting for the bell. She stood there, swaying with the wind whirring through her ears, waiting for the rest of her world to collapse, too heavy a burden for her to carry alone. This was too much. Her mother, Armand, Brianna, and her departed father had dragged her into a world her degree from Rice promised she could avoid. No amount of money could have saved her. The people failed her. Her relationships, once a source of strength and connectedness, had all failed her. She was not sure how much of herself she still possessed.

"I'm coming. I'm coming."

Michelle's temple throbbed, her body warm all over. She thought about the grandparents she never knew, wondered which of her mother's sins had soured the relationship, pondering how awful it must have been if it led to them disowning her. She shuddered, thinking of the ghosts lurking in her parents' histories that had inevitably made their way into the present. Mostly, she just wished she didn't belong to such a fucked-up family.

"LaCroix! LaCro—"

Armand swung the door open.

Smack! Michelle felt the sting of her hand connecting with his face before she could process it fully. "How dare you!" She charged, pushing past his body slumping in the doorway. "What did you tell her?"

Stepping into the trash dump that used to be her living room, Michelle shook her head in disbelief. He had destroyed everything. Couches were flipped over. Her treasured paintings now lay in pieces, ripped and scattered about the room.

Holding his cheek with his left hand, Armand pushed the door closed with his right. "Michelle, what are you talking about?"

"You destroyed my paintings? Really?" Michelle fumed. She glared at Armand, tracking his movement from the door to the couch, wishing she had Elle's powers to electrocute his steps. He flipped it upright and plopped down on the exposed springs to sit. Her breathing increased, awaiting an answer. "What the fuck, LaCroix? You know what they meant to me!"

Armand did not respond. He just looked at her with sunken eyes. She sprinted past him, hurdling random objects off the floor, and threw open the door to the room at the end of the hall, opposite their bedroom. Her book collection was still intact. Nothing in the room had been touched. She sighed with relief.

"I didn't touch it."

Michelle jumped at the sound of his voice, peeking over her shoulder into the room.

"I couldn't get past the door. It smells like you in here. I didn't want to lose this too."

Michelle ignored her urge to lean back into his chest, to fill her lungs with his cologne and drift into the future wrapped in his arms. She hated that she desired his love, something she could never accept from him again. Turning abruptly, she exited the room and walked back into the disaster area formerly known as the living room.

"So, what did you tell her?"

"What are you talking about?"

"Don't give me that bullshit, LaCroix. You know exactly what I'm talking about."

Armand sauntered, undetected again, behind her and returned to his seat on the couch. "Brianna?"

"My mother, Lacroix. What did you tell her?"

"I didn't tell her anything . . . nothing."

"Don't lie to me. I just left her house! Don't lie!"

"Shit! Listen!" He screamed in frustration. "You wouldn't talk to me! You wouldn't . . . you wouldn't talk to me, MK! So . . . so, maybe I said some things."

He sounded broken and helpless, but Michelle did not care. She saw him like a child, acting out, begging for attention. She was not his mother. "So! Whose fault is that? You couldn't get what you want, so what? You just lied? To my mother?"

Armand sobbed lightly and dropped his head between his legs, covering the back of his head with his hands. "I didn't mean to. I'm sorry. I just . . . didn't know what else to do. I miss you so much."

Michelle rolled her eyes, ruffled a handful of her hair. "What is there to discuss, LaCroix?" Michelle spoke, pacing back and forth in front of him. "I walked in on you fucking my sister!" Pointing to the foyer, she continued. "Right over there! You had her bent over my got-damn table!"

"If you'll just let me explain, Michelle. I know this is bad, but—"

"Explain! Explain what? I'm not confused. Things are very clear to me."

"That is not what I meant."

"I'd advise you not to waste your words, LaCroix. I have a character limit on bullshit. Tread carefully."

"Michelle, I have apologized. What else do you want from me?"

"Nothing."

"I've been praying for us. Asking God to help me fix things."

"There is no us. That is not happening ever again. Whatever that was . . . whatever we were . . . was not real. *We* were born on a big fat lie, and I tried to move past it, I did, but this . . . Brianna. I cannot and will not move beyond it. You are a liar."

"Please don't say that. You taught me everything I know about love."

"I hope you learn something from this. From losing me."

"You are the only woman I have loved besides my mother, Michelle. I just made a terrible mistake."

"A terrible mistake? No. Stringing me along for two years before revealing that you were hired to date me was a terrible mistake. Hiding an illegal gun with an unknown body count on it in our home was a terrible mistake. That thing you did with Brianna erased us. Do you understand? You erased us!"

Armand looked up at Michelle, still standing in the center of the room. His light gray eyes softened her approach as tears pelted his face. She felt them painting her face, too. She fell to the floor, bringing her knees tight into her chest as her anger faded, giving in to the hurt simmering beneath its cover.

"How could you do that to us? To me?"

"I was wrong, and I am so, so sorry Michelle. You mean the world to me. You are my everything."

Michelle dried her face with the back of her palm. "Quoting lyrics from songs now?"

"What are you talking about? I'm speaking from my heart, MK."

"Toni Braxton. How appropriate."

"Michelle—"

"Wrong song, though. 'Love Shoulda Brought You Home.' That's the one on repeat for me. 'See, it doesn't matter what you say this time 'cause our whole relationship is built on one lie.'"

"Give me another chance."

"That will never happen," Michelle answered through sniffles. "Death was imminent from inception. We never really had a shot."

Armand sat back on the couch, sinking farther toward the ground. "This is not the end of us. I won't let it end like this."

Michelle, now with her legs twisted like a pretzel beneath her, twiddling with a stray piece of thread hanging from her blouse, retorted. "From where I'm sitting, you don't have a choice."

CHAPTER 49

He wanted this to be over. He wanted Lisa to be better and Brianna to come home. Frank missed his family. He missed his dysfunctional, emotionally paralyzed family. He would give all the money he had to sit in the living room with his two favorite girls, cloaked in an uncomfortable silence, paying for the chance to look at them without fearing for their safety or needing to defend his loving them.

He lay in the bed, holding his wife's feverish body close to his, pretending to enjoy the full-blown sauna beneath his collared shirt as she scorched him with her heat. He feigned gratitude that he was not saying goodbye to her cold, lifeless body. The truth was far more difficult to contend with: he wanted her neither blistering hot, nor freezing cold. He wanted her healthy.

Besides, as warm as she made him, he could only imagine how magnified her discomfort was in comparison to his. She could not escape her 101.3-degree cocoon. She was trapped, much like he was, by his need to touch her, to glean what little strength she had to offer him. Together they lay like this for an hour each day. It was their time.

Lisa's body was failing her. Frank's untrained eye had not detected the infection the doctor suspected lived in her lungs after examining her. Her resting heart rate was over 90 beats per minute, far more than normal for someone engaged in little to no physical activity. She had become so frail in such a short period of time that Frank feared she might slip away. She received her nourishment intravenously.

Despite the fact that the private doctor promised to expedite the results from the screening and the other tests performed, there was still no word yet on what was taking Lisa away from him. *The wait* required Frank to tap into a kind of abstemious way of life that he was not accustomed to. He never waited for anything. Everything he had ever acquired, he did so by figuring out how to bypass *the wait*. His college degree, meeting the stipulations to get his inheritance, or even becoming a member of his family: he had found a shortcut. There had to be one out of this predicament as well, a faster way to heal Lisa, determine who was threatening her safety, and reunite his family.

Lisa had been without an anesthetic since Frank's conversation with Dr. Brunti. The private doctor could not prescribe anything new without knowing what was currently in her system. Lisa spent the majority of each day in dreamland, which Frank preferred to her being awake and suffering. He hovered over her, pressing his lips against her forehead until the heat became unbearable. Reaching over her body to the bedside table, he pulled the towel out of the bowl of ice water, wrung it out, and dabbed her cheeks and neck with it before stretching it across her forehead.

Frank tried to convince himself that all of this, the private doctor and the security, would amount to something, that his decision to keep her home was for the best, but he could not be sure. His wife was dying in front of him, and he felt powerless to stop it. He still had no contact information for his daughter, no way of reaching her, and perhaps that was best. Four days had passed since they returned from the island, and he was no closer to the answers he sought. Heavily armed guards flanked the house on all sides, no more than ten feet between each other, but Frank felt exposed.

I could use your help, Lisa. Tell me what to do, babe. Give me something, please.

"Frank . . ." Lisa's brittle voice broke into his thoughts.

"Lisa, baby, I'm here."

"Wa–wa–wa . . ."

"Water? I got it. One sec." Frank rolled off the bed, quickly walking around to her side where the table sat, holding all the comfort he could give her: a bowl of ice chips and a pitcher of water. After pouring Lisa a fresh glass, he held the neck of the straw between his fingers, keeping it in Lisa's mouth until she had her fill. This was the second part of their routine. The same time each day, plus or minus a minute, they would share this small moment. Frank was convinced that Lisa braved lucidity just for him. Frank spoke to her often, but she could not respond, and only faith envisioned her ability to comprehend.

"I . . . love . . . you."

"I love you, too."

Within seconds of him uttering those four words, she drifted back into the realm ruled by unconscious thought. He sat back in the chair, watching her rest for a moment. He could not see her organs slowly shutting down from the poison ravaging her system, but he knew it was happening. Lisa was depending on him, and he had to come through for her.

He rose to his feet, kissed her once more, and walked into the hall where he knew Simmy would be waiting.

"Yo, Frank, how is she today?"

"No change. Anything from the doctor yet?"

"This fax came in, yo. I didn't want to bother you." Simmy handed him the paper in his hand. "It's a picture or something."

"This is from Baptiste. This is from the surveillance footage at the hospital."

"Video from a hospital?"

Frank looked at Simmy. He could see the question before he asked.

"Yo, come on. You look like you seen a ghost or something," Simmy said.

"Someone is trying to kill Lisa."

"I guessed that much. Can a brotha get some details, yo?"

Frank waved Simmy down the hall toward his office. Maybe it was time to let Simmy in a bit on what was going on. "My office."

Simmy floated down the hall to Frank's office. Frank motioned for the return of the guards normally posted outside of his bedroom before joining Simmy. Once inside his office, Frank closed the door.

He took a seat behind his desk. Simmy sat facing him. "This information is for your ears only, Simmy. I am serious. I don't know who I can trust at this point. My best friend, Jacob, does not even know that I am back in town. No one knows anything until I get a handle on this."

"I don't know nobody but you, yo. Who I'm goin' to tell?"

"Simmy."

"I ain't sayin' nothing. What's up?"

"Resort in Saint-Martin. Someone broke into her suite, tried to stab her. I must have startled them. I found her when I came out of the bathroom."

"Yo, that is crazy."

"At the hospital, they tried to finish the job. Pretended to be her doctor, injected her with something. I don't know what yet."

"No wonder you got these CIA/FBI/DEA wannabes walking round here. Do you think they was following you through the airport?"

Frank shook his head. "No, I don't know. That was a different situation. They could have been, but that wasn't my main concern at that time."

Simmy's eyes grew wide. "It wasn't? For real, yo? Something bigger than some ninja chameleon assassin tryin' to merk yo' wife, yo?"

Frank had to laugh. The notion of something being worse than that was preposterous but no less true. "Yeah, something worse than that."

"Don't hold out on me, yo."

"Nothing more to tell right now." Frank trusted Simmy, but he was too unpredictable to be knowledgeable about everything. Frank needed to keep some things to himself. "Has Baptiste called back yet?"

"Nah, not yet. Why?"

"Nothing." Frank leaned back in his chair, thinking about his next move.

"What was on the paper?"

"I can't really tell. This fax is hard to make out. The quality is shit."

Simmy nodded in agreement. "This is off topic or whatever, but I heard you the other day, yo. Talkin' 'bout you know what I did."

"And?"

"So, what you know 'bout it?"

"I know enough, but my focus is on Lisa. Period. All else is irrelevant."

"Yeah, all right."

Ring, ring, ring.

Maintaining eye contact with Simmy, Frank answered the phone. "Hello? This is Frank Mason. . . . Right now? Gate number? I'll send someone to get you." Frank looked at Simmy, suggesting that he would be the lucky *someone*.

Simmy looked around the room, underneath his chair, and over both shoulders in search of this someone Frank would send to the airport. "Me?"

"I'm not leaving Lisa."

"But I'm not from here. I don't even know how to get to the airport, yo."

"Google Maps, Mapquest, Car Navi. Pick one and use it."

"You can't get Agent M or P or one of them to do it?"

"I am sure I want you to go get Detective Baptiste from the airport."

"Fine. I'll go. I'm takin' the drop top, though." Simmy got up to leave. "Wait, do I look po'? I need to look like I got money. I don't want no issues with DPD."

"Just go."

Ding, dong. Ding, dong. Ring.

Frank hit the intercom. "Doctor Utawa, I'll be there in a minute."

CHAPTER 50

She pulled into the circular drive, shifting the car into park, and sat for a while. Her emotions swirled like a little girl meeting her date's parents for the first time, except she was no little girl, and this reunion was nearly twenty-four years overdue. If there were some other way to guarantee her survival, she would take it, but she could not see a way around this. She needed him as much as she hated to admit it.

Her heart protested what she was about to do, but she turned that part of herself off. This was about strategy, not emotion. She had to make certain sacrifices to ensure her freedom, and this was one of them. She got out of the car, padding gingerly to the front door, and rang the doorbell. She could hear the tones echoing throughout the mansion.

She braced herself as a shaky hand slowly opened the door, welcoming her inside. "Mr. Freemont isn't expecting any company."

The tiny voice, fractured but tinged with the progression of time, was music to Sophie ears. A single tear fell from her eyes as she took in her old friend's aged, frail form. Standing before her was the only person she knew to have loved her unconditionally. Sophie stepped inside the door, admiring the old, massive foyer, while her old friend closed the door behind her. She had not yet realized who she was, and Sophie wasn't sure what it would mean to tell her right now.

"If you don't mind waiting, I can get him for you."

Sophie did not offer a verbal response. With a nod of her head, she agreed to wait. She followed the mild-mannered woman into the sitting room and took a seat before the woman disappeared into the house. Sophie stood, wandering about the room, touching and remembering her time there. Not much had changed, as far as she could tell. She was so lost in her thoughts that she did not notice when the person whom she had come to see joined her in the room.

"Sophie?"

His tenor, crusted from years of choking on cancer sticks, struck a nerve, sending the hairs all over her body to their feet.

"Sophie, my darling, is that you?"

Sophie turned to lay eyes on her father. "Hello, Daddy."

"Come here, child. Come here, now, please," Richard requested with his arms outstretched.

Sophie hesitated, not sure what to make of his kindness.

"Come on. It's been a long time. Such a long time."

Sophie relented and walked over to her father, allowed him to hug her for as long as he needed. "Daddy."

Time had been kind to him. Even in his old age, he still stood tall, towering above his daughter. His embrace was strong, like his age hadn't weakened him at all.

"You look good, Daddy."

"Today is good. Best day in a long time."

Sophie couldn't ignore the smile he wore. His eyes glistened like new diamonds.

"Come, sit. We can visit over here," he stated, pointing to the couches. Sophie followed close behind him. "I am very glad to see you, Sophie. Very glad."

"It's good to see you, too, Daddy. Honestly, I wasn't sure I would be welcome here, considering how I left." Sophie was still hesitant around him as they sat down and got comfortable. She still couldn't believe she shared the same space with him. The whole exchange was surreal.

Sophie watched a sadness interrupt his joy.

"I have done a lot of things I regret, Sophie. My biggest holes were with you and your sister. I cannot undo what I did, but I am sorry. I should not have run you away like that."

Sophie was so shocked that she couldn't respond. Out of all the things she had expected to hear, an apology was not on the list. She sat speechless and continued listening.

"It killed your mother. I thought I was doing the right thing for the Freemont name, but I was wrong." He grabbed her hand, held it gently. "I was wrong, Sophie. You are my daughter, and I love you. I am sorry, so very sorry that I ever made you feel different. The things that I made you do for me . . . awful things. Things no child should do. I am ashamed of myself."

"Daddy, this is a little hard to believe."

"Time has a way of breaking people, and when I lost your mother, it broke me. I am not that man anymore, Sophie, and I hope you can forgive an old man."

"Daddy . . ."

"The drugs, the lies, the fake relationships, and all the secrets I made you carry. No parent should do those things to their children. I was supposed to protect you, but I didn't. I made you vulnerable."

As much as she absorbed the confessional her father had doled onto her lap, she needed to stop the deluge so she could get to the heart of the matter. "I am not weak, Daddy. We can figure out the past another time. The reason I came here is that I am more like you than I care to admit. I have survived all this time, but I am in trouble now. I came here because I need your help."

"What kind of trouble?"

"The police are searching my home right now. Looking for evidence, Daddy."

"Evidence of what?"

"I am so scared, Daddy. I didn't know where else to go."

"You came to the right place. You came home. Tell Daddy what is going on."

"I killed a man, Daddy. I don't want to go to jail for it."

Richard sat up, rested his back against the cushions, and looked Sophie directly in her blue eyes. "Did he deserve it, child?"

"Yes, Daddy. Yes, Daddy, he deserved it."

"Good. Daddy will take care of it. No Freemont has ever seen the inside of a jail cell, and none ever will. Don't worry."

Sophie smiled, bursting into tears. "Thank you, Daddy! Thank you! I have something that might help." Sophie stood, reached into her pants, and pulled out the manila envelope she had hidden there. "I snuck this out of the house when I left."

Richard smiled. "I guess you are a lot like your father. What's in this?"

"My insurance policy, Daddy. If worst comes to worst, that is my get out of jail free card."

CHAPTER 51

Sophie's home was crawling with police officers when Dr. Baxter and Brianna pulled into the driveway. Brianna followed Dr. Baxter into the house in search of her mother. They had come to question her about their familial situation, but upon seeing the number of police officers present, it no longer seemed all that important, at least for the moment.

Brianna stopped an officer. "Excuse me, where is my mother? The owner of this house?"

"I am sorry. I don't know what to tell you."

"Has she been arrested for something?"

"I cannot speak with anyone regarding this case besides the owner of this house, but I can tell you that we have not taken anyone into custody today."

"So, my mother's here?"

"I don't know. Possibly."

Brianna felt her patience waning, but she needed to remain calm for the baby. She was still in her first trimester, and stress could complicate her pregnancy.

Dr. Baxter weaved his way through the crowd, back to where she stood by the front door.

"Anything?"

Dr. Baxter shook his head. "She is not here. An officer ran into her earlier in the bathroom and said that she told him she was leaving."

"Do you have any idea where she is?"

"Not a clue. Think your sister might know?"

"Maybe, but she isn't speaking to me right now."

"Want to talk about it?"

"No, I don't. I want to pretend like it never happened."

"Well, we need to find your mom. What's your sister's number?"

Brianna handed Dr. Baxter her cell phone. "Look under *Twin*."

As Brianna looked around the scene, something made her increasingly uncomfortable, but she couldn't put her finger on it. "What is going on here?"

Dr. Baxter looked at her, quickly looking away. She could tell he was hiding something.

"Let's go to the car. We can call your sister on speaker phone."

"That's fine."

Brianna and Dr. Baxter walked back to the car. Dr. Baxter turned on the bluetooth and dialed Michelle's number from his phone. She answered after three rings.

"Hello?"

"Yes, hi, Michelle, this is . . . your mother's *friend*."

"How did you get my number?"

Dr. Baxter shot a quick glance at Brianna, who remained mute. "That's a long story, but your mom is in trouble. I think it's really bad."

"That is too bad for her, I guess."

"I won't pretend to understand what is going on between you and your mom, but there are lots of police here, and she isn't. Do you have any idea where she might go?"

"To hell, would be my guess."

"Michelle, you don't mean that," Brianna interjected.

"Wait a minute. Brianna? What the fuck? I don't have shit to say to you! I don't know what the fuck is going on here, but leave me out of it."

"Michelle, wait. Your mother . . . she might be in very serious trouble here."

"She is a big girl. I am sure she can handle it. Now, I don't know how you two know each other, and I don't care. Lose my number."

"Michelle, wait—"

Click. Michelle disconnected the line.

Dr. Baxter took a deep breath, puffing out his cheeks in an exaggerated fashion. "So, Brianna, still don't want to talk about it?"

Brianna reclined the seat back. "Is this the therapist or the dad?"

"Both."

"I slept with Armand."

"With who?"

"Her fiancé."

"You did what? Brianna!"

"I know. I feel terrible about it, but she won't speak to me. I'm just trying to move forward."

"You are going to have to face this at some point. Maybe not right now, because I want my grandchild to be well, but eventually." Dr. Baxter cranked the car, pulling out of the driveway.

"I know. I will, hopefully." Brianna was not avoiding her sister, but she knew she was not in the right mental state to deal with the berating that would come with a confrontation. Part of her was glad that Michelle chose to ignore her; it allowed her to ignore the situation, too. She definitely wanted to make amends, though, and start this new phase of her life on solid ground. She needed at least one part of her family to begin with the truth.

"Where are we going?" she asked.

"Clearly, your mother is not with Michelle. She is not with you. I only know of one other place to look."

"Where is that?"

"Her parents' house."

Brianna got queasy, but she shook it off. She would be lying if she said she was not apprehensive about meeting her grandparents, but at least her father would be with her. She would not be going into this alone.

She looked at Peter. "So, are you going to make me ask?"

"Ask what?"

"I know you know what's going on. We cannot have secrets. My life was destroyed by them, and you and I cannot have them between us. So, you need to tell me whatever you know."

The worry lines in Peter's face increased with her demand. Sharing this information was clearly something he was not comfortable with doing, but Brianna did not care. The hardest lesson she took from her life exploding was the fact that loose ends covered with lies end up being the thread that destroys the fabric. She did not want that anymore. No more lies. No more secrets.

Peter still had yet to utter a word.

"Dad?"

Peter sighed. "Listen, Brianna, I don't want any secrets between us, either, but this really isn't my business to tell."

"She's my mother."

"I am aware of that. Trust me."

"Well, then, tell me."

"Fine, but I need to warn you that it's not good. Try and keep an open mind about it."

"It can't be worse than her selling me to some no-name stranger in a hospital," Brianna remarked. Peter countered with a look that suggested it might. "It's worse than that?"

"Well . . . maybe. If it's what I think it is."

Brianna got comfortable in her seat and prepared to hear the worst.

CHAPTER 52

Grayson shook his head at Michelle. She raised an eyebrow, trying to understand why he had given her such a disapproving glance. "What? What is it?"

"Why did you do that? Your mother could really be in trouble."

"I don't care, Grayson. She has squirmed her way out of any type of reckoning for her sins for too long. Maybe it's just time for her to pay up." Michelle paced back and forth beside the island in the kitchen. "What am I supposed to do, anyway? It's the police!"

"You could have at least talked to your sister or this Dr. Baxter guy."

"But I don't want to talk to them. If they are so worried about her, let them figure it out."

"You are worried about her, too. Look at you. The floor has grooves in it from you walking."

Michelle stopped pacing and sat down on a stool. "I am tired of them. That is a lot of drama, and I don't need it. If you could have heard the way she spoke to me this evening." Michelle shook her head in disbelief. "It was like she was someone else."

"But you said she was drunk. Drunk people—"

"Speak no lies."

"No, I was going to say that they do and say things that they don't mean."

"She meant it."

"You don't know that, Michelle. You're hurt, and you're being unreasonable."

"Grayson . . ."

"Seriously, I get it, but this . . . is not the way to handle things. You cannot keep running."

"I'm not trying to run."

"Sure you are. You have been running since the night I climbed into your car outside of Doug's Gym. Maybe even before then. That is just when you ran into me."

"I am not running."

"Michelle, keep it one hunnid. Have you talked to her, straight up? You told me you suspected something was going on between Bri—"

Michelle cut her eyes at him, forcing him to pause.

"Between Brianna and your ex. Did you ever say anything to her about it?"

Michelle did not bother answering. Grayson knew what she would say. She had told him as much previously.

"Rather than confronting the issue head on, you went on some goose chase to find your grandparents?"

"That was not a goose chase."

"It was busy work, Michelle. Come on." Grayson hit the countertop with his hand, emphasizing his point. "Finding them wouldn't have resolved anything. It literally would not have helped any of your relationships at all."

"I thought it was worth a shot."

"No, you didn't. You knew then, just like you know now, that the only way to mend things is by talking to your mother, or your sister, or both. Direct and deliberate conversation. But instead, you ran down a rabbit hole, trying to disappear."

"I did not run! I have never run from anything in my life. Ever."

"Really? You ran from your father. Your mother. You stayed with Armand even though he had been lying to you for two years. Why? He was an escape from the lie you grew up living."

Michelle shook her head, contesting his observation.

Grayson did not relent, intent on being the mirror she needed to look into to see the part she played in the whole production. "He allowed you to run from the lies your mother told. Hell, you even tried to run from us. Until life out there . . . sent you running back."

"I am not running."

"Then why are you here?"

"To get some love. That is why I came here. You're right. My life is crap, and it's chock full of crappy people—people that I call family—and I . . . I just cannot . . . I don't have anything to give them. I am running on empty. So, I came back because I didn't want to end up stuck in the middle of nowhere. I'd rather just be here."

"Come here." Grayson pulled Michelle up from her stool and wrapped her up in his arms. "Nothing changed since you left this morning. I got a lot of love for you right here."

"That's what I'm saying."

"I know you're concerned about my social activity, but stop."

"I left here with the best intentions, but the world is sooooo cold out there."

"Cute, but I'm serious, Michelle."

Michelle locked eyes with him, trapped by the intensity she saw in them.

"I can be a part of the movement for social justice *and* be here for you."

She closed her eyes to enjoy his embrace and let his words work their voodoo. "My happy place was destroyed hours after I left you. I should not have gone."

"Don't try and butter me up, being all soft and whatnot."

Michelle snuggled closer to him, burying her face in the nape of his neck. "I don't want to think about any of them."

Michelle forced her family out of her mind, delving into the moment, losing herself in Grayson. Giving into her desire for him felt a lot better than the hurt she couldn't escape without him. She planted a light trail of kisses with each breath she took.

"Michelle, don't get nothing started, now."

"But what if I want to?"

Grayson lovingly pulled her shoulders back, creating a little space between them. He peered intently into her eyes. "I know this sucks, but you are not alone. I know you don't really want this right now."

"Yes, I do," Michelle purred.

"No, you don't. You left here because this is not good for us. I didn't want you to leave, but you were right about that. We need to move slowly."

Michelle felt herself tearing up. She dropped her head to the ground, too ashamed to look at him. "I feel like I'm losing my mind."

Cupping her face with his hands, Grayson gently lifted her face until he had control of her eyes. That was what it felt like for her: like he had more control over her body than she did. "Aye, and if you needed me to pull a Martin Payne and drive all night from Detroit to Chicago to find it, I would."

Michelle chortled lightly.

"But you don't need that. The things that you have been through over the last few months would have been more than enough to break the best of 'em, but you are still here."

Michelle was not feeling like much of a fighter. She was tired of fighting, tired of being strong. She was exhausted with it all. "I am too tired. Too hurt. Too . . . everything."

"I know. I see you and what you need, Michelle. I will meet that need, but you cannot stop being who you are. If you stop, it doesn't matter what I give you. It won't ever be enough."

"Where have you been all my life?"

"Rescuing puppies, waiting on you."

Michelle took a deep breath and relaxed in his arms, freeing herself to be comforted by his touch. This, whatever was brewing between them, felt too fast for her, but she discarded the idea. She needed what he was giving her, and there was no crime in that.

Grayson's next suggestion was a long shot, but he put it out there for posterity. "I think you need to call your sister and talk to her."

Michelle's muscles locked for a moment.

"I felt that. Don't do that. Not right now, but you need to write that on your agenda."

"I will, Grayson. I need time. She is already fragile and . . . she doesn't need me to unload on her. I am angry with her, but she hasn't been fully functional in a while. I didn't know how to help her. She was going to counseling; she had Armand, my mother. I was alone, and I thought I could manage."

"None of us go very far trying to do it alone, myself included. I didn't know I needed you until you told me you were leaving. I started missing you. Common was sad, too."

Michelle smiled. "Thank you. Your words have healing power."

"Nah, I stole that from Iyanla," Grayson joked.

Michelle stood up, shrugged her shoulders, trying to rid herself of her uncertainty regarding her decision. "So, what would Iyanla advise me to do now?"

"Hey, my screen has only stopped on OWN while the remote was under your control."

Michelle rolled her eyes. *Arghh!* "I guess we are going to join the circus of clowns gathering at my mother's."

"Proud of you."

"Let's just go before I change my mind."

CHAPTER 53

"So, what are you saying? It was regular toxin?" Frank, the doctor, and Detective Baptiste sat in Frank's office, discussing the results from the tests administered to Lisa.

"I am not sure what you mean by *regular toxin,* but I am saying that it is likely that there was no toxin injected at all." Dr. Ojirika paused, allowing his words to resonate before continuing. "I know that you were convinced that someone poisoned your wife, but the tests I ran don't support that."

"Well, what happened? Something happened. She's dying in there."

"Upon my initial examination, I suspected that she had some type of bacterial infection, but I could not be certain where. Given her injury, it only made sense to start with her lungs. Indeed, my assumption was correct. She has a bacterial infection in her lungs."

"So, the difficulty breathing, the fever . . . lack of appetite. All that is from a lung infection?"

"Not exactly. The bacterial infection rooted in her lungs is the seed. From that seed, your wife is in the early stages of septicemia. I did not say anything the other day because I thought it more prudent to wait for confirmation. You seemed anxious enough, and I didn't want to make matters worse."

Frank was bewildered. He exchanged glances with Detective Baptiste, who seemed to have a similar thought.

"And this isn't anything someone could have given her?"

"It is possible that someone injected her with a bacteria, but it is more likely that it was something that developed as a result of her wound not being properly cared for."

"Septicemia?" Frank still did not know what to make of this news. "What does this mean for my wife? Is her condition reversible? Is this fatal?"

Dr. Ojirika shifted in his seat. "Fortunately, we caught it fairly early, and so I believe that with the treatment, she will be fine."

"That's great news! What is the treatment, and how soon can we get started?"

"My new intern is administering it to her right now as we speak."

Frank's heart dropped as he sprang to his feet. "What new intern? I have to personally clear anyone that sees her."

"He started working for me a couple of days ago. He has been vetted through the proper channels, and I assure you he is qualified for the position!" Dr. Ojirika yelled as Frank practically clobbered him, leaping over the desk to get out the door.

Frank bolted down the long hall and around the corner to his bedroom with Detective Baptiste a few steps behind him. "Move! Move!" Frank hollered to the guards he expected to find guarding his bedroom door. Not only were the guards missing, but as he turned the handle, he found the door locked from the inside. "Who locked this door?"

Together, Frank and Baptiste begin banging the door with their shoulders, forcing it open.

"Lisa!"

Lisa was unresponsive. The new intern stood over Lisa, pillow in hand. Frank had interrupted him again, but Frank was not letting him get away this time. Every muscle in his body twitched in anticipation. He stared at the intern with death in his eyes.

"Get away from my wife." Frank stepped farther into the room. To either side of him stood Detective Baptiste and Simmy, who had caught wind of the commotion. The three of them cautiously closed in on the would-be killer. Frank moved to rush the guy, but a strong arm across his midsection stopped him, forcing him to suppress his instinct to manhandle the youngin' in order to bear witness to Detective Baptiste's craftsmanship.

Baptiste gingerly stepped toward the intern, speaking to him with the authority of a father and the empathy of a young mother. Frank stood, mildly impressed with his ability to verbally disarm him. It was just like any movie Frank had seen.

"You can't leave, ya know? Just lay down, put your hands behind ya back. No one has to get hurt." Detective Baptiste lifted his arms in front of him. "Go on, now. Lie down. Don't make this any more difficult than it has to be."

"Listen to him. I cannot let you hurt her. I won't."

The three amigos made it within five feet of the intern, and he pulled out a knife, held it over Lisa's chest, halting their progress.

"I don't want any trouble. I just . . . he made me do it. I didn't want to . . . but he'll kill her . . . if I don't. I don't have a choice!" the intern sputtered with tears pouring from his eyes. He stepped away from Lisa a bit, pacing from the bed to the nightstand, indiscriminately swinging the knife as he spoke.

"Who is makin' ya do this? Who sent ya here?"

Frank kept his eyes on the intern but signaled to Simmy, who stood off to his left, to move toward Lisa. Without a second thought, Simmy dropped to the floor. Frank's legs nearly gave out, but by the grace of God, he managed to stay upright. Moving in complete silence, Simmy shimmied, out of sight, to the far side of the king-size bed.

Frank thought his eyes would pop out of his head as he watched in horror, praying Simmy's antics didn't attract any unwanted attention. He didn't know if he wanted to laugh or strangle him. Fortunately, the intern was too distracted to notice the activity. Baptiste had him under his spell.

Simmy would not be able to move Lisa very far with the IV chaining her to the bed, but Frank hoped that he could at least position himself to protect her. To avoid staring at Simmy, Frank watched through what felt like a complicated series of stolen glances, but when he spotted Simmy worming his way across the thick comforter to Lisa's side, he almost blew his top.

His heart pounded so loudly that it was all he could hear from the moment Simmy made his move. If the intern caught Simmy, neither of them would get to Lisa in time. He couldn't get caught, and Frank wanted to chuck something at his head for not finding another way.

Lisa shifted her head to the side, and before Frank could blink, he saw Simmy's hand cover her mouth, muffling her protest. Frank expelled the air in his lungs, relieved that Simmy had finally done something right. He shook off his nerves.

"You don't understand!"

The cry yanked Frank's attention away from Lisa and Simmy. The intern was getting irate. Baptiste was either losing the connection, or the intern was severing it. Frank couldn't tell, but he was nervous as hell. Simmy needed more time to develop some sort of an exit strategy.

Taking a cue from Baptiste, Frank studied the intern, searching for a shortcut into his mind. He was not the fake

doctor from the hospital, and Frank found it increasingly
difficult to believe that he was the guy from the hotel room.
This was a child standing before him, maybe a little older
than Simmy. He looked disheveled and completely out of
his element. He looked like the type of kid that would sing
in the Glee Club, not a professional killer. In fact, this kid,
seemed exceedingly ordinary, easily lost in a crowd. Frank
figured he and Baptiste could subdue him easily once Lisa
was out of the way.

"He'll kill her! I have to . . . I am sorry." The intern
pummeled the sides of his face with his hands, clearly
frustrated by the turn of events.

"I can help ya, but you have got to tell me who ya
talkin' 'bout."

"He's a monster. He has my sister, and he'll—" Suddenly,
the intern looked in Lisa's direction.

A panicked Frank looked with him, but to his amaze-
ment, he only saw Lisa. There was no sign of Simmy
anywhere. Frank didn't know what that meant, but seiz-
ing the moment, he decided to engage the intern himself.

"We won't let that happen. My name is Frank. I know
about monsters. My brother is a monster, and I have spent
my entire adult life hiding from him."

The intern locked eyes with him, and Frank instantly
felt uneasy. Something was off.

"I learned something, though. We can't run from our
monsters. We gotta face them. It's the only way to be free."

"I'm afraid. I'm supposed to protect her. I promised. I
promised, and . . ."

Frank continued trying to reason with him, inching his
way toward him. "We can help you, but you have got to
give us something. You're just a kid. You can still have a
life after this, but give us something. Who is it?"

He stood about three feet from him with Baptiste just behind him. He willed himself not to look directly at Lisa, but he could tell that she had moved a bit. She was not as close to the edge of the bed as she had been before. He wondered where Simmy had gone.

"No one can help me. I have to do this. She has to die." The intern lifted the knife he held in his hand, and in one swift move, plunged it into the feather pillow, inches away from Lisa's shoulder. Frank lunged forward, fist high in the air, cocked to swing at the intern. The intern ducked his punch, causing Frank to miss wildly. The momentum sent Frank colliding into the table.

Frank yelled as chunks of ice and water made their way inside his shirt. From the corner of his eye, he caught Simmy rising up from underneath the covers beside Lisa like a swamp monster in a lake. Both arms raised high in the air, Simmy threw his body over Lisa's, acting as her human shield. Frank tried to jump to his feet, but all he saw were fists. The intern attacked him with reckless abandon.

"Stop or I'll be forced to put ya down! Put ya hands up right now!" Detective Baptiste ordered. "Get down on the ground! Face down!" Detective Baptiste kept his gun aimed on the intern until he complied. Frank could hear the familiar clinking of cuffs.

Frank's vision was blurry. Every part of his face hurt. Even parts of his body that he didn't remember being hit ached. Tasting the blood in his mouth, he stood, staggering, trying to see, but all he could make out were colors—colors that did not mean anything.

"You had a gun?" Frank questioned. Frank stared in utter confusion in the area he thought Detective Baptiste to be in.

"I am a police officer, ya. Course I have a gun, now."

"Why in the hell were you doing all that talking? You could have just pulled it from the beginning."

"I told ya to wait. You made a different choice. Plus, drawing my weapon is a last resort, but I know you Americans think different than us backward island folk," the detective stated, winking at Frank. "Where should I take him?"

"Stick him in a closet. Can't do any harm there."

Detective Baptiste chuckled. "No, really, where do ya want me to take him?"

"Guest room is fine. Down the hall, third door on the left."

"All right, I will take him there and see what I can find out."

"You do that."

"Don't be angry, Franklin. Gun isn't always necessary." Detective Baptiste dragged the intern out of the room and disappeared from Frank's sight.

Frank mentally punched the shit out of Detective Baptiste before shuffling to Lisa's side. This had to be one of the most asinine few weeks of his life. He was in way over his head in this thing. Lisa was slipping in and out of consciousness. She had slept during most of the activity, but her condition was getting worse by the minute. For some reason, Simmy was still sitting on his knees on the bed beside Lisa.

"Simmy, go get Dr. Ojirika."

"I think OJ dipped out."

Frank groaned. "How would you know? And he told you not to call him that."

"I would split if I were him, and he ain't here, Raheim."

"Yes, *he* is, and I would appreciate it if you refrained from calling me that. If Ojirika is too difficult a word for you to pronounce, Doctor will do just fine."

Simmy whirled around to find Dr. Ojirika standing in the doorway. Simmy responded to his rebuke as he walked by him to tend to Lisa. "My bad, yo. No problem. No need to get upset. He didn't do it. The glove didn't fit, yo."

"Shut up, Simmy," Frank spat. He wanted Dr. Ojirika to focus on Lisa. Until those antibiotics were in her system, she was not in the clear.

"I'm just sayin' . . . it ain't like he went to prison—no, wait. Never mind."

"Simmy, go do something. Go find the security guards. I paid them good money to do nothing, apparently. Find them."

Dr. Ojirika pulled his bag from underneath the bed where it had been pushed during the commotion. Frank watched him take out his supplies to check Lisa's vitals.

"Cool. What do you want me to do when I find them?"

Frank cut his eyes at Simmy. "More than you did for me when one tree ninja started kicking my ass."

Simmy turned his face up. "What, I'm supposed to get beat up, too? Nah, bruh. I don't think so. You told me to protect Lisa. Nothing else matters. There wasn't nothing in any of your speeches about being twin punching bags."

Frank couldn't help but laugh. Simmy drove him crazy. He was the little brother he never wanted. "Figure out what happened with the two that are missing and let me know."

Simmy left the room. Frank returned his attention to Dr. Ojirika. "I need you to save her."

CHAPTER 54

"What in the hell happened here?" Michelle tiptoed through the door of her childhood home, astonished by the mess she saw. The police had left the house in shambles. Michelle chose her steps carefully as she surveyed the damage. "Wow. Are you seeing this, Grayson?"

"Of course. Hard to miss. Think they found anything?"

"I don't know. I'm not even sure what they would have been looking for."

"Evidence."

"*Ahhh!*" Michelle screamed, jumping back into Grayson, who quickly pulled her behind him. "Who's there?"

"Not important right now," the deep baritone responded.

"Where are you? Come out where we can see you," Grayson requested.

"I'm afraid that's not possible."

"Why not? What are you doing here?" Michelle inquired. She clung to Grayson for dear life. She could not remember being more afraid. "You need to leave, whoever you are, or I'm calling the police. This is my mother's house."

"Looks like the police have been here and left with what they came to get."

Michelle wanted to know what this stranger seemed to know. She was terrified but felt like Superwoman with Grayson, the Golden Gloves champ, to protect her. "Oh, yeah? And what was that?"

She and Grayson moved as one, slowly making their way toward to the faceless voice.

"Your mother will pay for what she did."

"Who are you? And what do you know about her?"

"You'll find out who I am soon enough."

"How do you know my mother?" Michelle could not tell if they were getting any closer. It was difficult to navigate through the debris.

"I know you, too, Michelle."

Michelle froze. She quit breathing and dared Grayson to take one. This was definitely not okay, and she was officially freaking out. She tried to search through the darkness, but it was too dark to see anything. The flashlight on her phone only lit so much, and none of it was this stranger.

"Grayson, let's go," Michelle whispered, pulling his arm back toward the front door.

"No need to fear me, Michelle. I would never hurt you."

Using the light on her phone to chart her path, Michelle hurdled and dipped her way to the front door and into the car. Her nerves were so shot that she accidentally locked Grayson outside the car. He banged on the window for a good thirty seconds before Michelle realized what was going on.

They sat in silence for a minute, parked in the driveway. She could not force a word from her mouth until she saw a shadowy figure, whom she assumed belonged to the faceless stranger, disappear into the night.

"Did you recognize his voice?"

Michelle shook her head. She had no clue who that could be. She didn't know of her mother having any friends, and she doubted that this person had good intentions. Nothing felt right about it. Why would he be lurking around her mother's home at this hour?

"This is crazy. My mother's house is a wreck. She is missing, and some random guy was in her house, and he clearly knows more about her than I do."

"I don't know what is going on, either, but you know you're safe with me."

Michelle knew that, but his words were of little comfort to her at the moment. She was not sure what, if anything, could calm her down. "He knew my name, Grayson. My name."

"I know. Something is up, and we'll get to the bottom of it. No worries."

I hate you so much right now. I hate you so much right now, Michelle's cell phone sang.

She looked at Grayson. "It's Brianna."

He motioned for her to answer it. Under the circumstances, she figured she better. "Hello, Brianna? What's going on with Momma?"

CHAPTER 55

Sophie was relieved that her dad had been so willing to help her. She thought she had accounted for any missteps, but the police showing up at her home was proof that she had not. The Freemont Estate was the last place she had expected to be, but such was life. She sat on the couch in the sitting room, perusing through old photo albums. She could not bring herself to go to her old room yet. There were too many painful memories there, and she needed to stay focused on the task at hand. Besides, she didn't think she could handle it given the current status of her relationship with the daughter she had given it all up for.

"Miss, are you sure I can't get you nothing?" the sweet, elderly woman who had greeted her at the door asked her from behind, standing just inside the entrance to the room.

Sophie turned and inquired with as gentle a voice as she could muster, "Nan, you don't recognize me?"

The wise woman smiled, dragging her feet across the carpet to the couch where Sophie sat watching her. Patting Sophie on the hand, she released even more of her smile, revealing the few teeth she'd lost over the years.

"Lucille Freemont, of course I remember you, but I figured I'd let ya come round in your own time."

"I am not who I used to be, Nan. I don't think you could be proud of . . . of who I have become. *She* is so far from who you desired me to be. So very far from her."

Nan rubbed her calloused hands against Sophie's cheek. "All I ever wanted was your happiness. Have you been happy, chile?"

"Sometimes." Sophie fought back tears. "I have had happy moments, but I think that's enough for me. I can't ask for more than that at this point."

Nan took a deep breath and, before shuffling back to her quarters, she said to Sophie, "Happiness is a choice. It is something you choose, Lucille. It does not happen on its own. No matter what life throws at you, you can always choose to smile."

Sophie watched Nan make the long walk to the other side of the estate where she had lived all of Sophie's life. Perhaps Nan was right; happiness was about the choices people made. What did that mean for her? More than twenty years had passed before she ventured to mend the relationship between herself and her parents. She missed her mother by an entire decade, and had this situation not come about, she probably would have missed her father and Nan, too. What had kept her from reaching out to them? It was a question she could not answer—or couldn't bring herself to answer.

She placed the photo album on the coffee table just as her father came back into the room.

"Sophie, I made a few calls. Thankfully, your old man still has a few bridges he didn't burn during his tenure as mayor of this city. I'm not going to ask you for any details. Plausible deniability. However, there is one thing I need to know, and I need you to be honest with me about this."

"Of course, Daddy."

"This man . . . was it that Leonard Lewis boy?"

"It was. You were right about him. I had no business running off to be with him."

"I don't know if you were wrong to leave, but . . . I am sorry for whatever he put you through. It is my duty as your father to protect you, and I sent you right into his arms. I have another question."

Sophie prepared her lips to answer. She knew he would ask eventually. "What happened to the baby? Did you raise the child?"

"Dad—"

Ding, dong, ding, dong. The doorbell cut her off. Richard turned to leave to answer it.

"I gave Nan the rest of the weekend off, so I'll need to get the door. Stay here. Don't move, and I'll be back directly."

Sophie thought it was a peculiar hour for her father to have visitors. He never used to entertain company after eight in the evening, but the circumstances were extreme. Concessions would need to be made. Still, she worried some about who it might be. No one knew she was there, or even knew to come look for her there. Maybe she was overreacting and the visitor had nothing to do with her at all. She decided she could make better use of her time than worrying about nothing.

Sophie lay down on the couch, trying to relax her mind enough to come up with a plausible story to tell her father. The truth could lead to a family meeting she was not sure she wanted to have. It was good that her father helped her now, but she didn't know if she was ready for him to be a part of her everyday life. If Michelle got wind of his whereabouts, Sophie would likely be forced to incorporate him.

Sophie was consumed by her thoughts when her father returned.

"Mom?"

Sophie's eyes popped open, and she jumped up from the couch. "Brianna? What are you doing here?"

Peter emerged from around the corner. "Sophie, we need to talk."

"Mom, we just left your house, and there were police everywhere," Brianna stated as she walked around the couch to hug Sophie. "Peter said that you would probably be here."

Sophie wrapped her arms around Brianna, squeezing her tight. "Everything will be fine." Pointing toward Richard, who had taken up residence in the Lazy-Boy, Sophie offered, "Your grandfather is taking care of everything."

Sophie tried to read Brianna's eyes but couldn't tell how she felt about him. She wasn't overly excited, but she didn't look horrified either.

"So, this is your child? My grandchild?"

Sophie shot a quick glance at her dad, hesitating before answering, "One of them."

"One of them?" he asked, obviously surprised.

"I had twins. It's a long story, Daddy."

"I would imagine so."

"Sophie, we need to talk, and it can't wait. I don't know what's going on, but this needs to be said. Is there somewhere we can speak privately?" Peter asked.

He looked exasperated, but Sophie's trouble far outweighed their relationship status, especially with regards to what had occurred over two decades ago, and Sophie did not have the energy for it. "Peter, we really cannot do this right now. I am in very serious trouble, and I can't do this with you."

Peter's face grew stern. "Either we speak in private, or right now. I am not waiting, and you cannot dismiss me again."

Sophie rolled her eyes in frustration. This was the opposite of what she needed when she had called him earlier. She didn't have energy to fight about what was. "Peter, seriously? My daughter is here, my father . . . do we really need to have this conversation right now?"

Peter and Brianna made eye contact, and that perturbed Sophie even more.

"What in the hell is going on here? Why are you with my daughter?"

Peter glared at her. "She is my daughter, too."

Sophie looked at Peter curiously. "What are you talking about?" Peter was out of his mind. "I buried her father."

Peter did not back down. "I am her father, and I have the DNA test to prove it."

Sophie's legs wobbled. She could feel Brianna staring at her, but she couldn't look at her. She could not believe it. It could not be true.

"Tell me you didn't know, Mom. Tell me you didn't know, and I'll believe you." Brianna's plea sliced her heart like a machete.

She could not lie to her. "I did not know, but I knew it was possible. That week changed my life, and I remember every little detail of it."

"Why didn't you say anything?"

"I don't know, Brianna. I couldn't." Sophie felt the color drain from her face. This was the worst possible time for this to be happening. "You were twins, and you look so much like your sister. I had no reason to believe that Lewis was not your father."

Brianna sat down on the couch without saying a word.

"Sophie, I cannot believe you kept something so important from me." Peter shook his head in disgust.

Sophie felt faint, and tiny beads of sweat covered her forehead. "Don't look at me that way. I didn't know. You cannot blame me for not sharing information I didn't have!"

"You should have made certain! I deserved that much! Any person does!"

"Peter, it was not intentional. I wasn't trying to keep her from you."

"Nothing ever is intentional with you. All incidental blunders due to circumstance." Peter eyed Richard observing from his seat in the corner. "Cannot blame this one on him, can you? Or on your late husband. Whose fault is this one, Sophie?"

"Peter—"

"You sold my daughter, Sophie! My daughter! You broke my fuckin' heart. I am hurting in places . . . I didn't even know existed before!" Peter leaned against the door frame.

Sophie recognized the look in his eyes. It was the same look he'd had that night she had to let him go.

"I thought about us . . . I thought we could be . . . again, but this . . ." Peter snapped himself free of the pain consuming him. Realizing where he was and who was present, he collected himself. "Brianna, let's go. Come on. I won't let your grandfather watch your mother rip my heart to pieces a second time."

Brianna stood confused as to what she should do. She looked to Sophie for an answer.

Sophie smiled at her daughter and pulled her close. "It's okay, Brianna. Go ahead. We can talk later. I promise I'll try my best to explain everything."

Brianna kissed Sophie on the cheek then left her mother to watch another daughter walk away from her. Her only comfort was in knowing that Brianna had Peter to help her. Sophie had left Michelle alone to strangers, just as her parents had done.

"Oh, daughter, I guess you made the same type of mess I did."

Sophie's face was wet with tears. She hadn't even realized she was crying. Richard joined her on the couch. She lay her head in his lap and sobbed aloud. "Daddy, everything is ruined. It was not supposed to be this way." She couldn't stop crying. "I thought I had it all planned, but . . . I don't think I can handle this, Daddy. My girls hate me. Peter hates me."

"Well, I think I know a thing or two about being hated. It does not feel good. I know that, but you still have time to salvage things. To repair what has been broken. Time has healing power if people want to heal. I don't know the other daughter—"

"Michelle."

"What's that, Sophie?"

"Her name is Michelle."

"Oh, okay. I see. Michelle and, uh, Brianna . . . I don't think they hate you. Probably very angry, maybe hurt, but I didn't see any hate here. Not even from Peter. That boy has loved you forever. He couldn't hate you if he wanted to."

"It doesn't seem that way to me."

"Just give them time. They will come around. You'll see."

Ding dong, ding dong. The doorbell chimed.

Richard leaned forward, kissed Sophie on the forehead, and lightly patted her back, urging her to sit up. Sophie looked at her father, her eyes swollen from hurt. She didn't think she had the strength to get through this.

"Come now. This is the beginning, and it won't be pleasant, but I am not leaving you. Daddy will be right behind you. Are you ready?"

"Daddy, I am scared."

"I know you are, but you don't need to be. I told you I would take care of this, and I will. Let's go, okay?"

Sophie nodded, took her father by the hand, and followed him to the front door. She marveled at the massive foyer again, as she had hours before when she first arrived. She kissed her father, laying her head on his shoulder, permitting him to open the door.

The detective flashed his badge. "Sir, we are here to execute an arrest warrant for a Sophie Lucille Freemont."

Sophie did not protest. Stepping from beside her father, she offered her wrists to the detective. "I am Sophie Freemont."

An officer stepped forward to take Sophie into custody while the detective rehashed the Miranda warning. "Sophie Lucille Freemont, you are under arrest for the murder of Leonard Brendan Lewis. You have the right to remain silent. Anything you say or do can and will be used against you in a court of law. You have the right to an attorney. . . ."

The officer's words faded into oblivion as Sophie felt the metal cuffs cutting into the soft flesh of her wrists. Her world was completely upside down, and the only person she had in her corner was the one person she had spent her life trying to avoid: her father.

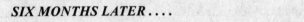

SIX MONTHS LATER . . . .

CHAPTER 56

"Ms. Vida, I think it's time that I moved out, got my own place." Micah threw out the notion in between bites. He and Ms. Vida were halfway through an excellent breakfast: two eggs, three waffles, four strips of bacon, and more, if he could find room for it in his stomach. "I appreciate you allowing me stay for so long, but I am in better health than I was even before the accident. Hannah cut me loose from OT months ago."

Ms. Vida peered at Micah from behind her round frames. "I know, Micah. I have been expecting this conversation for a little while now. I did not want to say anything . . . well, it's that . . . I do not wish to see you go."

"Ms. Vida, you know that I will be here to visit with you every day, and you'll always be welcome wherever I am. I may call you Ms. Vida, but I love you like a son loves a mother."

Ms. Vida reached across the small, oval table and patted Micah's hand. "I know, child. I am just used to you staying here. This tiny apartment will shrink a little with you gone."

Micah was not completely sold on the idea of leaving Ms. Vida. She was a staple in his life, and interacting with her had become as necessary as breathing for him. He didn't want to move, but he would be a father soon, and he needed to have a place of his own. Watching the sadness spread over Ms. Vida's face hurt him even more. He had anticipated her not liking the idea, but this was worse. Perhaps she would be open to his alternative.

"I have been thinking about this. I don't want to leave you, and you don't want me to go. I have a child that I need to prepare for. I cannot call myself a man and be living at home with my mother. I have to get a place of my own."

"I know that, Micah."

"Brianna and the baby need a place where they will feel comfortable to come and stay anytime. I'm not just thinking of me."

"You know I adore Brianna, and she is always welcome here."

Micah nodded his understanding. "And I appreciate you being a surrogate mother for us and grandmother for our child. You have been a huge support to us, and I cannot thank you enough."

"I love you two. Brianna is a great girl, and I am very happy that things are going well." Ms. Vida pushed herself away from the table. She rose to her feet and prepared to exit the kitchen. "Excuse me."

Micah knew she was attempting to hide her tears. She never wanted him to establish a link between his joy and her sadness. This was something she could not hide from him. Her despondence grew with his independence. He first noticed when Hannah released him from outpatient therapy. Being discharged from rehabilitation was good, but being officially cleared for take-off was something completely different. He figured Ms. Vida feared that she wouldn't be needed anymore, and she had started creating distance between them.

"Ms. Vida, don't leave. Please sit." He pretended not to see her wipe the tears from her eyes before she sat back down. "I was saying that . . . you should come with me."

Ms. Vida's eyes widened in surprise. "What?"

Micah smiled so wide his cheeks hurt. "I want you to come with me. You said it yourself; this apartment will shrink. You should just come."

"I have not lived with anyone since I was seventeen years old, Micah."

"I know, but I want to do this for you. You look beautiful, but you're no spring chicken, Ms. Vida. Let me be the one to take care of you. Let me be here for you. I can get a big house. You can have your own space."

"Micah, you are not working full-time. How will you afford any of that?"

"I'm an architect. I worked for one of the best firms in the city. I can find employment. Besides, it isn't like I am moving tomorrow."

"I cannot believe that you want me to come with you."

"Believe it. What do you say?"

"I retired to follow you from the hospital. I suppose it will not hurt for me to follow you into this phase of your life."

Micah beamed. "Excellent!" He could barely contain his excitement. Ms. Vida prided herself on being independent and having the ability to provide for herself. Micah had feared that she would not only reject his request but rebuke him for even suggesting it. The conversation had gone much better than he expected.

"I thought you would get rid of me because you did not need my help anymore."

"I know you did, but I cannot imagine a time when I wouldn't need you. I am not in the same condition that you found me in. I am better because of you, Ms. Vida. You helped me to help myself, and that is major. I could not have gotten here without you. We all need someone in our corner like that."

"That is very sweet of you to say, Micah."

"It's the truth. Plus, you're going to be a grandmother! I am pretty sure I'll need help with that. My father wasn't the best example."

"I am here for you, Brianna, and that baby, too. I think you will be a fine father, Micah."

"I hope so, Ms. Vida."

"Where is Brianna? I thought she would have come over for breakfast."

Micah cleared his throat. "She had court this morning, Ms. Vida. Remember?"

Micah knew she remembered. Ms. Vida did not forget things, particularly things regarding Brianna's mother's case. She consumed every detail and was convinced that Sophie Freemont was the devil incarnate.

Ms. Vida turned her lip up. *Hmph.* "I guess I had hoped that she would decide not to go."

"Ms. Vida, please. Not this again."

"Not what again?" Ms. Vida asked, offended.

"We only met the woman once. How can you deduce her character from five minutes of talking?" Their meeting had been uncomfortable, but Micah did not get the same corrosive vibes that Ms. Vida apparently picked up from her. Between that meeting and the story breaking about the arrest, Ms. Vida had abandoned all objectivity, relying solely on her flawless intuition.

"I do not need to meet her a second time to know the truth."

Micah shook his head. "And what is that, Ms. Vida?"

Ms. Vida leaned over the table, getting closer to Micah, like she was sharing a secret. "That woman is pure evil. She killed that man, and everybody knows it."

"We don't know it, actually, and that's why we have our grand judicial system. It is supposed to determine those types of things."

Ms. Vida reared back in her chair, folding her arms across her chest. "Courts cannot legislate evil. She has been all over the news, campaigning for her peers."

"Ms. Vida . . ." Micah knew he was wasting his breath trying to reason with her. Ms. Vida's mind was made up about Brianna's mother, but Micah felt obligated to try anyway, for Brianna's sake.

"She is not innocent, Micah. Brianna, that poor child, needs to believe she is because the truth is unbearable. She does not think that she can survive the sharp edges of living in a reality with a mother like her, but she is much stronger than she thinks."

"That we can agree on. Brianna is incredible, but can we drop this?" Micah pleaded. "If, and when, Brianna does come by, she does not need to hear from you about how her mother is a raving, murderous sociopath. She's at the tail end of her pregnancy and is under enough stress as it is. Let's not add to it."

"Now, Micah, you know that I would not do or say anything to harm Brianna. I love her like I love you. I just do not care at all for her mother. I hope she gets the chair for what she did to that man."

Micah sighed. "Ms. Vida, we all deserve an opportunity to be better. Is that not what you have taught me?"

"Some people forfeit their opportunity when they decide that someone else is not deserving of theirs. I know you think I am crazy, but I am not. Something is not right with her."

"You are probably right as you are about most things. That does not mean that you need to speak on it. Brianna does not need this. She needs our support right now. If what you say is true, she'll see it for herself."

"I hope she does."

"In the meantime, let's not jump to any conclusions. We don't know the whole story. We all play the defendant at different points in our lives. We should extend to others the same type of understanding and forgiveness that we would seek for ourselves."

"I will try and do that, for you and Brianna. I do not want to make things harder for her."

Micah was satisfied with that. "Well, enough of that. Let's go get the rest of the stuff for the nursery, shall we? We can meet Brianna at her place after."

Ms. Vida simply smiled and went to her room to get ready. Micah stared at her plate, full of barely eaten food. Ms. Vida put up a brave front, but he knew she was worried about Brianna, concerned about this trial and what it would all mean in the end. Brianna seemed a bit consumed by the showmanship of it all, despite her enlarged belly. She stood beside her mother at every press conference and visited with her each day. What if her mother was convicted of capital murder? What if she was found guilty? What would that mean for Brianna, for his child?

CHAPTER 57

Lisa was on the verge of a full recovery. Dr. Ojirika had pulled off a miracle, and Frank could not be happier to have his wife back. She was weak and could not move a lot, but she was light years away from where she had been. Detective Baptiste had taken a leave from work to stay Stateside for a while. Frank was grateful; the person behind the attacks on Lisa was still a bit of a mystery. He was well aware that Jacob had to have guessed that he was back in town by now, but he still had not said anything to him, so Frank didn't bother reaching out to him, either.

He was still not sure what to think of his old friend since that situation with his brother in New York. The entire evening felt like a setup. Of course, his brother had been expecting him, but there was something else going on there. Frank could not figure out what it was. That guy in the car looked familiar, but he couldn't place him, and Lisa had been so traumatized after seeing him that she pretended like he wasn't there. It was truly bizarre, and Frank figured he had better get them out of there.

Now, as he reclined in his office chair, that man's face came back to him. He knew exactly where he had seen him and understood what had frightened Lisa so. "Good gawd. Simmy!" Frank hurried out of his office toward the den, where he figured he'd find Simmy. "Simmy!"

Sure enough, he was lounging on the couch, watching some reality show. "What is it, yo?"

"I think I know who's trying to kill Lisa."

Simmy turned away from the television and met Frank's stare. "Who?"

"I think it was that guy in the car. The one from the airport ride to my brother's I told you about. Trench coat."

"Why do you think that?"

"I figured out who he is."

"Well, don't keep me in suspense, yo."

Before Frank could respond, the news broadcast interrupted his train of thought.

"Breaking news regarding the murder case involving ex-socialite Sophie Freemont Lewis, daughter of former Dallas Mayor Richard Freemont. The prosecution just introduced their star witness. Please stay tuned for a live feed into the courthouse. This is Fox 4 News."

"Turn that up," Frank instructed. He walked toward the screen, captivated by the hoopla. He hoped that he would not be pulled into her kind of trouble. He had enough dealings with the law and fully intended to stay off the radar.

"Well? Who is it, yo?" Simmy asked again.

Frank did not respond immediately. His eyes were fixated on the screen. He could not look away, but he was not sure what he desired to see.

"Yo, Frank?"

Frank was completely gone. His only thought was finding out who the man in the trench coat was. He was absolutely certain with each passing moment, until the news broadcast came back on.

"Welcome back. We are coming back from commercial break in order to cut to the live feed. We are headed into the courthouse now, where the prosecution is gearing up

to present their alleged star witness against the murder case involving Sophie Freemont. Oh, wait. We just received word that we have footage of the witness getting into an elevator at the courthouse. Here it is. . . ."

Frank could not believe it. There he was. The guy from the elevator, the prosecution's witness, was possibly the culprit behind the attacks on his wife.

"Here is a freeze frame of the witness. There, in the far corner of the elevator. That is the prosecution's alleged witness. This person's name and other details coming just after the break."

Frank pointed to the screen. "It's him, Simmy. That was the guy with my brother in the car. I think that's the guy trying to kill my wife."

CHAPTER 58

This was surreal. The courtroom was buzzing with reporters, gossip columnists, politicians, supporters, and enemies—people who wanted to see her mother go to prison. Others were in attendance for no real reasons; they had nothing else better to do.

"Michelle, this is insane," Brianna whispered into her ear, not out of a need to keep their conversation private but in an effort to be heard. "Look at these vultures."

Michelle considered ignoring her, as she had become quite adept at doing with every opportunity for months, excluding occasions such as this, when it could not be avoided. Though Grayson urged her to speak with Brianna about what had happened, Michelle had not found the stomach to broach the subject. She did not know if it was their mom facing a prison stint or the arrival of her niece or nephew that made skirting around the issue seem to be a more favorable solution. Not that it mattered much; the end result was the same. Michelle had not forgiven her sister and did not want to talk to her about anything. She did not want to fake a closeness that did not exist, but Brianna had been doing just that, pretending like all was well between them.

"Brianna . . . please."

"I get it, Michelle. You are still upset with me, but it's been months. You have moved on," Brianna whispered, pointing to Grayson. "I'm having a baby."

"With that crazy-ass Javan or Micah . . . whatever he's calling himself."

"Yes, with Micah. He was sick, just like I was, but we are both doing better now."

Michelle rolled her eyes. "He kidnapped you! Beat your ass and damn near killed you!" she retorted, trying to keep her volume at a reasonable level.

"He doesn't remember that, and . . . he is a different person now."

"You're delusional . . . and I don't care anyway. It's your life. Fuck it up however you want to."

"Michelle, I want my sister back. I need you. I haven't even talked to—"

"Don't you dare."

"All I'm saying is . . . he isn't a part of our lives anymore, but he's still separating us."

"Brianna, this is really not the time nor the place for this."

"We need to resolve this. Mom needs our support, Michelle."

Michelle cut her eyes at Brianna. "I could not care less about what either of you need. I am looking out for me. Besides, she has you and her new boo for that."

"Her and Peter are not . . . it isn't like that."

Michelle looked around, feeling fatigued over the whole exchange already. No one was paying any attention to their little spat. People were steadily filing into the courtroom to catch a glimpse of one the biggest stories in the city's history. It was only fitting that her mother lived at the center of it.

"Who told you that? Mom? She's a lying, narcissistic sociopath."

"Peter told me. I trust him." Brianna leaned over closer to Michelle.

Michelle suppressed her instinct to mush her in the face. "The boyfriend lying to protect the girlfriend? That never happens."

"He's my father, Michelle."

"Yeah, for a half a year, he's been a stellar dad."

"Ever since he found out. I have no reason to doubt him."

Michelle looked at Brianna. This child had gifted her sister with an annoyingly optimistic perspective on people. "Right, because we have such a good track record with truthful parents." Michelle wanted Brianna to leave her alone with this mess.

"Michelle, what happened to you?"

"This family happened to me. I am done, and if you keep dragging me through this conversation, I'll leave, and you can explain to your mother's lawyer why that beautiful family portrait he's trying to paint of us . . . isn't possible."

"Fine. I'll let it go . . . for now."

"Good."

Grayson nudged her, grabbed hold of her hand, and gave it a quick squeeze. She looked over at him. *I'm okay*, she mouthed to him. Nodding her head toward Brianna, her thumb and forefinger shaped like a gun, she mimicked the effects of being shot. *She's driving me crazy.*

Grayson leaned over and pecked her lightly on the cheek before bringing her hand to his lips and kissing it, too. "No worries. I got you."

Michelle smiled and took a deep breath. Grayson had really stepped up and proven himself. Living with him was a dream. She had never been around a more giving person, and all he seemed to require was her love. She did love him very much, but she still had things she needed to work through. He understood that and did not rush her into making any decisions. She appreciated that about him. They had not even "went there" yet. He had been extremely patient, and he was the only reason she bothered to come to court or entertain her family at all. She was there for him because he needed her to do this, to try to be a part of her family.

So, she could not let Brianna's impolite conversation get to her. She could not let any of this bother her. She was angry with her mom, but she didn't want her to go to prison. Her mother was a lot of things, but she did not believe her capable of murder, especially not of her father.

The judge brought the court to the order. The room went silent. Michelle's mind went into a vacuum. This scene was bizarre, something she had hoped her mother could avoid. She eyed her grandfather, Richard Freemont, entering the courtroom from some door in the back, one that average civilians did not have access to.

Their initial meeting had gone as well as could be expected. She had been summoned, along with Brianna, for a "family meeting" to the estate not long after her mother was arrested. There they were: she and Grayson, Brianna, Peter, and her beleaguered grandfather, Richard Freemont, all seated in the main room of the house, staring at one another, doused in an awkward, uncomfortable silence until dear old Grandad took center stage.

His steps were rigid, like he was reluctant to take them, but all of that disappeared once he hit his mark in front of the fireplace. Hesitation markers vanished as he assumed his role as the patriarch, orchestrating the merge of the Lewis, Mason, and Baxter clans. Harkening upon the importance of family, of releasing the pains of the past in pursuit of a better future, he spoke and paraded before them in the kind of grandiose manner people likened to public speakers, salesmen, or the occasional gifted politician she suspected he never ceased to be. It was quite the spectacle, but nothing compared to the silent film playing out before her.

Peter excused himself as he brushed past her, smashing her knees together, to claim his seat on Brianna's other side. Peter seemed very decent, a guy Michelle could have respected if he weren't *fucking her mother*. Not even Brianna's unsolicited, glowing character review could save him from the filth he covered himself with by aligning himself with her. She guessed that they were all a little dirty simply by being there.

Her grandfather had hired the best criminal defense attorney in the city to represent her mother, but the average person would not have guessed from his appearance. His suit was tailored, shoes Italian, but overall, he was very understated; likable but not overkill, much like her mother. Her dress was plain, simple but elegant. Both were seated in front of the assembly line of relatives.

Michelle looked around the courtroom, briefly making eye contact with a few people she knew, until she spotted Charlie. Charlie winked at her, and Michelle wished she could disappear. Dread took hold of her spirit as she flipped through a Rolodex of meanings for Charlie's *signal*. Her mouth went dry as her mind raced to the worst possible outcome.

She shot a quick glance at Brianna, engrossed in conversation with Peter. Charlie, with a wicked grin plastered across her face, vacated her seat when Michelle turned to look at her again. Michelle wiped the sweat off her palms onto her jeggings.

As regret filled her mouth with words she was too afraid to say aloud, Michelle looked at Brianna. The lon-

ger she watched her carrying on with Peter, the ease of relief slowly soothed her being, reasoning that if anything
had happened, Brianna surely would have mentioned it by
now. Embracing this line of thought, Michelle dismissed
her distress as paranoia. Her mother was on trial, not her,
and Michelle didn't need to worry about Charlie. She had
no power except for what Michelle may pass along to her.
Reprioritizing her thoughts, Michelle shook her head, settling into the conundrum that had been plaguing her for the
last six months: the question of how her mother had gotten herself into this mess.

Grayson shook her, demanding her attention. "Michelle,
where have you been?"

Michelle looked at him, puzzled. "What do you mean?
I'm right here. Why would you ask that?"

"I have been trying to get your attention for the last
thirty seconds."

"Really?" Michelle was more distracted than she
thought. "My bad. What is it?"

"I think the prosecution is about to bring that witness
we've been hearing about." Grayson was whispering, but
she detected a heightened sense of urgency in his tone.

Michelle nodded her understanding. The witness had
kept her up at night. She had no idea what he or she could
have possibly seen that would lead to the belief that her
mother had killed her father, but the thought of this witness
seeing anything made her nervous for many reasons. She
definitely wanted to get a good look at whoever this person
was.

"The prosecution would like to call our next witness,
Henry Benjamin Lewis, to the stand."

The doors at the back of the courtroom opened, and
the attendees gasped in collective shock as the individual

walked through the sea of people toward the witness stand. Neither Michelle, nor anyone near her, could see clear enough to identify the person yet. The man neared the witness stand, preparing to be sworn in. Michelle squinted and zoomed in as best she could, waiting for the guy, who currently had his back to them, to turn around.

The bailiff escorted him to the stand, instructed him to place his hand on the Bible and repeat the words, "I do solemnly swear to tell the truth, and nothing but the truth, so help me God."

The witness did as he was instructed, allowing his voice to boom against the walls of the courtroom. "I do solemnly swear . . ."

Michelle felt the tiny hairs all over her body rise. Her body temperature suddenly dropped, chilling her to the bone. She gripped Grayson's hand like her life depended on keeping her connection to him. Her eyes widened, round like teacup saucers. Her breath caught in her throat, and she couldn't speak. All she could do was shake him and hoped he understood.

When he found her eyes, she knew that he had. He heard it, too. That was the faceless voice from her mother's house, the voice that claimed to know her and her mother.

She glanced at her mother, who was visibly shaking. Michelle was not sure what to do. She did not know how to help her, so she waited for the guy to take his seat.

It was a very painful, aggravating twenty seconds, but when Michelle saw his face, she could not believe her eyes. *There's no way. This has to be some sick joke or something. This is impossible.*

Her mother jumped to her feet, waving her arms erratically, coming to the same conclusion as her daughter had. The crowd grew increasingly raucous as she verbally exercised her disbelief.

"No, no, no! It can't be!" She continued screaming over the judge's objections. "I'm not crazy! I'm not crazy! You're dead! I buried you!"

Sophie's lawyer and Richard struggled to get her back under control, but she was hysterical. She just kept yelling, not wanting to believe the sight in front of her. "Leave me alone! Leave me alone! He's dead! I know he's dead!"

The witness stood and, addressing Sophie, he pointed his finger in her direction, shaking it violently, his eyes showing the fire within him. "No! Never! You'll pay for what you did! You won't get away with what you did!"

Sophie collapsed, passed out cold on the spot.

Stunned, Michelle could not move an inch. She could not utter one word. She couldn't think straight. This did not make any sense. She saw the same thing her mother saw. Did that mean she was crazy, too? She looked at Brianna and Peter, who looked as confused and perplexed as she felt. Her eyes focused on Grayson, who seemed at a loss for words himself. None of what had transpired in the last ninety seconds made any type of sense.

The courtroom was vibrant, roaring with life again, but she could hear nothing. She saw lips moving, but there was no sound, except for the one voice that had haunted her since that night at her mother's. She looked at him, studying him from afar. He couldn't be her father, could he?

Then, it happened. He looked back at her, into her. He announced to everyone listening, but she knew the information was for her, an answer to the question he saw in her stare.

The witness offered a faint smile to her and stated for the record, so there was no further doubt, "Leonard Brendan Lewis was my twin brother, and I am here to get justice for his murder."